Toni Mount

Cover illustration by Dmitry Yakhovsky,
Copyright © 2017 MadeGlobal

The Colour of Cold Blood

A Sebastian Foxley Medieval Mystery
Book 3

Copyright © 2017 Toni Mount
ISBN-13: 978-84-946498-1-3

M
MadeGlobal Publishing

For more information on
MadeGlobal Publishing, visit
our website
www.madeglobal.com

Dedication

To Deborah and Rebecca

Why not visit
Sebastian Foxley's web page
to discover more about his
life and times?
www.SebastianFoxley.com

Prologue

H E GAZED at his handiwork and sighed. How sad. She'd been a beauty – once – but not now. He had enjoyed her company. On many a chilled night she'd warmed his bed and soothed his loneliness but, like all women, she had her faults, in particular, the inability to keep silent. That problem was solved forever now, he thought, wiping his soiled hands and the blade of his Irish knife on her linen shift, before concealing the weapon once more within his robes. He arranged her neatly, curled like a sleeping child, tidied her garments to preserve her modesty – not that she had bothered over much with such matters in life – nevertheless, she would be decent in death. No final confession for the likes of her, no last rites. Too bad. It was a task well done: at least one whore could lead the sons of Adam astray no more.

The pale, insipid moonlight cast the half-hearted shadow of the thorn hedge across the remains. Shaking his head, he left that unhallowed place. There was not a moment to lose; the solitary bell of St Michael's was already summoning the parishioners to the last service of the day, clanging like a cheap metal platter rapped with a spoon.

Chapter 1

Monday, the fourth day of November 1476, London

DAWN WAS breaking in the east, the rosy light shimmering on frosted roofs and walls, turning dirty old London to a place of magick and faery. Armed with his drawing implements and swathed in a grey woollen mantle, Sebastian Foxley stepped carefully along the frozen rutted ways of Panyer Alley and along the Shambles. There were few folk about so early. Greeted by the gatekeeper, still rubbing sleep from his eyes, Seb was the first to pass through Newgate as it opened for the day. He turned right up Giltspur Street towards Smithfield, inhaling the essence of the still-dormant city as it slumbered like a great beast, ready to awaken as the sun rose.

The late autumn grass, frost-rimed, crunched beneath his feet as he trudged towards his favoured spot beneath an oak tree, beside the Horse Pool. He noticed a good crop of oak galls attached to a low, leafless branch and collected a few, putting them in his purse. To a scrivener, they were as good as money for, together with a few rusty nails and a resin known as devil's fingernails, they made the best, blackest and longest lasting ink. He would send Tom and young Jack to collect more after dinner, then show them how to make the precious ink.

The hedgerow that ran alongside Chick Lane was aglow with jewels amongst the last yellowing leaves; each gem dusted with frost – haws and rosehips like rubies, sloes dark as sapphires, delicate-hued pearls of bryony. But his artist's eye was drawn to the diamond-strung cobwebs that draped the brambles. They could have graced a queen's throat if they did not disappear by dinnertime. He sketched quickly, capturing the beauty of a lacy leaf skeleton in the grass; a squirrel rummaging for acorns, flicking his rust-tinted tail and chittering a warning when he espied Seb invading his estate. He laughed at the little creature, scolding him like a Billingsgate fishwife, and moved away. His fingers were chilled and he chafed a vestige of warmth into them so he might continue with the silver point, drawing a redbreast warbling his joyful hymn of praise to the new day from a spindle tree in the hedgerow. The bright-eyed bird might later adorn the margin of a Book of Hours Seb had in mind. The spindle tree flaunted its bright madder berries like a Winchester goose, parting her skirts to reveal nether garments vivid as sunset: the precious seeds within, glowing among the few remaining russet leaves.

The water of the Horse Pool held a wafer of ice around the rim, freezing the faded reeds in place, upright as sentinels. Not a whisper of wind disturbed the unfrozen water further out where a lone swan sat serenely upon her perfect reflection, the feathers of her folded wings gilt-edged by the strengthening light. Seb drew what he saw but only in his mind's eye could he lock away the memories, the nuances of colour, light and shadow. He spent time, capturing the swan in her glory, but the light was changing, becoming brazen, revealing the less than lovely. A broken bucket lay discarded in the hedge; the bones of a fox's kill strewn in the grass like white pot shards and a lost shoe, split at the heel. Frost on the oak tree began to thaw, an icy drip finding a gap betwixt his cap and mantle, shivering down his neck. The spell was broken and Seb made his way home. Chimneys were now smoking, window shutters opening as his neighbours roused themselves to the day's labours; yawning and stretching and nodding a greeting as he passed by.

Just a few yards from Seb's door, a beggar sat hunched over his bowl, going through his beard, catching and cracking fleas between his thumbnails. A dusty heap of rags, he might have gone unnoticed, seeming more interested in fleas than collecting alms in his wooden dish, but Seb dropped in a groat all the same.

'God give ye good day, master.' The voice was hoarse and quavering.

'And also to you, Symkyn.'

The Foxleys' house in Paternoster Row

THE HOUSE welcomed Seb with the delicious scents of fresh baked bread and frying bacon. Setting down his drawing stuff, he shrugged off his heavy mantle, hung it on the hook behind the door and went to the laver to wash his hands before eating. The warmth of the kitchen and the hot water thawed his blood quickly, setting his fingers tingling and flushing his cold-bleached nails with renewed colour.

A noisy company was already at the table. Jack sat on his bench, eager as a hatchling for the first mouthful, whatever, whenever, it came his way. Tom, the apprentice, was older but no less hungry, tapping the board with his spoon, eyes watching Mistress Emily dole generous helpings of savoury pottage into the wooden bowls stacked by the hearth to warm. Gabriel Widowson was perched on a stool, telling some tale of a drunken fool he'd seen last eve, but only Nessie, the serving wench, was listening as she gave him the largest helping of pottage, giggling.

'Nessie,' Seb interrupted, 'After we have eaten, take some fresh bread across the road to old Symkyn, and a piece of bacon. God knows he needs food more than we. Aye, even you, young Jack,' he said, seeing the look on the lad's face: fear that a mouthful due to him might go elsewhere. Not that Jack was greedy; no, just that his days as a starveling orphan weren't yet quite forgotten.

Seb kissed his goodwife on the cheek and whispered in her ear, smiling, before taking the stool at the head of the board. She more than returned the smile, her azure eyes bright with pleasure.

'Good day to you all,' Seb said. The others returned the greeting, spoons poised. 'Jack.'

The youngster looked sheepish, his spoon already plunged into the pottage, before grace was said. Seb recited the usual Latin prayer that Jack never understood, but the 'Amen' was clear enough: permission to eat.

Gabriel resumed his tale between mouthfuls, setting the lads spluttering with laughter into their breakfast but Emily and Seb had attention for naught but each other, exchanging knowing glances from either end of the board.

'No Jude this morning?' Seb asked, noting the empty place where his brother usually sat. It was always an awkward arrangement: Seb, though younger, was the married man and this his house, so he had the place at the head of the board, relegating Jude to a lesser position. For the most part, it didn't matter but sometimes Jude, usually on a bad day, took himself off to the Panyer inn to eat. Perhaps this was one of those days. Sometimes it occurred to Seb that Jude might prefer to rent a place of his own, but neither of them had ever suggested it.

'Still abed, I dare say,' Gabriel answered. 'Heard him come home late last eve, later than me, even. He was singing some dirty ditty or other, stumbled on the stair. Reckon he was drunk. Probably still sleeping it off.' Gabriel sucked at his crooked front tooth, picking out a piece of bacon that had caught there. 'Hey, that was good pottage, Mistress Em, any chance of another helping?'

'You'll be as fat as a sow in furrow, you will, Gabriel,' Emily chided him, smiling, and turned away to see to the oatcakes on the griddle.

'Nonsense. Look at me.' Gabriel patted his muscular belly: flat as a platter.

The door from the yard opened, letting in a blast of icy air to announce Jude's arrival.

'You're late, as usual,' Emily said. 'Do it tomorrow and I'll give your breakfast to the pig. She deserves it more than you. Come next week, she'll pay for her keep, unlike some.' She slammed a platter of bacon collops, a bowl of pottage and two oatcakes on the board before her brother-in-law, flinging a spoon into the pottage so it splashed his tunic. He didn't seem to notice, saying nothing.

'Shall you be working for the coroner today, Jude?' Seb asked, referring to his brother's occasional employment by the city authorities.

'Aye,' Jude replied, swallowing bacon, 'Have to assess the value of a knife. The Lord knows why. Some damn fool ran into another fellow as they were playing at football, skewered himself on the other's knife and bled to death. Since the king demands the value of the murderous weapon be paid as a fine for breaking the peace, I have the fool's task of discovering whether the knife was of a bladesmith's finest workmanship or a cutler's cheapest, made after dark.'

'I thought the guilds made it illegal to work after cock-shut, when none can see well enough to ensure high standards.'

'Supposedly.' Jude shoved the last collop into his mouth and put the second oatcake into his purse for later, leaving the pottage untasted. 'Not sure if I'll be back for dinner, or no.'

'Well that's not good enough,' Emily declared. 'How am I supposed to be sure not to waste food when I know not whether I shall be feeding you? I'm tired of you, Jude Foxley. You're more bother than a babe-in-arms. I shouldn't have to put up with it. Tell him, Sebastian.'

'Now, Em, don't take on so. Jude never knows what the coroner may ask of him...'

'I don't care. My entire day has to be arranged to suit your brother.'

'Then don't bother!' Jude yelled, shoving past her. 'I won't be back.'

'Oh, Em. Why is it you two cannot live amicably together? As if his moods are not dark enough, you upset him...'

'So it matters not that he upsets me with his wayward time-keeping, his sulks and his cup-shotten tantrums.'

'Come now, sweetheart, 'tis not so bad, surely?' Seb put his arm around her waist but she stepped out of his embrace.

'Not now. And why do you always take his side, making excuses for him?'

'I do not. Or I don't mean to. I love you, Em. I want you, only you.'

When breakfast was finally done, Seb sent Gabriel and the lads to the workshop to prepare for the day's work, before taking Emily in his arms. Oblivious of Nessie watching from the chimney corner, they kissed tenderly. Seb was loosening the pins in Emily's cap, the thought of her autumnal tresses cascading freely quickened his breath as she pressed closer. Jude chose that moment to return. The happy couple pulled apart, guilty of a stolen moment. Seb clenched his fists and with the briefest gesture of both greeting and farewell, hurried towards the workshop, overcome by a hot rush of blood to his cheeks.

'Now what?' Emily demanded.

'Forgot my scrip,' Jude said, then called out after Seb, 'Though plainly some people have matters other than a day's work on their minds, eh, little brother?'

'You're disgusting. We *are* married, after all,' Emily said, straightening her apron and patting her cap back in place. Suddenly she had her broom – her favoured weapon – in his face.

'Get out of my kitchen!' She jabbed the business end of cut reeds at his chest, 'And there'll be no dinner for you this morning, nor supper tonight if you can't be on time. Just go away.'

Jude withdrew from his sister-in-law's temper to join his brother in the workshop. Seb sat at his desk, his inks and brushes ready set out, but he was frowning at nothing.

'Ah, so that's it, is it? A row and now you have to make amends, eh? What was it about? Money? Sex? It's always one or the other.'

'Neither. Why is it you have to make lewd remarks every time I so much as look at my goodwife. Just because you're not wed...'

'I've got more bloody sense.'

'Keep out of our affairs, Jude! Leave us alone, can't you?' Seb's anger was all but unknown in the workshop.

Jack, Tom and Gabriel kept their heads down so low their noses near touched their desks, feigning deafness.

Jude shrugged.

'Have it your own way then. What do I care?' He turned aside, selecting a new quill and taking out his knife to cut and prepare the point but then he threw it down and stomped out. Off to his other – and at present – more amicable employment with the coroner.

The Foxleys' parlour

'THE LORD bishop, in his wisdom, thinks I need help in my parish, though the Lord knows I must be twenty years younger than his grace... well, ten at least.' Father Thomas, the priest at St Michael le Querne in Cheapside, sighed deeply as he sank into the chair, grateful for the cushions Mistress Foxley provided, aye, and the good ale. He glanced around the comfortable room, smiling when he saw the elegant silver-gilt loving cup upon the shelf, a wedding gift to the Foxleys from the Duke of Gloucester, reminding the priest of that merry occasion a year past. 'But there you are,' he continued. 'Who am I to argue? I'm getting an assistant and there's an end to it. I am informed that the new man is most diligent about his duties.' The old priest puffed out his cheeks. 'Not too diligent, I trust. Don't want him upsetting my parishioners, do we? Some of them are quite set in their ways.'

'I'm sure you'll keep his enthusiasm within bounds, father,' Emily said, offering the priest a smile and another almond wafer. 'I hope so but a new broom sweeps clean, as my mother, God rest her dear soul, used to say.' He made the sign of the cross with gnarled old fingers and Emily did the same. 'Bishop Kemp insists he will seek out the roots of Lollard heresy wherever they may be found. Well, he'll be wasting his time at St Michael's in that case: none of my parishioners would dabble in that wicked nonsense, I can tell you.'

'Of course not. Why would the bishop think...'

'I don't know, my dear, some rumours about Gospel books in English circulating in the city. Well, that may be so, but not in my parish. My people, including you and your goodman, are all honest, God-fearing folk, obedient to the Holy Father in Rome. No question of that.'

'No question at all. More ale, father? Now what was it you wanted to see my Sebastian about? A new book, did you say?'

The old priest nodded, his tonsure a halo of wispy white hair encircling his skull cap. He reached for another wafer.

'Aye, what was it now? Mm, a psalter book, aye. I doubt my new assistant will want to share my ancient volume, seeing it's falling apart with age.'

'Sebastian could repair it. I'm sure he'd do it at a most reasonable price for you, as a friend.'

'Mm, most kind, but this new fellow – Weasel, or whatever his name is...'

'Weasel? That's a quaint name, isn't it?' Emily said, hiding a grin behind her hand.

'Well, something of the sort. He'll expect a new psalter at least, I don't doubt. Not that St Michael's can really afford it.'

'I'll fetch Sebastian from the workshop, so you may discuss it with him, here, in comfort.'

Emily bustled out, leaving Father Thomas seated before the hearth. Content, he helped himself to the last wafer, leant back upon the cushions and closed his eyes, thinking what a well-ordered, pleasant and pious household the Foxleys kept.

In the workshop, Master Seb wasn't looking his usual, cheerful self. Jack didn't know what was amiss but he didn't like bad feeling in the house for all too often, in his old life, other people had tended to vent their ill-humours on him. At least in the Foxley household, usually Master Jude was the only one who might do that but this morning Master Seb had a thunderous scowl upon his face. Jack's dog had made a mess in the middle of the workshop floor, not for the first time.

'Jack. I've told you before about...'

'Sorry, master, but Little Beggar's profleegate, ain't he?'

'What? Where did you learn that?'

'From you, Master Seb. Last week, you said the mayor was too profleegate with his coin, now he's got a new wife.'

'Hush, will you.'

'That's what you said. And Little Beggar's profleegate wiv his shit: spreadin' it all around.'

'Well, get it cleared up. I can't have the workshop reeking like a cess pit and customers treading in the muck all day.'

Jude, lately returned from interviewing various cutlers and bladesmiths on the coroner's behalf, left off sewing together the leaves of a new book and came to add his pennyworth, hands on hips:

'I've told you the same often enough, you little wretch. This time that bloody dog's for drowning. You hear me?'

'But he don't mean no trouble. Please don't drowned him, pleease.'

'No one's going to drown anything,' Seb said, seeing the lad on the verge of tears. Jude was always upsetting him about that blessed dog.

'You speak for yourself, Seb. I'm sick and tired of the damned thing. If I have to step around its piles of shit and puddles of piss once more...'

Jack was sobbing now.

'Leave it, Jude, for pity's sake. I'm too weary for this. I have to go down to Queenhithe, see what's happening about our cargo from Captain Marchmane. The *St Christopher* docked on Saturday yet we've heard nothing about the paper and pigments the captain was bringing in for us. Meantime, Jack! Clean up the mess and we'll say no more of the matter.'

'Until the next bloody time,' Jude added with a malicious look in his eye.

Seb went to his work desk, leafing through the sketches he had done by the Horse Pool that morning. Little Beggar came trotting over to him, sat on his haunches and raised his front paw. Whatever the Church said about creatures having no souls, with dolorous brown eyes looking up him, pleading, Seb could almost doubt the wisdom of the pronunciation. If that dog wasn't begging forgiveness for his sins... Seb found himself with a moist eye, scratching Beggar's scruffy little head. The dog's tail thumped the flagstones, as if he understood he was half-way to being pardoned for his crime. Jack was just finishing his unsavoury task.

'Take him over to Smithfield, Jack. You can collect those oak apples I told you about whilst Beggar may redeem himself and bring back a coney for the pot.'

'Aye, Master Seb.' Jack didn't need telling twice.

'Thought you were going to Queenhithe,' Jude said. 'Why don't you take one of these idle devils with you?' He nodded towards Gabriel and Tom. 'Christ knows why we employ either of them. When was the last time you moved your lazy backside, eh, Gabe?'

Gabriel Widowson gave a wry grin. He was not a handsome young man with his mousy hair and mismatched eyes – one blue, the other brown – and a lopsided mouth with a crooked tooth, yet his air of self-belief inspired confidence. Folk liked Gabriel without being able to say quite why. The rumour ran that he was the natural son of some person of rank, though whether bishop or baron depended on who told the tale and he did nothing to quell the rumours. In fact, he tended to encourage them with a knowing look, a wink, enjoying the harmless notoriety.

He had been the subject of endless hours of gossip around the conduit and at the back of St Michael's church on a Sunday for months, ever since the Foxleys had taken him on as a journeyman scrivener and illuminator at Paternoster Row last summer. Wenches were drawn like iron to a lodestone by the mystery surrounding this incomer from Kent. At least, that was where he claimed to have come from and he spoke like a man of that county. But some wondered when he told tales of Scotch moss-troopers and Irish slavers, Breton pirates and Moorish potentates. Gabriel was a gifted spinner of stories but which were true and which invented, none could tell. Like the rumours of his paternity – son of a prince or a pauper – somehow it didn't matter.

Gabriel laughed, seeing Jude scowling at him. There was no point in taking offence. It was just Jude's way. The journeyman set down his pen and closed the exemplar he had been copying from – a complex Latin treatise concerning the Old Testament biblical text of Leviticus, ordered by Thomas Kemp, the Bishop of London. It was a tedious task indeed, the text of uninspiring Latin did naught to raise Gabriel's spirit and he was glad to set it aside.

'Oh, I seem to recall doing a little work a week or two since, naught too exhausting. Why? What would you have me do?'

'Go with my brother to Queenhithe. He may need assistance to carry our reams of new paper. Oh, and see you keep him from the local brothels.' Jude, in better humour now, gave a snort at the thought of his straight-laced brother ever visiting a whore-house.

Just as Seb and Gabriel were taking down their cloaks from the hooks by the door, Emily hurried in.

'Oh, Seb,' she said, 'Father Thomas is here, in the parlour. I said you would speak to him about a new psalter book he needs for an assistant priest who is joining St Michael's. Could you see him now? He seems to think the need is quite urgent.'

Seb nodded, sighing.

'Aye. Of course. My thanks, Em. Tell him I'm coming,' he called as Emily returned to the parlour. 'Tom, fetch the pattern book for me and bring it along.' Seb turned to Gabriel. 'Our errand will have to wait until after dinner,' he said, removing his cloak.

'Or I could go alone?' Gabriel offered.

'Do you know the *St Christopher* out of Deptford? She has a bright blue and gold painted prow – a newish caravel.'

'I'll find her. What did we order?'

'A dozen reams of Bruges paper, water-marked with a hound's head, and a box of finest Venice pigments that Captain Marchmane promised he would bring. 'Tis all paid for in advance. If everything has been off-loaded from the ship, try the Customs House. You know where that is? Beyond the bridge, passed Billingsgate, in Water Lane, by the Wool Quay.'

'Fear not, Master Seb, I know the Customs House. I've lived in London long enough to learn my way around, even if I wasn't born here, like you.' In truth, he thought, I probably know the shadier parts of the city better than you do. But he smiled his lopsided smile and left, going out into the chill November street. Old Symkyn was still there, hunched behind his begging bowl, watching the world pass by, all but invisible.

• •

Over supper that eve, as the daylight was fading and the tapers were lit, Seb told the others about the new commission of a psalter book for St Michael's.

'I-I told Father Thomas we would make the book for him *gratis*.'

'What's gratis?' Jack asked.

'You did what!' Jude spluttered gravy on the cloth. 'How do you expect us to make a living, you dolt? We can't afford such generosity.'

'It will be good for our souls...'

'Bugger souls, Seb. I want a roof over my head and food on the bloody board. How dare you decide to do it for naught without my agreement?'

'I apologise, Jude. I thought you would wish to...'

'Well, I don't. Church robs enough from my purse in tithes as it is without you giving them weeks of work and expensive stuff for free. I suppose you intend to use gold embellishment?'

Seb nodded.

'Just a little, maybe.'

'You know they won't let us off a pennyworth of tithes in return. They're worse than leeches, sucking us dry.' Jude was wringing his napkin so fiercely the linen began to tear.

'It will be a fine opportunity to use those new pigments... when I receive them, eh, Gabe?' Seb tried to turn the conversation but realised that the mention of using expensive colours on the psalter was a mistake. 'How come you did not fetch them?'

'I went to the *St Christopher,* as you said,' Gabe replied. 'She was half unloaded already. I asked about your colours but the mate, Raff Scraggs, knew naught of them. Then I asked to speak with your friend, Captain Marchmane. Raff, I mean, Master Scraggs, said they hadn't seen the captain since soon after they docked on Saturday eve, so I couldn't ask him, could I?' Gabe returned his attention to his trencher, keen to get on with the succulent pig's trotter and peas in a good thick gravy.

'And our reams of paper? What of those?'

'Seb.' Emily interrupted, 'Can we discuss work after we have eaten, afore the food goes cold upon the platters?'

'This is important. We are short of good quality paper. That French stuff is thin and poorly made. Good enough for the lads to practise upon but not for the likes of Father Thomas's new psalter. I want the best for a Church book. So where is it, Gabe?'

'Fear not. It's at the Customs House, I made sure. We should have it by Wednesday, Thursday at the latest. You know how long such matters take, what with documents to be sealed, duties paid, tallies noted and all.'

'What else is fer supper, mistress?' Jack asked, pushing aside his trencher, cleaned down to the bare wood.

'Don't interrupt, Jack,' Seb said, rapping the board with his knife handle. 'This is business and you become more inconsiderate by the day. Now keep silent at table unless we speak to you.'

'Wot's 'inconseedrite' mean, Tom?' Jack whispered to his fellow apprentice, seated beside him on the bench.

'Do you understand what 'keep silent' means, Jack?'

'Aye, Master Seb.' For a moment Jack looked downcast but his eyes brightened like sunrise as Emily set a baked apple before him, stuffed with raisins and spiced sugar.

'At least one among you appreciates the food I spend all day preparing,' she said, jogging Seb's elbow, meaningfully. 'I believe you would hardly notice if I served you raw giblets and mouldy horse bread for every meal. Why do I go to so much effort, I wonder?'

'Because 'tis a woman's place,' Jude said without looking at his sister-in-law.

Everyone at table held their breath, expecting the worst. Mistress Emily and Master Jude rarely saw eye to eye as it was. Like fire and gunpowder, their near encounter could cause untold destruction.

'Supper is excellent, as always, sweetheart,' Seb said, hoping to diffuse the tension but Emily ignored him.

She was staring at Jude, wordless, but her eyes pierced him like daggers. Yet he gave all his attention to refilling his ale cup. Without warning, Emily struck his hand, sending the pewter jug flying, clattering onto the flagstone floor and spilling ale in his lap.

'You blasted woman!' Jude yelled, leaping up from his stool, 'You just wait until I get hold of you, you'll wish you'd never...'

'Enough, Jude!' Seb, too, was on his feet. 'I'll not have you threatening my wife in our own home. Now be calm, both of you. Sit down, finish your food.'

Emily obeyed, reluctantly, still glowering at Jude. He picked up his platter with the remains of his supper now swimming in ale, walked around the board to where Emily sat and with slow deliberation tipped it over her head. She flew at him, scratching and clawing at his smirking face.

It was over in a moment. Jude, far superior in strength, trapped her against the wall, pinning her arms at her sides but still she struggled.

'Seb!' she screeched, 'Get him off me!'

'Remember, I like 'em with a bit of spirit,' Jude laughed, a malicious sneer upon his lips.

'Jude!' Seb grabbed the heavy oaken stool on which he'd been sitting, raised it aloft, threatening to slam it down across his brother's shoulders. It was of such weight, it might have killed him if it had struck his head but, even in anger, Seb could not harm his brother. 'Behave yourselves, for God's pity. Is this a Christian example to set the lads?'

Jude was cursing as he stepped away from Emily.

'Don't you threaten me, little brother,' he said.

'And how else could I stop you?'

For a moment, the brothers faced each other, bristling like tomcats met in a midnight alleyway.

Emily sat, weeping into her apron, her gravy-stained cap and loosened hair dabbed at with a cloth by a tearful Nessie. Jack and Tom looked on, stunned into a silence such as Master Seb's demands could never have achieved. And Seb, still breathless from the effort of wielding his makeshift weapon, leant on a bench, shaking as his fury ebbed.

Only Gabriel sat calm and quiet, his stool removed to a far corner of the kitchen, shaking his head at the doings of his fellow man. 'Will us still get breakfast in the mornin'?' Jack asked. 'Hush,' Tom said in a whisper, 'Matters are dire enough without you make it worse with your silly questions. I think we should go to our bed.' The air in the kitchen seemed laden with ill-humours, along with the cooking smells. They were afraid of Master Jude's temper and eager to escape. As for Master Seb, such an act of violence from him the apprentices had not known before. It was quite unnerving. The lads crept out, hoping to avoid notice. Tom wondered if sleep would come to him at all with everything so unsettled. For Jack, the fear of no food for breakfast would be the worst torment in his dreams.

Chapter 2

Tuesday the fifth day of November

THE MIST was a wet sheep's fleece, compact and grey, draped from eaves and gables, enfolding London in its cold embrace. As if matters at home weren't chilly enough. Breakfast had been a dour affair. Indeed, hardly a word was spoken. Seb had done his best to cheer the lads, succeeding in coaxing a grin of sorts from Jack with an extra oat cake, but Tom was sombre as only a youth of seventeen years could manage. Emily had regarded him, red-eyed and accusing, though why she blamed him for last eve's hateful events he failed to comprehend. How did the fault lay with him? Only Jude's absence that morn had made the situation bearable.

And now the weather was as laden with misery as he. This was not a day to suit Seb's artistic temperament with all colour and form leached away from the familiar city, making it an alien place of muffled sounds and indefinite shapes.

A sudden figure loomed up before Seb, making him start as they near collided, each begging pardon of the other. It took a moment for him to recognise Father Thomas, swathed in a dark mantle.

'Forgive my clumsiness, father, I didn't see you.'

'Nor I you, Sebastian. Such a day as this, I can barely see my own shoes.'

'May I assist you anywhere?'

'Your kindness is appreciated, my son, but no. I am summoned to Foster Lane.'

'But you have come beyond it. Let me direct you, father, 'tis back this way.'

Father Thomas tutted at his mistake and allowed Seb to take his arm and guide him.

'I pray I'm not too late in that case. 'Tis a mother and babe, sadly, she in need of the last rites and the little one requiring baptism. Such a sorry event that should be a joyful one.'

Seb continued on his way, turning down Friday Street, towards the river. He knew the streets well enough, but it was a pity Gabriel hadn't been able to speak with Captain Marchmain yesterday, it would have saved him this horrible walk. He was in no mood to brave the fog and supposing the captain was unavailable as last time? It would be another wasted journey. Somewhere off in the murkiness, someone called out, their voice half-smothered. Probably they were lost. He should have brought Jack along. For certain, the lad knew the streets of London well enough to find his way through the alleys in darkness, so this accursed fog should hardly hinder him.

At the bottom of Friday Street, Seb turned left. The fog was thicker yet as he drew closer to the Thames, making landmarks invisible. He saw no one and had quite lost his bearings, having to trail his hand along walls to be certain when he should reach the turning down to Thames Street. It ought to be no more than a few footfalls away, following the wooden walls of the buildings along the south side of the street but, somehow, the turning into Bread Street didn't come. No matter. The next should be Sporren Lane, but when he found a passageway turning right, it led into someone's courtyard, a baby wailing behind a shuttered window.

A simple stroll to Queenhithe was becoming a nightmare, the city swathed in a devil's brew which stank of wood-smoke and the outpourings of a nearby midden. The next passage was narrow: it might be Trinity Lane but Seb was no longer certain.

At least it sloped quite steeply down, so he was definitely moving towards the river. The wider highway at the bottom must be Thames Street but, not knowing how far he'd come towards the east, he was unsure whether to turn left or right towards Queenhithe. A dog barked; a muffled curse as a door banged. A substantial stone building on his right hand must be the church of St Michael Queenhithe – or it might be St Mary's Vintry, if he'd come so far.

The fog tickled his throat, making him cough, the dampness dripped from his hair and seeped through his mantle. He shivered. The nearest passageway continued downwards. The fog smelled tainted with river mud. He should be hearing the sounds of ships bumping at their moorings, the shouts of stevedores and mariners, the squeak of windlasses, the thud of heavy cargoes onto the wharf, but all was silent, muffled by air as thick as oatmeal pottage. Perhaps nobody worked in such weather.

The wall he had been following on his right hand ended, leaving him groping like a blind man into a chill, colourless void. Nothing. Hands outstretched, hoping to feel a wall, a fence, anything, Seb stopped abruptly, gripped by a fearful thought. Suppose he was at the river's edge, one false step could see him fall in and drown. Nobody would know. He had no liking for the river which had almost claimed him once before. His saviour then, a ferrymen, had seen him by chance. That wouldn't happen on such a day as this.

Never mind Queenhithe. Seb just wanted to go home. He had to walk uphill, away from the Thames, yet whichever way he stepped, the ground beneath his feet seemed to slope downwards. His heart beat faster. Which way to go? In a panic, he shouted out, hoping someone would hear but the fog was a suffocating pillow pressed against his face.

'Is anybody there?' he cried, staggering a few steps forward. No one answered. And then he smacked into something solid. He explored it with his hands, feeling rough timbers. A ship!

Dear Lord Jesu, he was at the riverside. But no. The timbers' grain ran vertically. It was a paling fence. He moved along it, praying for an opening, a gateway or a door – anything. But the fence only turned a corner and, again, his feet told him he was walking down a slope, so he retraced his steps along the fence, reaching another corner where, once more, the ground went downhill. He would have to turn his back on the fence, there was no other way, but it meant venturing into nothingness. With little hope, he called out once more.

Of a sudden, his outstretched hand was clasped.

Startled, Seb jumped back, colliding with the fence.

'Fear not. Come with me.' The voice was young. A woman's voice or a child's perhaps. 'Come. I don't live far, just along the way.'

'I-I don't know where I am,' Seb said.

'This is Garlick Hill. I live just along from St James Garlickhythe. It's not far. They call me Rose.'

'Sebastian Foxley. I'm relieved to make your acquaintance, Mistress Rose.'

'Rose will do for me,' she said, giggling, 'Just Rose, Master Foxley. And here we are. It's not much but I call it home.'

Rose led her guest up a flight of narrow, rickety stairs and through a wooden door so warped that it protested as she leant upon it to force it open. The room was tiny, lit by the glow from a brazier basket and a sliver of gloomy daylight that sidled through a gap between the window shutters. But it was warm and dry and smelled clean. Seb made out a bed frame draped with a blanket, a box with a ewer and basin standing on it and not much else.

'Wait here,' she told him, 'I was on my way to fetch food and drink.'

'Surely you aren't going to venture abroad again in this fog? The shops and stalls haven't bothered to open on such a morning. I was foolish to try to reach Queenhithe.'

21

'I shall only go as far as the Pewter Pot next door. I work there.'

'Oh. I suppose you'll be safe enough then. Here, take some coins...'

'No need. I get bed and board for free, here, with my friend, Bessie.' She stared at his purse. 'I should keep that out of sight around here, Master Foxley. The weight of coin can be very tempting, if you take my meaning.'

'I had business with a sea captain at Queenhithe,' Seb explained.

'Shh. Walls are thin, master.'

In Rose's absence, Seb hung his dripping mantle from a peg behind the door, hoping it would dry somewhat in the brazier's warmth. He perched on the end of the bed since there was no stool nor bench but he felt uncomfortable, an intruder in a woman's chamber. How foolish. He laughed to himself, thinking how Jude would mock him, if he knew – Jude, the invader of so many bedchambers, if you believed all that was said of his brother. Seb wondered how much it was true these days, for Jude was a changed man since his time in Newgate and the narrow escape from the hangman's noose.

Rose returned, catching him still upon the bed. He leapt to his feet but could feel the hot blood in his cheek all the same. He hoped she wouldn't see it and think him, a married man, to be some silly innocent lad. On the other hand, he didn't want to seem as some lewd fellow who frequented women's bedchambers so readily on a first acquaintance.

'I brought us ale and bread,' Rose said, setting out the food on the wooden box. 'I'm afraid 'tis yesterday's loaf but, as you said, 'tis hardly a day to go a-marketing. There is a square of cheese and a morsel of black pudding to go with it. Help yourself, master. I'll find the cups.' She burrowed beneath the bed frame, showing the form of her neatly rounded buttocks through her skirts. Seb blushed again and looked away, taking out his knife to quarter the hunk of bread. It was dry and crumbled beneath the blade as he cut.

Rose reappeared with a worn linen bag from which she took two wooden cups and a platter.

'There! A feast fit for a cardinal. Well, good enough for now.' She poured the ale into the cups and handed one to Seb, smiling. He thanked her and drank deep, washing the fog from his throat. The ale was good, fresh and strong. They shared the food, dipping the dry bread into the ale. The cheese too lacked moistness but the black pudding was good and flavoursome, well spiced as Seb preferred.

As he ate, he kept glancing at Rose from the edge of his eye, not wanting to stare. He wondered at her age. It was hard to tell. She was plump-cheeked as a child but her bodice stretched tight across her small breasts. Her hips looked narrow as a lad's but, as he'd already been shown, her backside was rounded as a ripe apple. She was a pretty lass, there was no denying, fair hair straying from a jaunty little cap, determined in its escape.

She caught him looking and he took up his cup to hide his face.

'You like what you see, master?' She ran her hands over her bodice, smoothing out invisible creases in the cloth.

'No! I mean, aye, but I-I have to go now.' Seb hastened towards the door but caught his foot against the box, sending the earthen ale jug crashing to the floor where it shattered, spilling the last of the ale. 'Oh, no. Forgive me. I didn't... I'll pay for a new one.' He bent to pick up the broken pottery.

'It doesn't matter, master. Leave it be. It was chipped at the spout anyway. Master Roger expects breakages.'

'Who?'

'Master Roger Underwood. He owns the Pewter Pot tavern next door, where I work. Things get broken all the time in this business.'

'I'll give him money to replace it.' Seb began fishing in his purse for coin.

'Not 'til I've earned it, master.' Rose seized his hand from the purse and drew close, pressing against him. 'I could dress up for you, play the noble lady, if you want? See, Bessie has some fine things: a silk veil, a bejewelled girdle. Her priest customer likes it when she pretends to be a lady.' She shook out a piece of silk from the linen bag. It was frayed and stained but had probably belonged to a woman of high birth once, long ago. 'What do you think?' she asked, winding the veil elegantly about her head and swaying enticingly across the room.

'No, Rose. I'm a married man. I cannot do this.'

She pouted at him.

'You don't like me? You think I'm ugly.'

'Of course I don't think that. You're very pretty, Rose, but...'

'Is your goodwife pretty?'

'Aye. She's very pretty.'

'Pretty as me?' Rose's hand was warm against his thigh and sliding higher.

'Emily is the most beautiful woman in London,' he said, pushing Rose off more roughly than he'd intended but he had to get away. Now.

Rose dissolved in a wash of tears.

'I'll be in such trouble with Master Roger for not pleasing a customer, he'll beat me. Please stay, Master Foxley. I have to earn my keep. She looked up at him, her lustrous eyes like a begging dog's, pleading with him. 'Please stay.'

Seb had already glanced out of the door, sufficient to see the fog was a blank wall across the street, no less impenetrable than before. He could brave the weather or he could assist a beseeching wench in fear of her master.

'How much do I have to pay you?'

'I come very cheaply... for a virgin of so tender age.' She began to unlace her bodice with well-practised artistry.

'Stop that. I'm not interested in such... such goings-on.'

'Oh. You prefer other ways? I may have to charge more. You don't prefer lads, do you? I hope not.'

'Rose. Listen to me. I don't want bed-sport with you – not that you're not pretty – and I don't prefer lads. I am happily wed and I fully intend to keep faith with my wife, whom I dearly love. But afore you drown in tears again, I will pay you for your time... and the broken pot. Will a groat suffice?'

'You can have me, er, my time, all afternoon for that. But if you don't want any 'bed-sport', what shall we do?'

'We can talk.'

Having decided, they sat, side by side on the edge of the bed and the silence settled like an extra blanket.

'So. What manner of man are you, Master Foxley?' Rose said, shattering the silence.

'What do you mean?'

'I've taken an alderman and a serjeant-at-law to my bed, at least two friars and an Oxford scholar. So, what do you do? Let me hazard a guess: a lord's secretary? A parish clerk?'

'Not quite but...'

'Your fingers are ink-stained. Are you a lawyer? Perhaps you are another Oxford 'versity scholar?'

Seb laughed.

'Nothing so fine as that. I am a humble scrivener and illuminator of books.'

'I saw a book one time. A lodger left it as surety with Master Roger until he could afford to pay the rent. Master Roger let me look at it... so many words, too many, but the colours were lovely and there was an image of the Blessed Virgin, all blue and gold...'

'That is my trade: I write and make the images on the page, then bind the pages together to make a book. Was it a Book of Hours that you saw? Some are very beautiful.'

'I don't know, do I?' Rose said with a shrug, pouting her lips, 'I can't read, can I now? I wish I could, then I might better myself... be proper and respectable... find a decent husband maybe.'

'For once, I do not have my scrip with me, else I could draw the letter forms and teach you their shapes.'

'You would learn me how to read, master?'

'Aye. Why not? I don't suppose you have paper and ink, or chalk or...'

'Why would I? What would a whore like me need such things for?'

Seb shook his head, frowning at her using the word 'whore'. He found it difficult to label her so, tarnish her with so filthy a word.

'I tell you what I do have,' she said suddenly, jumping up from the bed. 'A customer left something behind one time. Said he'd come to the wrong door.' She giggled. 'Got cold feet more like, poor lad. I think I frightened him.' She rummaged in the linen bag that had held the cups and platter. 'Here. Lots of words already written for us. Now you can spend the afternoon learning me.'

'Teaching you,' Seb corrected out of habit. He did the like with young Jack all the while.

It was a gathering of a few sheets of poor quality paper, sewn together through the fold – not very straightly, his stationer's eye noted as he flicked through the pages. Printed in Flanders, most like, Mechelin, probably. A cheap import of low standard, off-centre in parts. He would have been ashamed to have made such a shabby job of it, but at least it was reading matter, so would suffice for now.

'This is the Gospel according to John,' he read, 'In the beginning was the Word, and the Word was with God and the Word... was... God.'

'What's amiss, Master Foxley? You've turned quite pale.'

Seb closed the pages.

'We cannot read this. 'Tis in English.'

'That's a good thing then, isn't it, so you can learn me, er, teach me to read English. That's what I want.'

'This is an heretical text, Rose, a Lollard tract. Don't you understand?' Seb shook the booklet at her.

'No. It's just words, isn't it?'

'Words from the Bible. The Church says the Bible must only be read in Latin.'

'But I don't know any Latin, only the Paternoster and Ave Maria.'

'That is the point. Priests read the Bible in Latin and interpret its true meanings for us. You must burn this in the brazier afore anyone else knows you have it.'

'What's inter-whatever mean, then?'

'Interpret. It means to explain to us what the words are telling us.'

'Can you read and understand Latin?'

'Aye. I have to for my work.'

'So you can read a Latin Bible. Why do you need a priest to tell you what it says then?'

'For fear I may misinterpret it, I suppose. I'm not trained for the priesthood.'

Rose took the booklet from him and smoothed out the pages that Seb had screwed up in his agitation.

'Why should I burn this when I could learn to read it and know what the Bible says without troubling a priest?'

'Because the Church decrees it.'

'Then the Church is an old, fat donkey and twice as obstinate.'

'Rose! Enough of this, I say. Now burn it. Forget you ever saw it. Next time, I'll bring you something suitable to read.'

'Next time? In English?'

'Aye. So long as I see you put that in the brazier. Now.'

With a heavy sigh, Rose pushed the booklet in amongst the glowing sticks. They watched the paper catch, flare, curl and blacken until it was naught but ash among the embers. Seb put a few fresh sticks to burn on top, making certain the evidence of heresy was gone forever.

He opened the window shutter and a few wisps of fog drifted in but he could begin to make out the form of the buildings across the way. The fog was thinning at last, wafting away on a rising breeze.

'I must leave you now, Rose,' Seb said, taking a shiny new groat from his purse and pressing it into her child-like hand with its dimpled knuckles. 'I'll come back on Friday, after midday, as a customer. Don't let Master Roger try to fob me off, selling you to me as a virgin, though I can see why many would believe it.' He smiled, removing the sting from his words. 'I shall bring what is needful for our reading lesson. Farewell, Rose.' He kissed her plump cheek, downy-soft as a day-old chick.

He was gone but Rose felt warm inside, hugging gladsome thoughts to herself. Here was a man who, for once, didn't want to make use of her for his pleasure but for her own sake.

• •

Seb made his way back to Paternoster Row through the thinning mist. It did not seem half so far as his walk earlier. Shop-owners were letting down their shutters onto trestles, setting out their wares for sale as a few customers began to appear. Seb bought some ripe pears from a huckster's tray. They looked golden and oozed juice as he bit into one, the syrupy sweetness trickling down his chin. He licked his lips. Em and the others would enjoy these – a peace offering to make amends – and at least he would have something to show for his venture out into the fog. He watched as the old woman, bent as an archer's bow at full draw, selected the best and put them in a sacking bag for him.

'I'll be 'ere t'morra, Gawd willin', so yer can return me bag,' she told him.

He thanked her and handed over two pence for eight fruits. As he turned from the huckster, something dark caught his notice, a flash of movement. Then it was gone, cloaked in the last of the fog. A bird perhaps? He looked up and round about at the rooftops and gable ends but saw nothing. He must have imagined it. Pleased with his purchases and still munching fruit, Seb reached his own familiar front door. What a relief. Old Symkyn was sitting opposite. Had he been there all morning, veiled from view by the fog? Seb hoped not. Surely the fellow could have taken refuge in St Michael's church else Death would catch him with a chill. Mentally, he counted out a fruit for everyone in the Foxley household and realised there would be one to spare, so he handed Symkyn a pear.

'Good day to you, Symkyn. I trust you'll enjoy it?' he said.

The beggar tested its ripeness, pressing the flesh with his thumb.

'God give ye good day, master. Aye, seems soft enough for my ol' teeth. Can't recall when I last ate a pear... must be years. And thanking ye kindly, master. Oh, and by the by, just so's ye be aware, master: they's follering ye. Follered ye yesterd'y, an' all.'

'Following me? Who? Why would anyone?'

'Can't say, master. Just know 'tis so.'

Seb nodded his thanks, certain the old man was mistaken or imagining things. After all, as an artist, he prided himself on noticing tiny details, observing things which others did not see, yet he had seen no sign of any felons lurking or miscreants concealed in shadow. Nothing. Poor Old Symkyn probably dreamt it.

He entered the house, hoping Emily would be in a less fraught humour but bracing himself for fear that was not the case.

• •

The workshop was in good order, Gabriel copying out the treatise on Leviticus – Seb could see he was nearing the final folios – Tom grinding azurite in a mortar, making the bright blue pigment, the first vivid colour of the day. Jack was attempting to look busy at the sand tray, practising his letter shapes with Little Beggar at his side, front paws upon the edge of the tray, slobber dribbling from his lolling tongue into the damp sand.

'Greetings, all.'

'Ah, Seb, I have a query for you in this Latin manuscript,' Gabe said, beckoning him to his desk. 'See here, there is a mistake by the previous copyist, or else by the original author, in which case he was addle-brained. Since we pride ourselves on our faultless copying, do I repeat the error or should I show that we are the better scholars and correct it?'

Seb read the passage and laughed.

'In truth, we cannot have a book leave this workshop with such foolishness upon the page. Put it to rights, Gabe, then come, I have some fresh fruit for you all. Ripe pears, one each.'

Of course, Jack needed no second telling when food was mentioned and left the sand tray. Beggar, less eager when fruit was the only new scent tickling his wet nose, still had his paws on the edge. Without Jack as a counterbalance, the inevitable mishap came to pass. As they all delved into the bag for fruit, Beggar upended the sand tray. It crashed down and the dog fled, whimpering, into the corner. Sand flew everywhere.

'Sorry, master. Beggar didn't mean no 'arm,' Jack said. 'He ain't in trouble, is he?'

Seb closed his eyes, praying that when he should open them again, the floor would not be covered in sand and all would be as before. It wasn't.

'Just fetch the broom and pray God that Master Jude does not come home as yet.'

The noise had summoned Emily and Nessie from their tasks in the kitchen.

'Ooh, mistress, what a mess,' Nessie said, fearing she would have to clear it up, even though the workshop was not usually her province.

Emily stood, hands on hips, observing the menfolk, all on hands and knees, doing their best to sweep the sand into a neat heap. They were not making much of a job of it. Men. Useless creatures for such a simple task, she thought and began to laugh. Seb looked up, irritated, but then he realised how foolish they all must look, so undignified, he joined in her laughter. Then everyone was laughing, even Beggar began yapping and dancing about in the sand. It would take longer to restore order in the workshop but at least good humour had been restored to the household which was a great relief to all.

Chapter 3

Wednesday, the sixth day of November
The Foxley's workshop

SEB WATCHED his brother, concerned for Jude. He had
come into the workshop after breakfast, sat on his stool,
leant back against the wall and closed his eyes. And there still,
an hour later, he remained, unmoving. Yet Seb did not think he
was sleeping, a clenched fist upon his desk suggested otherwise.
Jude, once so full of life, the man who had snapped his fingers
at the sumptuary laws of London and dressed as fashionably
and colourful as his purse permitted, was now dowdy as a dusty
starling, as slovenly as a clerk. How he had changed since his
time in Newgate last year. The lover of women had become a
lover of cheap ale. Seb couldn't understand what pleasure his
brother might derive from the nightly emptying of his purse
into the coffers of the local tavern keepers, draining their jugs
to the dregs only to piss the contents up the wall outside or spew
it into the gutter, crawl home, penniless, to suffer next morn
with a thunderous ale-heavy head. The shadows beneath Jude's
eyes were dark as candle soot; his once-bright fair hair like faded
straw and, Seb noticed with a start, sadly receding and thinning
beyond what seemed proper for a man not yet six-and-twenty
until the new year's turn.

'Stop staring at me as if I'm some mountebank's freak show.'
Jude opened one eye.

'Forgive me, Jude. I'm concerned for you is all.'

'Well, save yourself the trouble, little brother. Go, worry about someone else. I do well enough.'

'I know you still think of your time in Newgate, that it was terrible but...'

'Terrible? You hardly know the meaning of the word and 'tis best you never do. I tell you, Seb, wherever we go beyond Judgement Day, it can be no worse than that stinking midden of Hell. Sometimes I think it would have been better if you hadn't saved me from the hangman's noose.'

'Never say that, Jude. If I can help...'

'You can't. Forget it. I have work to do for the coroner this day, records to keep, witnesses to hear.'

Jude leapt from his stool, winced and clutched at the desk to steady himself.

Seb clasped his arm to aid him but his brother shook him off, took up his cloak and swung it about his shoulders. Collecting his scrip of pens, ink-pots and paper, Jude was gone, letting the door bang behind him.

'You know what he needs?' Gabriel said, having overheard much of the conversation.

Seb pulled a face.

'In the past, I would have said 'a good woman' but now... I just don't know what he needs.'

'Salvation.'

'Well, we all get that in the end, don't we? If we confess our sins to holy church, are truly remorseful and do penance, isn't that why our Lord Jesu died for us?'

Gabriel gave him a long, considering look, eyes narrowed. Then he shook his head, seeming to have made a decision.

'I mean True Salvation.'

And Seb knew that if the journeyman had written as he spoke, the words would have been scribed with large red capitals.

St Michael le Querne church by St Paul's Gate

IT WAS to be Father Hugh Wessell's first appearance at Wednesday Mass in St Michael's and, not surprisingly, the congregation was larger than usual for mid-week, braving the chill weather. The local gossips, who otherwise gathered at the conduit to exchange their news and views on all things, had come to church instead, not wanting to miss out on the new priest's first airing. The cold outside was just another good reason for them to huddle around the single brazier in the little nave for a sullen grey blanket – not quite rain; not quite fog – hung around St Michael's squat belfry tower like a dirty, discarded shroud on Judgement Day.

'Good day to you, Mistress Foxley,' Dame Ellen Langton had a cheery smile for her one-time apprentice. Emily bobbed a courtesy and Nessie tried the same behind her, wobbling.

'Good day, Dame Ellen. Have you come to measure up the new priest, like us?'

'You know full well, I always attend Mass of a Wednesday.'

Emily, having spent seven years working in the Langton household, knew no such thing, but she let it pass, forcing a smile in greeting for the other women she recognised, edging closer to the brazier that glowed with a dull red eye beside the font.

The summoning bell ceased and Master Marlowe, the churchwarden, hurried through from the belfry just as a faint rustling of vestments attracted their attention. Father Thomas and his new assistant stepped through beneath the carved rood screen. Was that a communal sigh of disappointment? No doubt every woman present had hoped for a tall young man, dashingly handsome with a dazzling smile. Or at least a pleasant countenance and a look of amiability.

Sadly, the new fellow's appearance was neither dashing nor pleasant, but his vestments were certainly dazzling, more befitting a bishop than a humble parish priest. He was a peacock to Father Thomas's sparrow, more than a hint of gold thread reflecting in the candlelight. Father Thomas introduced him to the flock with as much dignity as he could manage, since the fellow's appointment implied he could no longer do the job without assistance.

'This is Father Hugh Weasel, my children. I trust you will strive to make him feel welcome amongst us.' The elder man gestured to indicate the younger should speak.

'My name is Hugh WessELL,' he told them, his very first utterance irritable as sin. And, somehow, it seemed he had grown into the name – a short, broad, chinless face with small rounded ears; beady black eyes and, most oddly, little pointed teeth, spaced along his jaw like rusty pins pushed through old cloth. If the parishioners hoped Father Hugh would have a more agreeable nature than the vicious little animal whose name he bore, their first encounter dashed those hopes. He proceeded to lecture them on proper behaviour during Mass, even before learning of their short-comings.

'I will not tolerate gossiping during divine office and no late arrivals and interruptions. Do I make myself clear?'

The congregation muttered.

'And I see a number of you have brought your stools... well, there will be no sitting down for anyone until after the raising of the Host and then only when I permit it.'

'What about Mary's rheumaticks? She can't stand all the time,' one of Dame Ellen's cronies, Nell Warren, spoke up loudly for her friend. She wasn't to be cowed by this mannerless oaf; priest or no priest.

'And what about those with child?' Dame Ellen added, giving Emily a significant look that made the young woman blush. Little chance of that at present.

'No exceptions,' Father Hugh announced.

'We'll need his permission to drop dead next,' someone said, raising a laugh or two.

'And I will have no iniquitous back-sliders in this parish!' He was almost shouting.

'Thank you, Father Hugh, I think that will do,' Father Thomas said, ushering his assistant back to the chancel to proceed with the Mass. It was swiftly apparent that Father Hugh was wasting his breath anyway. Mary Jakes lowered herself onto her folding canvas stool, as did a few others, and the chattering began immediately the priests left the nave. There was plenty to say about the new man – none of it favourable.

'Iniquitous back-sliders, indeed,' Dame Ellen huffed, 'Who does he think he is, talking to us like that? Bishop's man or no, he won't speak to me in that tone.' And nobody doubted she meant what she said. 'Now, tell me what you've heard, Nell, Mary, about King Edward's new mistress. A goldsmith's wife, they say. Is that the case? Do we know her? Well, now, I don't listen to gossip-mongers, as you are aware, but I heard it said that...'

Queenhithe, by the *St Christopher*

GABRIEL WAS shivering, wondering how long he should wait. It had seemed that God was aiding this venture when Seb had asked him to come down to the docks, to search out his precious pigments, little knowing a message had already passed in the opposite direction, telling Gabriel to come. He had wondered upon an excuse to make for leaving the workshop but now none was needed.

Even though he was watching out for his coming, the tap on the shoulder caught Gabriel unawares, giving him such a fright.

'Gabriel... yer got my message.' The voice rasped like the incoming tide on gravel.

'You gave me a shock, creeping up like that.'

'Been a long time... too long. Yer've growed up, Gabe.' A strong, callused hand grasped Gabriel's and pulled him into an embrace. 'What've yer been up to, eh?' It was warm against his chilled flesh.

'Never mind all that now. What's this about? Your message mentioned packages?'

'Hush, keep yer voice down. Never know who's listening. Blasted bishop has ears everywhere. As I wrote: we need somewhere safe for the merchandise, just a few days. I heard tell the Foxleys' place is large. Would there be...'

'Aye, I have my own chamber above the workshop, room for these, er, packages, if they're not too big.'

'Small enough to carry. None shares yer chamber elsewise?'

'The serving wench makes my bed and brings me clean linen but she has the wits of a fish. She won't even notice. Besides, she fancies herself in love with me, dough in my hands, if need be. As for the Foxleys, they're as trusting as babes.'

'Good. Sounds well. I'll send yer word.'

'I'll be there. Come to the side gate. But there is another matter. Master Foxley ordered a box of pigments from Venice by the hand of Captain Marchmane. As yet, he hasn't received them.'

'Aye, well, that's another mystery, Gabe. We haven't seen the captain since the eve we docked, neither hide nor hair of him, and 'tis a worry because we have heard a rumour – plague, they say, on one of the other ships moored at Billingsgate, too close for comfort. But I'll see what I can find. Pigments from Venice, was it? If I find 'em, I'll send 'em up to, er, Paternoster Row, isn't it... to the front door.'

'Master Foxley will be most grateful, in coin, I dare say, knowing him as I do.'

The other man laughed and moved away but turned back.

'Gabriel. Take care and may the Lord God protect yer as a Known Man.'

'I will, never fear, and may He protect...'

But the man was gone.

• •

At dinner in the Foxleys' kitchen, Father Weasel – or rather Wessell – was the subject of the conversation. Over onion and leek pottage with fine white bread, the new priest's numerous faults were listed, examined and judgement passed.

'Not a pleasant man at all,' Emily concluded.

'Mayhap he was nervous about meeting you all: so many women,' Seb said, trying to excuse the priest he'd not yet met. 'I know the likes of Dame Ellen and her friends can put the fear of God into men of standing. Even Lord Mayor Bassett, he but lately stood down from office, has quailed before such goodwives and widows as they.'

'He called us 'iniquitous back-sliders' more than once and Dame Ellen won't stand by and let the Weasel get away with that,' Emily said, wagging her spoon to emphasise the point.

'Wot's ineekweetus mean, master?' Jack asked, wiping his bowl clean with the last of his bread – always the first to finish his food.

'It means 'wicked', Jack.'

'Then why didn't he say 'wicked'? Why do folks never say wot they mean? All them long words... it's stupid. Priests should speak proper so folk like me know wot they're talking about. 'Ow else do I learn stuff in church when it's all stupid, in Latin?'

'Jack! Mind your manners,' Seb said, setting his spoon and bowl neatly aside. 'Do not speak of holy matters in such words. You will make your confession tomorrow...'

'Not to that Weasel fella, I won't. Any'ow, 'tis true.'

'Jack! Enough! You will confess to Father Thomas and don't be surprised if he gives you a bread-and-water penance. I think you would be deserving of it. Now, Gabriel, what came to pass at Queenhithe? Did you discover the whereabouts of the paper we ordered and my precious pigments?

'The paper is on its way. Raff, er, I mean, Master Scraggs, the mate on the *St Christopher,* is looking for your pigments himself and will send them up when he finds them.'

'Still no word of Captain Marchmane, then?'

'No and the crew are concerned for there are rumours of a case of plague down by the river and they fear the worst for their captain.'

'Aye, that's the truth,' Jude said. 'The coroner was called this morning to confirm a case on a fishing vessel at Billingsgate. Saw the dark tokens upon the skin, so there was little doubt, though such a sickness is unusual in November. Seems we're all doomed to suffer in misery.'

Seb saw a look of horror on the young ones' faces. Such talk at dinner was not for their ears.

'Tom, Jack, now the mist has cleared, fetch your drawing boards and charcoal sticks and go to Smithfield. I want to see some drawings made from nature. Take your scrips and bring back some objects, leaves or twigs or berries or some such, that you can work on here tomorrow, if the weather is inclement – that means 'bad', Jack – and don't fall into the Horse Pool. And what of you, Gabriel? Could you take those sketches I did for the new sign for the Swan-on-the-Hoop Inn over at Holbourne. Get Thomas Luyt's approval for whichever design he prefers. The cost will be the same, whatever his choice.' Seb turned to Jude. 'Do you have business elsewhere?'

Jude shrugged.

'Maybe. There's always the tavern, to drown a few sorrows.'

Seb sighed to see his brother so forlorn but then, watching them all hastening to grab their cloaks and hurry out, he smiled. Nessie was up to her elbows, washing bowls, pots, spoons and cups.

Seb turned to his wife, eyebrows raised, questioning, hopeful.

'Remember, husband, 'tis Wednesday,' Emily said, sternly. 'Holy church forbids what you have in mind and yet more so in daylight.'

'We can always go with Jack tomorrow, to confess our 'iniquitous back-sliding' and I swear I'll keep my eyes closed all the while.' Seb took Emily's warm hand in his and led her towards the stair that went up to their chamber.

'I may have to give you a bread-and-water penance.'

'I shall make no argument against that... so long as I enjoy earning it.' They were laughing as Seb closed the chamber door behind them and dropped the bar in place.

Smithfield

A WATERY SUN was fighting its way through the last of the mist as Tom and Jack reached the open land of Smithfield, by St Bartholomew's where the monks tended the sick. Jack hurried past, fearing the stink of contagion that he was sure wafted out of the great oaken door. He skipped around the worst of the patches of mud and piles of dung left by yesterday's cattle market.

'Look, Tom, there's some o' them acorn fings up there.' Jack stood beneath master's favourite oak tree. 'We could draw 'em.'

'The only reason they're still there is because they're too high for rootling pigs to reach, or anyone else. If you want to draw them you'll have to do it from here.'

'But I can't see 'em proper, can I?'

'Well, then, find something else.'

'I could climb up an' pick 'em.'

'And break your stupid neck. I'm sure Master Seb will be well pleased with you then.'

'Nah. I can do it, easy.'

Jack took off his cloak and dropped it in a heap on the muddy grass.

Tom picked it up.

'Don't do it, Jack. I'm not carrying you home with a broken leg.'

But Jack was already climbing the trunk, seeming to find finger and footholds where Tom could see none. As he went higher, Tom could hardly bear to watch yet was fascinated all the same. Jack stretched out towards the twig on which the acorns hung, dangling by one tenuous handhold. 'Careful!' The little bunch of acorns landed at Tom's feet. Jack, still dangling, was grinning like a gargoyle on St Paul's.

'See. Told yer it was easy.' He came down the trunk, nimble as a squirrel, still grinning. He snatched his cloak from Tom and put it on, picked up his prize and tucked them in his scrip.

'Come on, Tom, don't dawdle like an ol' biddy.' Jack flapped his cloak and wheeled around some shrubby bushes Master Seb would have known the names of. 'Look at me, Tom, I'm flying like them birds up there.'

Tom glanced up, seeing a half dozen red kites circling.

'Kites,' he said, 'Must be some dying animal somewhere. They eat carrion, you know.' Tom, being the elder, liked to show off his greater knowledge.

'Wot, dead fings? Yuck.'

'Well, you eat dead pig and sheep soon enough.'

'But not dead dog or badger. I 'spect that's wot it'll be. P'raps we could draw it, like Master Seb told us too. Race yer!'

Tom sighed. Drawing a dead dog wasn't his idea of a joyous way to pass the time until supper. His nose was running and his hands were so cold he wasn't sure he'd be able to hold the charcoal properly. Still, they were free of the workshop without master looking over their shoulders all the while, so he joined his companion, running full tilt towards the far hedgerow where the birds seemed to be gathering, dropping lower with each spiral. Until Jack came near and they rose into the sky again, fading from sight among the last few threads of mist.

'Wot d'yer think? Ol' clothes is all it is.' Jack stood, hands on hips. 'We could take them bits, the fripperers'd give us a few coin fer 'em.' Always the street urchin, trust Jack to think of selling the rags to a second-hand dealer in such items.

Tom wasn't so sure. There was a strange smell about them as Jack moved the clothes with his foot and bent down for a closer look. Tom realised that kites were not going to gather for a feast of shabby cloth. He felt a shiver run down his spine that had naught to do with the November chill.

'Jack. Leave it be. Come away. I think we ought to fetch Master Seb.'

'Why? This is a goodly piece of cloth; it'll sell easy. And shoes... ah!' Jack leapt back, tumbling on his rump on the damp grass. 'Tom! It's a dead 'un, Tom. Wot'll we do?'

• •

The banging of the kitchen door and a frantic chorus of 'Master Seb! Master Seb!' disturbed the couple from a blissful doze.

'Oh, what now? I thought those two would be gone until supper.' Seb clambered out of bed, grabbing his shirt. He found one stocking under the bed but the other proved elusive. 'What've you done with my hose, woman? You wanton, irresistible temptress, you.' He leant over and kissed Em as she lay back upon the pillows. Her mouth was sweet as strawberries, her lips inviting...

'Master Seb, where are you?' Tom shouted from downstairs.

'Come quick!' Jack sounded agitated.

'Coming!' Seb called out. 'Never a moment's peace,' he muttered, tying the points on the one stocking he'd found. Em discovered the other among the sheets and threw it at him.

'I did warn you it was a sin of a Wednesday. Now you're paying the price.'

'Apprentices. Huh. More trouble than a cartload of drunken piglets. You just lie there, you seductress, you sister of Eve, and I'll return shortly. Keep my place warm for me.'

'Master!'

'I'm coming.' Seb stepped into his shoes and pulled on his tunic, not bothering to lace it up. 'Wait for me, woman... Don't dare move.'

Wait, she thought, aye, and for how long? Everything took precedence over her. Their marriage hardly seemed to exist these days. A snatched kiss here and there. In truth, her husband was a considerate lover upon these rare occasions but never exciting. No sense of adventure beyond the daring of a stolen Wednesday afternoon. Give him a new pot of pigment and he was giddy with delight and enthusiasm. Offer him bed-sport and calling her a sister of Eve was as boisterous as he got. Always, he seemed fearful of hurting her, apologising for every touch, as though she was fragile as glass and might shatter if he was the least passionate. Either that or he was incapable of feeling passion for aught but his wretched manuscripts.

• •

In the kitchen, Tom and Jack stood dishevelled and muddy. Jack was sniffing, wiping his snotty nose on his cloak.

'Jack, I've told you afore about that. Use the kerchief you were given. Now what is amiss? Where are your scrips, your drawings? And look at the state of you. Mistress Em will...'

'But master, we found a dead thing,' Tom gasped out the words. He was trembling, scrubbing away tears.

'A dead 'un fer sure,' Jack added, wringing his cloak hem in his hands. 'I seed it's foot. We thinked it was jus' rags but it weren't... t'was so 'orrible, master, an 'orrible colour. I was nearly sick it stunk so bad. I ain't never seen nuffin so 'orrible afore.'

'Aye, Jack, I believe I get the gist of your tale,' Seb said, seating himself on a bench by the kitchen board and pouring a cup of ale. 'Tom, tell me in sensible words, what you think you may have found. Take a sip of ale and calm yourself, first. You too, Jack.'

'You must come, Master Seb, over to Smithfield,' Tom began.

'Us ain't making it up, master, there's a real dead 'un stuffed under the 'edgerow. A woman, I b'lieve... it were a woman's shoe most like...'

'A woman?' Seb queried. 'I thought you meant some dead animal. You are sure it is a woman? Dead, not just sleeping?'

The lads nodded. Seb took the ale cup from Jack and drank what little remained.

'Very well. You must show me. Say naught of this to anyone.'

'Why master?'

'Because, Jack, as matters stand, you are first-finders and you realise what that means?'

'Nah.'

'It means you were duty bound upon finding a dead body to raise the hue and cry. The fact that you failed to do so could have you in trouble with the sheriffs. We must go to the place and remove all evidence that you have been there earlier. I take it that, in your haste, you left your scrips behind?'

'Aye, master. Sorry.'

'We must retrieve them. Then I can play the part of first-finder, raise the hue – pointless as that will be for one who died of cold, most like – and report my discovery to the authorities. You must keep silent about having found anything earlier. Do you both mark my words?'

'Aye. But wot 'bout the blood?'

'Blood? You did not mention anything about blood.' Seb turned to the stairs and called out: 'Emily! I have to go out. The lads are with me. We may be a while.'

'I might have known,' came back the muffled reply.

Seb put on his mantle and boots: Smithfield was no place for his best shoes.

'Lead the way, Jack.'

• •

The lacklustre winter daylight was already fading to dusk as they reached the place.

'The body is quite well hidden. Another half hour, we might not be able to claim to have found it by accident,' Seb said. He bent low, crouching beneath the bare, thorny branches of the brambles and briars in the hedgerow, parting the yellowing grasses of last summer to see what lay there like a discarded rag. The smell was worse than a slaughterer's yard.

Seb pulled the cloth of his mantle across his nose. Long strands of dark hair – there was too little light now to determine the colour more precisely – caught upon the thorns, indicated that the ravaged face might once have been that of a woman. The stiff blackness on the clothes, aye, he could tell it was blood even in the gloom of twilight. He surveyed the ground around. A patch of bare earth looked to have been churned up in a struggle. Now the mud bore footprints, testament to the presence of two persons: one with small dainty feet, the other larger. Seb traced the outline of a singularly clear print with his finger.

'Pass me your drawing stuff, Tom,' he said. In the last of the rapidly dimming light, with charcoal and paper resting upon his knee, Seb drew the footprint, taking great care over its uneven outline.

'If it wasn't for the kites, we wouldn't have looked, would we, Jack?' Tom said, keeping well away and upwind of the stink.

'Nah. Can yer see the blood there, master?' Jack pointed, moving closer.

Seb held the lad back and stood up, his left hip complaining as it still did sometimes on cold, damp days, his legacy of past times. He tucked his drawing away inside his shirt for safe-keeping.

'Leave it be. Gather up your scrips and come with me.'

'She is dead for certain, isn't she, master?'

'Aye, Tom. Beyond earthly help. Now come away.'

They reached Newgate just as the keeper was about to close the gates for the night.

'Good sir, hold off!' Seb called out, 'I'm raising the hue and cry. I found the body of a woman lying at Smithfield. I summon you as a witness and to heed me as first-finder.'

'Who's to be pursued? Did you see 'im?' the keeper asked.

'No. The body has lain too long. We will need torches to find our way.'

· ·

An hour later, by torchlight, Seb was returned to the site accompanied by the gate-keeper, Valentyne Nox, the under-sheriff, the coroner, Master Bulman, and, as it came to pass, Jude, as the coroner's clerk. The lads, making their grave disappointment most obvious, had been sent home to Paternoster Row, to warn Mistress Emily that her goodman would be late to supper.

'Too bloody dark to make notes,' Jude complained. 'Trust you to ruin my evening, little brother. Couldn't you have found the damned corpse tomorrow, after breakfast, preferably? Who is she, do we know?'

'I've no clue. In truth, I didn't look too closely.'

'Details, Master Foxley.' Under-sheriff Nox took Seb by the arm none too gently. He smelled of a long afternoon spent in the tavern, his breath sour with cheap ale. His pock-marked face was a devil's colander by torchlight. 'How did you find the body?'

'Red kites, sir, I saw the birds circling,' Seb said, repeating what Tom and Jack had told him. 'They attracted my notice. I came to see what may have caught their attention.'

'When was this?'

'Earlier this afternoon.'

'Before or after vespers was rung,' Nox asked.

'After. As I went to raise the hue and cry, the keeper was just closing the gates.' Seb gestured towards the gate-keeper who nodded his agreement.

'And it was nigh dark, you say?'

'Aye, sir. That is so.'

'And yet it was the birds which attracted your attention, Foxley? That seems remarkable to me. Not only were you able to see them in such poor light but that they should be there at all. Is it not the case that kites fly in the daylight and roost before dusk?'

'Well, I suppose so.' Despite it being so cold that his breath made clouds in the air, Seb was sweating beneath his shirt. How could he have made such a foolish error? Nox was going to pick his story apart, thread by thread, until it all unravelled. He should have thought his story through more carefully beforehand.

'So, tell me again when you found the body? Do you want to revise the time?'

'It must have been a little before vespers, then.'

'In which case, why did you wait – how long, an hour maybe? – before raising the hue. What were you doing all the while, Foxley? Think before you answer me because I'm smelling the reek of lies, here, the stench of fabrication, and I don't like men who play me for a fool, believing I won't know an untruth when I hear one.'

The gate-keeper stepped forward:

'Master Nox, I can tell ye, I saw them two lads, them as was with Master Foxley, earlier this afternoon, coming out the gate an' going towards Smithfield. Then, a while after, they come back, all of a lather, running like Old Scratch hisself was after 'em.' The keeper crossed himself at mention of the Devil. 'So I reckon it was they who was first-finders, not Master Foxley. Oh, and when they went out, they was carrying bags but came back without.'

'Is this the case, Foxley?' Nox demanded, his grip on Seb's arm tightening.

'Aye. I'm afraid 'tis true,' Seb admitted, 'But the lads were upset, knew not what to do, so they came to fetch me.'

'They should've raised the hue.'

'But they're only youngsters.'

'No excuse. And you're guilty of aidin' them in concealment of a crime.'

'But we alerted the keeper...'

'Aye and how long was that after you found the body, eh? More than time enough for the miscreant to make his escape.'

'But that is absurd. The body has lain for days...'

'And how would you know that? Unless you put it there? Did you kill her, Foxley?' Nox was twisting Seb's arm up his back, causing him to cry out in pain.

'Leave him be, Nox,' Jude said. 'My brother weeps over a fly caught in a spider's web. He couldn't kill a trapped rat, never mind a woman. Release him, I tell you. Now,' he growled, the threat hanging ominously, like a yet-darker cloud in the darkness between him and the under-sheriff.

With a curse, Nox let go of Seb. It was unlikely the murderer would ever be caught now and the stationer would have made a justifiable culprit instead. Perhaps the Foxleys were both involved? All the more reason to continue to keep a watch on them. No doubt they were up to no good somehow. Nox had an instinct for such matters, whether working in his official capacity for the city authorities or in his other, more lucrative, unofficial employment.

• •

'Trouble follows you, doesn't it, Seb?' Jude said as they made their way to Paternoster Row, carrying torches as required to show they were good citizens going about their lawful affairs.

'I was trying to protect the lads, spare them the obligations of first-finders.'

'And instead you almost got yourself arrested. How would that bloody help? You're a damned fool, Seb, always have been; probably always will be. You have to stop trying to do good by everyone. You're a one-man crusade and it's never going to work out. Just be a selfish bastard like the rest of us. It will cause far less trouble for us all.

'Now, I have business of my own to be about: a good evening's drinking at the Panyer which you've already cut short by an hour or more. I'll have supper there rather than put up with that shrewish wife of yours.'

Seb went home, exhausted, thinking Jude was probably right about him being a fool.

Jude made for the inn, to go in search of oblivion in the bottom of an ale cup.

Chapter 4

Thursday the seventh day of November
The City of London. Early morning.

THE THAMES had spewed this corpse onto one of the great starlings of London Bridge as the tide went out. Now it lay in a good, if faded, blue coat with tarnished silver buttons, discarded on the green-slimed stone, staring eyeless at the November sky. Valentyne Nox, under-sheriff of the City of London stood, hands on hips, by the Oystergate stairs, supervising, his breath puffed like smoke in the cold air as he yelled instructions to the boatmen on the water. They took no notice, knowing what they were about, the best way of hauling a body from the river, into the boat.

The boatmen wrestled it over the gunwale, immune to its stink, and rowed to the water stairs. As they lugged it up the steps, slick with weed, Nox covered his nose but his eyes missed nothing: the moment he saw the quality of the coat, the fine leather belt with a gilded buckle, the large purse still fastened shut, he knew this was no robbery. An accident: that was it. A drunk who had slipped and fallen into the river, aye, that was the case as he would tell it. Happened all the time. Not a week went by, they didn't have to retrieve a body or two. The greedy Thames swallowed anything, anyone, from unwanted by-products of the stews – poor little mites – to frail old biddies who fell in whilst washing their linen; from dead horses to foreign sailors. The Thames made no distinction. A pity the sea hadn't accepted this offering and saved him a deal of trouble.

The body was manhandled into the waiting hand cart and covered with sacking for decency's sake, to spare the good citizens from such ugliness. It was bloated from its time in the water, stretching the clothes tight, straining the laces and belt. As usual, the creatures of the deep had feasted on the eyes and lips first; 'til his own mother wouldn't know him. At least things had not gone so far: they could still tell it was a man.

'Usual procedure,' Nox instructed the men unnecessarily, making the most of his self-importance, 'Take him to St Magnus by the Bridge.'

The priest at the church of St Magnus the Martyr was used to receiving unexpected guests of this kind and made the sign of the cross over the body with little care and less compassion before it was carried down to the crypt. There it would lie for a day or two, in case it could be claimed by a relative or at least given a name, before the stench became unbearable and it had to be buried. With this one, that would be sooner rather than later. Worse yet, the coroner would have to be informed and that might well mean Nox would have to cross paths with those wretched Foxley brothers again – the one as coroner's clerk, the other as a blasted limner. Coroner Bulman liked to have the younger fellow draw the dead, especially when they needed burying quick, so relatives might see the likeness and put a name to the corpse even after it was underground.

Apparently, King Edward thought it was a good idea after one of his courtier's pages had been given a name for his grave marker, having been missing for weeks. The well-dressed lad had fallen foul of a runaway horse over by St Paul's. Nobody there recognised him so Seb Foxley had drawn his likeness, made copies and pinned them up in church porches. The courtier had eventually seen one and identified his servant. Drawing the dead didn't appeal to Nox in the least.

Nor to the man who drew those images.

The Foxley workshop

S EB WAS showing Jack how to whiten parchment with chalk, sprinkling on the powdered stone and working it in.

'Carefully now, we don't want it everywhere. You can use this means to make good after you've had to scrape off a mistake. Look, I'll show you.' Seb made an inky dribble in the corner of a parchment scrap, blotted it with pounce and then scraped it back with his knife. By the time he'd dusted it with chalk, the mark was gone. 'See? Now you try.'

Jack had no difficulty making the ink blot but the rest of the procedure was not so easy. The chalk dust got on his hands and up his nose. He gave a vast sneeze, blowing it in Seb's face, setting his master coughing.

Just then, a customer entered the shop, rapping on the door jamb.

'See who that is, Tom, please. I'll be there directly, when my eyes cease watering so.'

Tom returned in moments, carrying a wooden box of three hand-spans wide and a little less deep.

'A fellow came from Queenhithe, master, said this is yours, from the *St Christopher*. Might be your pigments, master.'

Like a child at New Year, excited over the prospect of a gift, Seb could hardly get the string untied fast enough, nor the latch undone. With a sigh of anticipation, he glanced around. Tom and Jack were crowding close to see. No sign of Jude, who had yet to appear this morning, unsurprisingly. And Gabriel wasn't to be seen either to share in his pleasure. No matter. Seb lifted the lid, revealing a layer of sheep's fleece protecting the contents. A mixture of odd, dry scents, earthy, pungent, wafted out as he removed the fleece and beneath sat a collection of small earthen pots, each with a waxed leather cover tied in place.

'Stand well back, Jack,' Seb said, 'You sneeze on these, you'll cost me a small fortune. Emily,' he called out, 'Come see what I have here.' He was sure that, as a silk-woman, she would appreciate the fine colours from Venice and Naples. The first pot was labelled 'terra verde' and contained a beautiful green powder, the colour of new spring beech leaves, perfect for the gown of the Magdalene he had in mind for Father Thomas's psalter. On the second pot, the ink on the label had run and his knowledge of Latin didn't help in this instance. He prayed that the pigment hadn't become damp as the label. It hadn't. It was a perfect blue and, once knowing that, Seb realised it was 'Egyptian blue'.

Em took the little pot, sighing over the exquisite colour.

'I would have a gown of such a hue, if only we could afford it,' she said. 'It would look so fine in church of a Sunday.'

'Aye, and probably cost a great deal in sumptuary fines, too,' Seb laughed, 'Wearing clothes so far above our status.'

'I can still dream, can't I? That at least costs naught.'

Seb was unveiling another pot marked 'terra rosa'. He gasped, having expected it to be an earthy red, as it said, but this was unlike any colour he'd ever seen before, one for which he had no name. If it were possible to take the tint of apple blossom buds before they open, the blush from a maiden's cheek and distil them together with the petals of a wild rose in the light of dawn, the colour might come close but still not equal the vibrant pigment in that pot.

'Look, Em. How would you like a gown of this hue, eh?'

'Oh, Seb, 'tis beautiful. Aye, I should be the envy of every woman in London clad so, would I not? Here comes Mistress Foxley, they would say, see how her gown outshines the queen's. It must be very expensive.'

'Mm, I had expected it to be a fine long-lasting red. Crimson lake fades so swiftly and I hoped this would be a good replacement. Oh, well, I'm sure I'll find a use for it one day.' He set the pot aside and took another from the box.

'Well, husband, some of us have more urgent matters to attend to, rather than playing with pretty powders like a royal mistress. I have marketing to do afore I cook your dinner, then some finished silk-work to deliver to Dame Ellen, I must repair your hose and beat the dust from the bed hangings.' Emily watched Seb, still engrossed in his pigments. 'You haven't heard a word I've said, have you?' No response. With a sigh, she left the workshop. Men!

• •

Seb was called from dinner by a visitor at the side gate. Valentine Nox, the under-sheriff, stood there, already tapping his foot despite having waited but a few moments since young Tom Bowen had answered his knocking and run to summon his master. Seb groaned inwardly. Was this about him having claimed to be first-finder of that poor woman's body?

'Master Foxley? I'm here at the coroner's behest. He would have you come to St Magnus church, to draw a likeness of a corpse, as you have done afore. It washed up earlier this day.'

Seb suppressed a shudder. His growing fame as a skilful draughtsman was proving to have a less pleasant aspect: this would be the third body the coroner had asked him to draw in the last six months. A likeness was only wanted if the deceased needed to be buried in haste, leaving no time for folk to come see if they knew the unfortunate. No one wanted an unnamed burial. It paid six pence a time but that didn't make the task any less awful. Seb collected his drawing stuff from the workshop and then returned to the kitchen where the rest of the household were dining on pottage and new bread.

'I'm going with Master Nox to St Magnus.'

'Now? But what about your dinner?' Emily asked.

'Can't be helped, Em, the dead cannot wait. I shall need a clean napkin and some lavender water, Nessie... now, if you please.'

The wench hurried to obey. Seb nodded his thanks and went with the under-sheriff, leaving Emily in a less than good humour. Another dinner spoiled.

St Magnus the Martyr's church

THE CHURCH of St Magnus beside London Bridge was larger than most places of prayer in the city but the broad nave was heavy with the miasmas of decay and putrefaction, welling up from the crypt. Little wonder Seb had been summoned. He pitied any parishioners having to breathe the stench during Mass, if they could stand it for so long. He doused the napkin liberally with lavender water, as he'd learned from previous times, and tied it round his mouth and over his nose before following Nox and the priest down to the crypt. Nox covered his face with his sleeve; the priest held a fragrant posy to his nose but Seb would need both hands for his work.

'Not much left to recognise,' the under-sheriff warned him, 'Not a pretty sight, but you can draw his scar; folk could know him by that alone.'

The corpse was stretched on a bier, set with a candle at each corner. Unlike the newly-dead who always seemed small, this was a great mound, swaddled like a pudding in its winding sheet. The smell grew worse. At arm's length, Nox lifted the face cloth and set an extra candle to better illuminate the ruined features. Seb closed his eyes for a few moments, willing his stomach to behave, having to swallow hard a couple of times before he had it under control.

'Scar?' he asked, steadying himself, leaning against the bier, silver point in hand, a sheet of prepared paper pegged to a drawing board wedged against his hip.

'Here.' Nox turned the head so Seb could see the other side of the face. From the right temple to the jaw stretched an old bluish scar, jagged as a lightning bolt. The drawing board crashed to the stone floor as Seb staggered to the steps and went up them as fast as he was able.

Seb sat on a stone beside the church porch, head in hands, sweating despite the chill of the day and the weakness of the winter sun. The river-dead were horrible to look upon at the best of times and he hadn't even recognised the man until he saw the scar. No drawing was needed: he could name Captain Philip Marchmane of the *Saint Christopher* out of Deptford, his friend and business partner.

An elderly woman, surely more frail than he, asked if he needed her to aid him home. He forced a smile, feeling it might slide off his face and splinter on the ground and thanked her for her kindness. Bracing himself, he returned to the nave. He could hear Nox and the priest laughing in the vestry. Probably laughing at him. Nox was tutting.

'Why the king foists a body so useless as that wretched artist upon us, I'll never know. I've no patience with the king's stupid notion of drawing the dead, anyway.'

'The fellow's pathetic but I warrant he'll be back,' the priest said, as short on sympathy as the under-sheriff. 'He'll want his six pence due and all his stuff's still down there.'

'Aye, and he can fetch it, too. I'm not,' Nox said.

'I've got wine, if you will...'

'A fine idea, father,' Seb heard Nox say.

Seb took the stairs slowly, pulling the lavender-scented napkin up over his nose again. Those uncaring devils had left Marchmane's ravaged face uncovered.

'My poor friend, may God be with you,' he whispered. The shroud had come unwrapped, would no longer meet across the bloated body. He pulled at the winding sheet, revealing discoloured skin marked with cuts and scratches from the stones and debris in the river. But then he noticed one cut, between the ribs, looked more intentional, precise. Trying to keep his hand steady, apologising to his friend for the indignity, he inserted his silver point into the wound and found it went deep, straight to the heart. Marchmane's death had been no accident. Seb crossed himself but the law said he must report his discovery. Though he knew the identity of the corpse, he drew the face anyway – not only as it was now, but how he remembered the captain from before. The sketches might prove useful yet. Then he replaced the face cloth, concealing his friend's features.

With dragging step, he went up to the vestry to tell Nox of his findings. The sheriff gave him a look of derision; the priest continued to sip his drink.

'The body is that of a sea captain, Philip Marchmane. He is... was... an old friend. His ship, the *Saint Christopher* sails out of Deptford but is presently moored at Queenhithe to discharge her cargo. We were business partners, importing goods from Venice. I don't know what happens about that now... the cargo, I mean. More importantly, my friend was stabbed.'

Nox hardly raised an eyebrow and shrugged without setting down his wine. 'What do you expect? All seamen are a pack of drunken brawlers. Mind you, I'm surprised they didn't relieve him of his purse, still full of coin. Too drunk to notice, no doubt. At least the coin will pay for his decent burial which is to be done at dusk, if you want to attend.'

Dazed, Seb said he would return after vespers for the brief interment.

'Now then,' Nox said, 'Come with me, Foxley.'

Seb went cold. He'd been right, thinking the first-finder business wasn't done. 'There's that other corpse, over at Grey Friars by Newgate, the one you claimed you found. Also needs drawing, coroner says.'

'Now?' Seb queried. He had seen enough of death for one afternoon.

'Ain't going to look any better t'morrow, is it? And you've already got your stuff fer drawing, ain't you?'

'I suppose so.' Wearily, Seb shouldered his scrip and followed the under-sheriff across the city. All very well for Nox on his horse, even if it was a sad-looking gelding with a tattered mane and a wall-eye, but Seb had to go on foot.

Grey Friars church, Newgate

THE BROTHERS' chant for the office of Nones, marking the third hour after midday, drifted under the door of the tiny chapel where the body of the woman lay beneath a sheet, her red shoes set neatly beside her as if she might put them on in the morning. She had yet to be washed and shrouded for burial. It seemed incongruous that her gown was a happy yellow colour of sunshine and saffron, now besmirched with her dried blood.

Like Marchmane's, her face was unknowable but in her case it had little to do with the activities of nature: her features had been ruined with hateful purpose by her assailant. Who could do such a thing? How could anyone loathe his fellow to such a degree? The poor woman. Seb could but hope she had been already beyond pain by the time... He couldn't finish that thought. There was no point in making a drawing but her family or friends might recognise the gown or shoes, so Seb took a sample of bright cloth, together with a lock of her hair and made a note of the dark mole on her left earlobe. He could find no other mark to distinguish her and, in truth, he had no intention of looking for one, partly out of respect for the dead but mainly because he could not bear it.

'Finished?' Nox asked when Seb met him outside the church, in the graveyard. 'Anything to report?'

'Nothing more than you know already. I haven't made a likeness – there seems little point – but I'll have my apprentices write out a description of her clothing and shoes, and the mole upon her ear, to be put in every church porch. Someone must know her. And if you have no other horrors for me...'

Nox shrugged but his eye was dark and he gave Seb a long, hard look, considering.

'No. You can go, 'til next time,' he said, counting out three groats and slapping them into Seb's hand, begrudging them as though they came from his own purse, rather than the city coffers.

The Foxley house

NESSIE WAS watching from the kitchen door as Master Seb came down the passage from the street door but her attention was on Gabriel, talking at the side gate to someone; she couldn't see who it was.

'Nessie, I'm dry as a desert, lass, what with the walk from St Magnus, then from Grey Friars,' Seb said, not mentioning that he could still seem to taste the foul stench of the dead. 'Some ale would be much appreciated.' He dropped his scrip on the floor beside a stool and sat at the board, kicking off his shoes and unfastening his mantle. 'Nessie,' he repeated when she took no notice.

'Oh, aye, master. Sorry, master.'

'Hang up my mantle for me, there's a good lass, and take some ale to Tom and Jack. They must be as dry as I am.' Nessie poured his ale but was concerned he would catch Gabriel – her light-of-love of the moment – up to something by the gate into the yard. Gabriel was looking over his shoulder before receiving a couple of heavy-looking packages from beyond the gate. One package he pushed behind the water butt, out of sight; the other he grappled with, glancing about, before manhandling it up the outside stairs to his room above the workshop. At the table, Seb wiped his mouth on a napkin.

'I shall be away to choir practice, shortly,' he said, 'Remind Mistress Em that we are to be singing a special anthem in St Paul's on Advent Sunday. The precentor may ask me to remain behind after, in which case, I might be late to supper. Can you remember that message?'

'Aye. More ale, master?' Nessie offered, thinking to keep him at the board, gathering up his cloak and draping it from the peg by the door.

'A little, yes.' Nessie took his cup to refill it, worrying over Gabriel. He would no doubt be back for the other package behind the butt. If Master Seb looked to the yard now, he might catch Gabriel in the act and there'd be trouble. Gabriel might even lose his place. She had to keep Master Seb in the kitchen a while longer.

Nessie remembered, at the back of the shelf, behind the dented copper pot they never used, cobweb-covered, was a tiny black vial. Her old mistress used to put the stuff in her husband's – and lovers' – wine when she was tired of their attentions. A drop or two in Master Seb's ale should make him doze off for a little while until Gabriel had done... whatever he was doing. It worked quickly: she knew that. She meant just to drip it in his cup but her hand shook and it trickled in. Too much. But it couldn't be helped now. She gave master the cup. It wouldn't matter if he slept an hour or two.

Seb emptied his cup, cleared his throat and went to push himself up off the bench. He struggled for a moment, a look of puzzlement on his face, then his features went blank. He fell forward, his head striking the board with a thump that made Nessie wince.

'Master? Master Seb?' No answer. One leg was folded under the bench, the other splayed out, the foot twisted over. His arms hung loose at his sides, dangling. His limbs looked formless as melted wax; boneless in his clothes. And his cheek lay pressed into the crumbs left from dinner; his eyes closed, a breadcrumb sticking to his lashes. Nessie peeked out into the yard in time to see Gabriel come down the stairs for the second hefty package, looking around before struggling back up to his room with it in his arms. She sighed: Master Seb could wake up now.

She tried to rouse him, shake him awake. He didn't move. She gripped his arm and pulled at him. His buttocks, barely perched on the stool, slipped off and he fell, cracking his chin on the edge of the board. He lay face up in a shapeless heap, his head under the trestles, his legs tangled round the overturned stool. There was blood all round his mouth and chin. Nessie screamed and screamed. Gabriel arrived first, clattering down the outside stair, took one look and dashed straight out again, shouting for Master Jude. But Jude didn't come. The two apprentices came running from the workshop.

'Help me shift the benches and dismantle the trestle board,' Gabriel told them. He straightened Seb's limbs and demanded a cushion, cradling his master's head on his knees.

'Come on, Seb, what's up with you, eh?' He wiped away the worst of the blood with his sleeve but it came again. Nessie wailed louder, her blunt features puckered in distress. 'Be quiet,' he told her, 'And fetch that cushion.' He smoothed Seb's hair off his brow with his fingertips, careful as a lover. 'Come now, my friend, don't do this...'

'Is it bad?' Jack asked, keeping to the doorway, not being able to see round Tom and unsure what had happened.

'Jack?'

'Here, Master Gabe.' The lad shoved past Tom.

'Run to Surgeon Dagvyle; tell him to come straightway. Tell him I sent you.'

'What if he ain't there?'

'Then find him!'

'It's bad then,' Jack concluded. He called to his dog and ran out, Little Beggar yapping at his heels.

'Where's Mistress Em?' Gabe asked Nessie as she handed him a cushion.

'She took them silk braids she finished over to Dame Langton's place. Should be back soon, I 'spect, master.'

'Tom, give me a hand with him: we'll get him upstairs to his bed.'

'What about me, master? What can I do?' Nessie asked, feeling helpless with no task to do.

'Set this kitchen to rights and for pity's sake clean up the blood before Mistress Em comes back.'

Seb lay on the bed, unmoving, looking more dead than alive. Gabriel and Tom were still sweating and blowing. It had been a real struggle to get him up the narrow stairs from the kitchen without knocking his head on the wall or getting his long legs hooked in the rope bannister.

'Least he's still breathing,' Tom said, straightening his clothes.

Gabriel sat on the bedside, staring at his master. He wiped away more blood from the deathly pale mouth.

'Where's Dagvyle got to? Why isn't he here?'

'Jack hasn't been gone long enough to reach Ironmonger Lane and come back again. Then Surgeon Dagvyle isn't going to run all the way. He might not even be there.'

'I know, I know, Tom, but look at him. He could be dying as we sit, watching. I wish I could do something.'

'Kitchen's all clean and tidy, master,' Nessie said from the doorway. 'What shall I do now?' Gabriel sighed. The maid was more trouble than she was worth.

'I don't know,' he snapped. 'Oh... go back to the kitchen: see if there are any worts to chop for supper. I don't know... think for yourself, can't you? What would mistress have you do?'

'Don't know, master.'

He was losing patience and about to clip the stupid wench around the ear but her stricken, woeful look and tear-filled eyes held him back.

'What shall I do?'

He shook his head, realising she was at a loss as much as he.

'Go, set out ale and cups. I think we shall all be in need. Tom, go down to the workshop, see if there are any customers waiting.'

'What shall I say to them, if there are?' Tom asked.

'Think of something, can't you? Tell them the truth, say we're closed for the day.'

'Shall I put up the shutters then, Master Gabe?'

'What? Oh, yes. I don't know. Just go.'

They heard the side gate shut in the yard below and voices bidding farewell: women's voices. Emily was home. After a few moments of Nessie's plaintive explanations, Emily came racing up the stairs, calling to Seb.

Gabriel met her at the bedchamber door, barring her way.

'Slowly, slowly, Mistress Em.'

'How is he? Nessie said... Let me by, Gabriel.'

He held her firmly, blocking her view of the bed.

'He's not too good, I fear.'

She pushed past him.

Gabriel didn't watch, not wanting to see.

'What happened?' Emily was on her knees beside the bed. 'My poor Seb...'

'We don't really know. Nessie says he just fell down.'

'Did he trip? Stumble on something?'

Gabriel shook his head.

'I don't think so.'

'Has he said anything?'

'No. He hasn't moved... hasn't made a sound... nothing.'

Emily took Seb's limp hand in hers, weeping silently.

'I've sent Jack to fetch Surgeon Dagvyle,' Gabriel told her but he wasn't sure if she heard.

John Dagvyle arrived, huffing and puffing. He was getting too portly for all this rushing about and his mule was in much the same case. Still, the Foxleys were always prompt in paying their bills so it was worth a bit of effort to keep their custom. But there were stairs! The bane of his life.

He paused before entering the bedchamber, taking a few moments to catch his breath and stop wheezing so much: it wouldn't make the most healthful impression if he went in red-faced and gasping.

'This is Master Seb's chamber, sir,' Jack said, wondering why the surgeon stood there, doing nothing. 'They put him t'bed, Tom said.'

'Go fetch wine,' Dagvyle ordered.

'We keep the wine fer important customers,' Jack said. The surgeon's scowl was fearsome. 'Aye, sir, I'll fetch some.'

The lad scurried off, down the stairs, three at a time.

'It would seem, Mistress Foxley, in my considered opinion, that your goodman has been taken with a seizure,' Jack heard the surgeon saying as he returned.

Nessie was bringing the wine and a set of pewter cups on a tray that rattled together in her unsteady hands.

'I don't want t' go in there,' she said, 'You take the tray.' She shoved it at Jack and couldn't get down the stairs fast enough.

He had no idea how to serve wine: it wasn't his job but he pushed the door wide with his foot and went in.

'But the blood?' Emily queried.

'Bit his tongue, cut his chin, mistress. There's no internal bleeding.'

'God be praised for that, at least.'

'I'll put a stitch or two in his chin before I leave.'

'Is... is it likely to happen again?'

The surgeon shrugged as he threaded his needle with dark silk thread. The stitches would show and thus be easier to clip through when the gash had closed over.

'No telling in a case like this. Depends upon the cause.'

'And what might that be?'

'Over-work... bad airs... an effluvium of evil humours eliciting brain fever,' he said without looking up from his needlework.

'Brain fever? Dear God. I had a cousin die of it.' Emily covered her face with her hands for a moment, trying to calm herself. 'But he doesn't seem feverish,' she added hopefully.

'No, not yet anyway. Or it could be the onset of the falling sickness.' Dagvyle clipped the thread on a fourth suture and eased himself up off the stool. 'I'll prescribe a potion anyway to sweat the ill humours out of him. Send for me if there's any deterioration, otherwise I'll send my bill over in the morning,' he said, slipping the needle back in its case, ready for the next patient. He packed away his little knife and his book of charts. 'His horoscope is fair, at least. He may require bleeding but not today, not with the moon in its present unfavourable aspect. So I'll bid good eve to you, Mistress Foxley.' He touched his cap; she bobbed her head. Gabriel showed him out.

• •

Supper was a miserable affair. Mistress Emily refused to leave her goodman's bedside and everyone was concerned for him. Gabriel disappeared upstairs at least twice an hour to see if his friend had regained his senses – which he hadn't – and Nessie snivelled constantly as she served an awful mess of tasteless stew which she said was rabbit. No one bothered to point out that since the coney Beggar had caught yesterday still hung, unskinned and whole as ever, on a hook by the chimney, it seemed she had forgotten to add the meat to the pot. Even Jack gave more than half his supper to the dog who sniffed it, turned his back on it and settled down under the board, keeping one eye open in the hope of some more tempting morsel coming his way. Tom chewed in ponderous silence and Gabriel's conversation was limited to a few insightful comments about Master Dagvyle's poor constitution for a man of medicine. Master Seb's name wasn't mentioned but no one was thinking of anything else. Brain fever? The falling sickness? Either long-term ailment could be a disaster for them all, for their business and their craft.

After the cloth was cleared – the bucket of leavings for the pig was full to overflowing – to cheer the company, Gabriel suggested he should tell them a tale. The lads were less than enthusiastic but there was naught else to do, so they remained, gathered close, elbows on the board, to listen as the cheap tallow wicks burned lower. Nessie, scouring platters, strained her ears to hear.

'Have I told you of the time I was sailing with a Barbary pirate captain, off the coast of Maroc?' Gabriel began, 'When the seas boiled with storm and strange birds dived upon us, trying to pluck out our very eyes...'

'You said they was pirates from Araby las' time,' Jack corrected, playing with a soft blob of wax, dripped from the single beeswax candle on the board – the household's symbol of affluence.

'Did I? Then it must be so. And you will remember that they tried to force me to aid them in boarding a fine Venetian merchantman, with a cargo of popinjays and monkeys and other strange beasts.'

'Was there unicorns?' Jack interrupted.

'Shh, wait won't you?' Tom said, nudging the younger lad.

'Indeed,' Gabriel continued, a smile pulling at the corner of his lop-sided mouth, 'There certainly were... and I found a sword among the pirates' baggage and determined they should not harm the Venetians, not a hair of their heads, if I might prevent them. So, I took the sword and crept to the captain's cabin...'

Gabriel related his tale, acting out all the parts, speaking with the pirates' voices, squawking like a popinjay and chattering like a monkey, as the story required. Eventually, he sat back, reached for his cup and found it empty.

'Then what?' Jack urged.

'As I told you, once the monkeys had aided me in slaying all the pirates, then the merchants, their popinjays, unicorns and other strange beasts went to their beds,' Gabriel said, rising from the bench, 'As will you. I must go see how Master Seb fares and I want you abed when I come down.'

But Seb fared the same: lying still, pale as a new moon, barely breathing.

Chapter 5

Friday, the eighth day of November

'ARE YOU certain you feel well enough for this, Seb?' Gabriel asked for maybe the fourth time since they had donned their mantles for the short walk along Paternoster Row to St Paul's Cathedral. 'I can buy what we need...'

'Gabriel, I'm grateful for your concern but, I swear on oath, I'm in good health as ever this morn.' In truth, his head throbbed and seemed stuffed with sheep's wool, his chin was sore, and the November gloom was too bright, making him squint, but Seb had things to do, an appointment to keep. Lying abed – which he'd felt desperately inclined to do earlier – wasn't going to achieve anything. 'I must make my apologies to the precentor for missing choir practice last eve. He will be most displeased with me...'

'Have you remembered what happened yet?'

'No. I don't recall anything much. I left Grey Friars, walked home, then... nothing.' Seb stopped as they reached St Paul's cross, bowed his head, briefly, and crossed himself, murmuring a short prayer before continuing their conversation. 'Then I woke this morn, feeling as one who'd spent the night guzzling cheap wine, finding Em in such a flutter you'd think I was Lazarus risen from the grave. And, no, I don't know what came to pass, despite her ceaseless interrogation over breakfast. I remember naught of last eve.'

They entered St Paul's by the south door, into the transept. The air smelled heavy with sanctity, clouded with incense smoke from the earlier celebration of the holy office. Seb usually attended Low Mass on a Friday but had woken too late. Another sin to be confessed. Before the rood, he bent the knee, repeating the same ritual as he had outside. Gabriel did not.

'I meant to ask you, Gabe, have you seen my brother of late? My mind may be fuddled somewhat but I don't recall seeing him yesterday, nor this morn?'

'I wouldn't fret about him. He most likely drank too much at the tavern and had to sleep it off somewhere. From what I know of your brother, Jude is well able to take care of himself.'

'Aye, maybe, but he's been so melancholy of late. I hope he isn't sickening for something. You know there has been plague reported, down by Queenhithe.'

They approached the stalls set out in the south aisle of the nave. Seb went to find the precentor, to apologise for failing to attend choir practice last eve while Gabriel went to a fellow they knew. Tall and skinny, with no more flesh than a length of string, Giles Honeywell always had the best quality quills for sale, along with much else. He left the plume of the feather intact for the customer to trim as he wished. Master Seb insisted on that, having his own preferred method of trimming. He said it also made it easier to judge the true quality of the feather, the health of the goose or swan from which it came and, therefore, whether the quill would wear well or have to be re-trimmed so often it would only last a few hours. Honeywell also knew exactly how to heat the quills, for how long to leave them in the hot sand to harden, so they were neither too brittle nor too soft. The Foxleys were among his best customers, so Honeywell greeted Gabriel with a toothless smile.

As Seb returned, looking relieved at having made his peace with the precentor, Honeywell's smile broadened.

'Master Foxley, good day to you. How may I please you this morn?'

'Giles. God's blessings be upon you. I hope you are in good health?'

'Aye, Master Seb, well enough, though I feel the cold in my old age. What can I get you?'

'Two dozen goose quills, if you have them, a dozen swans' and I'd like to see your finest brushes, squirrel hair, for preference.'

'Squirrel will be costly.'

'Aye, but I am making a psalter book for St Michael's. God will not appreciate poor workmanship. I need the best tools.'

While Seb was discussing brushes and examining quills, Gabriel was looking at Honeywell's other wares, picking over an odd assortment of objects, including scraps of cloth and what looked like horsehair of various colours. He was frowning over a small enamelled box, exquisitely wrought, but it was the contents of the box that had him scowling.

'What is this?' he demanded of Honeywell, interrupting as Seb was about to pay for his purchases.

'What it says on the label, master: the toe bone of Saint Margaret.'

'And this?' Gabriel shook a stained linen rag under the stallholder's nose.

'The tail-clout of Our Lord Jesu when he was a babe. A holy relic indeed for seven pence. A true bargain and guaranteed to reduce the pains of childbirth.'

'Disgusting. And the hair? From Pontius Pilate's horse, no doubt.'

'No. That is cut from the very beard of John the Baptist, master, when his head lay upon the platter, as demanded by Salome. Ten pence and I'll include the pen used by St Luke to write his gospel for another ha'penny. Precious holy relics all.'

'Relics! Chicken bones, rags and horsehair! You think this rubbish can work miracles?' Gabriel shouted. 'Filched from some backyard midden, you call this stuff holy? How dare you insult Our Lord Saviour and turn his house into a fripperers' market.'

'Gabriel. Be calm, I beg you,' Seb pleaded, taking the journeyman's arm. 'Folk are staring.'

'Let them stare. This man is deceiving them. He would have them believe these pox-ridden gutter-sweepings can perform miracles.'

'They're holy relics, Gabe. Honeywell has a license from the bishop...'

'Look at this,' Gabe put the relic of St Margaret's toe bone into Seb's hand. 'Go on. Look at it. Can you not see 'tis a chicken bone?'

'Well, I-I'm not sure...'

'I've heard how your lameness was cured of a sudden, Seb. Who do you suppose granted your miracle? Which saint did you beg to intercede for you? None. There wasn't time, was there? So you implored the Lord God and He heard you and answered your prayer. Not some useless saint's relic. No priest was needed as intermediary. God Himself and none other can work miracles.'

Realising that quite a crowd had gathered, Gabriel turned to them, arms open wide as a preacher's.

'Are you all as gullible and foolish as my friend here?' he yelled. 'Are you going to pay good money for things you could glean from your own midden just because this charlatan tells you they're holy? Well, are you?'

'I protest!' Honeywell cried. 'You're ruining my business.'

The crowd was muttering and shifting uneasily.

'I think we ought to leave, Gabriel,' Seb urged, tugging on his sleeve but Gabriel pulled away.

'And I'm about to ruin it further!' With that, he swept the cloth from the stall, bundled it up, threw it to the ground and began trampling on it. Honeywell was wailing at the sound of small bones crunching, pots shattering as his livelihood was destroyed.

'For heaven's sake!' Seb cried.

'It's for heaven's sake that I do this.'

'What's amiss with you, Gabriel? Come away, afore we are in trouble.'

But it was already too late for that.

The dean himself was coming down the nave, acolytes scurrying in his wake like ducklings behind their dame. Thomas Wynterbourne bore down upon them like an avenging angel, his dark robes flapping in his haste, his countenance forbidding.

'What is amiss here? Who is disturbing the peace of this house of prayer?'

'I am,' Gabriel said, 'And with good cause. This charlatan is...'

'Reverend, sir,' Seb interrupted, bowing to Dean Wynterbourne, 'There has been a misunderstanding betwixt my friend and...'

'Misunderstanding? It looks more like carnage to me.' The dean indicated the broken relics strewn across the tiled floor. 'You.' He shoved a finger at Seb's chest. 'I know you. You sing in the choir, don't you? Foxley, isn't it?'

'Aye, sir.'

'Aye, indeed. I never forget a name nor a face. But you,' he turned to Gabriel, 'Who are you? I haven't seen you before, have I?'

'No. I generally have little cause to come here. Master Widowson is my name.' Gabriel faced the dean without the least demonstration of respect, meeting him eye to eye.

'You show no remorse for your actions.'

'Why should I? I destroyed so much rubbish, all of it an affront, an insult to our Lord Saviour and to his people.' Gabriel indicated the crowd.

The onlookers had grown considerably in number.

'I should have you detained. Both of you.' Wynterbourne fixed Seb with a freezing glare.

'I'll make recompense, reverend sir,' Seb said, 'To Master Honeywell and to the church, pay for the damages.'

'How much?'

'Half a mark.'

The dean frowned.

'A whole mark? One pound sterling.'

The dean nodded.

'You'll do no such thing on my behalf,' Gabriel said, staying Seb's hand as he unlatched his purse. 'I will sweep up the mess myself but no one is going to pay a penny to Honeywell for his deception. As for the church, no damage has been done. I was simply pointing out the truth. Someone fetch me a broom and let that be an end to the matter.'

Seb stood slack-jawed with astonishment at his journeyman's manner. Gabriel was always so meek and mild yet he'd faced down the wrath of the dean. No good would come of it, for certain.

'I have you two marked down, in here,' said the dean, tapping his finger against his forehead. 'You cross my path again...' He left the sentence unfinished but the threat was ominous enough.

As they walked back to Paternoster Row, neither man had much to say to the other. Seb had not purchased quills nor brushes and supposed he would have to find someone other than Honeywell from whom to buy them. He was also concerned for Jude and had some idea that he ought to make enquiries as to his brother's whereabouts. But mostly he was thinking about Gabriel.

'You must take more care, Gabe,' he said as they went along Paternoster Row towards the Foxley house, 'Else they'll take you for a Lollard, eh?' He smiled at his jest, nudging his friend's elbow. Gabriel didn't reply.

They were almost at their door when Seb stopped to speak with Old Symkyn, asking after his health and dropping a few coins into his begging bowl.

'Beware!' Gabriel shrieked, shoving Seb aside with such violence that they both tumbled in a heap, the journeyman lying atop the master. Hooves thundered by so near at hand, splattering them with mud, the draught of their passage stirred Seb's hair. 'Are you unharmed?' Gabriel asked as he clambered to his feet and offered Seb his hand to assist.

Seb had had the wind knocked from his chest and took a moment to gather his wits and regain his breath.

'What was that? Who dares ride in so dangerous a fashion?' he asked, puffing. He stared down in dismay at his mud-soaked clothes and tried brushing off the worst of it. He only made it worse. They looked beyond saving without a deal of work. Emily would not be pleased.

'A Royal Messenger cares for naught but his mission,' Gabriel said, taking hold of Seb's arm, seeing him a little unsteady still. 'Be you certain you took no hurt?'

'A bruise or two maybe but no more than that, thanks to you. I believe you saved my life, Gabriel. I shall be forever in your debt.'

• •

It was a relief for Seb, after the morning's shocks, to go down to Garlickhill, armed with a slate, chalk and a book of *Aesop's Fables*. He had thought to cheer himself, teaching Rose her letters but, on the way, he enquired at the Panyer Inn, the Fleece Tavern and the Red Dog Ale-house – some of Jude's favoured watering holes – to find out if anyone had seen his brother of late. Nobody had, not since Wednesday eve, but all had suggestions of where else Seb might look, some places more enticing than others, from the brothels of Bankside to other city drinking establishments, to various church crypts: God forbid. 'Fish the Thames fer 'im,' someone had said. It didn't bear thinking about that Jude could meet such an end.

Seb entered the Pewter Pot. It was surprisingly wholesome looking, the tables scrubbed, the floor rushes fresh and the ale, when he ordered a cup, was clear and golden. Perhaps Jude had come here. But there must be two hundred or more places to drink in London. There seemed little chance but he'd ask all the same.

'Master Underwood,' he called, seeing a rotund fellow in a leather apron, wearing a red knitted cap. The innkeeper looked up and came over to Seb's table by the window.

'You know me? Have we met?'

'No, master. Forgive my boldness. I know Rose and she has spoken of you.'

'Ah. Then would you be the customer she is expecting this afternoon?'

'Aye, but beforehand, I wonder whether you might have seen this man?' Seb took a paper from his scrip, showed it to the innkeeper. He had drawn Jude's likeness to aid his enquiries. 'He is taller than most men; folk tend to notice him.'

'Nay. Never seen him. Is there reason to think he might come here? Who is he?'

'He's my brother, Jude Foxley. There is no more likelihood of his coming here than anywhere else, but I thought I'd ask all the same. Thank you for your time.'

'I'll keep a watch for him, if you want? Now. You want Rose or another ale first?'

• •

Rose's room above stairs had been swept and scoured. Seb could see the floorboards were still damp in places. He wondered if she went to such efforts for all her customers; he thought not. The lass had taken equal pains with her own appearance, her hair combed beneath her cap, a solitary stray tendril a little wet from when she'd washed her face. Her gown was neatly laced to the very top, showing she had no intention of enticing him, much to Seb's relief.

'Rose, I trust I find you well?' He kissed her forehead in greeting, as was mannerly.

'Aye, master. Thank you for asking. I'm very well.' She bobbed a little courtesy and then they stood, looking at one another.

'Would you...'

'Shall we...' They both spoke together. Seb shook his head, feeling awkward.

'What need for this, Rose? Let us get on with your lesson, shall we?'

'Di-did you pay Master Roger downstairs?'

'I did. We have the whole afternoon together. First, I shall read to you, then we will look at the letter shapes and how they make the words. Does that please you?'

'Aye, master, I suppose...'

Seb felt a twinge of disappointment. Rose had seemed so eager to learn just three days before but now she sounded no more keen than young Jack, being compelled to draw his alphabet in the sand tray for the hundredth time.

'Is something amiss, Rose? Would you rather we didn't do this?'

'Course not. I want to learn, truly I do.'

'I'm glad.'

Seated side by side on the bed, Seb began to read to her, telling Aesop's tale of the Fox, the Crow and the Cheese, running his finger beneath the words, so that she might follow them.

'The fox is foolish,' Rose said, 'Everyone knows that crows can't sing. Why is he praising her voice?'

'Shh. Let's wait and see.' As he finished the story, when the flattered crow opened her mouth to sing and the fox snapped up the tasty cheese that fell from her beak, Rose clapped her hands, laughing.

'So the fox was cunning and the crow was the foolish one. What a clever tale. Read me another.'

'Not yet. Now we are going to look at the letters. You see this 'F' that begins the word 'fox'. Take the chalk and draw the shape upon the slate, beginning with the upright stroke... that's it. Good. Now...'

They spent the time it takes to say twenty Paternosters, writing 'Fs' but Rose's heart wasn't in her task.

'I can't do it, master. I just can't. Not today.'

'But you're doing well, Rose. What is wrong with today? I can tell you're distracted.'

Rose sighed and set down the slate and chalk on the floor.

'I'm worried about my friend Bessie. I haven't seen her for days.'

'Where does she live?'

'Right here. We share this room, sleep in this bed. I've not seen a sign of her since we went to High Mass together on Sunday last, in St James. I'm afraid something might have happened to her.' Rose covered her eyes and sobbed. 'I don't know where she could be.'

Seb mulled over the coincidence.

'I know how it is, Rose. My brother has been gone for two days and I'm worried for him, as you are for Bessie. But let's not presume the worst. Mayhap, we shall find them together, in each other's arms...' He paused, realising he didn't know whether Bessie shared Rose's trade, as well as her room. He'd assumed she did but was relieved when Rose said:

'Aye, Bessie's lovesome enough.'

'What does she look like? See, here is my brother's likeness,' he showed her the image he'd shown the innkeeper, 'I could draw your friend's likeness so you can show it to other folk who may have seen her.'

'Your brother is a handsome fellow, master. Can you draw Bessie, even though you don't know her?'

Seb took up the slate and used his sleeve to wipe away Rose's attempts at letter forms.

'As with learning the letters, 'tis all about shapes. I'll draw as you tell me and we can erase and change the drawing until it looks like Bessie. Describe her to me.'

'Well, she's sort of, er, ordinary looking, like me,' Rose began. This wasn't helpful. Rose was a very pretty lass, not ordinary at all.

'Is her face long and thin, or round and plump? Or maybe heart-shaped?' Seb suggested, as would be the case if Bessie truly looked like Rose.

'Plump, maybe, but not too plump. Quite thin, really, I suppose.

Seb drew a simple circle with the chalk on the slate.

'Like this?' He put in a few lines to suggest hair.

'No, narrower. But not too thin.'

The short November afternoon was fading into dusk and it was becoming hard to see what he was drawing. Four times he'd wiped away the image and begun afresh but it was almost as though Rose had forgotten what her friend's face was like. In tears of frustration, she'd admitted as much, saying she could do no more. Her friend remained faceless.

'I'm sure she'll turn up,' Seb said, comforting the lass, 'With or without a likeness.'

'Aye,' Rose sniffed, dabbing at her tears with the hem of her dress. 'No doubt. Will you teach me some more letters now, master?' She dried her eyes, straightened her skirts and composed herself.

'Certainly. How would you like to write your name?'

• •

All through supper, Seb kept eyeing the empty stool and the platter set out for Jude, as if he thought his brother might materialise out of the ether.

'Did you make enquiries at market, Em?' he asked as he mopped up the parsley sauce that had accompanied the mackerel in a coffin.

'Aye. Mind you, the market was bustling, so busy, few were interested in looking at the likeness you drew of him. But I bought some pretty scraps of cloth for the doll.'

'Doll? What doll?'

'Do you never listen to a word I say?' Emily muttered, putting a second helping of fish on Jack's trencher, much to the lad's delight. 'As I told you, I'm making a doll for Dick Langton's daughter. 'Tis her first birthday next week. The doll's body and head are made – except for the face that you promised to paint for me... I don't suppose...'

Seb was frowning.

'A face? You never mentioned any such thing.'

'Sebastian Foxley! You have more fleece inside your head than the doll. Of course I mentioned it yester morn, and the day before and the one before that. Did I not?' she asked everyone seated at the board.

Gabriel nodded.

'You did, Mistress Em.'

'You reminded 'im this dinnertime, too,' Jack said, waving his knife to emphasise the fact.

'Stop brandishing that!' Seb said, slapping the lad's arm, 'You're splashing sauce everywhere.'

'Sorry, master, but you did too say you would,' Jack added.

Seb looked first to Tom and then to Nessie, hoping for their support but they both nodded. He rubbed his forehead, wondering how he could have forgotten so utterly. Perhaps the injuries he sustained last eve hadn't helped but it seemed Em had been asking and reminding him for days. Was he losing his wits or did he simply have too many other matters on his mind?

'I'll do it directly, Em, if you tell me how you want it to be, how big...'

Instead of thanking him, Emily sighed:

'I gave you the piece of white leather, cut to size. Don't tell me that you've mislaid it; I don't have any more. The trouble I had persuading the whittawyer to part with even a scrap of his finest kid skin without charging me the earth, even though his workshop was strewn with suitable off-cuts. He wanted to charge me a penny! A whole penny. Well, I told him, it was worth a fourthing and no more. So he demanded tuppence and I said I'd take my custom elsewhere, then he'd get naught for his scraps. In the end I got a piece from his wife, for no cost, so long as I make a repair to the sleeve of her Sunday best gown.'

Seb was still massaging his head, the ache having returned in strength.

'I'll see to it, Em, as soon as supper is done.'

As Nessie brought preserved plum dumplings to the table and Emily began describing, in detail, her marketing in Cheapside, the gossiping cheesemonger, the raucous hucksters and the angry poulterer, he decided that the silence of the workshop was preferable.

'In fact, I'll do it now,' he said, abandoning the dumplings, untouched.

Seb was surprised to see, lying on his desk in the workshop, an oval of fine kid leather, about four inches by three, with a smiling face already sketched upon it. Surely it ought to jog his memory, for it was obvious he had begun the task. Why couldn't he recall it?

Jude.

That was the problem: his missing brother filled his thoughts, driving all else from his head. He slumped onto his stool and closed his eyes, trying to picture the face he would paint for the doll, yet it was Jude's face that swum into his imagination, wavering and undulating, as if viewed through rippling water. Seb rubbed his eyes, hoping to dispel the vision. How could he concentrate on painting a pretty face? Rose. Aye, her face was perfect. And that exquisite new pigment would tint her cheeks and lips – just a miniscule amount to try out the colour, since it was so precious.

An hour later, it was done and Seb realised time had passed and he hadn't once thought of Jude. Rose's face smiled back at him and he was pleased with his work. He looked up and saw Jack standing in the doorway.

'Mistress Em sent you ale, if'n yer want it, master?'

'Aye, that would be appreciated, Jack, but shouldn't you be abed?'

The lad shrugged.

'We bin talkin' is all. Master Gabe told us a good tale. Is that the doll's face?'

Seb showed him. The pigments were almost dry.

'What do you think? Will it please a small child?' he asked. Jack looked doubtful.

'How should I know, master? I ain't a little maid. She's pretty though, I reckon, smilin' and cheerful. Who is she?'

'What?' Seb was shocked. How could the lad know he had based the likeness on Rose?

'Well, yer always use some real person's face, don't yer? That's what yer teached me an' Tom, so I...'

'Of course. You are correct but this is just a face I invented.' Seb wondered at himself. Why did he lie? 'Now, to your bed, young Jack. God keep you safe this night.'

'And you, master.' The lad scurried off, leaving Seb to his ale and a head full of disquieting thoughts. 'I likes 'er face, whoever she is,' he called out as he pushed open the door to the yard, making for the outside stairs that led up to the room he shared with Tom. Seb sighed. The lad's wits were too sharp; he couldn't be fooled. He could but hope Emily wouldn't leap to the same conclusion.

Chapter 6

Saturday, the ninth day of November

ACCORDING TO the bell at St Michael's, it was time for Low Mass but the watchful darkness had only reluctantly given way to a dreary daylight that painted the stone wall of the yard a sullen shade of grey. Seb returned from the privy at the far end of the garden, hearing the sow in her sty chomping and snuffling appreciatively at her breakfast of food scraps. He stopped to watch her, poor beast, nosing contentedly at the trough. Only one more breakfast before the Martinmas slaughter. It was as well pigs didn't know the calendar, how life slipped away, day by day. He shivered and it wasn't only because the rising wind whipped his hair and tugged at his mantle. The bare branches of the elder bush danced wildly and its narrow trunk groaned and creaked. He would have to cut it back, tidy it up. It would mean a better crop of flowers and fruit next year, both of which Em could turn into delicious cordials. He would make a note of the task but – far more important – was the search for Jude.

'I have to find him,' Seb said. Why was it that nobody else seemed to care that Jude hadn't been seen since Tuesday?

'What about the pig sty?' Emily stood in the midst of the kitchen, hands on hips. 'I told you the roof is leaking and the wall is crumbling. You said you would...'

'It can wait. The wretched pig will be gone in a day or two. My brother is of far greater importance to me.'

'Aye, and don't we all suffer for it? Your benighted brother gets more of your attention than the rest of us put together. I'm tired of hearing his name. He's a curse upon this house, Sebastian!'

Seb grabbed his wife's wrist.

'How dare you say that!'

'I dare very well, husband, because 'tis true. Now let go; you're hurting me.'

He flung her arm away and stepped back from her. His blood was up, his humours seethed. He hardly trusted himself to stay his hand from doing her some worse injury. He could barely spit out the words.

'I-I love my brother. If y-you can't see that... For all I know, he could be lying dead, somewhere, in a filthy alley, or drowned in the Thames, or dying from the pestilence. Oh, dear Lord God. I can't think of him so...' Seb tried to swallow but tears and anger near closed his throat. He had difficulty drawing breath.

'You have no reason to think any of those things,' Emily shouted back. 'The devil will return, like a bad smell to a midden when the wind drops.'

'I know not why you be so heartless towards my brother. What has he ever done against you? But I have no time for this now. I must seek him out, come what may. Don't expect me home for dinner, unless I find him first.'

• •

Cheapside was busy, as usual on a Saturday, but more so because a troupe of jugglers and acrobats was entertaining the crowd. Seb ignored them, trying to push through those who would linger to watch.

'Hey! Mind who you shove, fellow.'

Seb apologised and moved on, passed the Great Conduit. What was amiss with Em? Why did she care so little what happened to Jude? Did she not understand how close he and Jude had always been? Women! They never understood how a man felt. Oh, aye, women could be distressed, upset and worried, but not a man. No. He had to be strong, seemingly unaffected when his brother went missing. Well, too bad. He *was* affected; he was distressed. Em would just have to put up with it until Jude was found. However he was found... Seb mopped his eyes with his mantle, sickened by the horrors his imagination was inflicting upon Jude.

A sudden crash halted him in his misery. Tiles had slithered off a roof and smashed on the road at his feet. See? How easily a man might die in an instant? More earthen tiles cascaded down, lifted from the roof gable by the wind. Until now, Seb had hardly been aware of the rising wind but, as he hastened along Poultry towards Cornhill, he hugged his mantle about him.

He had already visited most of his brother's favoured alehouses closer to home but the inn at the sign of the Cardinal's Hat was one that Jude had used on occasion, admittedly, not often of late, but he knew not where else to enquire.

The Cardinal's Hat Inn in Cornhill

THE INN was well patronised, even so early as this, well before the hour of dinner. The gale seemed to have blown in stall-holders and their would-be customers alike. The din was deafening but the blazing hearth was welcoming and Seb stood, warming his hands, unable to find an empty stool.

'Master Innkeeper... Tapster!' Seb tried to gain someone's attention.

'Save yer breath, I should,' said a customer, lounging on his bench, taking up the whole of it that could have seated three. 'They's busy, as yer can see. Go elsewhere, I should. Ale's weak as piss, anyway. Waters it down, they does. Aye, waters it down.' The customer went back to his drink. Weak it might be but he seemed to be drunk upon it, nonetheless. Seb tried again and succeeded in catching a tap-boy's eye, waving him over. The lad handed him a brimming cup from his tray. Seb put a groat on the tray.

'I ain't got no time t'get change,' the lad complained.

'I don't want change; I want to ask you a question,' Seb said.

'I ain't done nuffin' wrong, master, 'onest.' He sounded just like Jack, always feeling he had to defend himself even before any accusation was made.

Seb took out the image of Jude from his scrip. It was becoming crumpled and grubby, he'd shown it so many times.

'Naught of that kind, lad. I want to know if you've seen this man in the last few days.'

'I ain't seen 'im. Don't know nuffin'. Wha's he done?'

'He's missing. He is my brother. Are you sure you haven't seen him?'

'Robin!' a voice yelled above the noise of enthusiastic drinkers, 'Get on wi' servin' or I'll bloody skin yer.'

'Aye, master,' the lad shouted back and went off to fetch more ale. Seb sighed at yet another wasted groat but sipped his ale. Might as well get something for his coin, even if the ale was watered down and all but tasteless.

'Show us it, then,' the drunkard said, stirring himself so Seb could share the bench.

'What?'

'The pitcha. The drawin' wot yer showed 'im. That lad wouldn't note a leper's wart on 'is own nose. Let's see it.'

Seb showed Jude's image yet again.

'Who drewed this, eh?'

'I did. Do you recognise my brother?'

'Good at drawin', ain't yer? How tall is 'e, yer bruvver?'

'About six feet.'

'Mm, reckon I see'd 'im recent.'

Seb nodded but wasn't hopeful. Drunks might see anything, from unicorns to faeries.

'Joined us in a round o' ale. The bugger took us fer nine pence ha'penny at dice and gived us no chance t' win it back, neiver. That's 'ow come I remember 'im; he owes us.'

That certainly sounded like Jude.

'When was this? Where?'

'Oh, let's fink, now... mighta been Thursday... or Friday. No, not Friday; that was yestereve an' I was 'ere. Thursday, then. Aye, I remember now.'

'Where was it? Where did you play dice with this man?'

'Wot man?'

'This man. My brother.' Seb shook the paper in front of the drunk.

'Oh, 'im. I fergit.'

'Please. I beg you. Try to remember.'

'Might've been at the Saracen's 'Ead, down Walbrook, or the Chequers Inn by Dowgate. Could be...'

'You don't know, do you? You're so in your cups, you wouldn't know if my brother sat here beside you.'

'No, no. I've a good mem'ry fer faces. I seen 'im... I need t' fink. Anuvver ale might 'elp...'

'No. More ale and you still won't recall, if you ever saw my brother at all, which I doubt.' Seb got up to leave.

'It were the Stag. I recall it now. In Bucklersbury. Now does I get more ale?'

'I don't believe you.' All the same, Seb put a ha'penny on the board before he went out into the gale once again. Was it worth trying the Stag? He'd never heard Jude mention the place but it was the first clue he had, however dubious the source and it was but a slight detour on the way home.

• •

Bucklersbury was a narrow street, home to the famous Barge Inn, but there were few folk around. Seb was surprised to see that the door to the Barge was firmly closed and no light showed within. Above the howling wind, every so often he caught the sound of hammering. In the midst of a storm hardly seemed the best time to make repairs. An elderly woman was sheltering in a porch. She caught at Seb's mantle.

'Don't go that way, master. It isn't safe,' she said, shouting to make herself heard above the gale and the sounds of workmen.

'Not safe, mistress? Why not?'

'They're boarding up the Stag Tavern. Pestilence's got them. I wouldn't be here if I didn't live here. Go away, master, 'tis the wisest thing to do.'

'My thanks to you, mistress, and may God bless you and keep you safe.'

'Amen to that,' he heard her say as he retraced his steps.

Unable to make enquiries at the Stag to confirm whether Jude had been there or not, having hardly believed what the drunkard had told him, Seb now felt the icy fingers of dread seizing hold of him. Walking back through Cheapside, a fear became a certainty and dread overwhelmed him. Jude had been there at the Stag, playing dice even as plague sauntered in through the door, turning a place of pleasure into a death house. That was how it must have been, he was sure.

The street entertainers were gone, defeated by the buffeting wind. The stall-holders had packed away their wares before the wind blew them skywards and the customers were retreating to the safety of their firesides. An old elm tree was down, blocking the entrance to Foster Lane but Seb staggered on. He was unsure whether it was the force of the gale against which he struggled or the shock of what he'd learned that had turned his legs so weak, his left hip throbbing. Whatever the cause, he reached home in Paternoster Row on the verge of collapse.

• •

At the door, Seb told himself he had to be calm. He mustn't scare Emily and the others needlessly.

'Where have you been?' Emily demanded, looking grim, arms folded as he entered the house. 'Never here when you're needed, are you? And you needn't think that dinner's on the board because it isn't. Bread and dripping is all you'll get. I told you the pig sty was falling down...' she paused for breath then turned and stalked back to the kitchen.

'What happened? What of the pig sty?' he asked. All he wanted was to sit quietly, rest his leg and think what next to do, to find Jude.

'As if you care in the least, unless it's about your precious brother.' She rounded on him, a kitchen knife in her hand but it seemed she was intent on chopping onions, not attacking her husband. 'The elder tree came down in the wind and took the wall of the sty with it. I told you how it was... Anyhow, the pig was terrified and bolted through the gap it left in between the stones. Me and Gabriel and Nessie and the lads have chased that animal twice round St Paul's and halfway to Ludgate. A merry dance it led us, while you – by the stink of you – were swilling ale at your leisure and now you return, expecting to be fed. Well, too bad. Look at the state of my gown: torn at the hem, and my apron filthy, my cap all awry. But do you notice? Of course you don't. If it was your brother who'd come home, all dishevelled, it would be 'poor Jude, what's amiss, dearest brother?' but with me, your wife, you just don't care. You never care!'

Seb let the tongue-lashing wash over him. He couldn't argue; it was too much effort. Instead, he sat on a stool, head in his hands, saying naught.

'By the way, if you be interested,' Emily continued, 'Which you will be at some time, we're using the public house of easement by the City Ditch for now because we had to shut the pig in somewhere and our privy is the only place, unless you want it sleeping in our chamber, which you might, in preference to me, if you'd even notice that I wasn't there...'

After a dinner which was far tastier than Emily had threatened, Seb retired to the peace and quiet of the parlour to do his 'penance', as he called it – the weekly accounts. It was a task he loathed and one he usually shared with Jude, checking incomings and outgoings which never seemed to quite balance. For the others, Saturday afternoon was a time free from work. The Church supposed that true Christians spent the time in contemplation, in preparation for a prayerful Sunday but, in truth, most folk found some more exciting activity. Children played, adults went to the tavern or visited friends but, with the weather blowing up a storm, upon this day most folk were safe by their hearths, doors and window shutters closed and barred.

In the kitchen, Tom and Jack had near come to blows over a game of nine-men's-morris and were now playing at fox-and-geese.

'Yer cheated, Tom. That weren't a fair move, that weren't.'

'It was! You always say I'm cheating when you lose.'

'No I never an' yer did cheat. I saw it. Yer moved them dice after yer rolled 'em.'

'I didn't touch the dice. You're telling lies.'

'No, I ain't. An' I ain't playing wi' yer any more, Tom Bowen, you cheater.' Jack grabbed the board and overturned it, sending the gaming pieces flying across the kitchen.

'Now look what you've done. You're a poor loser, Jack. Pick up those pieces afore they get lost.'

'Do it yerself.'

'You threw them.'

'That's enough, you two,' Gabriel said, coming in from the yard with more logs for the fire.

'Tom's a cheat.'

'No, I'm not.'

'Enough! One more word of dissent and I'll have the pair of you keeping the pig company out in the privy – which you can scrub spotless whilst you're there.'

'Tha's not fair. It weren't me wot started it.'

'Jack. Hold your tongue. If Mistress Em finds you quarrelling when she returns from Dame Ellen, she'll send you to bed without supper. You want that?'

Two young heads shook.

'Well and good. Put the game away tidily in its bag, sit down and I'll tell you a story.' Gabriel's last words worked like faery magick. Within less time than it took to say a Paternoster, the gaming pieces were collected up, even the one that had rolled behind the dough trough, backsides were upon stools and two eager angelic faces smiled up at the journeyman, all expectant.

'Once, many years ago, there was a lad, very like you two. He had no father – just like you – but he lived with his Mam and elder brother in a quiet village. Then, one day, an important man came to the village.'

'Was it the king?' Jack asked.

'No. But it was a man of high standing. And don't interrupt. The man visited the lad's mother and asked her a good many questions. Then he spoke to the lad and gave him a book, demanding that he read it aloud. Which the lad did, though not very well. Then the man gave him pen, ink and paper and told him to write his name. Which the lad managed to do, just. The important man patted him on the head, smiled and departed. After that, the lad's mother seemed all out of sorts, fussing the lad and often weeping of a night. The lad could hear her, sobbing in the dark.

'Meantime, his elder brother went off to sail the seas, apprenticed to a sea captain. And then, one day, a priest came to the village, riding a mule. He told the lad's mother that it was time. She gave the lad a change of clothes, bundled in a kerchief, kissed him and made him promise to be good and obey the priest. She wept as she waved farewell. He was going to school and would never see his mother again.' Gabriel paused to finger the corner of his eye. Only now did he realise his audience had grown: Mistress Em and Nessie had drawn up stools to listen. Nessie blew her nose on her apron.

'That's a sad tale, Master Gabe,' she said, sniffing. 'That poor mother, left all alone.'

'What wos 'is name, that lad?' asked Jack.

'It isn't important. Doesn't matter.'

'But everbody's got a name,' Jack said.

'Very well. We shall call him, er, Adam. Will that please you?' Jack nodded:

'So wot 'appened next t'Adam?'

'He attended a fine school, learned to read and write properly, in English, Latin and French. He was taught to read the Bible in Latin, learning much of it off by heart. And then, one day, the very important man came to see Adam, questioned him deeply about all that he'd learned and said he was most pleased. Then he told him that he was going to the university in Oxenford, to study for the priesthood – all at the important man's expense – so that one day he might be a bishop. "Like your true father," the man added.

'Then Adam understood. But he didn't want to be a priest. So he ran away. At first, he hoped to find his brother and go to sea but he had no way of knowing where his brother might be. So he journeyed all around England, visiting every port, hoping his brother would be there. But he never was. Adam made his way, working at any sort of task that needed to be done, earning his supper here and a bed for the night there. Eventually, a sea captain offered him a job aboard his ship. So Adam got his wish, though he hadn't found his brother. At least he had escaped the bishop's intensions for him.'

'Did Adam 'ave a'ventures, then?'

'Aye, Jack, he did. But I can tell you no more for the present as my voice is hoarse and Mistress Em will be wanting to set the board for supper. Go, fetch water to wash our hands – and no arguing.'

'That was a fine tale, Gabriel,' Emily said, brushing close to him as she spread the cloth upon the board.

He looked at her with his intriguing, mismatched eyes and smiled.

'Is it a true story?'

He shrugged and said naught before going out to the yard.

'Master Gabe tells such good tales, I feel like I'm there, watchin' the things happen,' Nessie said, 'He's so clever, isn't he, mistress? I think he's cleverer even than Master Seb.'

'You're neglecting the pottage, Nessie. Stop day-dreaming and stir the pot afore it burns.'

'Aye, mistress.'

Emily sighed. She had thoughts of her own concerning Gabriel and now she believed she knew rather more about the mysterious journeyman. She was certain that much, if not all, of Adam's story was Gabriel's own. The son of a bishop, eh? Well that was something to ponder on, wasn't it?

She followed him into the yard. In the fading light of late autumnal dusk, Gabriel was sitting on the steps that led up to his and Jude's chambers and the attic where the lads slept. Emily sat down beside him.

'Why did you call him Adam?'

'The first man; the first name that came into my thoughts, I suppose.'

'But it's your story, isn't it?'

'Just a tale is all.'

'Do you have a brother, as Adam does in your tale?'

'I do, as it so happens.' He leant forward, elbows upon his knees, cupping his hands, resting his chin. 'Our mother expected – or, more likely, hoped – that we would both be of an angelic disposition. My brother she named Raphael. I'm sure she must be gravely disappointed in us both.' He laughed.

'Why would you say that?'

'Would you want to own me as a son? I doubt it.'

'I don't see why not.' Emily rested her hand upon his arm and he turned to face her. They were sitting so close. 'I should be glad of a son like you. Any mother would.'

He turned away again but Emily slid her hand down his arm so it rested upon his fingers, a butterfly touch.

'I think you're a fine man, Gabriel.' Her voice was a sigh, a whisper of longing.

He tilted her chin and she smiled. Those eyes – one blue, one brown – being the windows of the soul, made him a man of contrasts, of mystery. She could feel his breath hot upon her cheek. His lips were so near. She closed her eyes, letting her senses drift. A touch.

'Emily, are you there?' Seb called out from the kitchen.

Of an instant, Gabriel was on his feet.

'Forgive me, mistress. This is too bad of me...' His anguish was evident in his voice.

'No, Gabriel.'

Then he brushed past her and raced up the steps to his chamber.

She heard his chamber door bang shut behind him yet the manly smell of him lingered for a few moments in the gathering gloom. She shivered. The night air was chill now the heat of their desire was gone, dissipating like smoke in the wind, but still she sat, waiting for the beat of her heart to steady.

'Em! Where are you?' Seb came out of the kitchen door. 'What's amiss, lass? You'll catch your death out here without your mantle.'

'It seemed too hot in the kitchen.'

'I pray you be not feverish. Come. The lads are already at the board, spoons poised. You know how Jack fears he will starve if his food be delayed by a moment.' He raised her up and wrapped his arm around her.

But it was not Seb's arm that she wanted.

Chapter 7

Sunday, the tenth day of November

AT LEAST the wind had dropped and, for the present, it wasn't raining. In fact, through the veil of cloud, a pale milky glow betrayed the position of the sun, peering between the gabled roofs of the house beside St Michael's, struggling to warm the wintry chill. Clad in their Sunday best, Gabriel joined Seb, Emily and the rest of the household, together with their fellow parishioners, for High Mass, summoned by the bell. All around, from All Hallows, Barking in the east to St Ewen's in the west, other bells rang out with the same message.

Gabriel, as an incomer, still could not appreciate the cacophonous din which the Londoners accepted as the song of their beloved city. It made his head ache and he was thus even less inclined to endure the tribulations of the divine office. Little wonder he made excuses. Last Sunday it had been a sore throat; the week before a chill had threatened. He only ever attended mass to avoid being noted as an absentee, forced to do penance and pay a fine. It was bad enough that he was obliged to pay tithes to those useless priests. Not that he was a godless man – naught could be further from the truth.

'God give you good day, Dame Ellen,' Seb greeted Emily's one-time mistress who had once been his landlady, 'I trust you be in fair health?'

'Thanking you, Master Sebastian, Emily. I am in as good health as age and weather allow. And your good selves?'

Gabriel rubbed his brow and made an effort to be courteous to the parishioners who acknowledged him. Did they not come to church to praise God? It seemed they didn't but rather to praise each other.

'What a fine gown you are wearing, Dame Ellen,' he heard Emily saying, 'Is that marten fur around the cuffs? 'Tis a most elegant cut.'

The older woman shook out her skirts and preened a little, beaming with pleasure.

'I trained you well to notice such details. It is indeed quite new, a gift from a, er, friend, an admirer, you might say. A man of taste and discernment.'

'Really? Who is he, may I ask?'

Gabriel sighed. As if it mattered one jot.

'Never you mind,' Dame Ellen said before moving on to greet a gaggle of women crowding around the brazier by the font. The summoning bell fell silent but, as usual, Gabriel saw that no one else seemed to notice. At least he was grateful.

'Did you hear that, Seb?' Emily said.

Seb was speaking to Churchwarden Marlowe who had just come from the belfry, asking if he had seen or heard anything of Jude – did he think of naught else?

'Sebastian!' Emily pulled at his mantle to gain his attention. 'Did you hear what Dame Ellen said?'

'No. I was making enquiries about my brother...'

'But Dame Ellen has an admirer! Is that not news indeed?'

'Well and good.'

'Well and good? At her age? What can she be thinking?'

'Disquieting news, then.'

'Why so? A woman is allowed to have an admirer, is she not?'

'What would you have me say, Em? I find you contrary this morn. What be amiss, eh?'

'You haven't even noticed, have you, husband?' With that, Emily turned her back on Seb, brushing close past Gabriel to join her fellows at the brazier.

'And what was I supposed to notice?' Seb asked Gabriel, seeming at a loss.

'The new trimming on her hood,' Gabriel told him. 'She wove it herself.'

'How do you know that?'

'She told me when I remarked earlier upon its fine workmanship and exquisite choice of colour.'

Seb shook his head. Failed again.

A young acolyte took his place by the font and then processed – if a lad followed by two men could be called a procession – the length of St Michael's little nave, wafting incense as he went. It made Gabriel sneeze as it usually did, wretched stuff, as though the odour of labouring folk wasn't good enough for the Almighty who created them. If God wanted perfume, men would sweat flowers.

Mercifully, Father Thomas and Hugh Wessell were standing beneath the arch of the rood screen, signifying that they were ready to begin the office.

As the priests murmured and mumbled their way through the Mass, Emily spent the time staring at the back of the men's heads in front of her – Seb's and Gabriel's. Seb was a little taller, his glossy dark hair just long enough to brush his shoulders, as was the fashion. He had the looks of a handsome fellow but he was as appealing and colourless as wet paper, a wilting weed. Gabe's shoulders were broader, sturdy beneath his mantle, his mousy curls unruly as ever. Emily smiled to herself, longing to run her fingers through those wild locks, to have his chest crushed against her, his strong arms embracing...

As though he felt her gaze upon him, Gabriel turned, his intriguing, mismatched eyes meeting hers for a moment. He half smiled, showing that crooked front tooth. The memory of last eve flared briefly between them, like a spark tossed from a fire. Then he turned away.

Guilty, she looked down at the floor. Beside her, she heard Nessie heave a sigh.

'He looked at me, mistress,' the plump little maidservant whispered.

'Who did?'

'Master Gabe, o' course. He likes me very well.'

'Don't be so foolish. He does nothing of the kind.'

'But he does. He told me so.'

'Attend to your prayers at once and stop this nonsense, you impudent child. I never heard so ridiculous a thing. Master Gabriel is a respectable journeyman and you're just, just a silly maid.'

Nessie sniffed loudly and inelegantly as Father Thomas rang the little silver bell, so the congregation should bow their heads and keep silent for the raising of the Host.

'Behave yourself. Use your kerchief, can't you?'

'Shh.' A woman behind them hissed.

When the office was done and the priests had blessed the congregation, folk could return to their conversations with their neighbours, whether business or gossip or a little of both.

• •

These parishioners were insufferable, so rude. Why did they insist on calling him Father Weasel? That accursed family name had been an unbearable burden he'd travailed beneath all his life. The proverbial millstone around his neck. He'd tried changing it as a scholar up at Oxford, but his fellows had found him out. Well, perhaps 'Bishops-nephew' had been a bit of a mouthful. But this morn, even Dame Ellen Langton, the respectable widow whom he had hopefully credited with better manners, had come over to him after Mass, fingered his fine stole and remarked upon it:

'Superb workmanship here,' she had said,' Beautifully done, though more likely a woman's fine stitchery than a man's. Workwomanship, perhaps we should call it?' She laughed. 'Good day to you, Father Weasel.'

She had left him fuming at her ill-manners; no better than the rest. Yet they always called the old priest 'Father Thomas', never 'Father Shuttlepenny' or 'Sweetha'penny' or whatever his preposterous family name was. Perhaps they didn't know it. Well, Father Hugh would have to inform them. 'Shuffleha'penny', that was it. Father Thomas Shuffleha'penny. That would amuse them. A small victory, but a sweet one. As for the parishioners' religious obligations, they behaved as badly before God as before His servants.

Two wenches – one the daughter of Churchwarden Marlowe who should have known better – had been giggling over a paper during his sermon. He feared it might be one of those devilish Lollard tracts, so he had confiscated it, only to discover it was some disgusting drivel written to one of them by a youth, declaring his fascination with her. It was difficult to read such an appalling hand, or the name at the bottom, unfortunately, else he would have taken the lad to task, given him a hefty penance. As for the wenches, those dirty little sluts, he could see full well where their destiny lay: in the Devil's den of the Bankside brothels across the river.

In St Michael's cramped vestry, Father Hugh hung up his vestments with the exquisite embroidery, taking care the folds went with the grain of the finest silk-linen cloth, so as not to crease it. He noted how Father Thomas, slovenly as ever, took no similar pains with his but why should he? In truth, his vestments were tattered rags in comparison. Hugh ran his hand down the cloth, almost a caress, before picking a lint fleck from among the gold and crimson threads of the stitchery, the image of a phoenix arising from the flames.

He went to sit by the brazier to warm his feet. Looking at his shoes, he realised they were no longer of such a fine appearance to match the rest of his attire. It was always the way, since he was a child, that he wore his shoes all unevenly upon his right foot, the legacy of two deformed toes that were his secret imperfection. He also noted a stain on the left one and, with utter distaste, realised what it was. New shoes were a necessity now to maintain his opulent standard of dress.

'Disquieting news from our flock, Father Hugh,' Father Thomas said, pouring them both a cup of wine, to finish off what was left over from the Mass.

'Indeed? ' Hugh might pretend indifference but he was as intrigued by gossip – the more salacious the better – as the older priest he was here to 'assist', or rather espy upon, him and his flock.

It had been Bishop Kemp's idea that his nephew should be at St Michael's and make the best use of the city's efficient rumour-mongering business. Old Father Thomas was well-liked by his flock and they were never afraid to share any titbits of gossip with him and, so long as it wasn't given under the seal of confession, the priest was always just as eager to pass it on. What better way to uncover the filthy seeds of Lollardy afore they had a chance to sprout and grow? That had been the bishop's intention, at least. So far, his nephew had been attempting to harvest a barren furrow.

'You recall the corpse of that unfortunate woman found at Smithfield by Sebastian Foxley's lads – may God have mercy upon her poor soul – well, rumour has it that she, an immoral woman, was last seen with a man of the cloth. A priest keeping company with a prostitute! Is that not a dreadful blotch upon the reputation of us all? The source of the rumour, as I heard it, was a tavern wench at the Pewter Pot, so it may not be reliable. If 'tis true, mayhap he was trying to persuade her as to the error of her trade? Aye, that must have been the way of it, no doubt.

'And the king's new mistress, the goldsmith's wife, is that not an appalling example for a Christian monarch to set his subjects? And Dame Ellen Langton, a most respectable widow, has a paramour, so they say... Hugh, are you hearing a word of this? A parish priest should keep abreast of the goings-on of his flock.'

Hugh had no interest in either mistresses or paramours. He snatched up his cloak and rushed out of the little vestry, leaving his wine untouched.

• •

'Dame Ellen's gown was fine indeed, was it not, Seb?' Emily was saying.

'Mm.' Seb was glancing around, wondering if there was anyone he hadn't asked as to whether they had seen Jude.

'I thought that deep murray colour suited her well. Don't you agree?'

Seb made some non-committal sound.

'I wish I might have a new gown. This one has faded so since I wore it as Queen of the May all that time ago. And then it served as my wedding gown.' It was true. The linen had once been as blue as heaven but the woad dye had not been so well mordanted and it was now more grey than blue – plunket-coloured, as it was known – and no longer matched her eyes as it once did. 'A new gown would please me well,' she said but Seb was busy, rebuking Jack for dawdling when his dog was annoying a neighbour's mutt, the pair yapping and snarling at each other with Little Beggar racing in circles whilst the other was tethered on a leash. Angry words were exchanged, the neighbour blaming Seb for failing to control the dog, although Beggar had no master but Jack, unless food was offered.

As they reached home, Old Symkyn, squatting by his beggar's bowl across the way, beckoned to Seb.

'I would warn ye, young master,' he wheezed, 'They're watching ye and your house.'

'Who is?'

'Fellow in a dark cloak, hood drawn close so his face can't be seen, but 'e watches, sure enough.'

'Thanking you for the warning, Symkyn. Why don't you join us at meat now? I be certain my goodwife has prepared sufficient for an extra platter.'

The old man nodded his thanks.

'You're a good Christian man, Master Foxley,' he said as Seb helped him to his feet.

'Set an extra place, Em,' Seb said, 'Symkyn is dining with us.'

Emily pulled a face. Charity was all very well and a veteran of one of King Edward's past battles Symkyn might be, but he stank like a privy and a few fingers weren't all he was lacking. Mad as a whirligig in a puddle and that was the truth of it.

• •

Being the Lord's Day, Gabriel left the house after a good dinner of stewed chicken and bacon in a coffin. One of Emily's hens had given up the ghost and made a welcome addition to the meal, even if it was an old bird, tough and stringy, it made a change all the same. Gabriel walked towards the river, down Garlickhill, to the Pewter Pot, but instead of entering the tavern, he went to a side door in a narrow alley. Having made certain none were watching, he knocked twice, paused, then rapped three times quickly. The door was opened barely an inch or two.

'Ah, 'tis you. Come in.'

The room was already occupied. Men and women sat around on benches, children sat upon the floor, all expectant except for a babe-in-arms and a bawling toddler, too young to understand. The place was lit by cheap tallow candles since the shutters on the windows were closed. The air was thick with their acrid stink and Gabriel coughed.

'You brought them?' asked the fellow who had opened the door to him.

'Aye. Ten copies. I hope 'tis enough for now. I did not want my burdened noticed.'

'It will suffice for the present. Pass them round, will you?'

Gabriel obliged. There was an unmistakable ripple of excitement among those gathered in the stuffy room. Folk looked at the pamphlets, handling the paper leaves with such care. Some stared, awestruck, at the first printed folios they had ever seen, let alone owned. Others turned the pages, frowning as they tried to fathom the words. Gabriel turned a pamphlet the right way up for an elderly woman with a young lad sitting beside her. She smiled at him.

'God's own words?' she asked.

'Aye, goodwife, they surely are.'

'Known Men... and Women, brothers and sisters all,' the doorman said, 'The Lord God has seen fit to grant us this blessing: the text of His own sacred words in our own tongue. Guard them with your very lives and let no one who isn't one of us know of their existence. We run a great risk, willingly, that you may hear and understand God's words, but if you reveal such things, our lives may be forfeit and there will be no more. Now, my brother,' he nudged Gabriel, 'I believe it is your turn to read to us.'

Gabriel nodded, cleared his throat and opened the pamphlet.

'This is the Gospel according to St John the Evangelist beginning at chapter one, verse one.' He coughed again before reading in a clear, sonorous voice: 'In the beginning was the Word, and the Word was with God, and the Word was God.

'... Hereafter ye shall see heaven open, and the angels of God ascending and descending upon the Son of man.'

He closed the pamphlet, emotions entwining his heart, before bowing his head. 'All thanks and praise be unto God.' He slumped on a bench, feeling drained of all but spiritual strength.

For a moment, the assembly sat silent, awed, absorbing the chapter he had read to them, then the elderly woman spoke up.

'And tell me why priests forbid us hearing those wondrous words in English? Why do they say Latin is the language of God when we all know well enough that the Almighty be as English as we?'

'You speak truly, sister,' someone said and there were general sounds of agreement.

After much lively discussion of the text and a prayer of thanksgiving to God for his benevolence in granting the same, the assembly broke up. They departed in ones and twos so as not to attract notice, the doorman's words of caution and the need for secrecy still in their ears.

Eventually, only four Known Men remained. Roger Underwood, keeper of the tavern next door and owner of the room, went around, snuffing candles, stacking benches and opening the shutters to let in the cold air and dispel the sour stink of tallow and crowded bodies. Naught must remain to betray the meeting. A weather-beaten man of middle years, a fisherman by his dress, still sat on the floor, studying his text.

'You did well, Gabe, it was beautifully read,' said the fellow who had served as doorman.

'The words give me strength, Raff, as well as a deal of pleasure and comfort. How sad it is that many of our brothers and sisters can't read the text for themselves.'

'Some of them can and are teaching the others. Master Fisher there...' Raff nodded at the fellow still reading, '...has learned well. The day will come, eventually, when God's words will be read by all. In the meantime, they enjoy listening to us, especially to you, Gabe. You have a fine speaking voice, always did. As lads, you could always shout louder than me.'

Gabriel laughed and gave his elder brother a playful poke with his finger. 'I had to, else our Mam wouldn't come to rescue me whenever I lost a fight, which was a daily occurrence with you, as I recall.'

'Those were hard times, Gabe. I had to teach you to fight, to stand up for yourself with no father to guide you, as I'd had, and our Mam a widow-woman.'

'I've done well enough all these years by my wits, rather than by brawn. Tell me: how much longer can you stay in London?'

'Not sure,' Raff shrugged, 'Now Marchmaine's dead, I don't know what will happen about the ship or when we might sail again.'

'We need you here, guiding us...'

'No. God is your guide, remember that. And Underwood is a good man, reliable. Master Fisher could help share the reading aloud. Betwixt you three and the Lord, the Known Men will grow in number and knowledge. Keep faith, Gabriel.

'You best go now, 'tis growing dark and you have no torch.'

'Shall you be here Wednesday?'

'Probably.'

The Foxley house, around midnight

'SEB... SEB, wake up.' Emily shook her goodman roughly. 'Seb, there's someone outside, in the yard.'

'Mm, probably one of the lads... can't sleep, needs the privy.' He turned over, pulling the coverlet up over his ears. The bed chamber was cold.

'No. I'm sure it's not. Remember, the pig is shut in the privy. Whoever it is, they're searching for something, poking around in our belongings.'

'A stray pig, then.'

'No, Seb, it's a thief, come to rob us.'

'On a night like this? Even a half-witted thief will be in his bed, sleeping sound. Unlike some.'

'Oh, please... you must go see. I can't rest until you do.'

'Leave it 'til morning. If there's anything missing, it won't be much. What do we keep of value in the yard? Now go to sleep, woman, for pity's sake.'

For a few minutes, Emily lay quiet and Seb drifted back to sleep.

'There! I heard it again! If you won't go look, I will.' Emily threw back the bed covers, letting an icy draught into their warm sanctuary, raising gooseflesh on Seb's naked body.

'Get back in bed, woman. You'll take a chill...'

'I don't care.'

'Well, I do. Stay warm in bed. You've won the argument: I'll go look.'

Seb left the bed, putting the blankets back in place to keep in the warmth.

'This is just your silly fantasy, Em. There's naught down there, I tell you. I'm catching my death for no reason, here.' He fumbled for steel and flint and tinder by the bedside. It took several attempts to light the rush wick. By its feeble light, he flung on his night robe, groped for his boots in the dark beneath the bed and went downstairs. If there was anything at all, it was probably cats or, as he suspected, a stray pig, rootling round the flour, ale and water barrels in the lean-to. Someone must have left the side gate unlatched.

In the kitchen, he used the rushlight to light a candle stub and set it in the lantern to shield it from the wind. Opening the kitchen door let in a frigid blast and a shower of autumn leaves skittered across the floor.

He pulled his night robe closer, tightening the belt, took up the lantern and an old staff, in case he had to persuade a pig to leave. The wind whipped at his hair and wrapped the robe around his legs, nearly tripping him. Even inside the lantern case, the flame danced and guttered as though it might go out at any moment. Its feeble light and the occasional glimpses of a young moon between tatters of racing cloud only served to further blacken the shadows.

Just as he'd thought: there was nothing.

But the next gust of wind set the side gate banging. It let onto the little garden through a high wall and also gave access to an alley that ran into Paternoster Row. It was used for taking deliveries without disturbing the house or workshop. Clearly, it hadn't been latched properly and was slamming in the wind. That was what had awakened Em. Probably, one of the lads had forgotten to latch it, or Gabriel had been careless upon his return from the Panyer or wherever he spent his time.

Seb battled the wind to get the gate closed, a lull giving him the chance to latch it properly. But the latch seemed loose; he would have to see to it tomorrow. Someone had likely forced it but, for now, he set down the lantern and the staff and rolled a half-full flour barrel from the lean-to in front of it, to keep it from blowing open again. He tucked a piece of canvas over the barrel to keep the flour dry, if it should rain again.

As he bent to retrieve the lantern, he thought he saw a flicker of movement from the corner of his eye, dark against the darkness. But it was nothing, just the wind tossing a few leaves in the corner of the yard. He went to take up his staff but couldn't see where he'd laid it.

There was a sudden flash of movement. Light splintered before his eyes in a ripped-ragged instant before he fell to the cobbles, the lantern flickering out in the rush of air.

• •

He had been gone for so long, his side of the bed was growing cold. Guiltily, Em moved over to warm it for him; he would be chilled to the marrow when he came back. She lay there, listening for his step on the stairs. Still, he didn't return. She got up, dragging the coverlet with her, and went to the window, forcing a shutter open against the wind so it slammed back against the wall.

'Seb! Seb!' The wind snatched her words away and blew the bed hangings like ship's sails. 'Seb, are you there?' There was no sign of a light in the yard but she could hear the side gate banging still. Perhaps he'd gone out into the garden, or was chasing that pig back onto the street. She waited. Nothing but the gate slamming back and forth. Since Seb had taken the rushlight, Emily had to find her robe in the briefest moments of moonlight and could not find her shoes. No matter.

The stygian blackness of the yard made it seem an alien place. Familiar things became terrible; everyday objects strange and threatening. The lean-to by the side gate lurked like a crouching beast; the stack of firewood grotesque and contorted beneath its canvas shroud. She lifted the torch from its sconce outside the kitchen door and took it to the fire to light it from the embers. The yard was recognisable now in the leaping light and she heard St Martin's distant bell ring for matins: the first monastic office of the day but the middle of the night for London's good citizens. Nothing seemed out of place but for a heap of canvas blown from somewhere, lying by the side gate. She cursed Seb, forgetting she had insisted on his mission in the night.

'Seb! Where are you? Answer me, you silly fool.' Her bare feet ached with the cold. Shivering, she made for the side gate, certain he must have gone out. She bent to pick up the canvas. The torchlight showed not some abandoned sailcloth blown in, but Seb's night robe, its frayed coney-fur edging dull against the wet cobbles. 'Seb! Oh, dear God. Seb...'

He groaned and stirred beneath her hand, struggling to sit up. She put her free arm around him and held the torch close.

'Can you stand? Shall I call Gabe to aid you? We have to get you indoors and warm.'

'Give me a moment... I'll manage. No need to...' He gasped, holding his head in both hands, sitting on the cobbles. She felt him shivering violently as he leant against her. She eased him down again, left him and flew up the outside stairs that led to Gabe's chamber and hammered on the door.

'Gabriel! Gabe, we need help. Seb's had another seizure. I can't get him up.' No sound from within. 'Gabe, for our Holy Mother's sake!'

Eventually, the door opened. Gabriel was wearing only a bed sheet, yawning hugely, his mousy hair stood on end. He blinked in the torchlight, his eyes those of some dazzled nocturnal creature.

'What's amiss?'

'Seb's had a seizure.'

It took a moment for Gabriel to think.

'Well, he can't fall any further than the floor. Throw a blanket over him 'til I get dressed.'

'But he's lying in the yard.'

'What's he doing out there at this time of night?'

'The side gate was banging; he went to close it.'

Gabriel disappeared into his chamber, leaving the door open, seemingly not bothered if Emily saw him naked. She turned her back anyway. He was already half dressed and pulling on his boots. He grabbed the blankets off his bed and was down the stairs in a couple of strides.

Seb lay huddled on his side, his whole body rigid with cold, twitching as he shivered. To Emily and Gabriel it seemed he must be in the throes of another fit.

'I can't lift him whilst he's like this,' Gabriel said, 'We'd both end flat on our faces. Come, my friend, easy now.' He tried to straighten Seb's legs but he resisted, pulling his knees up to his chest again.

'So cold,' Seb whispered as Gabriel swathed him in blankets.

'It's not a fit, mistress, else he couldn't speak. And his back would be arching, not curled up like this. I saw a fellow once... He's just frozen stiff, I think. Seb, come now, I can only help you, if you help yourself. Sit up.' Gabriel coaxed him into a sitting position then eased him up. But Seb's knees had no more strength than sodden paper and the journeyman had to carry him to the kitchen where they set a chair by the fire for him. Gabriel roused the fire to life while Emily chafed Seb's hands and rubbed his back to get the cold humours moving again.

'No more, Em,' Seb protested when her ministrations became too vigorous. 'My head is throbbing so...'

'But I have to get you warm,' she said, angry at him because she felt guilty, 'Else you'll get sick, suffer another seizure. You want that?'

'It wasn't a seizure.' He felt around the back of his skull, found the cause of his headache: a swelling the size of a duck egg at the very least, or so it seemed beneath his carefully probing fingers. 'Someone hit me.'

'What nonsense. You must have struck your head on the cobbles when you fell in the fit. You should have just closed the gate and come back to bed directly.'

'I did close it; wedged it shut with the flour barrel.'

'You couldn't have: it's still flapping and banging. You must have intended to shut it but were then taken by the seizure,' Emily insisted. 'There was no one else out there.'

'It was you who said there was.'

'Enough now. You need rest,' Gabriel interrupted. 'Shall I help you to bed, Seb, or will you manage?'

'I'll manage. Em will help, if I need it. I'm better now.'

'Aye, but no more late night forays, eh?'

'No, but the gate is still swinging.'

'I'll shut it on my way back to bed,' Gabriel said as he left the kitchen in a swirl of gusting leaves.

'Thank you,' Seb called after him. 'Sorry you were disturbed.'

With Gabriel gone, Seb tried to rally his strength. The chills were still upon him and his head swam and thudded.

'You want my help or not?' Em asked brusquely, her bare foot already on the bottom stair.

'No. I'll sit by the fire a little longer. Don't worry about me. I'll come to bed in a while.' Then he said: 'Do you have any of that meadowsweet potion... the one for headaches?' She sighed so loudly, he regretted asking.

'It's on the shelf, clearly labelled. Help yourself. Three drops in half a cup of ale.' He thought she was going to leave him to fetch it himself but then she sighed again, even louder, and set about preparing the remedy for him. She put the cup down beside him with a thump and marched up the stairs. Apparently, this was all his own fault.

He held his hands out to the cheerful blaze in the hearth and felt the welcome heat seeping up his arms.

But there had been someone in the yard. The lump on his head wasn't conjured from his imagination. And he had wedged the barrel against the gate. Someone had shifted it to make good their escape, probably the same someone who had damaged the latch getting in.

A thief.

But what did they hope to steal? A handful of flour? A swig of ale or water? Some firewood, maybe? If that was all, they could have simply asked. The Foxleys could afford a little charity.

No. Someone had wanted more than that; had expected to find... something.

But he was too tired to think now. His head was ringing like a blacksmith's anvil. He took a few sips of the meadowsweet and closed his eyes.

Chapter 8

Monday, the feast of Martinmas, the eleventh day of November

THE HOUSEHOLD was up and busy earlier than usual, preparing to take the pig to slaughter. The Shambles would be bustling and it was wise to get there before the neighbours, to avoid a lengthy wait for the butchers' services and have the rest of the day to joint the carcass and get it ready for salting, drying, smoking and pickling. Only Seb was still abed, oblivious of everything.

In the kitchen, it seemed that every pot, pan and bucket had been soaked, scalded and scrubbed, ready for use. Emily and Nessie had been hard at work since well before the pale November dawn crawled into the sky and the rushlights could be extinguished. It was a raw morning but at least the wind had dropped, the crumpled leaves had ceased their frantic dance around the yard.

'What are you snivelling for, Nessie?' Emily said, having no time for such nonsense. 'Blow your nose and get on with preparing those herbs. We'll want them directly after the pig's done for, to steep those chitterlings.'

'But poor Master Seb... and poor Maddie; they make me weep,'

'Master Seb will do well enough after a good sleep,' Emily said firmly, as much to convince herself as the servant, 'And who is Maddie?'

'The pig, mistress. All these months I been feeding her, we got to know each other. So I gave her a name. And now she's going for butchering.' Nessie sobbed loudly and tears cascaded down her plump cheeks.

'I told you not to name something that will end up served upon a platter, did I not?'

'Aye, mistress.'

'Well then, you were foolish to do so.'

'But she's such a friendly pig. I can't bear thinking what's going to happen to her.'

'Then don't think about it. Just get on with your work. Look. You've barely made a start on the sage and those precious pepper corns need grinding. Or must I do everything myself?' Emily blew a stray hair from her eyes. Her hands smelled fiercely of garlic and chives of which she had chopped a great mound with a half dozen strong onions still awaiting her knife. They would make her eyes water for certain.

Since the kitchen was given over to industry this morn, Gabriel, Tom and Jack had to be content to break their fast as they went about their tasks, ale cup in hand, gnawing on yesterday's bread and knobs of hard cheese.

Jack was excited by the prospect of visiting the Shambles on such a day. Visions of juicy sausage and thick pork chops were sufficient to quell any concerns about the less pleasant side of the matter. His only problem was that Little Beggar had to be tied up for the duration. It wouldn't do to have the dog loose, lapping up the blood they were saving for the black puddings, or running off with a piece of tripe about to be salted down. The trouble was that Beggar sensed the occasion and was as excitable as his young master, having no intention of missing out or giving in quietly.

While the women worked in the kitchen, Gabriel sat in the yard, sharpening the butchery knives on the edge of the back step that served as a whetstone. Tom had gone to tether the pig and Jack was attempting the same with his dog. Tom had the easier task. Beggar was flying in circles about the yard, as if possessed by a demon. He seemed to think this was a fine new game. Jack was shouting and waving his arms which did naught to calm the dog. Of a sudden, Beggar bolted past Gabriel on the step, into the kitchen, knocking the journeyman aside even as he had a great, gleaming cleaver in his hand.

'Get that beast afore I lose a limb!' Gabriel yelled, setting down the knife. But Beggar was now causing chaos in the kitchen, running among the trestles that supported the board and dashing between Nessie's feet. Jack followed, bawling the dog's name, as if that would help. Nessie squealed, throwing up her hands, scattering herbs and spices.

'I cut meself,' she cried.

Beggar was barking wildly, delighted with the chase, dashing down the passage, into the workshop.

'Jack, catch that blessed beast or it'll be next for the butcher's slab, I promise you,' Emily said. 'Show me, Nessie. What've you done?'

Nessie was flapping her left hand.

'It hurts, mistress. Ohh, it hurts so.'

'Keep still. Stop fussing.'

'The knife slipped when the dog near toppled me.'

Emily fetched a linen cloth they'd scalded earlier, ready to strain the pig's blood. Now she used it to bind Nessie's arm. It was a nasty gash, not too deep but nigh unto a hand's breadth long down her inner forearm, betwixt elbow and wrist.

'It isn't so bad,' Emily said, 'You can still use your right hand well enough.'

It seemed an age before order was restored. Their early start that morn now counted for naught. Eventually, Jack managed to tie Beggar to the tethering ring in the yard, Tom had the pig ready for her last short walk and Emily had calmed Nessie and finished most of the preparations for later. Gabriel had honed all the blades and was now gone to the workshop, just in case any customers should require attention.

Leaving Nessie still cradling her arm and feeling very sorry for herself, Emily and Jack, weighed down with bowls and buckets, led the way to the Shambles, Tom following on behind with the pig.

Seb awoke as the light from the open shutter fell upon his closed eyes, like lance tips piercing his brain. Such a sore head, yet he couldn't recall drinking so much. Some half-remembered image, the swirl of a dark cloak in the night, flitted into his mind, but he couldn't keep hold of it and it was lost again as an old dream. But the pain was very real, as was the tender lump, like an over-ripe plum, on the back of his head. It took more than one attempt to raise his head from the pillow. The bedchamber hangings swam and rippled like a green and gold sea, his belly churned and he lay down again until the nausea passed.

At the fourth attempt, Seb succeeded in sitting up and discovered he was wearing his night robe. That was a blessing. At least he was decent enough to go down to the kitchen, to ask Em to prepare another dose of meadowsweet for him. He'd already decided that calling out for her just wasn't possible at present; the effort would surely split his skull in twain. He shuffled to the door, placing his feet with care so as not to jar his head. At the top of the stair, he looked down – a mistake indeed – and had to lean against the wall and close his eyes.

'Em,' he managed to say. No reply. 'Em,' he called a little louder. The house seemed far too quiet. Where was everyone?

'There's only me, master, and I've got a poorly arm. See?' Nessie came to the bottom of the stairs, her face woeful.

'What's happening, Nessie? Where's my wife?'

'They've gone to the Shambles, master, but Master Gabe is here. Shall I fetch him for you?'

Seb was about to shake his head but caught himself in time.

'No need. Prepare me a dose of the mistress's meadowsweet potion, will you, Nessie, and bring it to me, please.'

'Don't know if I can, master, what with my poorly arm.'

'What's amiss with it?' Seb was desperate to lie down. He shouldn't have asked.

'A terrible bad cut, master. It does hurt so.' Nessie was holding out her arm for inspection, the linen still in place. 'Reckon I need a surgeon to stitch it.'

Seb trembled with fatigue by the time he reached the stair foot and staggered to the nearest stool. Having used the sleeve of his night robe to wipe the cold sweat from his brow and top lip, breathing deeply to steady himself and fight off the rising nausea, he beckoned to Nessie.

She unwound the cloth and showed him the injury, holding it close so he could examine it. That was the last thing Seb wanted. He shut his eyes and willed his empty belly to behave.

'See how bad it is. I do need it stitching, don't I?'

'Keep it covered.' It was meant as an instruction but sounded more like a plea.

Gabriel came from the workshop, summoned by their voices.

'Oh. I thought they'd returned from the butchering. What are you doing out of bed, Seb?'

'Dying, probably. But Nessie has cut herself.'

'From what Mistress Em said, you were to rest all day.'

'Do you think Nessie requires Master Dagvyle's services?'

Gabriel inspected the maid's arm, holding it gently, dabbing at the seepage of blood. Nessie gazed at him, quite forgetting why he held her arm. Neither man noticed.

'May be. I'm no expert,' he said, retying the binding. 'It doesn't seem that she'll bleed to death. Mistress Em said it would do well enough but you're the master.'

'I can barely think...'

Without being asked, Gabriel poured three cups of ale and handed one to Nessie. Into Seb's cup, he added three drops of the meadowsweet potion that Emily had left on the shelf.

'Drink up, Seb, then I'm helping you back to bed. Nessie, you will sit in your chimney corner, out of the way. When Mistress

Em returns there'll be work to be done and you two will hinder, rather than help.'

But a deal of noise in the yard, lads laughing, Emily telling them to take more care, meant it was too late for Seb to escape to his bed. Gabriel held the door wide as Emily lugged in a bucket of blood and a bowl covered with a gory cloth.

'Put those on the board, Jack,' she instructed, 'Tom, don't spill anything. Put that liver to one side, now, then take the barrow and fetch back the carcass, sprightly now. Nessie, set to and clean out those innards.'

'But, mistress, I can't, not wi' me poorly arm.'

'Get on with it and don't answer back. Ah, Seb, so you're up and about at last. Since you're not busy in the workshop, you can start washing the tripe...'

He looked at his goodwife, his face more pallid than parchment, glanced at the pig's stomach she was offering to him in a basin and knew it was too much. The speed with which he fled to the workshop defied the pounding agony in his head. Beneath his night robe, he was still naked as Adam was made, but it mattered not. He couldn't remain in the kitchen and buckets of blood and offal stood betwixt him and the stairs to his bedchamber. He wasn't of a mind to eat black pudding, sausage or liver ever again. And as for tripe... It was nigh unto a miracle that he managed to open the shop door onto Paternoster Row before casting up the ale he'd drunk, hanging onto the jamb to keep himself from pitching headlong, into the gutter. Passing folk tutted but he was oblivious.

'Come,' Gabriel said, taking hold of Seb as he retched feebly, 'Come inside. Folk are staring.'

Seb did not care, not until he realised Gabe was rearranging his robe which had come unfastened, showing, well, everything.

Having dressed in the clothes Gabriel fetched for him, Seb felt more composed and decided he ought to make an effort and work on the new psalter for Father Thomas, so neglected of late.

Tom and Jack were running errands for Emily, fetching endless buckets of water from the conduit, since Nessie claimed to be unable, and Gabe was being industrious, decorating the margins of the dire Latin treatise, a commentary upon the Book of Leviticus, which he had finished copying, at last.

In truth, Gabriel was enjoying himself. The text was acquiring some most irreverent marginalia. At the foot of the page, an animal-priest belaboured his congregation with a sermon to which none gave ear; a congregation of frolicking rabbits with naught but pleasure upon their minds. He was particularly pleased with the priest – a wicked-looking weasel, of course – contemplating his wayward flock as ingredients for his pottage pot, simmering in the right-hand margin. If the text had to be in a language few ordinary folk could understand, at least the image could convey a message with meaning for them. The page would be completed with a serpent, as malignant as it was magnificent, slithering down the left-hand margin, its tail coiled about the illuminated capital at the head of the page.

Seb too tried to settle with his brushes and pigments. The psalter was way behind its proposed date for completion but he was fretting about Jude, not seen since Tuesday last. And he was wondering who or what had struck him so hard last night. Em said he'd suffered a seizure but he didn't believe that. He'd seen something – or someone – before the blow had felled him like a sapling beneath an axe. He left his stool, thinking to fetch some ale from the kitchen but a sudden clattering of pots and his wife's voice raised in a cry of dismay reminded him it was a place best avoided at present.

He glanced at Gabriel, bent over his work, saw a smile twitching at the corner of the journeyman's mouth.

'What amuses you, Gabe?' he asked, drawing closer to look. The image was well done but Seb flushed hot. 'Remove that this instant!' he said, bringing his palm down hard upon the journeyman's desk, causing the shells of colour to rattle and jump. 'Where are your wits? You can't present Bishop Kemp with such as this; that creature has too close a likeness to his own nephew. The poor man will suffer an apoplexy.'

'I hope he does,' Gabriel said, chuckling at the thought, 'He deserves no less.'

'He's a man of the cloth of high Episcopal office. What were you thinking?'

'He's an old goat who believes money will cover all his sins; that he can pay to have them wiped from his soul.'

'You don't know that.'

'Do I not? I know more than you think.'

'In truth, it matters not what you know or think that you know, Gabriel Widowson. I will not permit such an offensive piece of work to leave this workshop. I have a reputation to maintain. Now, you will erase that image, if you can, or else you'll rewrite the whole folio. Do I make myself clear in this matter?'

Gabriel sighed and nodded.

'You do, Master Seb, and I apologise. I was carried away by my enthusiasm. It won't happen again.'

'Well and good. And, Gabriel...'

'Aye?'

'I think 'tis a well executed image. Show it to the lads afore you erase it: I know it will amuse them.'

Jack came in, looking sheepish. His dog at his heels seemed equally forlorn, its tail tucked betwixt its legs.

'What have you done amiss now?' Seb asked, knowing that expression all too well.

'Beggar 'elped hisself t' some chitterlin's, didn't he? Weren't my fault, it weren't, 'onest, master.'

'Is it ever, Jack? Well, make yourself useful: Master Gabe has pigment shells and brushes that need washing out. And don't give me that woebegone look, lad, 'tis your own doing. You were told to leave the dog tied up in the yard, away from the kitchen.'

'I did but Beggar got bored, didn't he?'

'And how bored will he be observing you washing out oyster shells? And be careful: you have broken so many of late that we have none to spare.'

'Me an' Beggar could go t' Billingsgate an' get some more, couldn't we?'

'Aye, I suppose you could and that would get you out of the house and keep you both out of trouble.'

'We'll go now.'

'No, you won't. You'll wash out the shells we have first of all, *then* you may go. And don't forget to leave the brushes to dry tip uppermost and worked to a good point, as I've shown you countless times afore. On the last occasion, one of mine was more like a scrubbing brush, impossible to use until I reshaped it.'

• •

Billingsgate on a Monday was at its least busy. The fishing boats, oyster-boats and shrimpers were out in the estuary, having rested on Sunday, and fish wasn't needed upon the board until Wednesday. The fishwives were fewer, many seeing to their butchered pigs, like Mistress Em at home but Jack knew one or two of the women from times past, when he had sought shelter from his uncle's wrath in their netting sheds. Ol' Widow Scally was sure to have a sack of empty shells he could buy for the ha'penny Master Seb had given him and, with luck, if the old woman was in the mood, he might get them for less and have money left over to visit a cookshop. The thought crossed his mind that whether he had a coin left or not, he might help himself to a hot pig's trotter, just like he used to. But no, he had promised Master Seb he'd never filch stuff anymore. Though, of course, Little Beggar had made no such promise and was as artful a thief as any creature upon four legs – or two.

As Jack made his way past London Stone along Candlewick Street, it seemed some fellow, hooded and cloaked, followed him like a dark shadow, flitting from one hidden refuge to the next but his efforts at concealment were not enough to keep him from the notice of a sharp-eyed, one-time street urchin. Jack had known he was there since he'd left Paul's Gate on Watling Street but why would anyone bother to follow him? A person so unimportant. It made no sense and even less when Jack was all but certain that he knew who it was.

Between St Botolph's church, Billingsgate and the Lion's Quay, stood a row of tall, narrow wooden buildings, lined up like men-at-arms to face the enemy. And the enemy was the elements. Within the buildings, the fishermen hung their nets to dry, safe from wind and rain. No fisherman worthy of the name would leave his nets to moulder and rot in a sodden heap. In his younger days, Jack had passed many a cold or stormy night in one of the netting sheds for the fisherfolk kept them in good repair – often better roofed than their own houses – since their livelihoods depended on the nets.

Determined to lose the man who followed him, Jack darted down the narrow space betwixt two neighbouring sheds. It was a tighter squeeze than it used to be when he was a starveling fleeing from an angry goodwife whose bacon pasty he had snatched or an irate tavern-keeper from whose ale barrel he had stolen a few sips. Even so, his skinny frame could go where a grown man's could not and, weaving around the sheds, Jack was soon free of his unwanted shadow.

'Well, lordy, look who turns up at my door after all this long while. If it isn't my much favoured ragamuffin, Jack Tabor.'

'Good morrow to you, Widow Scally.' Jack made a little bow to the old woman who sat upon a stool outside her ramshackle dwelling.

'Ooh, such fine manners, sir. I see you must have mended your ways,' she laughed without breaking the rhythm of her knife work: cutting off the heads, slicing the bellies and gutting herring faster than her actions could be described. She worked on a much-scarred flagstone before her door, sleeves rolled above her elbow even on a chill November day, her lap draped with a sacking apron, stiff with blood and stinking of ancient fish. Her sharp blade glinted in the pale autumn sunlight as she took a fish from one basket, deftly removed head and guts and tossed it into a second basket.

Around the flagstone sat a dozen or more sleek, well fed cats, each awaiting the chance to grab a fishy morsel, timing to perfection their lunges to avoid the widow's knife. 'Elijah! Get away from that basket. I've told you afore.' She shooed a fat tabby tomcat away from the gutted fish. 'That cat would rob me blind, if I didn't keep a watch. Now tell me, young Jack, what are you about these days? I feared you must be in the sheriff's lock-up I hadn't seen you for so long.'

'Nay, not me, Scally,' Jack said, standing up tall, 'I'm a proper 'prentice now to Master Seb Foxley of Paternoster Row, ain't I?'

'The scrivener? I've heard good things of him. Are you working hard for him?

'Mostly.' Jack mumbled his reply.

'What does that mean?'

'Well, I do try 'ard, 'onest I do, but all them letters look the same t' me, them 'bs' an' 'ds' an' 'ps' but I can spell me name: j.a.c.k. That spells Jack, see?'

'And who pays for your apprenticeship? Not your uncle, that be certain.'

'Nobody pays. Master Seb took me on fer no fee; teaches me fer nuffink, don't he? An' I get fed an' I got a proper bed, ain't I?'

'Then you are a most fortunate lad, Jack Tabor, and must make the most of it. You learn your letters and work hard for Master Foxley. You could have a good trade and be wealthy some day.'

A growl and a hiss interrupted the widow. Little Beggar, teeth bared, was spoiling for a fight with Elijah. The cat, fur on end and tail upright, looked twice as large as before, spitting and hissing at the dog. The two would-be combatants were now much of a size. Beggar leapt forward but the cat swiped a paw at him, clawing his nose. The dog yelped and retreated to cower behind Jack.

'You're such a coward, Beggar, ain't you? All bark an' no bite.'

'A wise creature, I would say. Elijah has done for far bigger dogs than he. I'm thinking I could make money if I put him to the bear-baiting.' The woman dealt with a few more fish while Jack watched, the rhythm of her work almost had him in a trance. 'Now, did you come all this way for the sake of passing the time o' day with an old friend, or was there some purpose to your visit, lad?'

'Wot? Oh, aye. Master Seb is in need of oyster shells fer mixing pigments, ain't he? I near forgot.'

'There's a sack o' shells indoors, in the back corner. Did you bring your own bag?

'Master Seb gave me one, aye.'

'Help yourself, then.'

Within, the single room was gloomy and smelled of fish, cats and, most of all, smoke. As his eyes became accustomed to the darkness, Jack could see that the roof beams were more than just soot-blackened from the open hearth in the midst of the earthen floor, they were badly charred. He found the sack of shells and rummaged through it. Winkle and whelk shells were no use but those of cockles, mussels, oysters and some of the larger limpet shells – though these last did not tend to sit straight – all made suitable pigment pots. With his bag full, as he turned to leave, he noticed that the lintel above the doorway was so badly burned it looked in danger of collapse.

'You 'ad a fire, Scally?'

'Aye. A week since, it was. One of the cats knocked a rushlight onto my mattress. The straw stuffing went up in such a blaze.'

'You weren't hurt, were you?'

Scally shook her head.

'Nay, but the cat lost a deal of fur. See? The grey one. She won't do that again.'

'But yer doorway looks near burned through, don't it?'

'Aye. I need a new lintel but when shall the likes of me ever be able to afford one? It'll have to do as it is.'

Jack recalled the ha'penny Master Seb had given him to pay for the shells, the coin he'd hoped to spend in a cookshop. The widow hadn't mentioned money but...

'Here, take this,' he said, pressing the half coin into her work-worn hands that glittered with slimy fish scales.

'I don't want paying for a few shells, lad.'

'I knows that, but it'll pay fer a carpenter's repairs, won't it?'

'No, I won't accept charity and, besides, where does a 'prentice get coin to spare?'

Jack shrugged.

'Take it fer a loan then, 'til Elijah earns money at the bear-baiting. Then yer c'n pay me back, can't yer?' They both laughed.

With his bag full and Beggar restored to his usual brazen self after his encounter with the cat, Jack made his way home, feeling very righteous for not having spent his master's money in a cookshop but in an act of charity. He was by the Walbrook before he realised that shadow was dogging him once again.

• •

'You took your time,' Tom complained when Jack reached home. Tom was now in the workshop, having finished helping Mistress Em in the kitchen. Master Seb was with a customer in the parlour and Master Gabe was engrossed in the Leviticus tract. 'You could help me trim these folios to size, if you ever did any work, you idle wretch. I had to help mistress and do my own tasks. And what do you do, Jack? Make such a nuisance of yourself folk prefer you to do nothing at all, rather than get under their feet. It isn't fair.'

'I *was* working. I was doing an errand for Master Seb. I wasn't idle at all. I had to go t' Billingsgate, didn't I? And you'll never guess what 'appened...'

'I'm sure, I'm not interested.'

'I was follered, wasn't I, all the way there an' back an' you'll never guess who it was wot follered us...'

'Why would anyone bother to follow you?'

'Dunno but they did. It were the under-sheriff, that Nox fella. Never liked 'im much, did I?'

'You're making it up. I'm sure Master Nox has better things to do than follow you around. Now hold these pages steady while I rule the edges straight. Steady, I said. Stop flapping about, you useless creature.'

'But 'e did foller me, 'onest. It's the troof wot I telled you.'

'Well, perhaps another woman has been murdered and he reckons you must be guilty of it.'

'But I never did nuffin, I didn't, I swear'.

'Never did nuffin? You never spoke a truer word, Jack Tabor, and I'm tired of it. I'm going to tell Master Seb that you're a good-for-nothing idle little liar and I hope he throws you out of this place, out of my bedchamber and out of the workshop, forever.'

'No, no, please don't, Tom. I promise I'll do your chores t'morrow an' the next day. Please don't say that t' master, pleeease. I ain't done nuffin *wrong*, wos wot I meant. Please Tom.' Jack dissolved into snotty tears, wiping his eyes and nose upon his sleeve, and Beggar whined and whimpered in sympathy.

'Why don't you go practise your letters? You're not helping me if you get snot on these pages Master Jude penned. He'll be livid when he returns if you do and you know what happens when Master Jude gets angry...'

Jack nodded. He knew only too well.

'Too much noise, lads,' Seb complained as he came into the workshop, sipping a drink. It was another dose of meadowsweet: his head was throbbing again.

'Tom said I was a liar and I ain't,' Jack wailed.

'Quietly, Jack, if you please.' Seb sat at his desk, taking another sip of his medication. He closed his eyes.

123

'Tom won't b'lieve me that I wos follered by ol' Nox. But I wos.'

'Why would the under-sheriff follow you?'

'Dunno, master, but I seed him anyhow. He ain't much good at sneakin' up on me.'

'I'm sure Master Nox was going about his reputable business and you just happened to see him.'

'I wager it weren't repertible, whatever that means. He was bein' inekwetus, like wot you said.'

Seb couldn't help smiling through his discomfort.

'Perhaps you are right, lad.'

'I knows I wos.'

Bishopsgate

FATHER WESSELL was in an ill humour. What was his uncle thinking of, using him as a mere errand boy to deliver a gift to the Abbess of St Helen's by Bishopsgate? It might be a fine salmon that he was carrying in the linen-draped basket but this was a task any menial could have performed. It was an insult to his office, no matter that the bishop had a favour to beg of the abbess, something about potted plums in wine, in case the papal legate should come to dine on his proposed visit to England. The visit was not yet a certainty and Hugh believed the plums – his uncle's favourite fruit – would end up being consumed in private by the bishop alone. Yet he was required to beg them from a woman. No matter that she wore a wimple and habit, she was still a sister of Eve beneath her dress, as wicked as any other woman with the morals of a bitch on heat yet pretending piety. It was all a sham, of course, a ruse that didn't fool Hugh, nor God, for an instant.

He was leaving St Helen's convent as dusk was falling, still fuming over the humiliation of delivering fish like a Billingsgate huckster and, having requested plums for the bishop, the abbess had smiled sweetly at him and said she had none to give. A lie, of course, but it humbled him still further that he would have to report his failure and the waste of a good salmon to his uncle. Having offered the fish as a gift, he could hardly demand that the abbess give it back, could he? But someone was going to pay, to compensate him for his trouble.

And there they were: a drunkard and his slut, sniggering together, creeping out of Bishopsgate just before it closed for the night, no doubt intending to find some secret den in which to fornicate and indulge in lust. Well, a priest ought to stamp out sin whenever it crossed his path and that was one task Hugh could go to with a will, especially in his present frame of mind. And this particular righteous act was indeed one to relish as he recognised the drunkard as one of St Michael's own iniquitous backsliding parishioners. He didn't know the slut but her sort was familiar to him as he followed the amorous couple out through the city gate.

Chapter 9

Tuesday, the twelfth day of November
The Foxley workshop

NESSIE HAD been complaining all yesterday and half the night about her 'poorly arm', as she called it. More worrisome for Emily, the girl was using it as an excuse to avoid work and there was still so much to do, butchering and preserving the pig's carcass.

'Seb. What am I to do with her?' Em asked, coming into the workshop to speak with him. At least she had contained her impatience until an important customer had departed.

Seb was busy, writing down the details he had just discussed with a wealthy merchant, recently raised to knighthood by King Edward as recompense for having excused his insolvent monarch a large sum of money owed. The man wanted his new coat of arms painted on an oaken panel to hang above his hearth to impress visitors.

'Mm, a Stafford knot. Is he entitled to that device, I wonder?' Seb closed the order ledger and turned to his goodwife. 'What's amiss, Em? What are you to do with whom?'

'Nessie: I cannot get a hand's turn of work out of her and her constant complaints about her arm are too distracting for me to accomplish very much either. What should I do?'

'Take your broom to her,' Gabriel suggested with a chuckle, 'That's what you do to Jude if he annoys you.'

'That won't help, will it?' Emily said. 'It will just give her another reason to whine. I'm tired of it... as if I haven't got enough to do.'

'Is her arm so painful then?' Seb asked. 'Have you looked at it this morn? She could be getting wound fever.'

'She tells me it pains her greatly but, in truth Seb, it doesn't look so bad to me.'

'Why not send for Surgeon Dagvyle, have him examine it? If he says there is no reason for concern then she'll have no cause to shirk her chores. If he thinks it requires treatment of some kind, at least she cannot complain that we haven't done our best for her.'

'It will cost.'

'Aye. Since when did aught come for no charge?'

• •

Surgeon John Dagvyle was all smiles: seeing to the ailments of the Foxley household was proving lucrative of late without the need to overcharge them by very much at all. And, better yet, payment was always prompt. He'd made ten pence ha'penny out of Master Sebastian's head injury for no treatment but a few sagacious head-noddings, expressions of concern and the time-honoured advice 'to rest'. They seemed to think they got value for their coin else why did they keep sending for him?

In the Foxley kitchen, Dagvyle's nose was besieged by so many aromas: savoury herbs and spices and meats stewing, along with the less pleasant stinks of blood and entrails. These last lay glistening in a large bowl, awaiting stuffing and turning into sausages. Fortunately, neither the sight nor the smell were unknown to a surgeon. Even so, the steam and heat from so many bubbling pots made the kitchen stifling.

The maidservant sat with her injured arm resting on the board.

'I pray you, cease your snivelling, wench,' Dagvyle said, 'I haven't so much as touched the bindings as yet. What will you do if the cut requires stitching, eh?'

'Behave yourself, Nessie,' Mistress Emily ordered.

Dagvyle began to unwind the length of linen from the lass's arm. What with her gasping and flinching and so many tears, he expected the worst. Yet the lifting of the last layer of lamb's lint revealed a clean, dry wound, naught amiss at all. But it was a lengthy gash and the surgeon thought it would heal more readily if he sutured it. He took out the little almanac that hung from his girdle and consulted the star charts. With most patients, he would have simply taken up his sewing kit and carried out the procedure but with this one he hesitated. He looked to Mistress Foxley.

'I think a little embroidery is called for,' he said. 'The astrological alignment is favourable. Just a couple of stitches to close the...'

'Stitches!' Nessie shrieked, leaping from her stool and upending it in her haste to flee the surgeon's needle.

'Sit down.' Emily would suffer no nonsense. 'Keep still and remain silent.'

'But it'll hurt, mistress.'

'It will hurt worse if you don't sit still.'

'Can't I have a sleepin' draught.'

'For a couple of stitches? Certainly not. Surgeon Dagvyle hasn't got time to spend, waiting for some potion to take effect and I see no reason to waste money on unnecessary medications. Just brace yourself; it will soon be over and done with.'

With a nod from Mistress Foxley, Dagvyle took up his needle and threaded it with a length of silk as deftly as any embroiderer but, at sight of it, the lass began to wail like a soul in torment.

'Noo, noo, mistress, I beg you, not wi'out a potion, pleeease.'

'I'm not paying for any potion and there's an end to it. Now be still.'

'But the potion won't cost and it works quick, I know. It worked ever so quick on Master Seb.'

'What did?'

'The potion my old mistress used to give to Master Bowen, he what was murdered. It's at the back of the shelf, behind that copper pot we never use anymore 'cos it's got a hole. It sent Master Seb to sleep for hours the other day. I could have a drop in some ale...' Nessie's voice tailed off. The look on Mistress Foxley's face was terrifying. Even Surgeon Dagvyle glanced away, flipping pages in his almanac.

'You gave poison to Master Seb? You wicked little...'

'No, mistress, 'tis only a sleeping potion but I-I gave him too much. A drip will suffice. I never meant to... I thought master looked in need of a nap, was all.'

'Where is it, this potion?' Nessie pointed and Emily found the little black vial behind a disused pot. 'This?' Nessie nodded. 'We will have words on this matter, later,' Emily threatened as she poured a little ale into a cup and added a solitary droplet from the vial, a greenish liquid, the colour of Thames river mud. Despite its unappealing appearance, it smelled of naught but fresh air. 'Drink it then and we shall see what comes to pass.' Nessie sipped. 'All of it.'

It worked. Within the time it took to say a half dozen or so Paternosters, the wench was sleeping, her head upon the board. Apart from a twitch or two, she snored softly, oblivious to Surgeon Dagvyle's ministrations.

Emily watched, seething all the while. Such wickedness had no right to untroubled slumbers.

Down by Garlickhill

'COME, JACK, hasten yourself. I promise you this afternoon will be more pleasurable than you expect.' Seb, despairing of his young apprentice's continuing lack of progress in learning his letters, no matter what means was tried, had decided the lad might do better if he had company for the task. If he and Rose – so apt a pupil – studied together, Seb hoped her diligence and enthusiasm would inspire Jack, make a competition of it. The lad wouldn't want to be bested by a lass.

'I don't wan' anuvver readin' lesson, master. Yer teached me 'm's and 'n's s'mornin'. Where we goin', anyways?'

'Garlickhill. We're going to meet someone who is also learning to read, only she is making far more rapid progress than you are. In but a few days she has already come to recognise at least half the letters of the alphabet and her penmanship shows much promise.'

'She, master? A wench?'

'Aye. Her name is Rose and I want you to be upon your best behaviour, Jack.'

The way was slippery with mud and uneven, so Seb took especial care. His hip was aching worse these days, suffering from the cold, damp weather. As they approached the Pewter Pot tavern, Jack pulled at Seb's sleeve.

'I knows this place, master,' he whispered, 'From when I lived wiv me uncle. Yer know it's an 'orehouse.'

'So I have been informed but, fear not, Jack, you will not be subjected to any sort of impropriety.'

'Wot?'

'There will be no wrong-doing whilst I am with you.'

'Pity,' Jack muttered, pulling a face.

'Did you say something, lad?'

'No, master.'

'Wait here by these steps whilst I go find Roger Underwood and pay my fee,' Seb instructed.

'But, master, yer said there wouldn't be none o' that imperiety stuff...'

'Impropriety. No, there won't be.'

'So wot yer payin' for, eh?'

'I pay for Rose's time, Jack. She has to earn her keep, you understand, whether any immoral acts take place or not.'

Jack was shaking his head. At the age of twelve years, or thereabouts – no one could be certain when he was born – he knew well enough how such matters usually went on.

'Yer pay but yer don't do nuffin.'

'I teach her to read. That is time well spent and I begrudge not a penny.'

Jack sat on the bottom step, thinking. Master Seb must be mad; fit for Bedlam. Paying over good coin and not getting any bed-sport: what a waste. Who could enjoy reading lessons better than wenching? In truth, Jack didn't yet know all the details but he'd seen it going on. As a street urchin, he'd watched many a couple down dark alleyways and, mostly, it seemed to be something folk liked to do. They called it 'taking pleasure', didn't they? There was certainly no pleasure to be got from learning letters, he knew that. Master was a strange fellow and hard to fathom.

'Come, Jack. I shall introduce you to Rose. You will like her.'

Seb climbed the wooden steps up to Rose's room above the tavern, Jack behind, dancing two steps up at a time and one back, keeping a rhythm. It made Seb envious.

Rose answered the door before he knocked.

'I was looking out for you, Master Seb,' she explained. He kissed her smooth forehead in greeting.

'How are you, Rose?'

'In good health, master, I thank you. I've been studying like you said to do. I did my best with another of Master Aesop's tales. One about a hare and some beast I never heard of. You'll have to explain to me about this tertise animal.'

'Ah, you mean the tortoise,' Seb laughed.

'Master will tell yer it's like a sort o' snail, a slowcoach creature,' Jack said, shoving in front of Seb. 'That's wot he telled me when I arst him.'

'Well! You're certainly no slowcoach now, are you, young master,' Rose said, hiding her surprise behind a smile.

'Rose, this is Jack Tabor, my apprentice, of sorts,' Seb said as Jack made his bow. 'Too forward in all things but learning his letters. I trust you have no objection to sharing your lesson with him? He is in sore need of inspiration.'

The dull November afternoon wore on. Master Seb and Rose were deep in discussion of letter shapes and sounds and he seemed impressed by the way she wrote her name on the scraps of paper he had brought for the purpose. Much neater than Jack could manage, however hard he tried. The hours at Garlickhill would have been tedious had Jack not found something else to interest him: Rose.

Gazing at her was better than staring at inky shapes. She was comely. Her eyes sparkled whenever she looked up from her lesson. She smiled all the while she wasn't chewing her nether lip in concentration. Jack could feel his heart pounding faster. His palms were sweaty so he couldn't hold the quill properly but who cared about writing anyway? He wriggled about as he sat beside Rose on the edge of the narrow bed, keeping his writing board across his lap so she could not see the stirrings within his breeches. No. He wasn't worried if she noticed, after all, as a whore she would know of such things. It was Master Seb he feared. Supposing he saw? It would be worse than showing a priest. Jack did his best to turn his thoughts to the lesson but his eyes kept straying to the curves of Rose's bodice and what lay beneath the pale green linen.

'Jack!' Master Seb's voice cut through his daydream. 'Show me your letters, please.'

Sniffing, he passed the paper. 'Is this all? Look at it. 'Tis a mess even worse than usual. What have you been doing all the while? Is this supposed to be your name? I don't know why I waste my time on you.'

'I'm sure he's doing his best,' Rose said, putting her arm around his shoulders. 'You are, aren't you, Jack?'

He felt sweat break out on his forehead. He nodded. 'I'm trying, master, 'onest, I am.'

But Master Seb wasn't pleased. He grabbed Jack's writing board and stuffed in into his scrip. Jack's hands flew to hide his groin but master didn't even glance at him.

'It was a mistake to bring you, Jack.'

'No, master. I really tried. I will try 'arder yet, if yer let us come next time.'

Exasperated, Seb turned his attention to Rose.

'You have done well, lass. I'm pleased with your writing. Have another look at the Hare and the Tortoise for next time and practise those 'g' shapes. I'll come by on Friday, as usual.'

'Thank you Master Seb,' she said, her face glowing with pleasure at his compliments.

'Oh, is there any news of your friend, Bessie? I meant to enquire earlier.'

'Not a word, sir, and I've asked so many folk. Even if they never saw her to recognise her face, they could know her by her gown alone. 'Tis such a lovely colour, so bright.'

Seb's blood turned of a sudden chill in his veins.

'What colour is it?'

'Golden yellow. I envy it so much.'

'Rose. Have you been to St James since Sunday?' he asked, attempting to keep his voice steady, remembering the piece of cloth, the lock of hair and the drawing of the large, uneven footprint, all tucked away for safe-keeping in his scrip. It might not be as he feared but he couldn't bring himself to show them to her.

'Wednesday, as usual, and earlier this day. Why?'

The copies Tom and he had made, giving the description of the woman found at Smithfield, were taken round all the churches, to be put up in the porches. Jack had delivered the last few first thing this morning. But then again, Rose couldn't have read it, if she saw it, but someone might have told her what it said.

'Tell me, Rose, does Bessie, by any chance – and 'tis no matter if she doesn't – but, er, is it the case that...' He couldn't do it. Not to that lovely face, those shining eyes. He turned away, mumbled the query to himself, rehearsing the words.

'Sorry, master? I didn't hear what you said.'

He turned back and began again.

'Tell me, does your friend have a mole upon her ear lobe?'

'Why, yes. She calls it her ear-jewel,' Rose laughed. 'Do you know her, then? Have you seen her?'

'We finded 'er,' Jack said quietly, hanging his head.

'Oh, sweet Rose,' Seb whispered and wrapped her in his arms. Jack looked away. He wanted so to do the same.

• •

It was dark by the time they had managed to comfort Rose, having shown her the scrap of cloth and the lock of hair. Sadly, there was no longer any doubt concerning Bessie's whereabouts. Seb would report his discovery to the sheriff upon the morrow, naming the unfortunate soul and telling of the man who had been her last known customer, according to Rose. Since she had no reason to lie about so important a matter, Seb had been shocked to learn it was a man of the cloth. He had quizzed her upon the issue, between her tears and lamentations, to be certain she was not in error but she was definite about the silk-embroidered cassock of finest wool, worn beneath a concealing cloak of plainer cloth. Besides, he had blessed them both upon entering the chamber, before Rose departed, as per their arrangement, to serve in the tavern downstairs, leaving Bessie to her work. That was the last time she had seen her friend, on that Sunday afternoon, before vespers, on the third day of November.

Reaching their home in Paternoster Row, Seb and Jack paused by the pigsty, empty now the pig had been butchered, to see how work was progressing in its repair. Tardily, it seemed. Only the lowest course of stone sat in its rightful place, as it had always been, but at least the old elder tree had been cleared away, chopped and stacked. As it dried – if it ever did in this everlasting damp weather – it would be fuel for the hearth. The rest of the stones were tumbled just as they had fallen.

'Ain't done much, 'ave they, master? Not fer an 'ole day's work.'

'No, Jack. Rather like someone else who comes to mind. Come now. I'm cold, weary and melancholy. Let us go warm ourselves by the fire afore supper and wear our more cheerful countenances for the others at table.'

• •

In the warmth of the kitchen, the savoury scents of onions, worts and boiled bacon reminded Seb how close to suppertime it must be. His belly growled appreciatively but then his wife left off stirring the pottage and confronted him. Her countenance was anything but cheerful.

'Wha's fer supper, mistress?' Jack asked, peering into the steaming cooking pot as it hung above the hot embers.

Emily slapped the lad away but otherwise ignored him, glaring at Seb.

'Where were you?' Her brow was drawn down, her eyes dark with anger, the hot ladle brandished in her hand. 'Father Thomas has been waiting to see you about the psalter. You said you would be but an hour.'

'Is he still here? Tell him that I beg his pardon and will be there directly.'

'Too late. He had the vespers service to conduct. If you don't take care, Sebastian, you're going to lose this commission, I warn you.'

Seb sighed. Em was right. He must give more attention to business and less to unprofitable pursuits, such as reading lessons and solving crimes. The latter should be the sheriff's and the beadle's concern, not his.

'Forgive me. I was delayed but have come by new information concerning a priest.'

'Aye, and you'll never guess, mistress,' Jack interrupted rudely, determined to make his contribution, 'Rose said the priest visited 'er and 'er friend at the 'orehouse where she works, didn't she, master? In that very room where we wos.'

Emily's frown deepened.

'Rose? At a whorehouse? What have you been about, husband?'

'Emily, dearest, 'tis not as it sounds,' Seb mumbled, knowing his face was turning fiery red, 'We were but visiting, briefly.'

'She's a lusty wench, fer sure,' Jack added, 'And so comely and buxom.'

Seb silenced him with a nudge on the shoulder.

'Lusty, eh? Buxom?' Emily's look turned Seb's innards to water.

'I-I'm teaching her to read is all.' The truth sounded so pathetic even to his own ears, she wouldn't believe him. What right-minded wife would?

'If you're going to lie to me, you might at least make the effort to have a decent story to tell. Reading? You expect me to believe that you spent three hours with a whore in her chamber, teaching her the alphabet?'

'Jack was a witness...'

'I don't care if the pope was a witness, you unfaithful dog.' Emily's action caught Seb off guard, the stinging swipe with the ladle sending him staggering back. Unable to keep his balance as his aching hip gave way, he ended slumped upon the floor.

'I swear 'tis true, Em, as God will judge me... please, Em...'

'You disgust me. As if going whoring isn't bad enough, you do so in the middle of the day when anyone might see you: the neighbours or Father Thomas or Dame Ellen. You could at least have taken the trouble to be discreet.'

'I was. No one saw us.'

'So, you admit you had cause to keep your visit secret. How much did you pay her?'

'Well, you see, er, as usual, I gave a groat for her time because otherwise...'

'As usual?' she snarled. 'You've done this before *and* paid good coin to give a whore a reading lesson?'

'Aye, I suppose that seems odd.' Seb realised he was damning himself whatever he said. Hunched on the floor, he looked up at her. 'I beg you, Em, believe me, I never bedded her. I wouldn't betray you, I swear upon the Gospels. Jack will tell you that I...'

'Jack will tell me anything to keep his precious apprenticeship with you, so spare your breath, Sebastian Foxley. I know you're lying to me. How dare you do this? How could you hurt me so, you wretch?'

Then came the tears, the wrenching sobs, the sound of a woman's heart torn asunder. She kicked at him as he lay there. The blow did not hurt; it was but a gesture of despair, a parting shot before she flung aside the ladle to clatter in the hearth, buried her face in her apron and fled upstairs.

Seb watched their happy marriage crumble and could do naught to prevent it.

• •

When Nessie had served everyone at the table, slopping pottage into their bowls with so little care – seeing her mistress was absent – Seb had to say something:

'Nessie! Don't waste our food in this way. I swear Beggar has the greater share upon the floor. Now take some bread and pottage to your mistress, upstairs, and be more careful with it.'

'Sorry, master. It's me poorly arm what does it.' It was an unconvincing apology accompanied by a shrug and a sigh as she nursed the bindings on her wrist as though the limb was so wounded it might need amputation any day.

'Did Surgeon Dagvyle attend you?'

'Aye, master, he did. But mistress isn't up there. Upstairs, I mean.'

'What? Where is she then?'

'Don't know, master.'

'Tell me, Nessie,' Seb demanded, abandoning his supper.

Jack mumbled something around a mouthful of pottage.

'What was that, Jack?'

'I said...' the lad swallowed down his food, 'Mistress said as she was goin' 'ome.'

'Home? This is her home.'

'Back to her father, probably,' Gabe suggested, sipping his ale to conceal a grin.

Seb pushed his stool back from the board. 'Jack, fetch my mantle, if you please. Tom, light a torch for me.'

'Master Seb, you're not going after her, are you? On a night like this? 'Tis raining like Noah's Flood again. You'll be soaked and catch your death. Let her stew for a while, that's my advice.'

'Emily is *my* wife and when I want your advice, Gabriel, I'll request it. Otherwise, this matter is none of your concern.'

'At least let me give you company.'

'There's no reason for us both to take a drenching.'

The Appleyard house in Cheapside

AT THE house of Stephen Appleyard, citizen, carpenter and Warden Archer, Seb stood in the porch, rain cascading from his mantle and pooling on the flagstones. He braced himself before knocking, unsure as to how he would be received. If Emily was here, what might she have told her father? If she wasn't, then he would have to admit that she had run away and he knew not where.

There was no need for words. The way Master Appleyard looked at him said everything.

'Forgive me for disturbing you at so late an hour...'

'I was expecting you. You'd best come in, out of the rain. Go through to the kitchen, 'tis warmer there. Let me take that wet mantle.'

Seb went down the screens passage to the kitchen at the back of the house, a cosy place, familiar from the pleasant times when he had been a-courting Emily. It seemed so long ago.

'Is Emily...'

'She's up in her old bedchamber, supposedly sleeping but weeping is more likely,' Stephen said. 'You've upset my daughter, Sebastian. I believed you to be a better man than that.'

'It's all a fearful misunderstanding. I explained myself inadequately in the heat of the moment. She hardly gave me the opportunity.'

Stephen set two beautifully carven stools of his own craftsmanship either side of the fireplace.

'Aye, women can be hasty sometimes, I know that, so I shall give you all the time you need to explain yourself whilst we share some of my elderberry wine.' He handed Seb a cup of fine treenware, again made by his own hands, and poured a generous measure of dark purple liquid from a pewter pitcher before filling his own cup and settling himself on the other stool. 'Emily spoke of a whore?'

Seb sniffed his wine, fruity and rich and, probably, more potent than he was used to.

'I admit, the lass in question is indeed a whore in that she earns her living by such means but 'tis not from choice. Four years since, Rose – for that is her name – was raped by one of her stepfather's apprentices. He was a glover by trade, in Canterbury. She complained to her stepfather, her mother being in her grave, but he blamed her for leading the young man astray and drove her from his house.

'Rose came to London, hoping her knowledge of the glover's trade might gain her some employment. In fact, she began to help out at a cordwainer's shop, selecting leathers, something in which she had certain skills. Only then did she realise she was with child by her stepfather's apprentice.'

He sipped the wine. It took his breath away and made him gasp. It was heady stuff.

'The cordwainer wanted no more to do with her and Rose was left wandering the streets, penniless. A young woman, Bessie Earnshaw, a lass from up North who had once been in a similar case, befriended Rose, kept her from starvation, shared her room with her. Bessie worked as a tavern-wench during the day and persuaded the tavern-keeper to give Rose a job – which he did. But at night, Bessie was a whore, her customers paying the tavern-keeper for her services. Then, when the time came, Bessie assisted Rose with the birth of the child. A boy, apparently. Rose gave him the name Edward, after the king's grace.'

Stephen refilled his own cup with wine but Seb's remained near full. A log settled in the fire, sending sparks rising in the chimney like fiery dust motes in a sunbeam. Seb watched them, letting himself be distracted.

'Drink up, lad. What does this tale have to do with you and my Emily?'

'I'm coming to that. Once she was no longer great with child and shapely as afore, the tavern-keeper told Rose she would now have to earn her bed and board, as Bessie did. And because of her youth, in order to pay for the child's keep, he would pass off Rose as a virgin maid and charge extra. Rose protested that because she would put him to the breast, the child would cost naught to feed but the tavern-keeper said that wasn't possible – only one Virgin Mother with milky paps had ever existed. Rose would have to stop suckling the babe herself. She was distraught. She bought goat's milk for the infant and did all she could for it but the babe no longer thrived. It died afore it was three months of age.

'Rose knew that the work she was forced to do might, inevitably, cause her to become with child again at any time and determined that little Edward's fate would not be repeated. So, she has been attempting to better her position, to learn to read and write, find some more respectable employment and, maybe, a husband.

'She and I met, quite by accident, in that thick fog the other week. We talked. She told me of her hope to learn her letters. I gave her an impromptu lesson and she was quick to learn. It seemed a pity to leave it at that but I could hardly invite her to our house, now could I? So I have continued to visit her, teaching her. But I swear that naught else has happened betwixt us.'

'Emily told me you were gone for hours, all afternoon, and that you admitted paying the tavern-keeper, whore-master, whatever he is.'

'Aye, 'tis the truth. I pay for her time, as I tried to explain to Emily, else the tavern-keeper would withhold her food, maybe throw her back on the street, if she fails to earn sufficient. And then, this afternoon, we were speaking of her friend – the one I mentioned, Bessie – who has been missing for a week and more. Rose said her friend wore a bright yellow gown. You may recall, a body was found at Smithfield...'

'By your two lads, if I remember rightly.'

Seb nodded and drank his wine. He felt in need of it.

Stephen put a fresh log upon the fire that had burned low, stoking it with an iron rod.

'What of it?'

'The body,' Seb continued, 'was clothed in just such a brightly coloured gown. I had a sample of the cloth in my scrip. Rose confirmed that it was very like Bessie's. Then I asked about the mole.'

'Mole?'

'The dead woman had a mole upon her earlobe. When I described it, poor Rose was in no doubt as to her dear friend's fate. She was distraught. I could hardly make some brief apology and leave her in such distress. I had to give her what comfort I could.'

Stephen looked up sharply.

'Comfort?'

'No, no. Do not mistake me. I offered her my kerchief, a shoulder to cry upon, a few words of condolence. That is all. That is what I was trying to explain to Emily when she struck me with her ladle.'

Stephen gave a bellow of laughter.

'With her ladle, eh? Sounds to me as though you got what you deserve. My Emily always was a feisty lass. Get you home to your cold bed, Sebastian. Let me rekindle your torch for you.'

'What of my wife?'

Stephen was still laughing.

'Fear not. I'll send the young tigress back to you in the morn, as soon as I have related your tale to her and convinced her.'

'So you believe me, then?'

'Maybe I do; maybe I don't. But you're her husband, so she belongs to you. It's up to you how you make a life together. I'll do what I can to plead your case but, knowing my daughter as I do, I have little doubt this will not be the last storm you have to weather, my lad. If you wanted a quiet existence, you should have chosen a more docile wife, as I warned you on your nuptial day.'

As Stephen helped him put on his soaking wet mantle and went with him to the door, Seb turned to him.

'Tell Emily I love her. She is more precious to me than mine own soul. I would never betray her trust nor be unfaithful. Tell her that, please.'

Stephen grunted.

'You can tell her yourself on the morrow, when I send her home.'

Stephen opened his door, the rain was still hammering on the porch roof. It disguised the sound of footsteps scurrying up the stair.

As her husband braved the torrents on his short journey from Cheapside to Paternoster Row, Emily returned to her chamber and softly closed the door before flinging herself on the bed and burying her face in the pillow.

Seb must love her, braving such foul weather for her sake, knowing how the cold and damp would afflict his poor bones. On the morrow, he would be stiff and aching, limping most like, and she wouldn't be there to rub in the goose-grease liniment for him. But was his tale true? It sounded unconvincing – passing three hours with a whore and doing nothing but reading. How believable was that?

On the other hand, why did he take Jack with him? Seb wasn't the kind of man who would want someone watching him sport with a woman, surely? And if anyone was thinking of aiding the lad in losing his innocence, it would be that rogue, Jude, not Seb.

Whatever had gone on in that whore's chamber, at least Seb seemed really sorry for it. Or was he just sorry that Jack had blurted out the truth? Was that it? Could she ever trust him again? And, of course, she had secrets of her own.

For hours, Emily lay awake, hearing her father come to his bed in the chamber next door, listening to the house-timbers settle, the rain beating against the shutters. Eventually, she slept but dreamt of Seb in another woman's bed, surrounded by loose papers with scribbled letters and discarded books.

Chapter 10

Wednesday, the thirteenth day of November

EMILY RETURNED home early, in time to prepare breakfast for the household. It was a meal eaten in silence as everyone pretended naught untoward had occurred yestereve. Only after he had dispatched Tom on an errand and seen Gabriel and Jack go to the workshop to open the shutters for the day did Seb take his wife aside. She sent Nessie to make the lads' beds in the attic, so they had a moment to speak together.

'Thank you for coming home,' he said. 'I'm so sorry about the misunderstanding.' He tried to put his arms around her but he may as well have embraced a tree.

'Let us declare a truce,' she said, pulling away from him. 'I haven't forgiven you but I don't want to fight.'

'Agreed. We'll take the matter slowly, Em. Just remember that you mean everything to me.'

'I'm not sure I believe that.'

The Foxley workshop

SEB RETURNED from his visit to the Guildhall, where he had the sorrowful task of explaining to Sheriff Horne the identity of the murder victim and how he had come by the information. Now he was fretting at the realisation that Rose would be questioned, probably by Under-Sheriff Nox. He felt he ought to be there at her side but, clearly, that would cause yet more strife betwixt him and Em.

It was quiet in the workshop but for the scratch of Gabriel's pen and Jack's shuffling of feet as he sat deep in thought, picking his nose all the while, supposedly reading a sentence Seb had written out for him.

'S'no good, master. Yer must'a spelled it wrong. Them letters don't make no sense t' me.'

'Bring it here, lad,' Seb said, beckoning the youngster over to his desk and setting aside his brush. 'Now tell me the words you can make out.'

'The first one says "Jack", I can see that.'

'Good, well done – and do stop investigating your nostrils while I'm trying to help you.'

'Sorry, master.' Jack gave his finger a surreptitious wipe on his breeches.

'And the next little word?'

'That's "is" and the next one says "a". But the next one's a word wot I never seen before.'

'You have seen this word but, I grant you, seldom in this context,' Seb said, sighing. 'Tell me the letters.'

'That's a "b".'

'No, lad, that letter is a "d". Remember, we wrote an entire page of "bs" and "ds" yesterday so you could see the difference.'

'But they look the same, master.'

'Don't whine, Jack. 'Tis a fault as unbecoming as nose-picking. Now try again.'

'D-i-l-i. Dilly, master. "Jack is a dilly-sumfing l-a-d." There. I readed it.'

'Diligent. The word is "diligent".'

'Wos that mean then?'

'Hard-working. And the saints know, Jack, what hard work it is forcing even a modicum of learning into that impervious skull of yours.' Seb blew out a breath and shook his head. 'We are never going to make a scholar of you, are we, Jack?'

'No, master.' The lad sounded pleased. 'But I'm good at uvver fings, ain't I? I c'n already pull a bow an' I c'n climb up fings an' run fast.'

'Aye, I dare say. Now show me how accomplished you are at fetching the ale jug and clean cups from the kitchen.'

'Wot's 'cumpleshed mean?'

'It means lessons are done for this day, Jack, I can suffer no more.' Seb took up his brush to resume work on the psalter, dipping it into a lustrous purple pigment – one of his expensive acquisitions from Venice – and began to paint the robe of Christ in Glory, the tip of the brush following the lines of the folds in the cloth. The colour was magnificent. He hoped it would not pale too much as it dried. He had hardly begun when Jack came rushing in, without the ale.

'Master, master, he's comed back, he 'as.'

'Who has?'

'Yer bruvver o' course. Master Jude's comed in the yard an' gone up to 'is chamber.'

Seb abandoned his work, for once unmindful of wasting expensive pigment. His uneven gait was almost a gallop as he raced up the outside stairs to Jude's chamber, without taking his customary care on the damp wooden steps. Not pausing to knock, he burst into the gloom. The window shutters were closed.

'Jude! Jude, I've been so concerned for you. I feared the worst.' As Seb's sight adjusted to the darkened room, he could make out the humped form of his brother lying on the bed. 'Jude. Are you quite well? Unharmed?' As he went to the bed, he almost tripped on his brother's discarded boots, his hood and mantle left strewn on the floor. He kicked them aside. 'Answer me, brother. Is all well with you?' He sat upon the edge of the bed and reached out to touch Jude. 'Your clothes be damp. You best take them off. I'll fetch you some dry garments.'

'I don't need bloody mothering,' Jude said. 'Let me be, can't you?'

'I've scoured the city for you. I did not know where you were.'

'Well, you know now, so leave me in peace.'

'Are you sick?'

'Sick of your bloody fussing. Get out.'

Ignoring the protests, Seb put his arm around his brother for a moment.

'I missed you so.'

Released from the awkward embrace, Jude turned away, facing the wall.

'Are you hungry, thirsty? Shall I bring you bread and ale?' Seb offered, going to the door.

'No.'

'I'll let you rest then. I'm truly glad you're home, safely.' He closed the door softly behind him so as not to disturb Jude further.

'Jude is home, God be praised,' Seb told Emily as she stood at the kitchen board, smoothing out clean linen, ready for the press.

'I saw.' She folded a napkin with unusual care.

'Such a relief to have him safe.'

'At least you can stop searching the streets now and get some work done.' Emily shook out a table cloth, making it snap the air, wafting the smell of boiling cabbage and leeks across the kitchen. 'Nessie. Give me a hand to fold this.'

Seb leant against the wall, smiling but his eyes were moist.

'It's so good to have him back.'

'Is it? To me it just means more linen to wash, more food to prepare and cook, more mending to do. You think I like being his unpaid servant?'

'He's my brother.'

'He's an ill-tempered, idle wretch. The only thing he works at is getting drunk.' Emily pulled so hard on the sheet they were folding between them, Nessie overbalanced and jarred the board, toppling the neat pile of linen onto the flagstones. 'Now look what you've done, you careless girl. This household is more trouble than it's worth, I swear. One of these days, Sebastian Foxley...'

He tried to immerse himself in his painting. Em was home and Jude had returned. The household was complete again, back to normal. Yet the two persons he loved most had both spurned him, turning from his affection. The beauty of his work was not enough. It could not touch his heart nor lift his spirit. Not this day.

Tom returned with news that the customer he had visited, taking Seb's message that the shop sign he had commissioned was ready for collection, was delighted.

'He'll come after dinner to collect it, so he said. And you'll never believe: they've found another dead woman, just like we found, but outside Bishopsgate this time. The story is all over the city. She's been dead a while, they say. You'll probably have to go draw her, master.'

'I hope not.'

'Shall I tell Master Jude?' Jack asked, doing a little dance.'

'He's home?' asked Tom.

'Aye, while you wos out. Shall I tell 'im, in case ol' Bulman sends fer 'im?'

Seb shook his head.

'No. Master Jude needs to rest.'

'Why? Where's he bin then? Wot's he bin doin', eh?'

'Never you mind,' said Seb, wishing he had the answers to those questions himself.

'So wot 'appened t' the dead 'un, Tom? Was she murdered like the uvver wot we finded?'

'So they say. They reckon she was stabbed, just like...'

'Tom. Jack. Stop this. Jack, wash out my brushes for me and make certain they're properly clean and don't forget to reshape the points and leave them to dry, tip uppermost, as I showed you. Tom, I believe you have pages to collate. Now set to your tasks, both of you and no more gossiping. Else it will be dinner time with naught to show for a morn's work.'

'You're hard on the lads, Seb,' Gabriel said looking up from stitching folios.

'I'm supposed to be training them as apprentices, not indulging their fascination with the macabre and gruesome.'

'Even so...'

'I'm going out,' Seb said. 'If the customer comes for his sign, Gabe, the cost is one shilling and tuppence three farthings. The bill is with the sign in the store room.'

Gabriel whistled through the gap beside his crooked tooth.

'Sounds expensive.'

'He wanted me to use gold paint.'

'On a shop sign? A bit lavish, isn't it?'

Seb shrugged.

'The customer is always right, Gabe. That's what they say.'

Seb ambled along Cheapside, towards Poultry and the Walbrook, favouring his left hip. The walk would cleanse his mind of the turmoil that swirled within. He told himself that he was happy to have Em and Jude returned but to have them under the same roof was never easy and now, with his wife and brother both at odds with him, the house was an unquiet place. Since he knew not what was amiss with Jude, there was naught he could do to improve the case at present. But with Em, perhaps he could do something. A gift; a peace offering. That was it.

She had mentioned of late how much she wished for a new gown; they'd even spoken of how much a rose-coloured gown might suit her – a change from the faded blue.

Newly inspired, Seb made his way down Walbrook to a mercer's shop by St Stephen's church, walking faster now, forgetful of his aching joint. The mercer was known to him as a friend of Dame Ellen Langton, a man with a reputation for selling good quality cloth at reasonable prices.

The premises smelled of scrubbing soap and new fabric with an underlying, less savoury odour, the faint reminder of various dyeing processes.

'Good morrow to you, master,' the mercer greeted him, raising his bushy grey eyebrows, a token of welcome. 'Ah! Master Foxley, 'tis good to see you. How may I assist? Or do you wish to browse a while?'

'Good morrow, Master Edmund. I have in mind to buy a length of fair cloth, enough for a woman's gown.'

'For your goodwife, is it?'

'Aye, and she has a fancy for a rose colour, if you have something of that hue?'

Master Edmund clicked his fingers at an apprentice who had been hovering at his elbow and the youngster leapt into action, up and down a ladder and balancing precariously on footstools, lifting down bolts of cloth: fustians, musterdevillers and tabby weaves, from high shelves. What a delight to see an apprentice so willing. Within a matter of minutes, nigh unto a dozen bolts of cloth were lined up along the counter board, all shades from the palest that was hardly more than white to the colour of deepest ruby wine. Seb instantly recognised this last – now a much reduced bolt – as the colour of Dame Ellen's gown in church the previous Sunday. He smiled, thinking he might just have learned the name of the widow's new admirer. Em would enjoy hearing such news but, of course, he couldn't tell her without revealing his business with the mercer and that would spoil the surprise. It was a morsel to savour for the future.

'May I see this in the daylight, please, and this?' Seb picked out two bolts that seemed closest in colour to his terra rosa pigment.

The apprentice picked up the heavy rolls, one under each arm, and carried them to the door where the November light did its best to illumine the day. Seb rubbed the first cloth betwixt his fingers. It felt fine and thick, closely woven.'

'A silk-wool mixture that one,' Master Edmund explained, 'New in from Genoa. Last a lifetime, that will. Hangs well, too. A good drape. Not cheap though.' He raised his brows in question.

'I like the cloth but the colour is amiss – too yellow compared to what my Emily has her heart set upon.'

'Ah. A woman who knows what she wants,' the mercer said with a chuckle, his adam's apple bobbing. 'What of the other?'

'The colour is closer but...' Seb could see the weave was more loose, likely to pull out of shape and wear less well.

'Much cheaper that one but customers like the hue. Fashionable in Florence, I hear.'

'I would rather pay a little more for cloth that will last longer.'

'You're a wise man, Master Foxley. William, fetch the stuff that came in from Venice last week, you know the one I mean. May I offer you some ale and wafers, master?'

After much scurrying around, the apprentice brought out a bolt of cloth, still wrapped in a roll of leather to protect it. The mercer set aside their ale cups and dusted off the counter board with his sleeve before laying out a length of the precious cloth and stepping back a pace.

'What do you think, Master Foxley? Fit for a queen, eh? The finest silk velvet in London, in the world, even.'

Seb wiped his hand on his doublet before fingering the raised nap. It felt soft as coney fur, almost alive. The mercer and his apprentice carried it to the doorway to show him how the light rippled across the folds as the cloth moved, like moonlight on water. The colour glowed, warm as a maiden's blush. It was perfect.

'I cannot afford such wondrous cloth as this, I fear. And besides, the sumptuary laws forbid the likes of me and my wife from wearing anything so...'

'Phh!' The mercer clicked his fingers again, 'Who gives a jot for those foolish rules anyway? Everyone ignores them these days. No one cares. I've seen strumpets in ermine and hucksters in gold-spangled baudekyn. Bought from fripperers, I grant you, but so what? If you like it; wear it. That's what I say.'

'No matter, Master Edmund, law or no law, as I said, I cannot afford it. 'Tis a pity but there's an end to it.'

'Maybe not. Perhaps we could come to some arrangement over the price?'

'I won't be beholden nor go into debt...'

'You mistake me, Master Foxley. I had in mind an exchange.'

'A book in exchange for the cloth?'

'No. My youngest daughter – she's a good lass and sweet natured – has a talent, to my eyes, at least, for drawing. With proper training, I think she might make a decent limner. Now, she is nigh unto her fourteenth year, come next spring, and I've been looking to put her to an apprenticeship, something that will use her talent. But I don't know much of limning and there are few artisans in London of such skill that they might...'

'You wish me to teach her, to tutor her in drawing and painting?' Seb said as realisation dawned. 'Or take her on as my apprentice?'

'Not straightway, of course,' the mercer said, eyebrows raised, 'You would need to assess her talent, her aptitude first. But if you agreed to look at her efforts with pen and charcoal, see if you think she may be worth the expense of an apprentice's indenture, I might find that a certain length of silk velvet has been much reduced in price, of a sudden. Three shillings an ell, shall we say?'

'Done.'

The deal had been sealed over a cup of good wine but during the walk homewards doubts began crowding in. Seb had agreed to pay an overlarge sum of money he could ill-afford for some cloth – exquisite as it may be and a bargain – that his wife could never wear and all but committed himself to taking on another apprentice, as if the two he had already weren't trouble enough. Throw a lass into the mix and the result was sure to be chaotic. He was a fool. Things at home were bad enough without making matters worse. The gown as a peace offering had been a bad idea. The package of cloth beneath his arm weighed heavier at every step. He hesitated outside Walter the tailor's workshop in Cheapside. Master Edmund had told him this was the man who had stitched Dame Ellen's new gown, the one that impressed Em with its fine cut. Such costly cloth shouldn't be left to some inexperienced fellow to chop about and stitch anyhow. Oh, well, so be it; he'd come so far, may as well complete the task. Seb braced himself, preparing to part with yet more coin, and went in.

• •

Back in his own workshop, Seb was irritated to find a customer, surrounded by Gabriel, Tom and Jack, discussing neither an order nor work of any kind, but the latest murder. The customer knew – or was inventing – some excessively gory details which had his audience wide-eyed with horror. Jack was a-quiver with excitement.

'Jack. Fetch a broom and go sweep outside the shop front. Someone has spilt a load of straw.'

'Oh, master...'

'Don't whine and wheedle. Get on with it.'

Jack stuck out a mutinous bottom lip but obeyed, slowly. Seb turned to the customer.

'May I help you, master?'

'Coroner Bulman sent me to fetch Jude Foxley to assist him.'

'Oh. I fear my brother is rather unwell at present.'

'Not so bloody unwell that I can't do my job.' Jude came into the workshop from the passageway to the kitchen, ale cup in hand.

Seb tried to disguise his dismay at Jude's appearance. His brother's face was puffy, his eyes sunken. Either he'd been drunk for a week or had been in a fight. His lip looked to have been split but had scabbed over. The black shadows beneath his eyes might well have been bruises. His shirt was filthy and stained with who knew what; his hair hung lank, uncombed.

'You can't go out like this, Jude.'

'Why not? The dead don't care what I bloody look like.' He went to the store room, took a few sheets of paper, folded them roughly and stuffed them in his scrip with his pens, writing board and ink pot. At least he'd not misplaced that this last week.

'I'll tell Em to keep your dinner for you,' Seb called out as Jude and the messenger left. His brother made no response. Perhaps he hadn't heard.

· ·

Dusk was falling early. The Foxley household was off to attend vespers at St Michael's, as was usual on a Wednesday, although last week had proved an exception. Jude could hear them down in the yard below his window. Seb had been right about one thing: he shouldn't have gone out to help the damned coroner. He ought to have stayed abed. Now he felt worse than ever. Interviewing witnesses to the death of a carter, flattened by his own cart as it rolled downhill, had made him nauseous.

Then the sight of his warmed-over dinner, presented by Em with such a glare, had set his belly roiling anew but maybe he should have tried a spoonful or two. God knows, he couldn't remember when he'd last eaten.

That was the trouble: he couldn't remember anything much at all. Where he'd been or what he'd done. How drunk did a man have to be to wipe away his memory? But then again, there were a few disjointed images. They made no sense. He might have dreamed them in a drunken stupor. He desperately hoped that was the case because if it wasn't... Don't even think about it, he told himself. There was no Irish knife. He hadn't heard any screams. He hadn't seen bloody Satan himself, looming over him. Of course not. Just a nightmare. But was it any wonder he dared not sleep?

· ·

The congregation at St Michael's had learned something of late – that Father Weasel was far too self-important to bother conducting vespers. High Mass, with the opportunity to wear his sumptuous vestments, was one thing, but vespers simply wasn't worth his efforts. Was it any wonder then that the humble evening office was increasingly popular with the parishioners, rather than Mass?

'I find dear old Father Thomas so much more bearable, don't you, Emily?' Dame Ellen said. 'That other pompous creature quite puts my teeth on edge.'

'I think we all agree with you, good dame,' Emily replied as they filed out into the porch to wait while the menfolk lit torches at the brazier to light the way home.

'By the by, if you have a moment or two to spare, Emily, I have the stuff ready for you for those new braids you said you'd do for me. We could go now, once we have a torch.'

Seb and Gabriel came out together, each carrying a torch, as the law required after dark.

'Seb,' Emily said, 'I have to go with Dame Ellen. It won't take long.'

'Sorry. I must get home. I'm so worried about Jude.'

'Your wretched brother! You worried about him when he was missing, now you worry still more when he's home.'

'Something's amiss with him...'

'Something's amiss with you, more likely.'

'Gabriel can escort you and Dame Ellen. I'll go home with the lads and Nessie. I have to see Jude; make certain he isn't ailing any worse.'

Emily stamped her foot.

'Do as you will then. Come, Gabriel, light the way to Dame Ellen's house, if you'll be so kind.'

Gabriel didn't really have time for this either but he dare not protest. He had planned to eat his supper in haste and then rush to the meeting in Garlickhill, taking a few more of the precious pamphlets with him. Now he would have to linger while the women chattered about inconsequential things, wasting his precious time – time that should be given to God. He'd already spent an hour hearing a priest mumbling meaningless Latin that no one paid heed to, least of all the Almighty. He only went

St Michael's to avoid the fines for non-attendance and, more important, so as not to arouse any suspicions concerning his true beliefs.

'Now you may escort me home, Gabriel,' Emily said when her business with Dame Ellen was completed. She had a bundle under her arm from which a strand or two of thread hung loose. As they walked, she linked her free arm through his. 'I don't want to slip and drop the good dame's work here. This is a fine mantle that Dame Ellen would have me stitch a silken border to for Lady Josselyn, the Lord Mayor's wife. She would be most displeased if it was muddied. Please don't walk so fast; my legs are not so long as yours.'

In truth, she wished to hold him back, in no hurry to go home. She liked the feel of firm muscles beneath his sleeve, the manly odour of him, hot even on a chill night, potent. Her inner fire, lately reduced to cooling embers, burst into flame as he pulled her closer to his side.

'Beware that puddle, Mistress Em.'

Let there be more puddles; a veritable flood, betwixt here and home, she thought, visions of him carrying her, so she shouldn't wet her shoes, tip-toed into her head. Hold me. Touch me. She glanced at him. His face was solemn in the torchlight. She pretended to stumble and he caught her. They faced each other. She could see his jaw clench, the sinews of his neck tauten and knew he wanted her.

'Thank you,' she whispered.

His mismatched eyes met hers and she felt her knees might fail her in truth.

'We must hasten,' he said, 'I fear it will rain again soon.'

Emily cared not if they were caught in Noah's deluge but pressed herself into the folds of his cloak, soaking up his warmth and breathing deep the animal scent of his body. Yet it seemed he had quite forgotten the other eve.

Women were a distraction that a Known Man had to avoid. Mind you, it was no easy thing when a beautiful woman tempted you but Gabriel had resisted her advances – just. It was a relief to escape the Foxley house but it had been a near thing on that walk home. He hadn't succumbed. He'd turned away once more from those inviting lips. Yet he had broken the Lord God's Tenth Commandment: he certainly did covet his neighbour's wife and his loins still ached with desire.

The meeting in the room beside the Pewter Pot was well attended as usual. Gabriel sat on a bench in the far corner. Roger Underwood, the taverner, was reading this eve but despite the wonder of the sacred words, his voice was hardly inspiring. He cleared his throat after every sentence it seemed, detracting from the meaning. Gabriel found it hard to concentrate, his thoughts kept straying to far less righteous matters and the second chapter of the Gospel of Saint John the Evangelist quite passed him by. Another reason to feel guilty.

'I always appreciate that story,' Raff said when the meeting was done and folk were leaving in ones and twos, so as not to attract the attentions of the Watch. 'Don't you, Gabe?'

'What?'

'How our Lord threw the accursed money-lenders out of the Temple. P'raps we should do the same, eh? Cleanse St Paul's.'

'Mayhap.' Gabriel shrugged and sighed.

'What's amiss with you? I swear you never heard a word of the reading, did you? Your thoughts were afar off, I could see that. What's distracting you, eh?'

'Naught. I just found the reader difficult to listen to.'

'Aye. He's not the best, I admit, but it's God's holy words, all the same. You must try harder. Give the text your full attention, as it justly deserves.'

'You're right. I will next time.'

'You'd better,' Raff said, grinning. 'It will be my turn to read, unless we put to sea afore Sunday.'

'So soon as that? Oh, no, Raff, stay a little longer, can't you?'

'Time and tide, brother, you know how it is. And if I am gone, then you should practise chapter three so you can read it in my stead. Remember what is said in that chapter, Gabe: "Whosoever believeth in Him shall not perish, but have life everlasting". Those words will lift your soul and inspire you, whether I'm here to remind you or not. You should leave now, get home afore they start to wonder where you are.'

'I'm at the Pewter Pot, aren't I? Drinking myself witless,' Gabriel said, laughing.

'Is that what you tell them?'

'They never ask but, if they did, that would be my story. 'Tis close enough to the truth.'

'Aye. Well take care, Gabe. These be dangerous times for us Known Men.'

Having lit his torch from the brazier, Gabriel stepped out into the darkness. It was a clear night for once, so quiet he could hear the sounds of laughter from the Vintners' Hall across the way. Some folk were enjoying themselves in this life, if not in the next. A sad thought indeed but there were those who didn't want to be saved. People of whom he was fond, like the Foxleys. Jude was a lost cause already but Seb, as a man of learning and good sense, might yet see the light. Not that the young master had agreed with him destroying those filthy relics the other day, but in time... And Mistress Em; what of her?

Walking up Bread Street to the Cheapside Cross – a memorial to some long-dead queen – Gabriel found the image of another woman filling his head. God aid me, he prayed, to think on Thee, on Thy sacred words. But thoughts of Emily could not be dispelled and so filled his senses he was oblivious to all else. Oblivious to the figure that had shadowed him all evening in his comings and goings.

Chapter 11

Thursday, the fourteenth day of November
The Foxley workshop

WITH JUDE returned, all seemed well in Seb's world, even though Em was not yet in the best of moods with him. Still, the new rose-coloured gown should put that to rights when he collected it in a day or two. He looked up from the image of the Magdalene he was completing for the psalter – it was progressing well – and smiled to himself, seeing the lads, both industrious for once, Jude collating and stitching the commentary on Leviticus that Gabriel had finished yesterday and the journeyman in question was gone to Lombard Street to deliver a finished piece to a client.

Besides that, two customers had come in to place orders earlier and a third – a priest from St Margaret's, Lothbury – had purchased five cheap little Latin primers for the pupils at his school with money bequeathed for the purpose. A successful morn, indeed.

The shutters were down, to let in the light on this first bright day for what seemed weeks and Seb noticed Father Hugh Wessell and Under-Sheriff Nox – a strange pairing for certain – approaching the shop door, shouldering their way through the crowds off to market in Cheapside.

Having washed out his brush of terra verde pigment, Seb left his desk to welcome them but there was no need. Father Wessell had come in and stood before him. The only word Seb could think of to describe the man's expression was smug.

'Good morrow –,' Seb began.

'I didn't come here for pleasantries,' Wessell announced, ignoring Seb's out-stretched hand of welcome. 'Nox. Get on with it.'

'What is it? How may I help you, sirs?'

In reply, Wessell waved a paper at Seb.

'Know what this is?'

'No. How would I? Hey! Leave that be,' Seb cried, rushing to protect his work as Nox began sorting through the finished pages of the psalter that represented so many hours of painstaking work.

Jude came from behind the collating table and gripped Nox's shoulder hard.

'My brother said "Leave that be", or are you deaf?'

'This is a warrant, signed by the Lord Bishop, giving us the authority to search this place,' said Wessell, showing his pin-like teeth in a serpent's smile. 'Now stand aside... all of you whilst we execute the warrant!'

'But what is it you seek? What do you think you'll find?' Seb tried to shield his work desk on the one hand and Tom and Jack on the other. 'Go to the kitchen,' he told the lads, 'Tell mistress to remain there also. I'll deal with this.'

'We both will,' Jude said. 'What in hell's name do you pair of jackanapes think you're doing? The mayor will hear of this, rest assured. I take it, this is church business, in which case you, Nox, have no right to be here.'

'I am assisting the bishop.' Nox pushed past Jude, towards the storeroom but the tall scrivener grabbed him by his jerkin.

'No, you're not. Now get out afore I fling you out!'

'Look in the paper store,' Nox yelled as Jude opened the shop door and propelled the under-sheriff into the street with a well-placed boot to the backside. 'You haven't heard the last of this Foxley!'

'And neither have you.' With that, Jude shut the door, grinning. He hadn't enjoyed himself so much in an age.

Seb looked on, helpless, as Wessell poked about and thumbed through reams of paper and rolls of parchment on the shelves of the storeroom. The room, being hardly of a size to contain two men at once, did not take long to search.

'Ah. What have we here? Just as I thought...' Wessell looked like a man granted a vision of heaven as he brandished a handful of papers.

'What are those?' Seb asked, frowning. He didn't recognise the paper type nor the size.

'As if you didn't know. Heresy. That's what these are.' Wessell shoved a fistful of pamphlets into Seb's face. 'Lollard pamphlets written by you. You are in grave trouble now. Nox!'

The under-sheriff had not gone far but waited by the door. At Wessell's call, he marched back into the workshop, mud-smeared but triumphant.

'Arrest him,' Wessell instructed, poking a finger at Seb, 'Take him to the bishop's lock-up.'

Seb staggered a little, as one struck by a thunderbolt. This made no sense. What were those papers? What were they doing in his workshop?

'How dare you lay hold of my brother,' Jude said, barring Nox from coming closer to Seb. 'He's innocent of any charge you might concoct against him. No man is more law-abiding than he.'

'You wish to join him in gaol?' Wessell asked.

Of a sudden, Jude did not feel so courageous, his past experience of such a place made his belly churn.

The priest must have seen him turn pale.

'Then move aside.'

Jude stepped back, shaking his head and wringing his hands.

'Forgive me, little brother. You know I'd do anything but that. I'll sort this matter out, fear not.'

'Jude. I understand. Do not be concerned. This is all some absurd mistake.'

Seb managed a smile, if not a very reassuring one, as Nox pushed him into the street and there, in full view of passers-by, humiliated him by tying his hands like a common felon. By the look on Nox's pocked face, revenge must be tasting sweet indeed. Fortunately for Seb, the under-sheriff would have little time to gloat: it was but a short walk around St Paul's Yard to the bishop's lock-up they called the 'Lollards' Tower.

With a leering smirk, Father Wessell took a final look around the workshop. The elder brother and two apprentices stood in stunned silence but a little dog, its head cocked in curiosity, trotted over to sniff the stranger in its territory. Wessell, alarmed at the prospect of dog hairs upon his fine vestments, would not tolerate such familiarity and lashed out with his well-shod foot, sending the creature whimpering into a corner.

'You leave my dog be,' the smaller apprentice yelled, rushing to tend the animal, 'Yer just a bully, ain't yer, kickin' my dog like that wot never hurted yer? I hate yer, I do.'

Wessell raised an eyebrow. Well, one at least in the Foxley household was not so spineless after all.

The Lollards' Tower by St Paul's

IT WAS nowhere near so bad as Newgate, Seb thought, recalling his visits to Jude in that fearful place. He sat upon the floor in the empty room. It looked to have been recently lime-washed, the floor boards scrubbed. It was as clean as Em's kitchen but it was still a prison cell. Utterly bare of comfort. Not so much as a spider in her web for company. He expected that situation would change soon enough.

His breath made white clouds in the chill air. He had no mantle and his teeth chattered. He hoped they – whoever they might be – wouldn't mistake that for a sign of fear. Huh. That was a foolish jest: of course he was fearful. Innocence didn't always prove enough to save a man, as he knew all too well. Jude had been innocent of murder, yet had come within a hair's breadth of dying in the hangman's noose.

And the penalty for heresy could be far worse. An image of flaming faggots heaped about a stake wavered before Seb's sight but he drove it away, wiping his eyes upon his sleeve. No. It wouldn't come to that. It could not. He was guilty of no crime against the Church. He was a true God-fearing Christian and the Almighty would protect him, wouldn't He? Well, his own namesake, St Sebastian, had come to a terrifying end, shot full of arrows, despite being an innocent man. He shook his head, dispelling such morbid thoughts. This matter would end well. It must.

The sound of a bolt withdrawn brought Seb from his disquieting reverie. A servant came in, carrying a chair, followed by another fellow with cushions. The chair was set down and the cushions plumped and placed.

'Not there. Away from the draughty window, you fool.' Father Hugh Wessell came striding in, Under-Sheriff Nox at his heel. 'Get up, Foxley. Stand when your betters enter. Pretend you have manners, at least.' The priest seated himself, arranged his fine vestments so they should not crease and folded his arms. 'Proceed, Nox. I want this done afore dinner.'

Valentyne Nox grinned. It was not a comfort to Seb. He felt like the sacrificial lamb espied by the wolf as he stood in the midst of the room.

'Afore you accuse me, I know naught of those papers...' he spluttered.

'I know.' Nox stood so close, Seb could smell his stale breath.

'You know? Then – then why am I here?'

'Yours was not the only arrest made this morn. We have others in custody, among them your journeyman, Gabriel Widowson.'

'Gabriel?'

'A Lollard,' said Nox. 'A Known Man, as those heretics call themselves.'

'I don't believe what you're saying. 'Tis not true. My friend isn't like that. How could he be? All of us in our household are God-fearing Christians. We attend St Michael le Querne regularly. My friend is no Lollard. He couldn't do what you would accuse him of.'

'Are you saying I'm lying?' Nox took out his knife, polishing the blade upon his sleeve. 'Why would I lie about such a thing? I see how much your friend means to you but I cannot deny what I saw for myself: he was there, close as I stand to you now.'

'Where? Where did you see him?'

'Last eve. Coming from the place beside the Pewter Pot, where those devil-worshippers meet.'

'You are mistaken. It couldn't be him, not then, not there. He wouldn't be.'

'How can you be so certain of that? Do you know his whereabouts every moment of last eve?'

'Well, no. But I know he wasn't there.'

'Then where was he? At home with you all evening, no doubt?'

'No, not with me, not *all* the while, at least, but he couldn't be there... with them. I know.'

'How long have you known this man?'

'He joined our workshop a year ago last springtime.'

'Not so long then. Where was he before that?'

'I don't know his last abode but he is a Man of Kent. He has travelled widely, I believe. What has this to do with last eve?'

'I'm merely pointing out that you know very little of this man's past. And what of his family? What do you know of them?'

'Naught. But I know my friend well enough to be certain he cannot be involved in this matter.'

'Well, so. And if not him, then who? Someone in your household is involved. How else did these heretical texts come to be stored in your workshop?'

'They weren't stored there at all. They must have been brought by accident, packaged with the blank paper I ordered from Bruges. It was a mistake made by those who delivered my order – naught to do with my friend.'

'Yet your friend was there last eve, at the place where these texts were being shared among the heretics...'

'I told you: he couldn't have been. He's no heretic but a true Christian.'

'Then perhaps *you* are the heretic?'

'Of course not. Ask Father Thomas or the precentor at St Paul's. They will vouch for me.'

'Your brother then... or could it be that pretty wife of yours?'

'Never. Never on both counts. That's a diabolical thing to suggest.'

'Diabolical indeed. But someone took a number of those texts to be shared among the heretics, the same as the ones we found in your workshop? Perhaps they flew there by themselves – after all, who knows what filthy magick the devil has wrought to confound us?'

'I cannot explain it. As you say, maybe the devil is behind these things, but you do wrong to accuse my friend; you do him a grave injustice.'

'Far from it. Gabriel Widowson has freely admitted his crime. He boldly declares himself to be a Known Man – a heretic. He says you have no knowledge of his devilry but why should I trust the word of a stinking blasphemer? We found bundles of those pamphlets beneath his bed in *your* house. Are you so ignorant of the goings-on under your own roof? Are you truly master of that house of sin?' Nox struck Seb hard across the cheek, knocking him sideways.

'Enough!' bellowed Wessell. 'I think we have our answer. Pledge him, get someone to grant surety and release him. He is simply a fool, deceived by the journeyman. I will waste no more time on him.'

The ropes around Seb's wrists were cut and he was escorted down the spiral stair by Nox.

'This won't be our last encounter, I promise you,' Nox said, sneering.

'How did you know those pamphlets were in my storeroom when I did not?' Seb asked.

Nox laughed. A disturbing sound indeed.

'You think you be better than the rest of us, you damned Foxleys. Ever since the Duke of Gloucester became your patron... well, he isn't in London now to speak up for you, is he?'

'I don't know why you have taken against me and mine. What have we ever done to so offend you?'

'You made a mockery of the law that time and a friend of mine died at your brother's hand. The Newgate gaoler who fell and broke his neck when your wretched brother pushed him down the steps; he was a close friend to me.'

'That was an accident.'

'So you say but you'd best watch your step on these stairs for fear the same accident befall you.'

Having made his way to the bottom of the steps without mishap, Seb and Nox encountered Dean Wynterbourne.

'Sebastian Foxley,' the dean said, frowning. 'Now why am I unsurprised to find you involved in this heretical business. You and that journeyman of yours destroyed those relics – an action typical of Lollard scum. I should have arrested you there and then.'

'But we are both of us innocent, sir, 'tis a grave mistake,' Seb protested.

'A grave matter, aye, but a mistake? Somehow I doubt that.'

• •

Seb returned home to a barrage of questions he did not feel ready to answer.

'You're back then,' Emily said, putting a platter before him, 'They let you go. It was a mistake, wasn't it?'

'Aye.' Seb moved the platter aside. That blow from Nox had bruised his face and loosened a tooth. He could not eat.

'I don't know where Gabriel's got to. I saved dinner for him too but I don't know why I bother.' Em pushed Seb's platter back at him.

'Gabriel won't be coming to dinner... nor supper.'

'What's he doing then?' Jude asked, 'He's supposed to be helping me this afternoon.'

'Gabriel has been arrested.'

'Him too? Another bloody mistake then.'

'They say he confessed.'

'To what? You believe those conniving bastards? Their lips move; they must be lying.'

'I don't know what to believe anymore, Jude.' Reluctantly, Seb told the household all that Nox had said. But was any of it true?

'One thing concerns me...' he said.

'Only one?' Jude queried.

'Apart from others. You heard what Nox said as you threw him out. He told Wessell to look in the paper store. I think he knew those wretched pamphlets were there but how? Later, he said – when questioning me – that they found bundles of the same beneath Gabriel's bed, if that be true. Why were they not kept all in one place, secrecy being so vital? Why would just a few be hidden amongst our blank paper and how did Nox know where to find them? Unless he put them there?'

'Couldn't have,' Jude said, 'I never let him in there, did I? But maybe that serpent Wessell had them hid within his vestments?'

'No, not that, else why would Nox have to tell him where to look? It was Nox who knew of them, I be certain.'

'Has he come by on a visit any time whilst I've been away?'

'No. Not to my knowledge, at least. Unless...' Seb rubbed at his sore face, thinking.

He turned to Emily, touched her hand. 'Supposing the other night, when the banging of the side gate awoke you, Em...'

'When you suffered another seizure: how could I forget? Seeing you lying on the wet ground, unmoving, I thought you were...'

'But I wasn't. Did I not say at the time that I thought I saw something? That something struck me out of the dark?'

'You said naught, husband. That's why I feared for you so.'

'Well I *did* see something and I know you believe it was a seizure that felled me but... what if it was Nox, sneaking around like a thief in the night but, instead of taking our valuables, he secreted those pamphlets in our store?'

Jude puffed out a breath:

'I suppose he might have. Could have put those packages in Gabriel's chamber too.'

'No, that wasn't possible,' Em said. 'I called to Gabe as soon as I found Seb lying there and he came straightway to aid your brother. He would have seen Nox in his bedchamber.'

'Mayhap, he went there first and put the packages – and remember, we cannot be certain they even exist apart from Nox's claim – he could have crept in whilst Gabe was sleeping. What do you think, little brother, is that likely?'

Seb looked doubtful but it made sense of the tangled facts, so far as they knew them.

'Must'a bin Nox,' Jack chimed in. 'I never liked 'im.'

'Anyhow, who stood surety for you?' Jude asked.

'Surgeon Dagvyle. He was there, tending one of the other prisoners.'

'Not Gabriel, I pray,' Em said, crossing herself.

'I don't know who needed Dagvyle's services, I was hardly in a position to enquire, but Nox is a man of violence upon the least excuse.'

'Aye. He's made a mess of your face, husband. Nessie, fetch the violet oil, that will ease the bruising.'

'I'll ask Coroner Bulman,' Jude said.

'Oh, please God, Gabriel cannot be dead,' Em said, her voice quivering.

'No, no. You mistake me. The coroner has contacts,' Jude explained, 'I shall find out what's going on, what exactly Gabe is supposed to have confessed to – which I don't bloody believe for one instant – and see about getting him released.'

'You'll do that for Gabriel?' Em asked, sounding surprised.

'I'd do it for any man I knew to be wrongly accused, well, almost any man. There's a few buggers I wouldn't trouble myself about but Gabe is a good fellow.'

The clement weather and the sun casting its pale beams across the yard mocked a day turned to disaster after such a promising beginning.

'Tom, Jack, take your drawing stuff to Leadenhall, sketch what you observe, whatever takes your eye.'

'Shall I draw animals or folk?' Tom asked.

'As many animals as you wish,' Seb said, knowing such a task would please the lad. 'And you draw anything you like, Jack, just something I might comprehend... know what it is.' It was better that the youngsters have something to keep them busy, away from the gloomy house. It felt like someone had died. And more so when Jude returned.

'I spoke with both the coroner and Surgeon Dagvyle,' he said. 'Ale, Nessie, for God's sake.'

Seb, Emily and Jude sat at the kitchen board.

'Afore you ask, Em,' Jude went on, 'Dagvyle wasn't there to tend Gabe but some other fellow. However, Coroner Bulman confirmed that he too has heard that Gabe confessed to being one of those Known Men. All I can think is that they bloody tortured it out of him.'

Emily gasped and covered her mouth with her hands.

'Why else would he admit to being a sodding heretic?'

Seb said not a word but his palms were pressed together in an attitude of prayer.

'You did it once before, Seb,' Jude went on, 'I think we have to save Gabe, afore they torture him into implicating us in their damned scheming. Those devious bastards don't like us and would do anything to ruin us. As it is, they've made inroads on our good reputation by arresting you this day. By the time word gets out about Gabe, the name of Foxley will be buried in the bloody mire. We need a plan, Seb. That's your strong point: planning.'

The Lollards' Tower

GABRIEL SWAYED upon his feet, his hands secured with rope behind him. Almost too weary to stand, he yet faced his accusers with a bold eye. Nox seemed near demented with frustration; Gabe could see that and knew he was going to pay dearly for his silence. Wessell sat, calmly observing, as though he cared not whether the information they demanded was revealed or no. In truth, Gabriel suspected they knew everything already. Even so, a grubby little clerk scribbled down every utterance, useful or otherwise.

'So, tell me, how are the Foxley brothers involved in this devil's scheme of yours?' Nox was prowling, playing with a birch rod, swishing it through the air, as a schoolmaster might to frighten his pupil.

'I have told you, repeatedly, the Foxleys have no part in this. They know nothing.' Gabriel was not to be intimidated. Every bone in his body ached from the beatings but God would aid him.

'Then name those who *are* involved,' Nox shouted, 'Name your fellow heretics and spare yourself more pain.'

'I cannot tell you any names for I do not know them. We do not use names. Our names are known to God and that is all that ma– '

The rod caught him hard across his chest, knocking the wind out of him.

'Names!' shrieked Nox. 'We will have names.'

Blows rained down upon Gabriel until his assailant stepped away, gasping from the effort. Driven to his knees and bleeding from numerous cuts, he would not betray his fellows but closed his eyes, beseeching God to help him keep a still tongue. He tried desperately to dispel thoughts of his brother, Raff – whose name alone he certainly knew – for fear it might escape his lips, unbidden.

His tormentor, having rested, began the questioning again.

'Who wrote these disgusting tracts that you were distributing, corrupting good Christians with your devilry?'

'They are not written; they were printed abroad. I never asked where or by whom. And I would ask how *you* dare say God's own words are disgusting? How can the Holy Gospel corrupt?'

The rod struck him in the mouth. Blood spurted and he spat out a tooth. No longer would he be known for a smile with a crooked tooth because it was gone, a gaping hole in its place.

'Then who paid for them? Who imported them?'

'I don't know.' Gabriel's words were slurring through rapidly swelling lips and tongue. His mouth filled with the rusty tang of blood. He crouched on the floor, rocking in agony but praising God who had rendered him no longer capable of forming words.

'You've gone too far, you fool,' Wessell was saying, 'How can he answer with a ruined mouth? Leave him to recover. Put him back with the others; they'll tend him.'

'I'd sooner let the devil choke on his own blood,' Nox said, swishing his rod again.

'I said, leave him! Go and get drunk or whatever it is you do of an eve.'

'Aye. I suppose I could. Thirsty work, this questioning business.'

'Indeed. And we learned naught that we didn't know already. Bishop Kemp will not be pleased when I inform him of your failure.'

'My failure? You miserable cleric. Don't you dare blame me. You're the one who said we had to beat it out of him.'

'Don't write that down.'

The last things Gabriel heard before he slipped into darkness were the frantic ripping of paper and the clerk's cry of protest.

The Foxley house

WITH HIS face throbbing, Seb just wanted to sit quietly by the blazing hearth in the parlour. Jude was gone to the Panyer, as usual. The lads had gone to their beds in the attic, Nessie was snoring in her corner by the kitchen chimney, so Seb and Em were alone. To distract his thoughts, Seb had lit an extra candle to read, yet the book lay open at random upon his lap and the page remained unturned. Emily sat opposite, across the hearth, sewing by candlelight. She was putting the finishing touches to the rag doll for Dick Langton's little daughter. Seb watched her deft needle fly.

'Em?'

'Mm?'

'Could you sew a much larger rag doll for me?'

'And why would you want a doll, husband, at your age?' She continued to stitch.

'For a noble purpose, I promise you.'

Emily frowned.

'How much bigger?'

'The size of a man.'

'What?' She looked up at him, 'Why? How could a doll serve any purpose other than a play thing?'

'It would needs be sewn in secret. Do we have sufficient linen? It would be better not to purchase any.'

Emily put down her needle whilst she considered.

'An old bed sheet might do. That young wriggler Jack put his foot through his sheet last week. I was intending to repair it but I suppose I could use it to make your doll. Does it matter if it be patched?'

'Not at all.'

'When you have finished with it, I can probably find some other use for the cloth, for patching and mending other sheets.'

'You will not see it again, once it has served its purpose.'

'And what purpose is that?'

'If the worst should befall him and he be condemned, I think I may have a plan to rescue Gabriel.' Seb went back to his book, turning a page at last. 'Oh, and tell those fellows who are supposed to be rebuilding the pig sty wall not to bother. The task can wait 'til we buy a piglet next spring.'

Chapter 12

Friday, the fifteenth day of November
The Foxley workshop

'JACK. COME here a moment,' Seb said.

Jack groaned, certain master would have more letters for him to copy or brushes to wash. Master had been mixing pigments all morning but, as far as Jack could tell, hadn't done any work on his precious psalter. Master's desk was littered with scraps of parchment, everyone daubed with blotches of paint of every shade of purple, red, rose and black.

'Roll up your sleeve, Jack.'

'Why?'

'Just do as you're told for once.'

The lad pushed up his sleeve, the cuff already grubby despite his shirt being clean but three hours since. Master took up a brush and, holding Jack's wrist, put a small circle of paint on his forearm, just below the elbow, then another of a different hue beside it.

'Wot yer doin', master? Looks like I got the pox or a plum puddin' on me arm or sommat.'

The line of spots grew longer, down to his wrist, each one a different colour and size.

'There now. Don't touch the paint and don't pull your sleeve down until it's dry. And stay out of sight of any customers. Go, tidy the storeroom.'

'Again? I did that yesterday, didn't I, after ol' Weasel-face messed it up?'

'Well, do it again. And don't smudge the spots.'

Jack sighed so heavily his shoulders slumped but he trudged off to the storeroom, thinking he'd spend a while in there, doing nothing.

'What are you up to, little brother?' Jude asked, having watched the procedure.

'If the worst should come to pass, we may not have much time to save Gabriel. I need to be ready.'

'And painting that rascal's arm is part of your plan?'

'An idea; no more than that.'

'You want to tell me about it? Talking it through may help.'

'Not yet; 'tis all too vague. Probably a foolish idea in any case. But there is one thing I need to ask of you, bearing in mind what you said yesterday when Nox arrested me...'

'Oh? What did I say?'

'That you would do anything to aid me except set foot in a gaol.'

'I said that?'

'Something like, aye. But if we have to rescue Gabriel, it may well require us both to enter the Lollards' Tower.'

Jude scratched his chin, thinking.

'You mean we get ourselves arrested? I don't want that.'

'No. Just as visitors.' Seb draped a damp cloth over his oyster shells of pigment mixtures, hoping they wouldn't dry out too much.

'Do they allow visitors there? I've heard that they keep the heretics confined, away from good Christians for fear of bloody contaminating them and, if their own kind visit, they don't come out again.'

'But would you, if it was a matter of life or death for Gabriel?'

'In truth, Seb, I don't know. I just don't bloody know if I could. Not after Newgate.'

175

'The Lollards' Tower is much cleaner, so far as I saw yesterday.'

'Still got sodding turn-keys, I'll wager.'

'Well, yes, but...'

'God rot the lot of 'em. Bastards, every damned one.' Jude turned away and went back to his desk, cursing gaolers to damnation and back.

Seb still didn't know if his brother would be able to assist in rescuing Gabriel – if matters went so far.

'Jack. Leave what you be doing in that store room and come with me.'

• •

'Where we goin', master?' Jack asked as Master Seb hurried him along Cheapside to Ironmonger Lane, by the Hospital of St Thomas of Acon.

'You have a nasty rash, lad. Where do you think we be going?'

'But I 'aven't.'

'Indeed you have, sufficient that we must enquire of Surgeon Dagvyle, ask his opinion of your complaint.'

'No, master, pleeese. I don't wanna 'ave t'swallow any 'orrible potion, like when I 'ad the measles. Yer know there's nuffin' wrong.'

'Be quiet.'

'But a bit o' paint's not gonna fool the surgeon, is it?'

'Silence! You will say naught of what occurs this day to anyone. Do you understand me?'

'Aye, master, s'pose so.'

John Dagvyle ran his prosperous barber-surgeon's business from a rambling old house opposite the hospital. The brethren at St Thomas's called upon his services occasionally in tending the poor and sick who were their patients and Master Dagvyle obliged, often for no fee, certain his charitable acts ensured his place in heaven.

The door of the house stood open and beside it, pinned to a board, was the image of a 'wound man' who, despite being beaten with a cudgel, pierced by an arrow, sliced and stabbed by every conceivable kind of blade, struck by a cannonball and stumbling on a caltrop, smiled a welcome, advertising the services available within. Jack kept well away from the hideous picture.

'Good morrow, masters,' said a benevolent-looking woman of middle years, wearing a veil that had a great complexity of pleating, kept in place by so many pins, Jack reckoned she must have a pin-cushion for a head. 'Master Surgeon is with a patient at present but I be certain it won't take too long. May I fetch you some ale while you wait?'

Jack's look of pleading was such that Seb said a cup of ale would be welcome. They sat on stools purposefully shaped to make your backside uncomfortable, Jack was sure. The ale wasn't much good and the place smelled faintly of evil potions, mixed in with the stinks of sweat and piss and Christ knew what else. Jack for one did not want to know. He fidgeted and squirmed on his stool 'til master told him to be still, then sat, staring at the cob-webbed pots lined up on the shelves – Mistress Em would have a fit at the sight of so much dust and grime. This turned his thoughts to mistress's kitchen and, inevitably, what would be for dinner. Friday. So it must be fish. Mackerel, may be. They hadn't had that for weeks. It was one of his favourites, except for the bones. Still, better than stockfish and a change from salt herrings.

A half-strangled shriek and a terrible howl from another room broke in on Jack's reverie.

'There. All over now,' he heard the surgeon say as a door opened. 'That tooth won't bother you ever again. That'll be half a groat. Pay my goodwife on your way out. Good day. Next!'

As Master Seb pushed Jack towards the back room, a poor fellow stumbled passed them, a blood-soaked rag held to his mouth. A grown man, yet tears streamed down his cheeks like a babe.

Master Dagvyle was tidying his instruments. A grisly pair of tongs looked wet with gore. The surgeon's apprentice threw sawdust on the floor to soak up the previous patient's blood. Was it any wonder master had to drag Jack over the threshold and close the door?

'May we speak in confidence, Master Dagvyle?' Seb nodded towards the apprentice.

'Everything said in this room is in confidence, Master Foxley,' Dagvyle replied.

'Even so.'

The surgeon nodded and sent his apprentice off to sharpen blades or some similar gruesome task.

Seb pulled Jack close and folded back his sleeve.

'At a glance, what do you see?' Seb asked.

'A spot, inflamed, possibly infected.' The surgeon took Jack's hand and rubbed his thumb across the spot. The pigment smudged. 'Hey, what's this? Are you playing me for a fool? This is paint of some kind.'

'Aye. That is so, but please do not be offended.' Seb rolled up Jack's shirt sleeve so that all the spots – large and small, faint and intense – were visible. 'Good master, which of these spots appears the worst to you? Which might signify an ailment that a man is most like to die of?'

'I don't have time for such foolishness.'

'I will pay for your time. Please, oblige me. Tell me what you think. Does any seem to be the pox?'

'No. The pustules are raised in the pox, full of matter. None looks the least like it.'

'What of the plague?'

'Don't be ridiculous. How can a few drips of paint look like a case of pestilence? You waste my time.'

'Yet in the first instance, you thought I had brought the lad here with an infected spot. Just for a moment, it was convincing enough. Please. You see, a man's life may depend upon his supposed death from some dreadful contagion.'

Seb feared the surgeon was about to order them to leave but then the plump fellow went to the door, bellowed for his wife to bring some decent ale before seating himself upon a cushioned bench.

'A surgeon's business is about saving lives, I suppose,' Dagvyle said as his wife bustled in with a tray of ale cups and a platter of oat cakes. He nodded his thanks to her, selected a cake and took a sip of ale. 'So, whose life may depend upon a few daubs of paint? I'm intrigued.'

Seb suffered a moment of gravest doubt but realised he had no choice.

'All that I tell you must be in strictest confidence.'

The surgeon frowned.

'I'm a man of medicine, Master Foxley. Everything a patient tells me remains as close a secret with me as any confession made unto a priest.'

'Forgive me. I did not mean to question your integrity.'

'Good. Now tell me.'

Over ale and cakes, Seb divulged his plan to secure Gabriel's escape, should the need arise. As the tale unfolded, Jack's eyes grew wider in wonder and disbelief. Master must be a lack-wit to think it could ever work.

When the explanation ended, the surgeon looked again at the pigment spots on Jack's arm.

'This one,' he said, pointing to a mixture of terra rosa and candle soot smeared just below the lad's elbow. 'The worst kind of pestilence, the one that kills infallibly, sometimes within a day or two, sometimes within hours, causes bleeding beneath the skin, producing what look like bruises that quickly blacken with a reddish purple tinge. This colour is most like but the edges need to be less distinct, blurred. This deadly form of pestilence is also the most contagious.

'But, of course, there are other symptoms beside the black tokens: severe headache, black vomit, fever, bleeding from the nose and other orifices, prostration... How will you fake those? And finally, death. What of that? A man can only hold his breath for so long and cannot stop his heart for a moment.'

'I know. I'm relying on fear, Master Dagvyle, on the terror instilled in us all by the word 'plague'. I was not fully aware of these other symptoms you describe – except that they be terrible – so I trust that my fellows are equally ignorant and also too fearful of such horrors to look closely at a victim. As to fever, you prescribed a potion for me the day I seemed to suffer a seizure, to sweat the evil humours out of me, and there is enough left over for a dose or two. The would-be victim is capable of playing a part and the potion that put my maid servant to sleep whilst you stitched her arm will feign death – so long as no one feels for his pulse or listens close for his breathing and, again, I trust to fear to prevent that.'

Walking home after, Jack, for once, had naught to say. He even forgot to think about dinner. He didn't want to ask, but hadn't Master Seb forgotten something? How was Master Gabe going to get the paint and potions; how was he going to know he was supposed to pretend to be sick with the pestilence?

• •

After dinner, Seb slipped out of the workshop, saying naught of where he was going. He wanted to avoid any arguments with Em concerning his visits to Rose but was determined to keep his appointment. He had mulled over whether it was safer to take Jack, or maybe Tom, along as a chaperone, or just to go alone, with the least fuss, and hope Em didn't notice his absence. On this occasion, he chose the latter but decided he should not stay too long.

Rose opened the door and welcomed him in but her smile lacked its normal sparkle.

'What's amiss, Rose?'

'You can tell?'

'Aye. I can see you've been weeping. You be missing your friend?'

Rose sat on the edge of her bed and Seb took his usual place there, setting out the writing stuff and the book of fables on the threadbare coverlet between them.

'Not just my poor Bessie,' Rose said, dabbing her eyes with her sleeve. 'Haven't you heard? Another of our sisters was found without Bishopsgate, dead. And Under-Sheriff Nox came to question me about both of them.'

'You knew her also?' Seb patted her hand.

'Not so well as Bessie, of course. Her name was Beatrix, Beatrix Whitehead, which is queer 'cos her hair was red as strawberries.' Rose gave a feeble laugh. 'She was more Bessie's friend than mine but I knew her well enough. Oh, Master Seb, I fear someone is trying to kill us all off. I be so afeared. Will I be next, mayhap?'

'No, Rose, of course not. But you must take care. Don't go out alone. Don't have to do with strangers.'

'You ask the impossible. In my work I have little choice. Every other customer that Master Underwood sends up those stairs is a stranger to me: mariners and foreign merchants mostly. Of course, I have a few who keep returning – like you and certain officials and priests I must not name.'

'I wish you could find some other means of earning your living, lass, besides this.'

This time, Rose's laughter was genuine:

'Then find me a wealthy husband and I'll live like a lady.' She stood up, twitched her skirts, held her head high and processed around the little chamber. 'Will I suffice, master? I warrant I have airs and graces enough. I could wed a grand lord or a handsome knight, could I not?' Then she crumpled to the floor, sobbing. 'I'll never be free of this place.'

Seb picked her up, dried her tears upon his kerchief and sat her back beside him on the bed.

'You will be free, Rose. I don't know how but we'll make it so.'

'You promise?'

'Aye. I promise.' Even as he spoke those words – words he so much wanted to be true – he realised he was probably setting himself a task he could never accomplish; a promise he could never keep. At least he had put a smile back upon her lips and rekindled the light in her eyes. 'Do you wish to have a lesson now?'

'No time like the present, as they say, master. I'm sorry though, I haven't practised my letters much this week.'

• •

Back home, Seb was greeted by an alarming billow of smoke that filled the passage through to the kitchen. Coughing, he made for the kitchen. Chaos prevailed. The floor was awash, the board and trestles overturned. Emily was stamping and pouring water on a sodden pile of linen. Soot motes floated like black flies in the smoky air. Tom rushed in from the yard with a brimming bucket and emptied it over the linen. Jack followed with another.

'Hold off, Jack. I think the fire is out now.' Emily wiped her brow with her begrimed apron, righted a stool and slumped upon it.

'What happened?' Seb asked.

'Oh, you're back then,' Emily said, 'As usual, you're not here when your aid is needed.'

Seb found a cup, wiped the soot from the rim and fetched some fresh ale from the lean-to in the yard. When he returned, Em was washing her hands in Jack's bucket. He gave her the cup.

'How did the fire begin?'

'Nessie. The foolish wench thought to hasten the drying of the linen – the tablecloth on which one of your customers spilt his wine so I had to soak it. She was impatient for it to dry and hung it in the chimney... my best tablecloth. And now look at it.' Emily waved her hand at the burned heap of cloth by the hearth. 'Ruined. All my beautiful embroidery. Naught but charred rags and ashes.'

'And where is Nessie? She can set about cleaning up the mess.'

'No. She can't. I told her to go, to get out of my sight, else I'd thrash her 'til she screamed for mercy. I've had enough of her foolishness and idle ways. After she near poisoned you...'

'Where has she gone?'

'I don't know and I don't care. Serving wenches are ten-a-penny. I'll get someone new.'

'But this is her home. Nessie has lived here for longer than we have. You cannot expect her to beg her bread on the street.'

'I don't care what she does. She deserves to be punished for her carelessness.'

Seb went to the row of pegs by the door to the yard, where they hung their cloaks and mantles. He took down Nessie's cloak. It smelled of smoke. He went to lift the latch but Emily barred his way, hands on hips.

'Don't you dare go out and find her, Sebastian. Don't you dare undermine my authority as mistress of this house. Don't you da...'

'She'll freeze to death out there, Em. Do you want that upon your conscience?'

'My conscience is clear. She has brought it upon herself.'

'Let me pass, please.'

'No.' She folded her arms and scowled at him. Straggling strands of hair had escaped her cap and clung to her face. 'I'll not have her back in my kitchen, ever. And there's an end to it.'

'Step aside, wife. I'm being reasonable here, but...'

'But what? You'll strike me? Beat me? You'd do that but won't let a stupid scullery wench be out in the dark?'

'I won't do either of those things but don't goad me, woman. Now get out of my way.' He pushed past her and near collided with Jude coming into the yard but strode on without greeting his brother.

'Who put a wasp in his breeches?' Jude said. 'Lord. Who burned the bloody supper? This place stinks. Ow!' The blow that caught him hard across the ear seemed to come out of nowhere.

'Keep silent, you.' Emily shook her broom at him. 'There is no damned supper. Not for you nor anybody. You can all starve and go to hell for all I care.'

'So that's the way the furrow lies, is it?' Jude muttered, sighing. But then he grinned. 'Come along, Tom. You too, Jack. If we're not going to get fed here we can sup at the Panyer, leave mistress to indulge her misery and choler by herself.'

The lads needed no second telling but grabbed their cloaks and followed Jude.

Emily flopped onto her stool and surveyed the mess that had been her neat and spotless kitchen before dissolving into tears. She just might go to her father's house again and leave the menfolk to fend for themselves, damn them. God knew why she'd ever involved herself with the wretched Foxley brothers, let alone married one of them. She must be mad.

• •

Seb didn't have to search very far to find Nessie. She was huddled behind the fallen stones of the pig sty wall. Her snivelling was not a heartening sound.

'Nessie,' he said gently, holding aloft his torch so she could see his face and not be scared. 'Here. Put your cloak around you, afore you take a chill.'

'C-can I come home n-now, master?' she asked through chattering teeth.

'Not for the moment, lass. I fear your mistress is too upset.'

'She clouted me wi' the broom, master, said I was a curse on the house. I'm not though, am I, master? I didn't do it of a purpose, honest I didn't.'

'Of course you didn't.'

'You b'lieve me, master?'

'Aye. Now come, we must find you somewhere to sleep for the night, somewhere warm and dry.'

'But me bed got scorched.'

'Which is why we must go elsewhere.'

Seb rapped on the once-familiar door of a house in Cheapside, a few steps along from the conduit. After a lengthy wait, he heard a woman call out:

'Who's there? 'Tis late to come a-calling. Whatever it is, I've got one already, don't need one and I'm too old to want one.' The door opened slowly and a wary face appeared.

Again, Seb held his torch to illumine his face.

'Good eve to you, Dame Ellen.'

'Sebastian? Is something wrong?'

'Nothing to concern yourself, good dame. Rather I would beg a favour of you.'

'Indeed? Well, you'd better come in. And who's this?' Dame Ellen ushered Seb and Nessie into her kitchen – her one-time lodger and some wench or other weren't of sufficient rank to warrant using the parlour. Besides, the kitchen had a good blaze going in the hearth.

'You may remember Nessie, dame? You see her at church with us.'

'May be I do but why is she here?'

'There was an, er, incident at home. A fire...'

'Oh, dear. Anyone injured?'

'No. It was naught of any consequence but, as a result, Nessie is in need of somewhere to sleep.' Nessie bobbed a little courtesy.

Dame Ellen considered for a good few moments.

'A fire there may well have been, Sebastian, but your house is of a size to find some corner for her to sleep, bed or no bed.' She turned to Nessie. 'Your mistress has thrown you out, hasn't she? What did you do, eh?'

'It was an accident,' Seb explained whilst Nessie blubbered and bawled. 'I'll pay for her board and lodging, just for a few days, until Emily sees sense.'

'Cease your howling, girl, you sound like a whipped dog. Very well. Three days, Sebastian, no more.'

'Thank you, Dame Ellen, you are an angel.' Seb kissed her wrinkled cheek.

'Well, I don't know about that. Can she cook and clean? My scullery could do with a thorough scrubbing down. In which case, I'll only charge tuppence a day, all found. That'll be six pence, Sebastian, in advance.'

Seb fished in his purse, depleted of late, and found a groat and two pennies which he pressed into the old woman's hand.

'Behave yourself, Nessie. Obey Dame Ellen in all things. Understand? I'll be asking Dame Ellen to report on your conduct.'

As the good dame saw him to the door and he was thanking her again, he looked back. Nessie stood there, dumbfounded, bewildered as a newborn lamb, her thumb in her mouth. Women, he thought. What a merry dance they led him. And he still had to face an irate wife in her fire-blackened kitchen. Was it any wonder that the rushlight, spilling from the door of the Panyer, looked so inviting?

• •

'Ah! The hen-pecked husband has made his escape. Welcome to my kingdom, little brother. We don't see you in here too often.'

'Jude. Have you and the lads eaten supper yet?' Seb looked about for an empty stool.

'Aye, if you could bloody call it supper. Friday's not the best day to eat at the Panyer.'

'Bloody stockfish, agen,' Jack moaned.

'Mind your tongue,' Seb said. 'Just be thankful. Stockfish is more than you'll get at home this evening.' Having found a stool, he joined Jude and the lads at the board.

'If Master Gabe was here, he could tell us a fine tale now,' Tom said.

'Well, he's not and I think you'll have to get used to that. He's probably going to languish in that sodding hell hole for a while yet.' Jude drained his cup and waved at a tap-boy to refill it.'

'Wot's lankish mean?'

'Trust me, Jack, you don't bloody want to know. Now why don't I show you how to cheat at dice?'

'Jude, for pity's sake. I'm doing my best to teach these lads how to live righteously.'

''Tis just for fun.'

'Let Master Jude show us 'ow, pleeease.'

'No. I forbid it. Now get you home to your beds, both of you. And no dawdling. I want a decent morning's work out of the pair of you on the morrow.'

A platter could have stood upon Jack's nether lip and Tom's doleful face would turn milk sour but they left, grumbling about Master Seb treating them like serfs and making life a misery for them. They slouched off, Little Beggar yapping and trotting behind.

'I believe you're none too popular in that quarter at present, little brother,' Jude said, laughing.

'I dare say but it cannot be helped. I meant what I said about raising them righteously. 'Tis too bad that they would rather learn to cheat at gambling and how to drink a tavern dry than how to earn a living by hard work. You're not setting them a good example either, are you? I have no idea where you've been or what you've been doing this week past.'

Jude took a couple of hefty swallows of ale.

'Are you going to tell me?' Seb prompted as his bowl of stockfish arrived. It looked like bits of shattered greyish pot floating in a thin, colourless gruel with a greasy scum on top. Appetising it was not. He stirred it about with his spoon. It smelled of onions and old shoes. No wonder even Jack – who would probably eat roasted toad, if it was set before him on a hunk of bread with a sprinkling of salt – complained about the food, but the alternative was to go without.

'I don't know.'

'Well, when you be ready, I'd like to hear of your whereabouts of late.' On second thoughts, Seb pushed his bowl aside: going without was probably preferable, safest for his belly.

'I mean, I don't know where I was. I can't remember. That's the trouble.'

'Jude, don't jest with me. Drunk you may well have been but you must recall something.'

'I'm not jesting. My mind is a blank page. There's naught but a few flashes of – I don't know – dreams, may be, nightmares, ghostly apparitions. It makes no damned sense to me at all. I don't want to talk about it, or even think about it, so don't ask me. I can't tell you what I don't know.'

'Someone said they saw you at the Stag by Bucklersbury. Might that be the case?'

Jude shrugged. 'How many times, Seb: I. Don't. Know.'

'There were cases of plague there. The Barge Inn was shut up. I was so worried about you, fearing you might have fallen sick... died, even, and I wouldn't have known.'

'Sweet Christ's sake, Seb. I'm not bloody dead so you can stop whining about it.'

'What is the last thing you do recall?'

Jude pulled a face and rubbed his cheeks: 'We were at the city gate, you claiming to be first-finder and Nox proving otherwise. Then I came here to the Panyer. Nox came too, unfortunately. We shared a jug, rolled a few dice. I seem to remember a fight broke out, maybe. That's all.'

'And what is the first thing since then? You remembered to come home, eventually.'

'I woke up. Huddled in a cattle byre outside Bishopsgate. I knew not the day, the hour nor where I was 'til I crawled from the byre, found myself behind St Botolph's church. I thought it was dusk but then the light grew brighter in the east and I realised it was daybreak. Reckoning by that, I must have been out all night, so it seemed. Until I came home and you yelled at me for being gone for a week... I didn't believe you. Not at first. And I still find it impossible that a whole damned seven-night has gone missing from my life and I know naught of it. Where was I? What was I doing? Was I lying in that bloody cowshed all that time?

'I could have been to France and back, met the Emperor of Cathy, flown to the moon. I could have humped the king's mistress, won a hundred marks at dice... I just don't know.'

He laughed, attempting to make a jest of it. 'Clearly, the king's mistress made so little impression upon me, that I have forgotten her utterly and I must have spent my prize money, or been robbed of it. That's more bloody likely.

'Whatever happened to me, little brother, it did me more harm than good, I can tell you that. I felt so bad when I got home... thought I was dying... thought that wife of yours might get her wish and see me in a shroud.'

'Em doesn't want that no more than I do, Jude.'

'No? You think not? Well, she certainly plays the part convincingly. Told me this morn she was disappointed at my return, that she'd have been content if I'd gone to hell.'

'Just words. Em doesn't mean it. She's not been herself of late. Ever since that poor woman was murdered at Smithfield. And now there's been another. Such happenings are sure to distress the womenfolk.'

As his brother spoke, Jude swallowed hard and clenched his fists beneath the table. The air in the tavern seemed suffocating such that he could hardly draw breath.

'Jude? Are you quite well? Shall I order wine?'

'No. I do not intend to drink wine ever again.'

'But you appear in need of a restorative: you look so pale of a sudden.'

'I am fine, little brother. 'Tis just a bad dream half remembered. Nothing more.'

'Do you want to tell me of it? That may help.'

'No. I want to forget it.'

'But...'

'Let it lie, Seb. Ask me no more.'

The Foxleys' kitchen

'THERE'S BREAD and cheese, or you can go without. I don't care which.'

It wasn't much of a welcome but neither man expected any better. Jude cut a wedge of cheese, tore off a hunk of bread and patted Seb on the shoulder to bid him 'good night'. Then he was gone to his chamber, leaving Seb to face his wife, alone.

'You have made a good job of putting this place to rights. Apart from the smoky smell, you'd hardly know...'

Without warning, she slapped him – hard.

'And what did you do to help, eh? Abandoned me to see to the mess by myself. Thank you so very much for your assistance. Found that useless maid a bed, did you? Afraid she'd be alone in the cold, were you? What about me? Did you even think about me for one solitary heartbeat?'

Seb reached out to her.

'Em, my sweet...'

'Don't you 'my sweet' me, you uncaring, ungrateful, unfeeling... oaf! Get away from me. I don't want you near me. And you can sleep in the parlour, you wretch. Or share your brother's bed since he means far more to you than I do.'

'That is not fair. Jude needs...'

'Of course. How could I forget? Jude's needs always come first, don't they? Or the lads' wants, or Nessie's, everyone's but mine. If Gabriel was here, he would've stayed to help, I know.' The tears came in a flood.

Seb was about to take her in his arms. But no, that would surely make matters worse. Weeping women confounded him. What was a fellow to do?

Chapter 13

Saturday, the sixteenth day of November
City of London

UNDER-SHERIFF NOX was in an ill-humour and exhausted. A generous purse only weighed so much and he was tired of doing Bishop Kemp's bidding, sneaking around the city, keeping an eye on those wretched Foxleys, their journeyman and apprentices. At least Widowson – the Known Man – was now locked up, safe. But what of the brothers? The bishop was convinced that they too were involved in this damned heresy? In trying to uncover their dirty little secrets – of which there seemed to be many – the scriveners had been leading him a merry jig indeed. And it hardly seemed right that he, an officer of the city, responsible for civil law and order, should be doing the work of the Church.

Besides, that miserable 'Weasel' was an unbearable, sanctimonious pain in the backside, more of a hindrance than a help. No wonder the bishop had required Nox to assist his nephew. Assist? More like do all the work himself. When was the last time that prideful priest went creeping down a shit-strewn, rat-infested alleyway, eh?

Aye, that was where the trouble had begun, in a stinking alley down by Queenhithe. If that self-righteous do-gooder, that ship's captain, whatever his name was – Marchmane – that was it, hadn't discovered and reported those damned pamphlets he'd found on board, Nox could have avoided becoming involved.

But no. Marchmane had shown him the heretical texts, saying he feared they would infect London with the Devil's ideas, but then refused to reveal who among his crew was involved in smuggling them in. If he knew who it was? Perhaps he hadn't known but then he'd become angry when, having told all to the bishop, the bishop determined to put a watch on Marchmane's crew. The captain had refused to co-operate further. In fact, he said he would warn the men that the ship was being espied upon.

That would have ruined the bishop's plan to discover who among London's citizens was also involved in the heresy. It was then that the bishop had given Nox a most generous purse and ordered him to see to it that the captain never had the chance to warn his crew.

And as for the wretched taverner, Roger Underwood. Calls himself an espier? He couldn't espy St Paul's steeple in broad daylight. And now, here was Nox, yet again following Seb Foxley along Cheapside for God alone knew what purpose. Did the bishop expect Foxley to stand at Paul's Cross and give a sermon of a sudden, proclaiming his heretical beliefs? It wasn't going to happen that way, was it? This espying was a complete waste of his time. Indeed, Under-Sheriff Valentyn Nox could think of far better ways of spending a cold, drizzly Saturday morn. There was to be a bear-baiting at Smithfield at ten of the clock and he intended to be there to see it.

Seb Foxley turned into a tailor's shop in Cheapside. Nox sighed. Following the fellow as he tried on a new gown was pointless. Unless the tailor was another Known Man. But Nox knew the proprietor, a harmless old man, Walter, whose skill with a needle was unmatched but with naught else to recommend him. Foxley was in the shop for some time, long enough that the tailor's apprentice tried to lure Nox within, proclaiming his master's near-magical skills in making well-fitting hose even for the knock-kneed and bandy-legged. Nox sent the pesky knave off with a swipe on the ear. The cheek of it: these were his best hose.

He hid around the corner, concealed by a brewer's dray. The horse betwixt the shafts eyed him with suspicion and blew through its nose, pawing up the mud as it waited. Nox could sympathise with the creature's impatience.

At last, Foxley reappeared, looking very pleased with himself, a package tucked under his arm. Nox was instantly alerted. Was it more pamphlets, he wondered. Catching Foxley red-handed with heretical texts would be worth an extra reward from the bishop. But the package was wayward and unwieldy, flopping about. A tail of ribbon escaped the wrappings and he realised it was just a piece of clothing, naught more. He heaved a sigh, shoulders slumped, cursing the bishop, and made for the nearest tavern. Foxley could read Lollard tracts until he went blind; Nox was too tired to care whether he did or no and to hell with the bishop.

The Bishop's Palace beside St Paul's

BISHOP KEMP reclined in his cushioned chair, sipping fine wine and helping himself from a silver comfit dish. His many chins wobbled as he chewed.

'You have always been a grave disappointment to me,' he said, taking another sugared plum and admiring it before he popped it in his mouth. 'And now you have shown your true nature...' He wiped his fingers upon a napkin. '...my disappointment knows no bounds. When I think of the time and money I've wasted, attempting to give you a good living...'

'As a priest!' Gabriel spat the words. 'Blinding good Christian souls with your blasphemous doctrines that have no place in the Scriptures. Leading them by the hand to hell where you'll be first...'

'Silence! You will not speak to me in this manner. I am a prince of the Church.'

'The devil's minion.'

'You are a worthless piece of offal.'

'I am a man known to God, as all men may be who see the light.'

'Don't you preach to me!'

'Why not? Do you see yourself already beyond redemption, a man of the cloth who raped a respectable widow women?'

The bishop flew out of his chair with surprising speed for one so heavy of flesh. His hands began to close upon Gabriel's throat but good sense intervened. They were alone within the chamber but there were servants within summoning distance.

'It wasn't like that. Your mother was my house-keeper, lonely in her widowhood. We were both of us young and she was an attractive women. It was but a moment of madness. I admit, temptation got the better of me but I did what I could for her – aye, and for her dead husband's son, your brother – when I learned she bore my child. I saw to it that you never starved – '

'We lived in the meanest hovel in the village, went bare-foot even in the snow.' Gabriel's voice was barely more than a whisper but it over-brimmed with contempt. 'My mother worked herself nigh unto death to keep bread in our mouths whilst awaiting your occasional hand-outs, when and if you remembered us. But she taught us that, no matter what became of us in this life, God would save us in the next, if we were prayerful and paid heed to His Word. She told us the wondrous stories from the Bible, explained the tales told in the wall-paintings and the tiny stained glass window in the village church. We survived on her simple faith which she passed on to us – in English. We understood and took to heart every word.' Gabriel paused to wipe away a tear. 'And then you, thinking to 'educate' me, would corrupt me with your contorted Latin doctrines, confuse my very soul with your words written by men – not by God.' He summoned up his strength and cried aloud: 'I reject your Church and all its evil works of Satan!'

The bishop took up his oaken footstool and brought it down upon his son's chest. Had the cleric been taller, it should have been the younger man's head and, in all likelihood, he would now lay dead upon the floor. Rather, he was badly winded, his ribs much bruised.

'Guards! Guards!' the bishop screamed. A servant and a turn-key came running. 'Take this filthy heretic away. He attacked me, so I had to defend myself.'

With Gabriel gone, Bishop Kemp collapsed back into his chair, gasping for breath and mopping sweat from his brow with a silken sleeve. The ungrateful wretch had caused him much distress and would pay the ultimate price. All the same, he shed a private tear for the waste of a prodigious talent and the loss of his natural son.

• •

Seb found his goodwife in the kitchen amidst a cloud of flour, pummelling the bread dough into submission, scowling at it as if it were a Frenchmen. Why was she making bread mid-morn? Then he recalled that Em had dismissed Nessie yestereve and now had no help with her work. No matter, a new gown would cheer any woman. He went to kiss her flour-dusted cheek but she elbowed him aside.

'Can you not see I'm busy? Get out of the way, you'll get flour everywhere.'

'I have a gift for you.'

'Gift? I don't have time for gifts. If you wanted to please me, you could have aided me last eve, when I had to clear up the mess after the fire. But did you think to do so? No. Of course you didn't. You were concerned only for 'poor Nessie', that useless wench. And did you so much as consider me, scrubbing walls and floors and boards and benches? Now you think you can buy back my favour with a gift. Well, I don't want it, whatever it may be. Just get out of my kitchen!'

Jude sauntered in, went to the ale jug and found it empty.

'What? No bloody ale?' he said.

Emily turned to face both brothers, one bearing a large package, the other a pewter jug.

'Fetch your own ale, Jude Foxley,' she screamed, throwing a huge lump of dough at him. 'And as for you...' She slapped Seb as hard as she was able, sending him stumbling back. He dropped the package which split open to reveal yards of exquisite rose-coloured silk velvet. The gown lay crumpled amongst flour and lumps of dough upon the kitchen floor. 'What is this?' Em demanded.

'Your gift.' Seb held his face, his eyes watering with the pain.

'You've wasted our money on these useless rags, cloth forbidden by the sumptuary laws so I can never wear it. How witless can you be?' She struck his other cheek for being so foolish.

'Enough of that, sister.' Jude grabbed her arm.

'Don't you 'sister' me, you scoundrel; you wastrel. Take your hands off me.'

'Not until you calm yourself. Get a hold on your bloody temper.'

'Leave it, Jude,' Seb said, his voice little more than a whisper, 'Em is right. I shouldn't have spent so much.'

'She's an ungrateful hell-cat who needs to learn some manners. She wouldn't bloody speak to me that way, if she was my wife.'

'But I'm not your wife, so you can mind your own business. Get out of my house and don't come back, ever.'

'Em, you forget, this is Jude's home as well as ours.'

'No, it isn't. Not anymore. I warn you, husband: you have to choose. Either Jude goes, or I do. It's your decision. I won't live under the same roof as the man you care for more than you care for me, Sebastian. And that's my final word. You have three days to make up your mind.'

Slowly, Seb stooped to bundle up the silk before leaving the kitchen. Jude helped him catch up the ribbons so they didn't trail in the flour. Knowing Tom and Jack, supposedly about their Saturday chores in the workshop, had probably heard every word, the brothers sought the privacy and comfort of the parlour.

'You think she means it?' Jude asked, stretching out on the cushioned settle and putting his feet up.

Seb took the chair close beside the hearth, feeling the cold. His face hurt – yet again, his cheeks burning.

'Who knows? I do not. I can never comprehend the way women's minds work. They're a mystery to me.'

They sat in silence for a while. Jude was thinking about wanting ale – still – since none had been forthcoming in the kitchen.

'Shall we make a start on the accounts?' Seb suggested, seeing the ledgers lay awaiting the usual Saturday task of construing the weekly tallies of incomings and outgoings.

'Can't it wait? I'm not of a mind to tussle with numbers. I'm more inclined to go to the Panyer. Coming?'

'With my face like this?'

'Why not? My friends will probably buy you a drink out of sympathy. Besides, mine isn't much better. What a bloody pair we must make.'

With Jude departed for the tavern, Seb sat with his head in his hands, tears coursing down his swollen face as he wept in silence.

'Master? Master, there's a customer in the shop,' Tom said, creeping into the parlour. 'Shall I tell him we be closed?'

Seb roused himself, wiped his eyes on the sleeve of his doublet. It was unusual to have customers on a Saturday afternoon when most businesses were closed.

'No, lad. I'm coming.'

The customer was a grocer from Candlewick Street who was compiling quite a library for himself, twelve volumes at the last count.

'Good day, Master Wilkins, how may I help?' Seb tried to sound welcoming but his voice would hardly oblige.

The grocer frowned, staring at Seb.

'Are you quite well, Master Foxley?'

'Toothache.'

'Oh, an unpleasant complaint, indeed. I advise oil of cloves as a remedy. I wish to discuss a new book I would have you produce for me but, mayhap, I should return another day, when you have recovered from your indisposition?'

'No, no. Our discussion will divert my thoughts from my discomfort. Shall we go into the parlour?'

'If you be certain?'

'Aye. Tom, ask Mistress Emily to serve ale and wafers in the parlour. Tell her we have an important customer.'

Master Wilkins smiled.

Seb tried to return the gesture but his face was too swollen.

Seb guided Wilkins to the chair where there was most benefit from the fire. He sat on the settle, armed with a wax tablet and stylus, ready to note down the customer's requirements. Customers were notorious for changing their minds, so the wax tablet was the best way of recording the preliminary discussions before the final version was penned in the order book.

They were talking about the relative merits of paper and parchment when Emily came in with a laden tray. All graciousness, she set the tray upon a stool and offered Wilkins a platter of hot oatcakes before pouring him a cup of ale. Seb noted that there was but a solitary cup. She offered him neither ale nor oatcake but glared at him from the doorway as she left. Fortunately, the customer was enjoying his repast and did not see.

With the customer's order carefully noted and copied into the ledger, Seb bade farewell to Master Wilkins, pleased to see that he had left some of his ale in the cup. Seb drank it before Em could whisk it away and then settled down to wrestle with the accounts. This was not a favoured pastime. In fact, he dreaded it every week. Somehow, no matter how diligently he had recorded every penny earned or spent, the double columns never quite balanced.

Occasionally, there were a few too many coins but, more often, as this day, money was missing: the considerable sum of one shilling and nine pence three farthings seemed to have vanished into the air. But Seb was not of a mind to interrogate the household. Not this time, at least.

Last week he had been short by six pence ha'penny but the time before that there had been eight pence more than he could account for, so it would probably work out in the end. He closed the ledger and put down his pen. He'd done his best. Jude could check the numbers later, if he could be bothered.

He set aside the purse containing the wages that Gabriel had earned earlier in the week, wondering if the journeyman would ever be able to collect it. Poor Gabe. How he must be suffering in that prison. Seb rubbed his sore face, certain his friend was most likely in a far worse case. He would go to St Michael's at vespers, say a prayer and light a candle for him.

Emily interrupted his sorrowful thoughts. She wore her mantle and hood and carried a covered basket.

'I'm going out,' she announced.

'Marketing?'

'No. I'm going to Deptford. I shall visit the Langtons. I have the doll I made for their daughter.'

'That's quite a walk to undertake, Em.'

'I know. Which is why I want six pence to pay for a wherry, there and back.' She held out her hand. 'The tide is on the ebb: I shall be there in no time.'

'Aye, but you'll be returning in the dark. Wait whilst I fetch my mantle: I'll come with you.'

'No. I don't want you to. I am quite capable of going alone.'

'I don't want you out after dark. There's a murderer on the loose out there, somewhere.'

'Do I look like a prostitute?'

'Of course not.'

'In which case I shall be perfectly safe since he only attacks women of that sort.'

'There is no certainty of that. You must not go unaccompanied, Em. I forbid it.'

She snorted in derision.

'*You* forbid it, husband? Oh, I quake in my shoes at the thought.'

'At least let young Tom go with you, so he may visit his sister. Here. Here's a shilling that you both may take a wherry. Please, Em, for my peace of mind, if naught else.'

'Oh, very well.' She snatched the coins and put them in her purse. 'Tom! Where are you? Hurry, else we'll miss the tide. We're going to Deptford.'

The Panyer Inn

JUDE SAT on the bench in the corner – his customary seat in the Panyer, nursing a cup of small ale. He had at least learned his lesson to some extent. He drank to drown his sorrows, as he had done ever since the trauma of Newgate, but no longer would he drink himself into oblivion. Not after what happened – or may not have happened – this last week past. He still did not know. Ragged shreds of images hung at the edges of his mind but he could not gather them into any semblance of a true picture, telling what had befallen him. If he was honest, he was afeared to try too hard, scared of what he might find, lurking in the dark recesses of his memory, if it did return.

He had killed before: once unintentionally, in a fit of rage, with his bare hands; once by design in cold blood, though in the latter case it had looked to be an accident. It had certainly done for that bloody deserving bastard of a gaoler. In both cases, he felt he had obliged the city with a service, but now... Drink could numb the senses but in this present situation, it couldn't erase the possibility of guilt.

There had been a woman. He could still hear the echo of her merry laughter; glimpse the haunting shadow of her smile. If he had ever known her name, that was now lost to him, but the scent of lavender upon her hair remained, tantalising. They had drunk too much; fucked too much. And now she was gone. When he closed his eyes, he saw the glint of a blade in the darkness. The distant sound of angelic plainsong chant, carried on the wind, lingered too. He was certain of those things without knowing how or why he knew. But in whose hand was the blade? His?

Whatever had come to pass, someone had put up quite a fight. He had bruises aplenty for which he couldn't account, including his split lip, a fading black eye and deep purplish bruising to his ribs in the shape of someone's boot. This last was tender still and he thought his ribs might have been cracked. Had he had the victory? It seemed unlikely but who was his unremembered assailant? And why the recurring vision of Satan, cloaked in black? Had the Devil been at his side, driving him to commit murder?

He sipped his ale. Afraid of the truth. A man alone.

The Foxleys' kitchen

TOM WAS bursting with excitement upon their belated return from Deptford.

'My sister was so pleased to see me, I mean Mistress Em and me, she baked a fine pie for our supper and little Janie so loved the doll mistress had made for her. My niece has grown since we saw her last. Toddling about. She makes me laugh. And the wherryman was quite a clown too – '

'Where have you been?' Seb asked his wife when he could fit a word in around Tom's enthusiastic report. 'I've been that concerned. 'Tis so late, I feared something dreadful had happened to you.'

'Well it hasn't so you can stop fretting, can't you? I told you where I was going. Bella cooked us a good supper, as Tom said, then Dick Langton escorted us back to the quayside and even paid the wherryman to row us back home. Here.' Emily threw six pennies into Seb's lap. 'Since I didn't have to pay, you'd best have that back to keep your precious accounts straight. And I hope you don't expect me to cook supper for you and Jack. I'm weary now and I'm going to bed.'

Seb shook his head.

'I bought something from the cookshop for Jack and me. No need to concern yourself for preparing a meal.'

'I wasn't going to.'

God be thanked, Seb prayed silently, that Em and Tom had returned safe from Deptford. He should never have allowed such a journey and he'd been sick with worry until well after curfew when she had breezed into the kitchen, flushed with triumph. He had a feeling she delayed their return purposefully, just to spite him and cause him so much anxiety. Now he lay abed upon an unforgiving pillow, torturing himself with fears of what might have been: the boat upturned, armed foot-pads lurking, losing their way in the unfamiliar streets of Deptford. He should have forbidden it but knew he never would.

Emily lay beside him, a hand's breadth away, but it might as well have been an abyss betwixt them for there was no way he could cross the divide. What had gone so wrong in their marriage? He was a good husband, wasn't he? And now she had given him three days to make an impossible choice: her? Or Jude? No man should be forced into a decision like that by his wife. A wife was supposed to obey her husband, wasn't she?

She snuffled and murmured in her sleep and he wanted to reach out, touch her skin. But he dared not. Why not? He was a fool. It was his right in the marriage bed. But words spoken on both sides had built a fortress wall to keep them apart. He loved her deeply but was no longer sure she felt the same towards him.

In fact, he was becoming convinced that she loved another – a possibility that tore at his soul.

'I love you, Em,' he whispered into the darkness of the chamber, 'And I always will, I swear.'

There was no reply. He didn't expect one. Just a small sound that may have been the wind betwixt the shutters. All was silent for a while.

'Have you decided then?' she asked, turning in the bed.

Seb could tell she had been crying from the quaver in her voice.

'How can I? You would have me tell my brother to leave but you know that cannot be. This house is his home and Jude is part owner of the business...'

'You could purchase his share from him. He's always in need of money.'

'The business is doing well enough but there isn't sufficient profit that I can afford that.'

'Then borrow it.'

'No, Em. You know my ruling on debt.'

'So break your foolish rule. You would, if you loved me.'

Again, silence hung heavy as the bed curtains that surrounded them in deep, miserable darkness.

'Then I shall take my case to the Court of Arches, have this wretched marriage annulled.'

'Why? Why are you so unhappy, Em? Anyhow, you can't have our union annulled: we are not related in cousinhood to the least degree and our marriage has been consummated, so you have no grounds.'

'Only you know that. It would be my word against yours. I shall claim to be a virgin still.'

'Don't be ridiculous, woman, of course you're not a virgin. You are making no sense.'

'How would they know, those celibate churchmen? I am most certainly not with child. I shall tell them you aren't capable...'

'You would humiliate me with such a lie? You'll be on oath before the court. You'd put your soul in jeopardy just to escape our marriage? Whatever have I done to make you hate me?'

Seb was half out of bed, sitting on the edge of the bed-frame, naked and without blankets, yet he didn't notice the cold.

'What happened to us, Em?'

'I used to love you. I thought you were special: kind, thoughtful, gentle. I believed you were different to other men but you're not.' Em was sobbing. 'I was wrong. You're just as selfish, uncaring and unmannerly as all the rest. What kind of husband lets his brother bully his wife? What sort of man loves his brother more than her?'

'I'm sorry. I cannot turn against my brother. He has been there for me, stood up to those who used to torment me. He's cared for me for my whole life. I owe him...'

'And you owe me nothing? I helped you save him from the hangman's noose not so long ago.'

'For which I shall be forever grateful.'

'Grateful? Is that the most you feel for me? Gratitude?'

'Of course not, Em. I love you. I've said so often enough, haven't I?'

'Then prove it. Tell your brother to leave.'

Seb fell back upon his pillow and dragged the blankets to him. He was shivering now. The argument had come full circle. And still there was no answer he could make.

Chapter 14

Sunday, the seventeenth day of November
St Michael's church

SEB'S UNQUIET mind was greatly in need of the solace
of prayer in a holy place. He rarely attended Low Mass
so early on a Sunday morn but he knew the congregation would
be few and, most likely, only Father Thomas would officiate.
Seb had no desire for another encounter with Father Weasel.
He entered the hallowed place, crossed himself with holy water
from the stoop and found a shadowed corner where he might
pray in peace.

Upon his knees on the ice-cold stones, he did his best but
endless Latin Paternosters weren't helping. So he spoke to the
Almighty in English, begging aid in his time of trouble. A
Lollard practice much frowned upon, he knew, and hoped the
Church would forgive him in his desperation.

Was it a coincidence that, when he opened his tear-filled
eyes, the aged wall painting above him seemed to shimmer and
change. Christ Jesu was in the Garden of Gethsemane, alone,
praying for aid from his heavenly Father, knowing he was about
to be betrayed by those who should have loved him. Was it Seb's
imagination or was his vision blurred by salt tears? For it seemed
the figure of Christ was looking down, gazing at him with the
compassion of one who understood his suffering so well. Then
he blinked and looked again at the faded image. As before, for

centuries, the kneeling Christ had his eyes upturned to heaven. But Seb felt stronger.

'Sebastian. Is all well with you? 'Tis unusual to see you here so early but I'm glad.' Father Thomas smiled sadly. 'I barely expect a handful of souls to attend divine office at such an hour, it seems an insult to God, and Churchwarden Marlowe – he of the powerful voice – is afflicted with a sore throat. Thus the responses will be thin indeed, such that even the Almighty may need his hearing trumpet. You can help me, Sebastian. I know you have a fine voice. You can stand by the rood screen and read from the missal, if you cannot recall the correct wording of the responses.'

'Of course, father, I shall be pleased to assist. I shan't need the missal: I know the words well enough.'

'Good. Then the Almighty shall not be insulted.'

'Will Father Hugh not object, though?'

The old priest pulled a wry face.

'Father Hugh is probably still abed beneath a purple canopy and silken sheets, sleeping off a surfeit of good wine and an over-generous supper with his uncle, the bishop. Forgive my interruption of your prayers, Sebastian. I must go prepare for the office.'

The Lollards' Tower

SINCE THEIR enforced incarceration meant they were together upon that Sunday morn, Gabriel and the other Known Men held their meeting much as ever, if earlier in the day, for no one was going to be required to attend Mass just to avoid a fine. Of course, there were none of their printed texts available to read from, but Gabriel's word-perfect memory supplied the lack.

He proclaimed the third, fourth and fifth chapters of St John's Gospel, pouring his heart into the telling of the Saviour's baptism and healing miracles. But most of all, bearing in mind that upon the morrow they would stand trial before the bishop, Gabriel stressed – and repeated – the eighteenth verse of the third chapter, to remind the Known Men that 'he that believeth in the Saviour shall not be condemned.' At least, not by any heavenly authority, whatever the bishop should decide.

With no need to hasten from the meeting, their deliberations and discussions could go on for as long as anyone had points to raise or comments to make. Their prayers could be made in full. Surprisingly, no one came to try to prevent them or silence their supplications to God. Gabriel found a strength and courage he hadn't known he possessed and wondered if his companions had too. Only the elderly woman seemed distressed and it was the matter of who would care for her young grandson that worried her, rather than any fear for herself.

'The Lord God will see that your lad is kept safe, sister,' Gabriel assured her, patting her wrinkled hand with its spattering of liver spots. He managed a smile for her a little more easily now his swollen mouth was mending. It still felt strange to be missing his crooked tooth.

'You're a kind man to reassure me, brother. I wish I had as much faith where the lad's mother is concerned. She's as foolish as a wet sheep and has no idea how to care for her own child.'

'His Father won't let him down.'

'Huh, his father – that wastrel son of mine – is too far gone in his drinking and dicing...'

'I meant his Heavenly Father,' Gabriel said.

'Ah. Of course you did.'

'That was quite a recitation you gave us,' Roger Underwood interrupted, pulling his red knitted cap lower over his ears to keep them warm in the icy chill of the heretics' prison. In truth, the owner of the Pewter Pot seemed hardly put out by imprisonment.

'The Lord's words, not mine, brother.'

'Mm, speaking of which, your brother – your brother by blood – seems not to have been taken with the rest of us. For which mercy, God be thanked, naturally.'

'Aye. I pray it is so; that he isn't under guard elsewhere, suffering alone. We at least have each other's support here.'

'I'm sure he's still free as the wind,' Underwood said, gesturing to the sky beyond the single window, 'Else we would have heard. Where could he hide, I wonder? Where would be safe? It would be as well to know, if any of us could manage to escape.'

'I don't know.' Gabriel frowned. 'I haven't given the matter much thought.'

'Doesn't every fellow behind a locked door think of little else but the possibility of escape?'

'May be so. I prefer to turn my thoughts to more reliable hopes.'

'I see,' Underwood said, sounding unconvinced. 'So you don't know where your brother might be?'

'No. And as for escaping this place, I shall put my trust in the Lord, as the Scriptures tell us.'

'I thought Scripture told us that 'God helps those who help themselves.'

'Does it? In which book?' Gabriel asked, trying to recall such a phrase from the years of his youth, spent copying out and learning by heart great biblical tracts – in Latin. Perhaps the words lost something in translation.

Underwood shrugged.

'No idea but it sounds well enough to me.'

St Michael's church

JUDE, NOT much of a one for regular church-going to the extent he had been fined more than once for the omission, nevertheless made the effort on this particular Sunday.

It was worth trying anything to keep the devilish waking nightmares at bay.

Why was he not surprised to find Seb already there, perched upon a column base, gazing at the wall?

'Why so early, little brother?' Jude tapped Seb's shoulder, making him jump, he had been so unaware. 'It seems we are first to arrive.'

'I needed to think. 'Tis quieter here than at home.'

'Away from that bloody wife of yours, you mean.' Jude wedged himself on the base of the column opposite.

Seb sighed. 'Aye, I suppose so. She has set me such a dilemma.'

'If I was you, I'd take a birch to her back, knock some sense into her.'

'I know you would and that be part of the problem.'

Jude was silent for a while, scratching his chin in thought.

'She wants me out, doesn't she? Expects you to tell me to leave.'

Seb looked up quickly from studying a broken fingernail.

'Did she tell you that?'

'Not in words, no. But in looks and actions, could there be any doubt? I'm right, aren't I?'

Seb nodded.

'Well, I might just oblige her,' Jude went on, 'I'm more fortunate than you, little brother, in that I'm not bound to the harridan by ties of marriage as you are. An hour or two in the scolds' pillory is what she needs. Teach her better bloody manners.'

Their conversation was cut short by the arrival of other members of the congregation. Dame Ellen and her fellow gossips had come to hear High Mass. Or, more likely, the latest city scandal.

'I heard about your journeyman, Sebastian,' Dame Ellen said, bustling over. 'I wouldn't have believed it of him. He seemed such a good Christian fellow, to be a heretic! There's just no telling these days, is there?'

'Gabriel has yet to stand trial, Dame Ellen. Thus far, he is accused but that in no way means he be guilty.'

'Oh. No. I suppose that's true.' The elderly woman looked much deflated. 'But what of this second murder, eh? Now some devil is certainly guilty of that and I'm sure I have a fair notion of just who that might be.' She tapped her forehead. 'It's all in here, Sebastian, I can tell you. Now where's Nell got to?' She turned away. 'Nell! Mary! I would know what news you have. Is the king still up to his tricks with the goldsmith's wife, eh?'

The office of High Mass began but Jude paid little heed. Dame Ellen's claim that she thought she knew the murderer was worrisome indeed. Yet how could she know? Had she seen something? More to the point: had she seen *him*? Bloody hell, what a mess was his pitiful life. Not knowing whether he'd committed a felony or no.

He was still racking his brain, trying to dig out memories that might not even be there, when the bell rang, signifying the moment of the Elevation of the Host. Jude stood by the centre aisle in the nave and had a good view of the altar through the rood screen, to see Father Wessell officiating. The priest had his back to the nave as he raised high the Host before the Cross. The weak winter sun, a pale beam of light through the east window, glinted on the priest's hands for an instant.

Jude gasped and fell back with a cry.

'Jude! Dear heaven! What be amiss?' Seb had near been knocked off his feet as Jude fell against him. 'Are you unwell?'

Jude clambered to his feet, groaning, mumbling to himself. He was paler than candle wax. Then, without explanation, he bolted from the church.

Seb left rather more discreetly but hastily, certain Jude was taken ill.

At first, he could see no sign of Jude. Only Old Symkyn squatting by the churchyard wall.

'Have you seen my brother?' Seb asked him.

'Aye,' Symkyn pointed back along Paternoster Row. 'Went home, I reckon. Ran like the Devil was at his heel. Looked like he'd seen him, too.'

Seb found Jude seated at the kitchen board, making rapid inroads on the ale jug.

'God be thanked, you're here. What happened Jude? Are you sick?'

Jude drained his cup and tried to refill it but his hands shook so he spilled the ale. Seb took the jug from him and poured ale for them both.

'Bloody Revelation,' Jude muttered.

'Revelation? What has that to do with aught?'

'I've seen the Beast. Never did make any sense when I had to copy the book out.'

'I don't understand. 'Tis you who are making no sense.'

'But then I saw it all, Seb. The Devil has been revealed to me. I remember.'

'What do you remember? Tell me.'

'He left me for dead. I was a witness and he thought to kill me too. I was so drunk, incapable of preventing it. I couldn't protect her, could I? Bloody useless... And now look. I'm doing it again!' Jude picked up his ale cup and threw it at the wall where it shattered, spilling ale everywhere.

Seb ignored the mess as his brother buried his head in his hands, sobbing. He had never seen Jude do that afore.

'Jude.' Seb embraced his brother. 'I'm sure all will be well. We'll put matters to rights, won't we? Together. The two of us. You're not alone in this, brother. You know I'll help; I'll always be at your side.'

'I saw who killed the woman at Bishopsgate, Seb.'

'Dear God in heaven. How fearful for you. Do you know his name?'

Jude nodded and turned to him, hiding his face against Seb's chest, like a child desperate for comfort, his tears soaking into Seb's doublet.

And, upon her return from church, that was how Emily found them.

'You finally told him then,' she said to Seb.

'Told him?'

'That he has to leave.'

'What? No. I've said naught of that. Now let us be, can't you? My brother is sore distressed.'

'Your damned brother!' With a cry that melded anger, frustration and distress of her own, Emily stalked out of the house.

'Who was it that you saw?' Seb asked, speaking gently.

'It is of no matter for now. You'd best go after her,' Jude said, making a visible effort to compose himself, drying his face on a napkin and trying to straighten the damp creases in Seb's doublet. 'Sorry. Seems I've spoiled your Sunday-best.'

'I'm tired of her tantrums, Jude,' Seb said, pushing himself up from the board with a sigh. 'She wears my patience so thin of late. 'Tis fast reaching a point where I'm not sure I care any longer.'

'You will care come dinner time, when we have to risk our bellies on the fare at the Panyer.' Jude forced a grin that was more of a grimace. 'Go on, fetch her back, little brother and, to make amends, tell her I shall be leaving, as soon as I find – '

'No, Jude. I will not have her send you from your home.'

'She isn't sending me; I'll go of my own free will. You know it makes bloody sense, Seb. This was never an ideal arrangement, was it? Now, go. Bring her home and let's have a decent dinner. I'm half-starved. I'll even sweep up the mess I made afore you get back.'

Dinner was a strange affair, indeed. Tom and Jack were mystified: Masters Seb and Jude and Mistress Em all smiling and laughing round the board. And yet it seemed that each played a part, a mountebank's pretence. None of them felt the joy they showed. Master Seb was thin-lipped, his jaw taut as hempen rope. Mistress's laughter sounded desperately close to weeping. Only Master Jude seemed somewhat at ease but he watched the other two as if fearful they might explode like ill-primed cannon.

Jack took solace in the diced pork with apples and chopped hazelnuts in a pastry coffin, served with onions, turnip-tops and sage, followed by apple dumplings with spiced honey.

Tom ate quietly, keeping his eyes upon his trencher, averted from the adults' faces that betrayed so much but explained so little.

As soon as the meal ended and Master Seb had given thanks to God in crisp, faultless Latin, the lads begged leave to escape.

'We c'n go drawin' stuff, master, couldn't we? Jack suggested.

'No, 'tis the Sabbath day,' Seb said.

'But drawin' ain't like workin', is it, Tom?'

At first, Tom made no reply, trying to think of some other reason for being elsewhere.

'We could go to St Lawrence by the Guildhall, look at that new wall-painting you told us about, master: the one you said was poorly done. We could study it so we know how *not* to paint images in future.'

Seb nodded, well aware how much the lads wished to be elsewhere.

'Very well but woebetide you if you make nuisances of yourselves for be sure I shall get to hear of it.'

'Aye, master,' they chorused, scampering off to fetch cloaks and hoods against the November chill.

'And do not be late back for vespers,' Seb called out as the door banged shut behind them. He eased back against the wall, savouring his ale and a moment of peace before Em began clattering empty pots and dirty platters, washing them in the cauldron of hot water that hung above the flames. 'I could fetch Nessie back to aid you,' he suggested.

'Or you could give a hand here, yourself.'

'Mm, I suppose. What has to be done?'

'You can put those pots to soak in that bucket of lye over there. The pewter dishes you can scour with sand to get them clean, thoroughly, mind, no bits to be left stuck upon them, else they'll discolour,' Em instructed. 'And when I've washed them, you can dry them, sand them again and buff them 'til they shine like silver.'

Seb grunted, having doubts as to whether he should do women's work or no, but put the pile of pots into the lye.

'Make certain the lye gets to every part.'

Seb looked at Jude who was still seated at the board, taking an overly long time about finishing his ale. The faces his brother was pulling, trying not to laugh out loud, proved how much he was enjoying his younger brother's efforts to play the kitchen wench.

'Mind you don't soil your apron,' he chuckled.

'Why don't you do something useful for once, brother?' Emily said, putting a sack of worts into Jude's lap, slamming a long-bladed knife and a large bowl of clean water on the board in front of him. 'You eat it, so you can help prepare it. Those worts need chopping and washing, ready for supper, so wipe that smirk off your face and get busy. No slugs. No bugs and no dirt. Understand?'

'Indeed, madam. Your every command shall be obeyed, your highness.'

Jude set aside the bulging sack and made a deep, mocking obeisance.

'Don't get clever with me, Jude Foxley, just get on with it.'

Emily had completed her task and gone up to their bed chamber for some purpose.

'No work upon the bloody Sabbath, eh, Seb?' Jude complained. 'How many damned worts can one household eat? Look at me: I'm turning green just thinking of it.'

Seb had barely started sanding and buffing the pewter.

'Well, I've worn away all my fingernails with this scouring sand and my hands are that sore. Shall we exchange tasks?'

Jude took one glance at Seb's red-raw fingertips and shook his head.

'Nah. I've nearly done here. I know more about knife work than I do about washing pots.'

'Aye. I never realised it was such hard work. Whatever Em says, I'm bringing Nessie home tomorrow, inept or not. I can't be doing this again. I doubt I'll be able to hold a quill for a week 'til my skin grows back.'

'Poor ol' Seb.' Jude ruffled his brother's hair with green-stained hands. 'I'm going to the Panyer. Coming?'

'I thought you were avoiding too much ale?'

Jude shrugged.

'Cutting down will suffice. Now, you coming or not?'

'How can I? I've still got three dishes and five bowls to polish. This is going to take me 'til supper time. It would be quicker if you helped.'

'Huh, not likely. I've done my appointed task for her highness. That's quite enough for me for one day; for a bloody lifetime come to that. Enjoy your labours, Hercules.'

The Panyer Inn

IT WAS a good deal later that Seb finally got to the tavern. He had certainly earned it: his fingertips would probably never be the same again.

'Come to make certain I'm not too drunk, have you?' Jude said as his brother sat beside him on a bench. 'This is but my second cup, I swear.'

'How much you drink is entirely your business. I came to discuss what we spoke of earlier.'

'About me getting out from under your wife's broom?'

'Perhaps, but I was more immediately concerned with what you were saying about seeing the Beast from Revelations. Just what did happen to you at Mass this morn, Jude?'

'It was naught. A momentary thing. 'Tis over and done.'

'No, it isn't. It troubles you still. Tell me. I want to know.'

Jude sighed and stared into his empty cup.

'I saw something, or rather, I *thought* I saw something. But it was just a trick of the light. Nothing at all. But it brought back memories. Or more likely, a bad dream. It wasn't real so can we talk no more of this?'

'I want to help you,' Seb said as Jude moved away along the bench. 'What was this trick of the light that brought back memories? Was it something you've remembered from those days when you were missing? It is, isn't it? What did you see?'

'I need another ale. You want one?'

'Aye. And I also want you to answer my questions.'

'You're a persistent bugger, aren't you, little brother?'

'When it's important, aye.'

'And what makes you think this is important?'

'Because you are not a man to become distraught over a bad dream, as you call it.'

'Distraught? You mistake me. I was no such thing.'

'I won't argue the case.'

A saucy tavern wench served them more ale. She was a favourite of Jude's yet he ignored her smile, the swing of her hips, even the knowing wink. Seb knew he was correct about this matter being important to his brother. Though Jude's bruises were beginning to fade, his worries were fresh as ever. It concerned Seb greatly that his fastidious brother of old was still unshaven and unkempt – clean linen had hardly improved his appearance.

'I was with a woman.' Jude spoke quietly, barely above a whisper. 'Don't ask me when for I cannot tell. I was too drunk. And so was she. She was a pretty thing with red hair, if my memory serves me at all. A whore, of course, but a sweet lass. Can't recall her name, if I ever knew it. It was getting dark, the city gate was about to close as we went out. She said she knew of a place where we could... do what you usually do with a whore.

'It was a cattle byre or some such and we were about to get busy and then... the world went mad. Something, someone dragged me off her. Like a fool, my first thought was that it must be her father. He yelled at us and screeched as he struck me in the face, kicked me and trampled on me. I was too drink-sodden to fight off this-this black demon that was attacking us. My senses were reeling but, afore I was lost in the void of nothingness, I saw the creature standing over her, his hands raised high. A shaft of moonlight – devil-light for all I know – glittered on something. A knife that he held? A ring on his finger, maybe? That's the last I saw. Or the last I remember seeing. I almost believed – for a while – that the raised hands, the knife... were mine. I truly feared I had run mad with drink and killed her.

'But during the Mass, when he raised the Host and the light glinted... It wasn't me, Seb; it was him.'

'The black demon.'

'No. Don't you understand what I'm saying? It was him: the bloody priest. He killed her.'

'Dear God, Jude. Be you certain?'

'Yes. No, not really. That's why I'm scared. I might have done it but I don't think I did. In that instant this morn, I *knew* he was guilty but now... I'm not so sure again. What am I going to do, Seb? What if I did do it?'

'You didn't. I suspect the woman may have been Beatrix Whitehead who, according to Rose, had hair as red as strawberries, and what rumour says was done to her couldn't be your doing... such terrible things.'

'You know that?'

'Of course. You're my brother and would never take a life.'

Jude looked away. If only Seb's faith was justified.

'We will prove it, you and I, together,' Seb was saying. 'Come. Let's drink to our success.'

Jude nodded and raised his cup as Seb insisted. But his doubts remained.

Their crime solving would have to wait.

The Foxleys' kitchen

THE HOUSEHOLD was still at supper in the kitchen, enjoying bowls of excellent pottage, when a clattering and crashing in the yard made everyone sit up.

'I'll go see,' Jack volunteered, 'Come on, Beggar.' The lad was gone before Seb could warn him to take care or make to follow.

Barking, squealing and shouting could be heard. Then all was quiet by the time Seb had reached the door.

'A stray pig, it wos, a huge hog,' Jack announced, holding his arms wide to show how enormous had been their adversary and flushed with success, 'But Beggar seed 'im off, didn't yer, lad? Chased 'im well away.' He roughed up the little dog's fur and held him close 'til the animal squirmed.

'Saw, Jack,' Seb corrected out of habit, 'Beggar "saw" him off. There is no such word as "seed".'

'Yes, there is: we sowed seed last spring fer worts in Mistress Em's garden, didn't we?'

'The lad's got you there, Seb,' Jude laughed.

Seb swallowed another spoonful of pottage before answering.

'That "seed" is a noun. The past tense of the verb "to see" is "saw". If you see something on a past occasion, then you saw it.'

'Why is it? If I *be* good this day, then I must'a *bore* good yesterday, an' I know that ain't right. Boar's a wild pig.'

'God give me strength,' Seb complained, 'If I wanted to be a pedagogue, I would have set up school. It's just the way it works, Jack. Now finish your supper.'

'Finished it hours ago, didn't I?'

'Don't exaggerate, lad.'

'I never zaggerate. Wotever it is.'

'I think, husband, that you should have got that gate latch mended afore now,' said Emily, 'Then you could avoid such meaningless discussion.'

'Aye. I cede you the point on that, Em.'

'There!' Jack yelled, gloating in triumph, 'Master said "seed". I knowed it wos a word.'

Seb sat, shaking his head at his unfortunate choice of word but everyone else was laughing. It hadn't happened in the Foxley household for a long while and it felt good.

Later, after Tom and Jack were abed, Seb and Jude retired to the parlour while Emily disappeared for a while. Probably scouring the supper dishes – something the brothers would assiduous avoid, if they could. But when Jude returned to the kitchen to refill the ale jug, the pots were still soaking in the bucket and there was no sign of Emily.

Back in the parlour, Seb was about to broach the matter of Gabriel's trial upon the morrow when a whisper of cloth caught Jude's attention as he sat facing the parlour door.

Jude whistled.

'Well! That's quite a sight,' he said.

Seb turned to look.

Emily stood in the doorway, framed by candlelight, wearing her new rose-coloured gown.

'What do you think?' she asked, spreading her skirts and turning on the spot.

'A bloody duchess at the very least,' Jude said. 'What's it for? You planning to be the king's next mistress? I hear he has a preference for citizens' wives.'

'Take no notice, Em,' Seb said, finding his voice at last, 'You look astoundingly beautiful. You outshine the stars.'

'Quite the poet, aren't you, little brother. What did you do: rob the Lombards? How else can you afford this?'

'Em is worth every penny,' Seb said, on his knees like a lady's maid, arranging the hem to best effect.

Jude snorted.

'I can think of more important things to spend a small fortune on than a gown you dare not wear outside these walls. The workshop could do with more storage shelves and a new stitching block would help.'

'Just this once, Jude, I admit to being frivolous with our money,' Seb said, 'Just once. And if it gives pleasure to my wife, well and good. I shall forego the new hose and hood that I promised myself to compensate, in part, at least.'

'Well, thank you, husband. 'Tis a wondrous gift. I shall treasure it, even if I may not wear it.' Emily gave Seb a resounding kiss upon the lips. 'And also...' she hesitated, 'In truth, I have been unfair to you of late and am sorry for it. I'm also grateful to you, both of you, for your help in the kitchen. 'Tis not men's work, I know, but you made a fair job of your tasks.'

She gave Jude a kiss which was more of a vague brush of his stubbled cheek but a sign of her deep apology. 'You be in need of a visit to the barber, brother,' she added, ensuring Jude knew he was not utterly returned to her favour. 'Now I must change out of my finery: there are tasks to be done, so that I am at liberty to attend the trial tomorrow.'

'You won't let her be there, will you?' Jude asked, putting another log upon the fire, for the night had indeed grown chill.

'And if I forbade it? You know Em: she would attend despite me and make of it yet another cause for dissent betwixt us. I shall most certainly attempt to discourage her but I don't see how I may prevent it without tying her to the chair and barring the doors from without, do you?'

Jude made a wry face as he pulled his stool closer to the hearth.

'Probably not but she won't understand a word of the proceedings, being all in Latin. Why is she so keen to attend, do you know?'

'She has a soft spot for Gabriel, I think.'

'Mm, I wonder what it is about him that has women drawn to him like iron to a lodestone? Even Nessie, who used to love me like a newborn now dotes upon him. Do you see the size of bloody helpings she gives him at dinner? I used to be her favourite. Not that I'm complaining: I prefer the silly wench's affections to be elsewhere, but I just don't see what is so damned special about Gabe.'

'Not jealous, are you, Jude?' Seb warmed his hands before the blaze.

Jude just laughed. Ridiculous question.

'Seb, take care if you go out to the yard, the flagstones are already slick with frost. 'Tis colder than a hermit's bed out there.' Emily fetched her sewing basket, even though it was a Sunday.

Seb moved a second stool beside the fire for her, setting a cushion upon it.

'D-do you think I should continue to sew the large rag doll you wanted? I know not what purpose you think it will serve but...'

'Aye, lass,' Seb replied, 'It would be as well to have it ready in case 'tis needed.'

'I cannot see what use it could be.'

'I dare say my brother has some outlandish bloody scheme in that otherwise empty pate of his. 'Less its sole use be as somewhere to keep his cap. What say you, Seb? Are you going to reveal to us humble folk the mighty plan you have in mind to save Gabe?'

'I pray it will not come to that. Even if found guilty – which would be a nonsense – most likely it will mean a hefty fine, seeing the Church loves money even more than souls. Either that or a brief imprisonment and severe penance.' Seb looked at Em, stitching away at a seam in the linen. 'Whatever befalls, I would prefer that you not be there upon the morrow, Em; a court is no place for a woman.'

He couldn't have worded his plea more poorly.

Emily looked up, eyebrows raised.

'No place for a woman? Why ever not? A woman has as much right as any man, if the accused be a member of the household. Of course, I shall be there. Gabriel will need to know he has the support of us all.'

'But there ought to be someone in the shop to attend to customers.'

'Tom is capable enough for an hour or two.'

'It will all be in Latin, anyway.'

'Then you can explain it to me. You may as well cease trying to dissuade me, husband. I shall attend and there's an end to it. Now, pass me my snips, if you please.'

Chapter 15

Monday, the eighteenth day of November
St Paul's Cathedral

IT WAS just such a morn, when cobwebs hung with crystal and even rotting dung heaps were disguised in virgin white, that Seb would have been enraptured by its beauty. But not this day. The Bishop of London's court was convened in the nave of the huge minster. Five Lollard heretics – calling themselves Known Men – were to stand trial. Gabriel Widowson was one of them.

There was a large eager crowd of on-lookers, citizens gathered to witness this rare event. The heavy frost might have glazed the cobbles of St Paul's Yard but the chill had not deterred the spectators. Now their wintry breaths issued forth from betwixt woollen hoods, thick cloaks and muffled chins, making little clouds of fog in the nave.

Seb and Jude came to give their friend and journeyman moral support. Seb had done his utmost to persuade Emily to stay at home, telling her the proceedings would be mostly in Latin so she wouldn't understand what was being said anyway. But she was determined all the same, disregarding his pleas that it would be too distressing if, by some grave miscarriage of justice, Gabriel was found guilty.

Seb had been through the like before, more than a year since, when Jude had been wrongly accused of murder and, in truth, had no wish to repeat the experience. He also wondered at Jude's own courage in attending the trial – what horrific memories it might resurrect for him.

The early sun streamed through the great east window, casting jewels of coloured light upon the black and white tiled floor. Christ in Judgement gazed from the glass upon the bishop's opulent procession, led up the northern aisle by a gleaming golden crucifix, studded with gemstones. If the bishop meant to impress, he succeeded, his cope and mitre weighted with gold and silver embroidery and decorated with still more precious stones and pearls.

Seb wondered, briefly, whether the Lord Christ was similarly influenced. He hoped not. Surely, the Ultimate Judge would be impartial, persuaded only by the innocence – or guilt – concealed within a man's soul and visible to His eyes alone.

The crowd, noisy with anticipation, fell quiet as the bishop's bailiff called for order. Two dogs, spoiling for a fight beside the font, were kicked into silence. The bishop, seated upon his carven cathedra, indicated to an acolyte that a brazier basket be moved closer by his feet for his greater comfort before the five prisoners were brought in.

An elderly woman was wrapped in a threadbare blanket but all four men were in their shirts and hose alone and looked to be perishing of the cold as they were lined up across the nave before the bishop. Gabriel stood at the midst of the line, upright and unbowed despite the occasional shiver that shook his frame. His hands were tied behind him, as was the case with his fellows. Only the woman had her hands free to clutch the blanket about her.

At a nod from the bishop, Dean Wynterbourne conducted an interminable litany of Latin prayers, mostly listing the torments in store for all sinners and then beseeching God to look upon the fallen with mercy, provided that fully repent of their heresies.

Seb watched the bishop's face above its many chins and saw that the man was impatient of so much preamble. In fact, just as the dean drew breath to begin another Latin recital, Bishop Kemp spoke out loudly.

'Now you are made aware of what awaits all those of an heretical turn of mind in the life to come, does any one of you wish to admit your great sin? Here is your chance to recant, to renounce your errors. Well?'

With little hesitation, a man in a knitted cap stepped forward. Seb recognised him as the fellow who ran the Pewter Pot tavern, Rose's employer: Master Roger Underwood.

'I freely admit my gross error, your grace. I fear I was led so far astray as to follow this abomination of falsehood. But I now see how wrong I was to give credence to anything other than the true teachings of Holy Church.'

'As do I,' said another of the prisoners.

Seb did not recognise him.

With a look of sadness, the lone woman turned to Gabriel who gave her the smallest of nods.

'I too recant my past beliefs.' She spoke so quietly, few could have heard.

'Speak up!' demanded the bishop, forcing her to repeat her words.

Tears poured down her old cheeks:

'I too recant,' she sobbed.

'Take them away. I will deal with them later,' said Kemp, turning his attention to the two remaining prisoners. He beckoned to the bailiff and a few words were exchanged. 'So, you two prefer to cling to your devil-damned heresies then, or will you also see sense? No? Ah, well, in which case...' the bishop raised his voice:

'Gabriel Widowson and Michael Fisher, you stand accused of gross acts of heresy on numerous counts. Of causing to be written, imported and distributed scriptural texts, in English, as forbidden by Holy Church. That you did read aloud the aforesaid forbidden texts to others, in order to mislead and misinform them of the teachings of Holy Church, against the rule of his Holiness the Pope as God's intermediary on earth. That you did usurp the office of Christian priesthood to lead astray from the path of righteousness those of simple faith whom you could influence. '

Seb saw the man, Fisher, shrink before the bishop's recitation of their crimes. But Gabriel did not flinch. Why should he when none of it was true? Even so, it was admirable that he could remain so calm in the face of these many false accusations, such that Seb wanted to cry out on his friend's behalf against the unwarranted slanders.

Thus far, the case had been conducted in English for the benefit of the crowd.

'Do you still wish to maintain your heresy?' the bishop asked.

'Why does Gabriel not speak out?' Emily asked Seb and Jude. Jude shrugged.

'I suppose he regards the accusations as so utterly absurd that they deserve not the effort of making reply,' Seb answered, although, in truth, he was as puzzled as Em.

Fisher was weeping openly, sniffing back the tears, attempting to wipe them away on the shoulder of his shirt, his hands being tied. For a moment, it seemed as though he too would recant but Seb saw Gabriel turn to the fellow, whispering a few words.

'Silence!' bellowed Kemp, but Fisher seemed to compose himself, strengthened by whatever Gabriel had said to him.

The case then proceeded in Latin. Although few in the assembly could understand what was said, other than clerics and some of them knew little enough of the tongue, no one left the nave. All wanted to know the outcome.

'This is not going well,' Jude muttered.

'Is it too late for Gabe to speak out?' Seb wondered aloud.

'What are they saying,' asked Em.

'Shh.'

At length, the bishop conferred with Dean Wynterbourne and two other clerics. Their grey tonsures nodded together, burdened with wisdom and responsibility, until they broke from their deliberations.

One cleric had a worried expression but the other, along with the bishop and the dean, looked well satisfied with their decisions, whatever they were.

'Michael Fisher, step forward to receive sentence,' instructed the dean.

'You!' Kemp pierced the air with a fat finger, 'Have been found guilty of the charge of heresy. You will be fined one hundred marks...'

The crowd gasped at such a sum.

'And imprisoned until it be paid, after which you shall be banished from this city for life. Then someone else can deal with you, if you persist in your erroneous ways. Take him out.'

'Gabriel Widowson, step forward to receive sentence.'

'You are guilty of heresy to its utmost extreme,' Kemp snarled, his voice jagged with rage and vindictiveness.

This all seemed very personal, Seb thought, and wondered what reason the bishop could possibly have for loathing Gabriel so.

'You have been indoctrinating Christian souls with your satanic corruption and filth,' the bishop cried, spraying spittle, 'Of dragging innocents to the pit of eternal damnation along with you. You are an abomination, unfit to soil this sacred place. There is only one means of destroying your sin and cleansing the world of this contemptible perversion, so abhorrent to Almighty God. Sentence is given that the law *De heretico comburendo* is to be implemented in your case. Sentence shall be carried out three days hence at Smithfield and may the Lord Christ have mercy on your worthless soul, for I shall have none.'

A shudder rippled through the crowd, whether they knew Latin or not.

'What does that mean?' Emily asked, her voice trembling.

'Gabriel has been found guilty,' Seb whispered.

'It means he's condemned to death by burning at the stake,' Jude said.

'Jude.' Seb had wanted to tell Em the awful truth in more gentle fashion, if such was possible. Of course, there was no kindly way to say it but Jude should not have been so brutal, so plain speaking.

Em's face was the colour of death. Too shocked even for tears.

Seb made no attempt to stop her as she forced her way through to the front of the crowd. As the guards led Gabriel away, she cried out:

'I love you, Gabriel!'

He looked back. Their eyes met and he smiled his sad, lopsided smile and shook his head, just once, saying nothing.

Jude and Seb exchanged glances.

Seb's mouth was agape in bewilderment. He must have misheard. His mind was reeling from the double shock. Gabe condemned? Em in love with him? How? When?

Jude took a firm grip on his arm.

'Steady, little brother,' was all he said but Seb understood enough. Now was not the time.

'You still think he's worth risking our necks to save him from the flames?' Jude asked. The crowd was departing from St Paul's. News of the bishop's chosen punishment for the Foxleys' journeyman would soon wing its way into every part of the city, from rotting lodging houses to royal palaces, from quiet cloisters to raucous taverns. Everyone would know. Their reputation would be deep in the mire, as far beyond saving as Gabriel's flesh and bones.

Seb felt sick at heart on both counts. And worse yet, it seemed his wife loved another but a debt was still a debt.

'Gabriel saved my life not so long ago. I said I owed him. I cannot renege upon that.'

'Despite what Em said just now?'

'Aye. I heard her words to him but... I suppose she thought they would give him solace, comfort him at a time when he be in sorest need.'

'You don't believe that no more than I do. They're lovers, you bloody fool.'

'Where is the evidence for that?' Seb demanded, turning on Jude. 'You be as eager to condemn as the bishop. I will not listen to your nonsense. Gabriel is innocent and I would set him free and save our reputation.'

'If I were you, I'd let the bugger burn but I'm in agreement with rescuing our good name, if such is possible.'

'I have a plan of sorts. It may result in our name being somewhat tarnished but by no means so infamous as it would be, if one of our household goes to the fire. In which case, we all must work together, Em as well. Where is she? I lost sight of her in the crowd.'

'Does she have to be involved? Women always bloody complicate matters – as already proven this day.'

'She must finish stitching the doll; the manikin.'

'Why? A child's toy?'

'Because, Jude, we will need a dead body to bury.'

Jude laughed, though there was no humour in it.

'Dear God. You don't expect anyone to be fooled by a doll being tied to the stake in place of a living, breathing man? Even you're not so stupid as that.'

'If my plan works, things will not go so far as the stake. Now, please, help me find Em. She must be distraught.'

The Foxleys' kitchen

'YOUR GOODWIFE needs to rest, master,' Surgeon Dagvyle was saying over a cup of wine, 'I've given her a sleeping draught that should keep her abed for the rest of the day. Too much upset has put her humours badly out of balance. I've bled her which should help settle her. Does anyone else here need my attention? Your recent shock could affect you all.'

'No, thank you. I believe the rest of us have come through, shaken indeed but not overwrought. But there is another matter.' Seb took the surgeon a little aside. 'You may recall my visit to you upon Friday last, when you examined the rash on my apprentice's arm?'

'I have not forgotten,' Dagvyle said, scowling at the memory of being professionally deceived, however momentarily.

'How much would you charge me, if I asked that you diagnose a somewhat similar rash as a symptom of plague?'

'Impossible. You would have me look a fool.'

'How much?' Seb repeated, weighing a leather purse in his hands, chinking the coins within.'

When the surgeon departed, the purse was a deal lighter.

'What did you pay him?' Jude asked, taking the purse to test its weight himself.

'Four pence ha'penny for Em's treatment.' Seb sighed as Jude raised a questioning eyebrow. 'And three marks for his aiding our plan.'

'That's two pounds sterling: are you quite mad, little brother?'

'I know. It leaves a great hole in our savings, but...'

'Is Gabe bloody worth it?'

'He *and* our good name, remember. I pray so. And it will probably cost as much again afore we be done.'

'Master Seb,' Jack interrupted their conversation, tugging at Seb's doublet and looking sorrowful indeed.

'Aye, Jack, what is it?'

'When's it gonna be dinner time, master? Me an' Beggar is starvin' t' death, ain't we?'

'Food! Is that all you can think of at such a time: your belly? Your mistress is sick and a man's life hangs in the balance and you demand dinner! There be far more important things. I have no patience with you, Jack.'

231

'Eatin' is important,' the lad moaned, pouting. 'Tom's 'ungry too, ain't yer?'

Tom shrugged, then nodded.

'I'll take 'em to the Panyer; food's not usually too bad there of a Monday. At least, it won't be stockfish,' Jude said.

'Jude. Could you fetch something back for me too, please? I daren't leave Em here alone. And, one other thing – another favour, if you will – '

Jude sighed. What was he, a damned errand boy?

'Go to Dame Ellen's place and tell Nessie to come home. At least we may get some supper, if you do.'

• •

That afternoon, Seb was busy at his desk in the workshop. The remains of a boiled pig's trotter in gravy sat in a bowl by his elbow. Jude, too, was at his desk but no work was being done. Seb was too preoccupied to allocate jobs to Tom and Jack and Jude was content to watch, intrigued by what his brother was doing. Meanwhile, work of some sort was going on in the kitchen: the sound of Nessie clattering and rattling pots implied that supper might be forthcoming, eventually, in some form or other. The lads were hopeful.

'What are you doing?' Jude's curiosity got the better of him as Seb held an empty copper pot over a tallow candle, filling the workshop with the stink of pig fat and heated metal. Then he began scraping soot from the bottom of the pot into an oyster shell. 'You could buy lamp-black from the apothecary, if you need it.'

'Better not to involve anyone else in the plan, unless I have to,' Seb muttered, 'Too many are involved already.'

'So how does lamp-black fit into your wondrous bloody plan?'

'Plague.'

'What? How so?'

'Lamp-black and terra rosa mixed in the correct proportions make a reasonable semblance of the tokens of plague – at a glance, at least. Surgeon Dagvyle said it looked most like the fearful spots but the edges must be smudged, not clear defined. I've found a thumbprint of pigment works well. What do you think?' Seb held out his left hand for Jude's inspection. Upon the back of it were three purplish-black marks, like deep bruises.'

'How can I tell? Mercifully, I've never seen a bloody plague token.'

'That be the point, Jude. I'm trusting to fortune that no one within the Lollards' Tower has seen them either. I just need to know that they would make you wary, have you keep your distance.'

'Aye, they would, if they weren't just painted on.'

'But no one but us and Gabriel will know that.'

'Mm.' Jude began to understand at least part of Seb's idea. 'And how will Gabe even learn of your plan, never mind his part in it?'

'I have written the instructions for him.' Seb handed Jude a neatly written paper. 'Read it through, if you will, see that I have explained matters clearly for him, since he will have no opportunity to ask questions.'

Jude read the letter – twice.

'So, in short, he daubs himself with pigment spots and swallows Dagvyle's prescription that will make him sweat. Then, after Dagvyle is summoned to attend him – how can we be certain they won't have some other surgeon?'

'Because Dagvyle will be there already upon some pretext of his own devising. I have paid him for his service, as you know.'

Jude nodded uncertainly.

'Then Gabriel swallows the sleeping draught to assist him in playing dead: a state that Dagvyle will confirm. Is that it? Your entire plan?'

'The first part. Aye.'

'You know it's going to fall at the first obstacle, don't you? Any letter sent to a prisoner will be read before he gets it. Gabe is never going to receive his bloody instructions or, if he does, it will be so they can catch us all in the act, since they will know everything.'

'Ah, which brings us to Jack's contribution,' Seb said, grinning.'

'Me, master?' Jack skipped across the workshop, tired of doodling in the sand tray, making out he was practising his letter shapes. 'Wot's my conterbition, then? Will I get supper, still?'

'You will, lad, but on the morrow, afore dawn, you will need to be up and ready. You must be nimble as a squirrel, slicker and more silent than a stoat. Can you do that?'

'Aye, master, course I can.' Jack was bouncing with excitement. 'And Beggar'll be ready too, won't you, lad?'

'Sorry, Jack. There is no place for a dog in this enterprise.'

'But Beggar's good at empty-prizes.'

'Not this time. Remember, Master Gabriel's life depends upon us. Besides, I never saw a dog as could climb, did you?'

'You want me t' climb? I can do that. Sorry, Beggar. You c'n lie late abed t'morrow but I'll tell yer all about it, after, I promise.'

'Afore that, though, you can rummage through the sack of shells you fetched back from Billingsgate. Find two identical limpet shells with smooth rims.'

'Dentackle?'

'Exactly the same size and shape, so they may fit together. Tom, warm some of our best rabbit-skin glue for me, just a little will suffice.'

'Nessie,' Seb called as he went through to the kitchen. The wench was tipping sliced leeks and diced bacon into the pottage pot that hung above the fire. 'Smells good,' he added.

'What did you want, master?'

'The sweating remedy Surgeon Dagvyle prescribed for me when it was thought I'd suffered a seizure: where is it?'

'In mistress's medicine chest. I'll get it for you. Are you sick again, master?'

'Not at all. And that notorious potion of yours, Nessie. Where do you keep it?'

The maid wiped her hands on her apron but hung her head, saying nothing.

'Come, now. This be not the time to pretend you know naught of it. If you want to assist in rescuing Master Gabriel... You know he be imprisoned?'

'Oh, aye, I do, and I soo want to help him. He's soo fine an' he loves me true, I know he does.' She reached up and took the little black vial from behind the dented pot upon the shelf. 'Not much left now.'

'How much is needed to render a man senseless for three, maybe four, hours?' Seb took the little flask and unstoppered it. It was difficult to tell how much remained. He tipped it, holding it to the light. The dark liquid glinted. There was enough, he hoped.

'Three drops should do, I s'pose.'

'Be you certain? How much did you put in my ale that day?'

Nessie shrugged.

'Don't know. It just poured out; more than I meant.'

'Four drops, then? More?'

'P'raps.'

He could ask Surgeon Dagvyle but then even he would not know how potent it might be, or not. It was a risk they would have to take and, God willing, he would guess the dose correctly. If not, the man's life was forfeit anyway and for the sleep of death to come peacefully upon him by such means was surely better than death by fire? Too much would be more welcome than too little. All of it, then. So be it.'

In the workshop, Seb was making up what he hoped would be a life-saving package, Gabriel's passage to freedom. He wrapped both the potion to cause sweating and the black vial in scraps of leather. Then a pair of limpet shells, fixed together with rabbit-skin glue, held the special pigment he had contrived, then they were folded within a square of waxed linen. Together with his letter of instruction, he put the items carefully into a small leather purse. Finally, he attached a length of strong cord to the purse, long enough to go around Jack's neck and under one arm. The lad would wear it 'neath his shirt, so it was out of sight and would not hinder his climbing.

'Dear Lord Christ, I beseech thee to let these things do their work in order that thy faithful servant, Gabriel, be safe delivered from his undeserved imprisonment and unwarranted and untimely death. In the name of the Blessed Trinity, I ask this. Amen.' Seb made the sign of the Cross.

Jude was watching.

'I suppose it can't hurt to have the Almighty on our side, can it?' Jude said. 'There's little enough hope of bloody success for such a wild plan otherwise.'

'You don't think we have much chance, then?'

'Do you? Honestly?'

Seb remained silent which was answer enough. There were too many crucial details that were going to rely upon good fortune.

'Em? Be you awake?' Seb held high the candle to illumine his wife's face as she lay abed. It was after supper and the chamber in darkness. She stirred beneath the coverlet. 'Do not feign sleep, Em: you have work to do, if we are to save Gabriel.'

She lifted her head, drowsily. The sleeping draught had but lately worn off.

Seb refused to see her eyes, swollen and red-rimmed from weeping for another man. He threw the half-stitched linen manikin upon the bed.

'It will be needed upon Wednesday eve. Nessie is bringing your sewing basket and another taper. The pair of you can work on it here.' He almost added 'to save the man you love', but managed to hold his tongue. 'Get it done.' His tone was terse and he did not wait for his wife's response – if she made one.

Emily was not pleased to learn in such a fashion that Nessie had returned without so much consultation as a by-your-leave. Seb had overstepped the mark this time. There would be words betwixt them, again. Why had he brought the foolish wench back? Without her permission! He had no right to undermine her authority in this way. But she would set that matter aside for now. Her wretched husband was right on one score: saving Gabriel was more important.

Nessie came in with the sewing basket and an extra candle and plumped herself down upon the bed.

'What we doing, mistress?' she asked. As if there had never been anything but amity between them.

Emily swallowed her anger, telling herself this was for Gabriel's sake.

'You can fetch me some ale, then I'll instruct you.'

'Aye, mistress. I don't know why everyone is so sour-humoured,' she muttered to herself.

'And don't think I've forgiven you your crimes nor your stupidity, because I haven't!' Emily called out as Nessie went back downstairs to the kitchen. It was easier not to say it to her face and those doleful eyes, so ready with their false tears.

Later, the two women sat stitching on the bed, both cross-legged like tailors. Emily wore her night robe but Nessie was fully dressed. Emily was sewing around the doll's head while Nessie plied her needle to its left foot.

'How's this going to help Master Gabe?' Nessie asked, sniffing back tears.

'I don't know,' Em admitted. 'I'm not privy to their plans. In truth, I don't see what use a doll, however large, can be?'

'Is it s'posed to look like Master Gabe? They could leave it in prison in his place, couldn't they?'

'Don't be absurd. Even you couldn't be fooled into thinking this was a real man, not for one moment.'

'No, mistress, but s'posing it was wrapped in a blanket in a bed, then it might pass for a man asleep, mightn't it?'

Emily thought about it. Nessie had a valid point but she wasn't going to admit that.

'Only an idiot would be convinced. You think the bishop could be that stupid?'

'Well not him, o' course, but his guards might be.'

Emily continued stitching at a furious pace. Was that what Seb had in mind, the witless oaf? But she was intrigued nonetheless.

Nessie had pricked herself with the needle so many times and both women were weary and yawning but the manikin was finished, all but the back opening where it would be stuffed. St Paul's bell rang for matins. It was after the midnight hour.

Emily went to the window and opened the shutter. Roofs glittered with frost in the faint starlight, the moon, just passed full, had not yet risen. Somewhere in the city a dog barked, answered by another. A door banged. A baby wailed closer at hand and, in the darkness, a woman's laughter rang shrill. The sounds of the city at night. Like a wary beast, it was never quite deep in slumber.

'Have we done, mistress? I'm falling asleep as I sit?'

Emily picked up the empty linen shape and shook it out. It was well made but looked sad: a skin without substance; a body without a soul.

'Aye. The candles are near burned down anyway. Get to your bed now.'

'We will save Master Gabe, won't we mistress?'

'I'm sure we will, Nessie. No doubt, Master Seb has everything planned out.' Emily surprised herself: her voice sounded so confident. It was a pity neither her head nor her heart felt likewise.

The house fell quiet. Jude and the lads slept in their beds. Nessie curled up on her pallet beside the kitchen hearth and was soon snoring softly. Emily lay awake in her lonely bed until the after-effects of the sleeping potion reasserted themselves.

Seb sat downstairs in the parlour, staring into the embers of the fading fire. It was growing cold and he reached for his mantle and huddled into it. There was no point in seeking his bed. Sleep would not come this night, he knew. He had too many worries and doubts churning inside. Not least of which were the questions about Em and Gabe.

Did she truly love him, or were they just empty words, spoken in the moment when horror struck? Had they been lovers? Had he been cuckolded under his own roof, in this very house? Had Emily betrayed him? And Gabriel too? He couldn't believe it. These people were precious to him. They wouldn't be so cruel, so heartless. Would they?

As the night hours crawled by, Seb's thoughts grew blacker and more despairing. It could not be so. They could not break his trust in so callous a manner. Yet he feared, more and more as approaching dawn summoned the cocks to crow, that it just might be that they had.

But he must set such matters aside for the present. It was time to rouse young Jack afore it was light.

Chapter 16

Tuesday, the nineteenth day of November
St Paul's Yard

DAWN WAS no more than a pale brush stroke in the sky downriver when Seb and Jack made their way with utmost caution across the frosted cobbles of Paul's Yard. The Lollards' Tower rose, threatening and ghostlike, in the silvered light of the moon. Seb would have accounted it beautiful, the moonlight glistening upon the ancient stones, if he had not been preoccupied with so many matters of greater import.

'Which windah, master? Where d'yer want me t' climb?' Jack whispered.

Seb pointed upwards at a darker shape within the shadows of the grey stone.

'That one. I believe that be the room where they kept me that day. One of the window bars be bent, sufficient that one so slight as you should be able to squeeze through.'

'And Master Gabe will be there?'

Seb sighed, puffing a fog of breath into the icy air. This was one of the too numerous points at which his plan might fail.

'In truth, lad, I know not but, as a condemned heretic, I think it likely he will be imprisoned alone, for fear he may infect others with his misconceptions.'

'Miscon...'

'Never mind. My fear is that, if there be someone else imprisoned in that room, the door will be barred from without.

In which case, our cause may be lost afore it begins since you will not be able to search for Gabriel.'

'Don't worry, master, I'll find 'im,' Jack said with the optimism of youth.

'I know you'll do your best. Have you got the purse?'

'Aye, master.'

'Then God be with you, Jack, and see you safe. Go now, afore it gets too light.'

'I'm on'y climbin' a wall, not sailin' t' France.' Jack grinned impishly, his teeth showing white in the gloom.

Seb smiled back, wishing he had as much confidence, and patted the lad's shoulder.

'Up you go, then.'

He watched as the lad climbed, hand over hand, one step after another, from a jutted stone to a clump of ivy to an unevenness in the mortar betwixt the blocks. Further than that, it was too dark to make out what precarious hand- and foot-holds Jack was clinging to. As he reached the embrasure, he seemed to hesitate. Perhaps the gap betwixt the bars was too small. Seb held his breath. But then the little distant figure was gone, disappearing inside the tower. Now Seb could only wait, hope and fret.

• •

It was even darker in the room where the moonlight could not reach. Jack had to wait until his eyes became accustomed but he used his ears, his nose and every other sense instead. The place felt empty: no body warmth nor snuffle of breath. Not a fart nor a rustle of straw. No smell of sweat or body stink. He could now make out the door, just. His past skills as a thief now served him well. He moved to the door but indirectly, tip-toeing around the edge of the room, where the floorboards were less likely to creak and betray him. As there was no prisoner here, Jack was unsurprised to find the door hadn't been barred outside. Master Seb need not have feared. He looked out through a hole cut in the door so the turnkeys could espy the prisoners. Beyond the door, nothing stirred.

The door opened onto a spiral stair, lit by a torch in a cresset. Up or down? Jack considered for a moment. Up. He crept upwards, his heart hammering so loud in his skinny chest that he feared someone might hear it. As he reached the next landing with another door, there came a sudden noise. Jack stifled a gasp. It was only a rat, scurrying about his private business as dawn neared.

Peering through the hole in this second door, he could hear movement, the grunts and snores of sleepers, see the moist clouds of their breath. Master had said he thought it likely that Gabe would be imprisoned alone, so he probably wasn't in there. Silent as a moth, Jack went up another stair, sensing that this must likely be the last, that the tower went no higher. Again, he stretched up to see into the room through the turnkey's spy-hole. This time, he could hear a man's voice, speaking so soft and low. It sounded like praying but in English. He knew he'd found Master Gabe.

Quietly, he lifted away the heavy oaken timber from its rests on either side of the jamb and opened the door just the width of a hand.

'Master Gabe,' he whispered, 'Master Gabe, it's me, Jack.'

The prayer ended abruptly.

'Hush, you'll wake Master Fisher.'

And there he was: Gabriel. Jack's quest was accomplished.

'Take this,' Jack said, removing the purse that had hung inside his shirt and passing it round the door. 'Master Seb said you wos t' foller them 'structions exackerly and we'll do the rest. That's wot he telled me t' say.'

Gabriel took it but held Jack's hand for a moment as he did so. The man's hand was corpse cold already and Jack shivered but the grip was still strong and firm.

'If it be the Lord's will, I shall do it. I know not how you come to be here but thank you, Jack. And God be with you.'

'That's wot Master Seb said an' all.'

Then the lad left, making his way back down the stair.

Seb had remained at the foot of the tower, staring up at the embrasure, waiting for Jack to reappear but such a position was likely to draw attention as folk began to go about their daily tasks. As the light strengthened, Seb removed himself deeper into the shadows. It felt as though hours had passed since Jack had climbed the tower and still no sign of his return. Seb's anxiety was mounting.

'Master? Wot you doin', lurkin' like a felon?'

Seb jumped back.

'Heavens above, Jack, you startled me. I was expecting you to climb down.'

'Nah. I comed down the stair, didn't I? Turnkey's too busy scoffin' breakfast to notice me. I sneaked by like a fief, quiet as a cat, weren't I?'

'Come, Jack, we best not linger here. You've earned a good breakfast this morn, for certain, then you can tell me of Master Gabriel's situation.'

'Siterayshun? Wot's that?'

'After breakfast.'

While Michael Fisher slept still, Gabriel opened the purse Seb had sent. Jack's sudden appearance had been a surprise indeed and he was heartened that the Foxleys hadn't abandoned him in his plight.

Seb's letter was succinct but clear. It was a dubious plan at best and might end in disaster for them all. As he hid the pigment and potions beneath the pile of straw upon which he had been supposed to sleep – not that he had – he wondered what was God's will for him? He was prepared and resigned to his gruesome fate, if the Lord intended that to be his destiny. But now, perhaps that was not the case, else why had God put this idea into Seb's head?

Or was it the Devil's handiwork to lead him from the righteous path and a martyr's death? He couldn't tell. He would pray about it but could not spend over long before deciding, for the plan required that he act this day.

He read Seb's letter again before concealing it in his shoe. There was only one thing he could believe: if the plan worked – insane as it was – then it must be that God intended it should. That the Almighty still had a purpose for him in this world and it would be wrong to deny it. He would have to take the risk.

He was still coming to terms with the thought of counterfeiting death and considering if he should paint the spots on his skin now, while he was fit and well, or whether to swallow the potion to make him sweat first.

In the letter, Seb warned from his own experience that it would make him feel weak and feeble. How long would he have before the draught took effect? There was also the difficulty that Seb's instructions said both potions should be taken in ale and none had been provided. Only sour, greenish water that he was wary of drinking. But then there was no opportunity.

Father Wessell entered, followed by an acolyte carrying a small silver bell, a Gospel book and a candle. Gabriel knew what that meant. In the eyes of the Church – though certainly not in his own – he was about to suffer a fate even worse than death: excommunication. Yet for a Known Man, being expelled from the succour of Satan's minions was more a blessing than a curse.

The priest looked self-satisfied as he began to intone the words that supposedly would deny Gabriel salvation. Meaningless Latin cant. That's what it was. He may as well save his breath. Gabriel wasn't listening but dwelling upon the irony of it. Did this smirking priest even know he was excommunicating his cousin? They being nephew and natural son of Bishop Kemp. Gabriel laughed at the foolishness of it.

'You'll not be so merry, heretic, come Judgement Day, when you be condemned to an eternity, blistering in Hell.'

'Indeed? I was told by the bishop that a blistering at Smithfield in this life would save my soul from suffering in the hereafter. Mayhap, I heard him wrongly. Or is it you that be mistaken?'

'The flames will put an end to your jests. I can barely wait to watch you burn.'

'Have you finished your excommunication of me, only I have better things to do than harken to your prattle.'

Father Wessell stepped so close that Gabriel could smell the breakfast ale upon the man's breath.

'Two days, heretic, then I'll see you roasted like a pig on a spit, hear you scream as your entrails boil, your skin melts and your hair catches afire. And I shall be the one laughing.'

'I'm sure you'll enjoy the spectacle; I'll do my best to entertain.'

Father Wessell's neck was red as a cock's comb, a vein pulsed in his temple beneath his tonsure. He looked upon the verge of apoplexy as he stormed out, vestments flying, with his acolyte tottering after with his symbols of excommunication. He then dropped the little bell which clattered and tinkled as it rolled in a circle. The priest was gone and Gabriel picked up the bell and gave it to the acolyte who, far from seeming grateful, muttered something about having to wash the bell in holy water to cleanse it of a heretic's touch.

'I don't know why you taunt him so, brother,' Michael Fisher said, bestirring himself from his bed of straw. He had lain there, silent and unnoticed, while the priest did his worst.

'Why not? I have precious few pleasures left to me now and even fewer hours to enjoy them.'

'A Known Man is not supposed to harbour hate against another but it seems to me that you do in the case of that particular priest.'

'Hate? No. I would not go to so much effort for him. Utter contempt is what I feel for my cousin.'

'Your cousin! I would never have believed it so.'

'No. We are hardly alike and I am deeply ashamed that I share so much as a single drop of blood with one such as he. Fortunately, God in his mercy spared me the misery of knowing we were close kin until recently. Not that I would have invited him to dine, if I had known.'

'But I heard he is the bishop's – God wash my tongue in vinegar – nephew. So how are you related? Upon his mother's side, eh?'

'His mother is Kemp's sister and… well, it matters little now if I admit it, but Kemp is my father.'

Fisher covered his mouth to prevent unchristian expletives escaping unbidden.

'And he condemns you, his own son, to suffer so hideously?'

Gabriel nodded.

'Aye, and will take pleasure in it, I suspect, unless I foil his plan…'

The Foxleys' kitchen

'YER SHOULD 'ave seen it, Tom, a rat big as a sheep, it wos. Made me near jump outta me skin, it did.' Jack took another hefty bite of new bread smeared thick with honey – his reward for the morning's efforts. The household was gathered around the board, watching him eat and hanging upon his every word. 'An' then I creeped up them stairs like a ghost, so nobody 'eard me. An' then I finded Master Gabe. He wos sayin' 'is prayers, weren't 'e, but I gived 'im the purse, like wot Master Seb told me to. An' then I creeped all the way down agen, right passed the fat turnkey wot wos 'avin' 'is breakfast. An' that wos it! I wos out, weren't I? Safe an' sound.'

Seb, whilst itching to correct the lad's grammar, didn't interrupt. Jack deserved his few moments of glory for a job well done – one beyond the skills of anyone else he knew and vital to set the escape plan in motion.

'Was Master Gabriel alone in his cell?' Seb asked.

'Nah. That fella Fisher wos wiv 'im. Is that a bad fing?'

'Maybe not. When Gabriel begins to pretend he is unwell, it is perhaps fortunate that there be someone there to raise the alarm, yet I fear Gabriel may have difficulty applying the pigment to his skin without Fisher knowing of it.'

'P'raps Fisher'll 'elp. They's friends, ain't they?'

'I do not know, Jack. I never heard of the man afore yesterday. Who can say what he may do? Either way, you and Tom have another task to do this day.'

'Not more letters, master, pleeease.'

'Do not whine, Jack, 'tis most unbecoming for a hero. No, not letters. I need you both to take earth and stones from the pig sty wall and stuff the manikin – the rag doll Mistress Em has made,' Seb added, seeing Jack frown. 'It must be heavy as a man but the stones must not rattle together, so the earth should be packed tight around them. Use straw too, if that will aid you. And work quietly when you be outside. Do not attract attention for this must remain a secret matter. Do you understand?'

'Aye, master,' the lads said together.

Emily began tidying away the platters, passing them to Nessie to put to soak. Seb was relieved that his wife and servant seemed to have called a truce, even if the peace treaty had yet to be sealed.

'What can I do to help?' Emily asked without meeting his eyes.

'The manikin will need stitching up once it be stuffed.'

'More than that. I want to be part of this.'

'You shall be. At some point, afore the burying, there must be a diversion to distract any on-lookers. It may be a plague burial and therefore to be avoided, but I don't doubt there will be a few come to gawp – there always are. And what better distraction at such a moment than a fine lady in distress? You, Em, will be that lady.'

'In my new gown! Aye, that will do. Oh, but Seb, everyone knows me. How can I pass for a lady?' She sat down upon a stool opposite him, abandoning a tottering pile of unwashed pots.

'It will be dusk, as it must be by law for a plague burial. You will be wearing a silken veil...'

'But I have no such thing.'

'You will have. Then 'tis up to you how you draw folks' attention: swooning, maybe, wailing like a lost soul? I know not how a woman may act.'

'But what if I swoon and someone rushes to attend me and removes my veil? Then they will know me as plain Mistress Foxley.'

'Indeed. Someone will attend you. Your lady's maid, of course.'

'Not Nessie. Everyone knows her too and she couldn't pretend to be anything but... but Nessie.'

'Yes, I could,' came a protesting voice from the doorway to the yard. 'I'd do anything for Master Gabe 'cos he loves me.'

'He most certainly does not, you witless wench,' Emily cried, fists bunched in rage. The pots began to topple.

'Calmly, calmly now, for pity's sake,' Seb said, leaning across the board and making a grab, saving the pots from falling. 'No, not Nessie.'

'So what can I do?' Nessie asked.

'Gabriel will need your aid – both of you – in recovering from his ordeal and the potions he will have swallowed. He will require a decent meal and provisions for a journey after. Can you work together, in harmony, for his sake?'

The women nodded, agreeing that they could.

'But where's he going on this journey, master? Why's he going?'

'Better you know not, Nessie.'

'When'll he be coming back?'

Seb said nothing. He was no more ready to admit the truth, even to himself, than to the womenfolk. But Emily was quick witted and read the facts in her husband's face.

'He isn't coming back, is he? Not ever.'

'I fear his life would be forfeit, if he did. I am so sorry, Em.'

She nodded and turned away so he should not see her tears. 'Are you truly sorry?' she asked.

'He's been a good journeyman and a close friend to me. That's all I need to know. I shall be sorrowful not to see him again. Now, I have matters to attend to elsewhere.' Seb went towards the workshop. 'Jude! Be you there, brother? Will you accompany me?'

Queenhithe

'DON'T KNOW why you need me,' Jude said. 'Surely you're more than capable of arranging a passage aboard ship on your own?'

'You know full well I have no liking for the quayside nor for ships which never stay still. They make me queasy. Besides, last time I came here, I got lost upon the way. Granted, it was foggy, but I still feel easier with you at my side.'

'There,' said Jude, pointing, 'I can read *St Christopher* painted upon the bow. But what makes you think they'll give passage to Gabe? Your friend, Marchmane, isn't its captain any longer, is he? You know who is?'

'According to Gabriel, the ship's master is a fellow by the name of Raff Scraggs. Gabriel seemed to know him quite well. I am hoping he has taken Marchmane's place.'

The ship seemed quiet with little activity on board, just the sigh of the breeze in the rigging and the forlorn cry of gulls wheeling overhead. Seb found the stink of pitch abrading his nostrils – a nasty reminder of past events – and the cargo was of untreated fleeces, to judge by the stink of sheep that accompanied it.

'Shall we find out?' Jude stood back so Seb might precede him up the gangplank.

'I hate this,' Seb muttered as he stepped onto the plank just as it lurched upward in the swell of the river beneath.

Jude was but a step behind and took a grip on Seb's arm.

'I've got you, little brother.'

'What d'you want?' a voice demanded as they reached the ship's side and peered down at the deck.

Seb was still poised upon the plank's end, trying to build up the courage to jump down.

'We're looking for Master Scraggs,' Jude said, 'Raff Scraggs.'

'Not 'ere.' A broad-chested fellow, his features like leather, long since tanned by wind and sun and salt water, stood four-square before them, barring their way.

'We must speak with him upon a matter of urgency,' Seb said, having finally got onto the deck without coming to grief.

'If yer the bishop's men or the mayor's, yer ain't welcome 'ere and can get off right now. Go on; get you gone.'

'I swear to you, we be neither,' Seb said, clutching at Jude as the ship rocked under his feet.

'This about Scraggs' appointment as our new captain?'

'Aye, it is,' Jude lied, wanting this matter done with before his brother turned a worse shade of green.

'What is it, Hal?' A man came up from below, his mouse-coloured hair snatched by the breeze.

'These two say they've come about your new appointment, master,' Hal replied, tugging his forelock to the newcomer.

Scraggs gave them a long look, then shook his head.

'No, they haven't. You're the Foxleys, aren't you? I've seen you around. I think you best come below.'

Seb wanted to refuse. On deck was bad enough but down into the bowels of the ship – he did not dare to even contemplate it. But the man was already leading the way down a narrow ladder. Jude followed, pulling at Seb's mantle so he was forced to follow.

The cabin was small but spotlessly clean and tidy. There was hardly room for three men and they all had to stoop. Seb, all unwary, had already clouted his head on the low lintel in the doorway.

'Aye, you need to mind the beams in the hatches and below deck,' the man warned – too late. 'Sit down, that's safest.' He pulled down a kind of folding shelf that formed a bench. 'Will you take ale?'

Jude said he would.

Seb kept his hands over his mouth.

'So, what business do you have with Raff Scraggs?'

Jude looked to Seb but realised his little brother wasn't going to say anything.

'We come about a friend of his, a man who will shortly be in need of safe passage abroad.'

'And the man's name?'

Again Jude glanced at Seb to answer but his brother's eyes were tight shut.

'Gabriel Widowson.'

The man looked surprised.

'He who was t-tried by the bishop and c-condemned?'

There was no mistaking the tremor as the question was asked.

'The same.'

'But how?'

'My brother has devised a foolish plan but, if all works out as he intends, Gabriel will need to leave the country right swiftly. A ship would be best.'

'Where would he go?'

Jude shrugged.

'Anywhere the bloody bishop's writ doesn't run, I suppose. The Low Countries, the German Lands, maybe?'

The man smiled.

'Well, if my appointment is confirmed by Marchmane's people in time, the tide will be with us just after midday on Thursday. Our cargo is loaded and ready. We be bound for Bruges in Flanders and just await the arrival of their warrant.'

'And you would take Gabriel?'

'I have a purse to pay you,' Seb said, laying a bag of coin beside his untouched ale cup before covering his mouth again.

'No need. I'll take him for no charge since he will work his passage. He knows his way about a steerboard and a forecastle well enough. Besides...'

'He is your brother, isn't he?' Seb said suddenly. 'His stories make sense, if that be the case. You are Raphael. There is some likeness...' As the ship rocked gently, his words tailed off. He leapt from the bench and bolted back up the ladder, cracking his forehead on the lintel again.

Both Jude and Scraggs winced in sympathy.

Jude found Seb hanging over the ship's side, his face a horrible shade betwixt virdigris and cold ashes, sheened with sweat.

'Scraggs said you should drink this,' Jude said offering Seb a cup. 'An old mariner's receipt, apparently.'

'What's in it?'

'No idea. Smells like bloody cat's piss, if you ask me.'

Seb turned away, groaning, and Jude threw the contents of the cup into the Thames just as Scraggs appeared from below.

'Feeling better?'

'Aye, he's much improved, aren't you little brother?' Jude handed Scraggs the empty cup.

'Before midday Thursday, then?'

Jude nodded.

'Come, Seb, let's get you onto good solid ground, shall we?' Jude took hold of his brother's shoulders with both hands to guide him down the gangplank.

'I never want to see another ship, as long as I live.'

Garlickhill

'SO HOW did you, of all people, come to know a whore?' Jude asked as they walked the short distance from Queenhithe to the Pewter Pot.

'It was the same day I mentioned afore, when I lost my way in the fog. Rose found me, guided me. And please do not call her a whore. 'Tis not her fault she cannot live otherwise. This is the place though I more usually arrive later. She may be busy elsewhere.'

'In the tavern? Good idea, Seb. You look to be even more in need of ale than me. Your face is still the colour of uncooked pastry. I thought you'd recover as soon as we left that bloody ship.'

'I'm doing well enough. Better by the moment.'

'Good, then you can buy the drinks, since you didn't have to hand over a penny to pay passage to Scraggs. His brother, eh? Well, that was a bloody surprise.'

'Shh, Jude. You never know who may be listening.'

Sitting upon a bench that kept perfectly still beneath him and with some decent ale inside his belly, Seb recovered swiftly.

'Well, that's a vision to cheer any man in low spirits,' Jude said, nudging Seb as a pretty wench came through the tavern door, laden with a tray of bread. 'Baker's wife, no doubt. Oh, watch your manners, little brother, she's coming our way.'

'Good day, to you, Master Seb,' she said, making a little courtesy.

Jude's eyebrows disappeared beneath his hat.

'Good day, to you also, Rose,' Seb said, rising from his seat. 'This is my elder brother, Jude Foxley.'

'And a very, very good day to you, Mistress Rose,' Jude said, hurriedly standing and offering his hand.

Rose took his hand, laughing at so much formality.

'Jude. Cease staring.' Seb dug his elbow into Jude's ribs. 'Close your mouth: you be gaping like a fish.'

'Shall we go up to my room, masters? You cannot pay Master Underwood at present, he isn't here.'

'She's a little jewel, Seb, you lucky bugger,' Jude whispered as they climbed the outside stair.

'Stop it, Jude, 'tis not like that betwixt us, as I told you. I'm teaching her to read and write.'

'Huh, well I never heard it called that before. Come on, you can tell me: she's as good a fuck as can be bought, isn't she?'

'No! I mean, I'm not saying she isn't but I've never... Oh, stop it, just stop pulling that face. I don't care if you don't believe me.'

Jude was laughing so hard, he near tripped upon the top step.

Rose's room surprised him. For one thing, it didn't stink like a whore's chamber. It was clean and neatly kept.

'I do apologise,' Rose said, 'But there is only the bed to sit upon. I don't have a stool.'

'Jude will be content with the floor. Won't you, brother?' Seb said.

'Let me make you comfortable, Master Jude.' Rose hurried to put the pillow from her bed behind his back as he leant against the wall. She bent close to him such that he might glimpse what was hidden beneath her bodice, the delicate pearlescent skin of her breasts. She smelled like flowers – Jude wasn't sure what kind – and that smile of hers lit up the day. But then she moved away, rummaging beneath the bed to retrieve – God knew what and who cared, anyway – that beautiful little arse was so enticing.

'Here, master,' Rose was saying, presenting Seb with a few papers. 'I've been practising my letter shapes, as you told me to. I hope I'm improving. What do you think? I had trouble with 'r'; it seems to disappear into the other letters when they join up. Am I writing them wrongly?'

That came as a shock to Jude. Seb was telling the truth! For certain, such a waste of so luscious a body must be a crime. He ought to be in the bloody cloister if he couldn't think of some better thing to do with such a woman. Jude knew exactly what he'd like to do with her, as many times as life might allow.

'That was indeed well read, Rose, I commend you. Do you not agree, Jude?'

'What?' Jude was dragged rudely from his reverie, his blissful contemplation of what might be. 'Oh, aye, no doubt. Are you done with the lesson yet, brother?'

'If Rose be agreeable, we are, for there are matters to be discussed, concerning tomorrow's eve.' Seb tidied the papers and handed them to Rose.

Jude hoped she would put them back beneath the bed, but she set them aside on the worn blanket that served as a coverlet.

'What of tomorrow, masters? Tell me. I am intrigued.'

So Seb told Rose about the plan with numerous interruptions from Jude that helped not at all.

'It be the case then, that my goodwife, in playing the part of a fine lady, will need some accoutrements and assistance...'

'And you want my help,' Rose concluded.

'If you would, I should be so grateful,' Seb said. 'Of course, I shall pay you for your time, as always.'

'We need to think this through thoroughly,' she said. 'Does your goodwife have a suitable gown to wear?'

'Aye, she does, and a cloak that may be borrowed for the once.'

'What about gloves? The first thing that will betray a working woman is her hands. No lady would have rough skin and broken nails. Your wife must wear beautiful kid-leather gloves, preferably white with silken tassels.'

Seb shook his head, knowing there was no such thing and he could never afford them.

Rose laughed.

'Then how fortunate it is that I was training to be glover at one time, long since. You see, I went so far as to begin my apprentice piece.' Again, she burrowed under the bed and drew out a small wooden box. 'I never quite finished them. The tassels still need to be stitched in place.' She gave the box to Seb. 'I thought I might sell them but, somehow, I still hoped they might serve their purpose, show a master glover what I can do. Foolish, I know. They're of no use now so you may as well have them for your goodwife's disguise.'

'They're exquisite, Rose. Your stitches be so small as to be near invisible. I cannot take them.'

'I will stitch the tassels in place and bring them to you in the morning, if you allow me to come to your house?'

'I cannot pay you what the gloves be worth.'

'Master Seb, you have been teaching me for no cost to myself, yet paying Master Underwood for services you don't receive. I believe I owe you far more than a pair of gloves. They will be a gift to your goodwife from me, a payment in kind, if you like, to her for letting you spend so much time with me. How else may I show you my gratitude?'

'I'm sure I could think of something,' Jude murmured under his breath.

'And a veil of silk,' Rose said, 'She must have one of those.'

'Indeed. I was hoping you would supply that also, if you be willing?'

'From Bessie's belongings. Of course. I shall wash it and repair it and bring that also.'

'And you do not mind playing a lady's maid as I explained?' Rose smiled.

'I've done it before, for customers. This time, I shall do it because I want to.'

• •

Every step of the way home, so it seemed to Seb, Jude talked about naught but Rose.

'You have taken a liking to her then?'

'Well, she's a fine looking lass. What man worthy of the name wouldn't take a liking to those, er, her. How much does she charge?'

'Jude. We have a friend's life to save. Can you not turn your thoughts to some more relevant matter?

In Paternoster Row, Old Symkyn was there, as usual with his begging bowl.

'Nobody watching ye today, masters. Makes a change for ye.'

'You must be so cold, Symkyn. Come round to the kitchen and warm yourself,' Seb suggested.

'Nay, master, thanking ye, kindly, but I got new shoes now, see? My feet be warm for once.' The old man pulled up his tattered robe to show his shoes. 'Came from St Michael's alms box they did. Comfortable too, if a trifle large. But that means I can stuff them with straw which is better yet.'

Seb admired the shoes to please the old man. They looked to be of good leather although the right foot was oddly worn and scuffed at the toe. The other bore a stain but Symkyn was content with them.

'I'll send young Jack to you with some mulled ale to warm you, at least,' Seb told him.

'You're a good Christian fellow, master. God's blessing be upon ye and your house.'

Amen, to that, Seb thought.

Chapter 17

Wednesday, the twentieth day of November
The Lollards' Tower

GABRIEL'S HUMOURS were churning, like cream being turned to butter, and he hadn't even swallowed a potion as yet.

'There. I trust I've done that right,' Michael Fisher was saying, 'Your back is now well spotted. It would convince me.'

'My thanks for that, brother,' Gabriel said. They were both upon the floor of their cell, Gabriel seated and naked from the waist up while Fisher made thumbprints upon his back and neck with the pigment Seb had sent. Gabriel had already done the same upon his own arms and chest. Once the pigment was dry, he put his shirt back on. 'I hope they don't rub off on the linen.'

'Now you take the sweating potion. Wasn't that what the instructions said?'

Gabriel nodded. The letter of instruction was gone now, torn into tiny pieces and cast out betwixt the window bars on the wind. It wasn't worth the risk of a turnkey finding it. Even if he wouldn't be able to read the words, he would certainly pass it on to someone who could. Besides, Gabriel knew every word by heart.

Fisher took the little green container from beneath his bed of straw and handed it to Gabriel.

'How long before it has an effect?' he asked.

'I don't know.' Gabriel unstoppered the potion. Wisely, he didn't sniff it. Having murmured a heartfelt prayer that this plan of Seb's would work out successfully in every part, he closed his eyes and swallowed a mouthful of the stuff. 'Take it with ale,' Seb had written but there was no ale. He gagged and choked on the bitter herbal taste that burned the back of his throat. 'I can take the rest later,' he gasped, 'If the symptoms abate too soon.'

St Michael's church

S O AS not to arouse suspicion, the Foxley household attended Low Mass, as they usually did on a Wednesday. Yet there was one surprise in that Father Wessell was conducting the office – he who only officiated at Sunday High Mass, lesser services being beneath his notice.

'Where's Father Thomas?' Emily asked Dame Ellen.

'Abed with a nasty cough, so I heard, too breathless, they say,' the dame answered.

'I hope that doesn't mean we'll be treated to one of the Weasel's endless rants about fire and brimstone. I have much work to do at home.'

'Have you finished Lady Josselyn's cloak yet? She would have it directly. Apparently the Lord Mayor and she are dining at Westminster with the king on Friday. She must have it by then.'

'I'll have it done by tomorrow morn and bring it to you directly.'

'Today would be better.'

'No. It will have to be tomorrow, dame.'

'Well, just be sure it is done to my highest standard, then. There won't be time enough to correct anything amiss. You should organise yourself better than this, Emily, as I taught you. Never leave things until the last possible moment, remember that, for you never know when fate may intervene and things not get done at all.'

'I'll remember, Dame Ellen. It's just that the workshop has been so busy of late.'

'That's not what I've heard,' the dame said. 'And will you look at that. Jude Foxley, all clean and kempt. I haven't seen him so respectably turned out for weeks. He was becoming scruffy as a beggar. Have you had a hand in this sudden change of his, Emily?'

'No. 'Tis as much a mystery to me as it is to you, dame. All I know is that last eve he demanded Nessie heat enough water so he might bathe. And this morn, even before church, he must have visited a barber. It is a considerable improvement, isn't it?'

'Well, mark my words: there's a woman behind it and if not you, then who else? I shall make it my business to find out.' With her eyes and ears alert as a questing hound, Dame Ellen went off to chat with her friends and glean any news-worthy tit-bits they might share.

Emily need not have feared an interminable sermon for Father Wessell was as eager to be done with the holy office as anyone in the congregation.

'New shoes, I see,' commented Dame Ellen, back at Emily's side as the priest administered a final hasty blessing upon them. Beneath his vestments, the piked points of his footwear showed – as he fully intended they should. 'Points greater than two inches, I warrant – against the laws of sumptuary, of course. Perhaps I shall make report to the sheriff?'

'You could but then the poor shoe-maker will be fined also,' said Emily, 'Which is hardly fair to my mind. I do like the blue colour of the leather, though, don't you, dame? I wonder if he gave his old shoes to the poor, as a priest ought?'

'Unlikely. That one wouldn't give a sip of water to Jesu Christ upon the cross. He sold them to a fripperer or a cobbler for a good price, I'll wager.'

'You be looking very fine this day,' Seb said to Jude as they were all walking home after church.

'Man's got to make an effort.'

'Has he? It has not bothered you over much of late to go unshaven and unwashed. Meeting Rose has had quite an effect upon you.'

'What rubbish you speak. I barely noticed her. Why would a whore affect me in any wise?'

'Because you have a liking for her and would impress her when she comes a-calling later, to bring the stuff for Em.'

'You've got your head in the bloody clouds as usual, little brother. She is nothing to me, I tell you: just another prostitute of my acquaintance.'

'I do not like it when you call her so. Her trade is not of her choosing but was forced upon her.'

'Oh? You know her story then? How did she come to be in her present situation, if not by choice?'

As they walked, Seb told Jude Rose's story, much as he had told it to Stephen Appleyard not so long ago.

'So that's why you teach her to read and write? Because she thinks such skills will make her more marriageable?'

'Aye. She desperately wants to be a respectable man's wife but feels she has so little in the way of assets to recommend her.'

'I can think of a few assets of hers that would come highly recommended. Bloody hell, Seb, a respectable marriage would almost be a waste – one selfish bugger keeping her all to himself.'

'You may have cleansed your body, Jude, but your mind be as filthy as the Fleet River. This morn, I have been praying so ardently for Our Lord's aid in our enterprise. I think it would be as well if you also turned your heart and thoughts to higher matters, just this once.'

As they reached home, Old Symkyn was still there, as ever, looking as though he hadn't moved.

'Still no one watching ye, masters. I think that under-sheriff fellow has despaired of incriminating you two, now he has your journeyman under lock and key. Have ye seen the great mound o' faggots they're building for him over Smithfield way? Enough to roast a half dozen oxen, let alone a solitary man.'

Seb felt his stomach lurch at the image conjured by the old man's words. He didn't even want to think about it; what would happen to Gabriel if their plan foundered this day. What was Gabriel doing now? Did the pigment spots look convincing? Had he taken the potions yet? Supposing the excess of sweat washed away the pigment? He hadn't thought of that 'til now. In a state of turmoil, he threw a coin into the beggar's bowl, as was his habit, not looking to see what it was. He was trying so hard to have everything seem normal yet a half mark, an angel thrown to a beggar, could hardly fail to be noticed. He stumbled into the house, ill with worry.

The Lollards' Tower

S EB WAS right, Gabriel thought, the sweating potion was making him feel weak. Too weak. How could he make his escape if he could hardly stand? His head seemed to spin and his limbs weighed heavy as lead.

When the cell door opened and two men entered, Fisher jumped up.

'A good thing you've come. I fear my companion is very sick.'

'He'll be a lot sicker t'morrow,' laughed the turnkey, scratching at a louse in his armpit. 'Go to your task, Master Smith.'

The second man knelt down beside Gabriel.

'Raise yer arms, so I can measure yer,' he demanded.

Gabriel did his best to oblige.

'What for?' he asked.

'Now, see, there be no point tyin' yer t' the stake 'cos rope'll burn through in no time. So I'll make yer a nice new girdle outta iron, just the fashion, see, t' hold yer up agains' the stake. Don't want yer runnin' off when yer sees them flames, do we?' The smith passed a length of string around Gabriel's chest, beneath his arms and tied off a knot to mark the size needed. 'Gawd, but yer sweatin' up proper, ain't yer?'

'Fear, that's what it is,' said the turnkey.

'Now, see, I can make it so it fits yer, nice and comfy.'

'He needs a surgeon, I tell you,' Fisher insisted.' He's very sick. Look.' He lifted Gabriel's shirt to show the purple spots across his chest. 'Could be the pox... or worse.'

The turnkey took a long step back.

The smith looked scared of a sudden.

'But I touched him, jus' then, I put my hand on him. Gawd. I'm gonna die.' The smith fled, shrieking.

In no time, every denizen of the tower would know about the sick man. The turnkey followed, muttering.

'Will they fetch a surgeon to me?' Gabriel asked Fisher when they were alone again, his voice faint. 'How will a man of medicine be fooled by paint?'

'I don't know, brother. We're just following your friend's directions. See what comes to pass. If the Lord Christ wants you to escape this place, be sure that He will make it so. If not... who can say what will happen?'

As promised and paid for in advance, Surgeon Dagvyle and his apprentice happened to be loitering near at hand by the Lollards' Tower. How fortunate then that a smith, in a state of near apoplexy, ran from the doorway, screaming that someone had afflicted him with the pestilence.

Dagvyle grinned and sauntered over to intercept the fellow.

'I'm a surgeon. May I be of assistance to you, master? You seem quite distracted.'

'As would yer be, if yer touched a body wi' plague.'

'Go and rest, would be my advice. Make your will and confess your sins to a priest. And you may have that advice for no charge.' Dagvyle wanted to laugh out loud. 'Someone said there was a case of the pestilence here,' he shouted, entering the door from which the panicked man had run.

'Ah, Master Dagvyle. Whatever brings you here,' the flustered turnkey said, 'You've chosen the right moment. As you say, there may be such a case among the prisoners. I'm not sure if it is, but since you've come, you may as well see for yourself. Then, if it be just some spotted fever or other, we need not worry and can sleep well in our beds this night. This way.'

'There have been a few cases of pestilence of late around Bucklersbury, as you may have heard. As you say, 'tis best to be certain but I advise caution all the same.' Dagvyle was quite enjoying himself, watching the turnkey's expression change from mild concern to deep anxiety to outright fear as he listed the symptoms in every gruesome detail. That was until the turnkey told him that the prisoner in question was in the cell at the very top of the tower. Stairs! So many accursed stairs! The bane of the plump surgeon's life. He would demand extra payment of Master Foxley for this.

Wheezing and gasping painfully for every breath, Dagvyle reached the last stair. The stench of sweat and foul straw didn't help as he struggled to breathe.

'That's him,' the turnkey said, making a hasty retreat.

Fisher looked at the surgeon, an expression of grave doubt upon his features.

Dagvyle too had his doubts. Was this other man privy to the plan?

'He is a very dear friend to me,' Fisher said, 'I know not what may ail him.'

Was there a message hidden in those few words, Dagvyle wondered as he paused to recover from the climb. The last thing he wanted was to look a fool, identifying painted on spots as a dread disease in front of this man. On the other hand, he didn't want to ruin the plan for which he'd been paid so generously. The surgeon eased himself down beside Gabriel, still wheezing.

The journeyman looked ill in truth, slumped upon a scraped together bed of unwholesome straw, sweat oozing copiously from every pore. His shirt was wet as a dish clout. Quite convincing, if he didn't know otherwise.

'I know this man's master; Seb Foxley,' Dagvyle said. 'He knows I am here.'

Fisher sighed with relief.

'The Lord God be praised. Then you know of this.'

'Aye. I see the turnkey was convinced.'

'And the smith, poor fellow. I could hear him screaming in the yard below, even from here. He truly believes he will die upon the instant.'

'He does. Serve him right.' Dagvyle struggled to rise. 'Aid me, damn you!' he yelled at his apprentice who waited outside, as fearful as the turnkey because his master had told him naught of any plan.

'Is it the pestilence, master?' the lad asked as they made their way down the winding stair.

The surgeon was already silently cursing that he would have to climb these devil-damned stairs again before the day was done.

'Aye and as bad a case as I've seen. The fellow is like to be dead before tonight.'

Seeing the lad falter and blanch, Dagvyle took pity on him. 'Fear not, in this form 'tis hardly ever contagious, especially for a young, fit, black-haired lad like you. Your humours would dictate you suffer a sniffle at worst. But for a mouse-haired man beyond his twentieth year, 'tis another tale entirely.'

'What of you then, master? You're beyond your twentieth year, aren't you?'

'Aye but no hair, see? A bald pate precludes it.' This was becoming over complicated. 'Run to the Foxleys' place in Paternoster Row. You know where it is. Tell Master Foxley I shall be there directly.' After a drink at the Panyer to assist my own recovery, he said to himself.

The Foxleys' house

'JACK, DID you fetch your uncle's barrow and fill it with straw?'

'Aye, master, but 'e weren't 'appy about it 'til I gived 'im the groat wot you sended. An' the manikin thing – wot I don't much like the look of – is well hided in it, under all the straw.'

So far; so good, Seb thought. Dagvyle had reported that their deception had succeeded beyond expectation. He ought to be relieved but he wasn't. For himself, personally, the worst moment had come: the first meeting betwixt Emily and the woman she feared to be her rival. It was nonsense, of course, but where women were concerned, Seb felt that nonsense seemed to fill their heads as often as not. He'd tried to explain to Em but she refused to believe him still.

Rose came to the side gate in the alleyway off Paternoster Row, as Seb had told her, so as not to attract notice. Difficult indeed. Rose tended to draw attention wherever she went, so she wore her hood up and pulled close about her face. Such concealment may, of itself, have caused folk to look at her. There was no help for it. Now she stood in another woman's kitchen.

Emily stood with her arms folded: a protective shield against the intrusion of the enemy.

'Ah, Rose, there you are. A chill day is it not?' Seb tried to make light of the situation. 'Emily, this is Rose from Garlickhill. Rose, this is Emily, my goodwife.' The air seemed to prickle betwixt them, as if two lionesses were trapped in a narrow passageway. 'Ale, anyone?'

The silence was agonising.

'Mistress Foxley,' Rose began, 'I know not what you think of me but I'm come to assist in the rescue of your journeyman. I have brought some things that may be of use.' She put a linen-wrapped package upon the board and unrolled it before stepping back, to make way for Emily, so their skirts wouldn't touch.

'Why?' Emily did not move. 'Why would you want to assist a man you never met? How much is my husband paying you?'

'Not a penny, mistress, so if you don't want me, no doubt you will manage without...'

Rose began to roll up the linen again.

'No. Please. If you can make Gabriel's chance of rescue more certain...' Emily was in tears and Rose went to her, put an arm around her shoulders as she sobbed.

Seb was wise enough to realise his presence was no longer needed and he left the women alone. Soon he could hear them and Nessie talking of the best way to drape a veil and gasps of admiration for a wondrous gown, a fine cloak and a splendid pair of gloves. He smiled. Women! They went from anger to tears to laughter in less time than it took him to shave his chin.

The messenger, though expected, came as a surprise, for it was Father Wessell who stood upon the front step, demanding to speak with Sebastian Foxley and none other. St Paul's bell had just rung the third hour after midday. Seb had thought it would take longer.

'Foxley.'

'Father Wessell, won't you come in? In what manner may I assist you? Will you take wine?' Did he sound like a man with no idea of what was to come? Would the Weasel suspect?

'This won't take a moment. I have to inform you that your heretic journeyman is dead.'

Seb staggered slightly.

'Dead? But that's not supposed to be... I thought...'

'Bastard died of plague not an hour since.'

'Be you certain?'

'You doubt my word, Foxley?'

'Well, I...'

'Surgeon Dagvyle confirms it. The bishop thought we should burn him anyway but I argued that we don't want a plague victim lying around, spreading contagion. Besides, the fire would cleanse his soul of its sin of heresy, making it fit for heaven. I prefer that it shall go straight to hell where it belongs.

'The bishop says you must send for the corpse directly, if you wish to bury it – in unhallowed ground, of course. In fact, to save you any expense, you may use the grave ready dug for the devil at Smithfield, beside the hospital of St Bartholomew. There will be no last rites, no services of a priest for an excommunicate.'

Seb nodded. Thinking of such a sorry plight proved more than sufficient to bring tears to his eyes.

'I will make the necessary arrangements,' he said. 'And thank you for your courtesy in permitting us to bury him, at least.'

'Get it done tonight else I'll have him thrown in a ditch, like a dead dog, which is what he deserves.'

With the priest gone, Jude applauded from the workshop doorway.

'Well done, little brother. You nigh had me weeping there.'

Seb wiped his eyes upon his sleeve.

'You were truly in tears! This is but a ruse, remember.'

'Aye, I know, but the thought of it... Come, we have much to do. Tom! Tom! Ah, there you are. Ready? Wear your most solemn face and go ask Master Appleyard to bring the parish coffin to St Paul's Yard. And do not look so excited: a man lies dead of plague. Oh, Jude, Em, what if we ruin it now?'

'All will be well. My father will not fail us,' Emily said, 'You can trust him.'

'Aye, lass, but I wonder if I can trust myself.' With an effort, he straightened his doublet and breathed deeply. 'Of course. Your father will bring the parish coffin, as he always does. Now you and Rose must dress yourselves and make your way to Smithfield. Jack will take the barrow.'

'I know. You have explained a dozen times and more, as if we be witless fools. We will be there to play our parts, won't we, Rose?'

Seb and Jude, with sorrowful step, walked the short distance to Paul's Yard. Tom was there already with Stephen

Appleyard, Warden-Archer, carpenter and keeper of St Michael's parish coffin. They climbed down from the cart. The horse whickered, softly.

'My deepest condolences to you,' Stephen said, bowing his head. 'I don't hold with Lollardy or whatever your Gabriel believed in, but no man deserves to die so sudden of plague, with no chance to make confession. I'm truly sorry for it.'

'Thank you,' Seb said, 'On behalf of us all.'

'Where have they laid him?'

'I shall ask. Away from other folk, I expect.'

The turnkey directed them to the very top of the tower. It was no easy task, even with four men, to get the coffin up the spiral stair and it would be worse coming down when the wooden box weighed more heavily.

'You sure we can't just carry him down and then put him in the coffin?' Stephen said.

'A plague victim,' Jude reminded him, 'Best not. Sooner we get him boxed...'

'Oh, aye, I suppose.'

At the cell, they were met by Master Fisher.

'They just left us,' he explained, 'Never barred the door after, just fled. I could have walked out, except that I didn't think he ought to be alone.'

'That be a kindness indeed,' Seb said. 'Would you help my brother and I to shroud him?'

Tom and Stephen waited outside since the cell was so small.

Seb had brought a winding sheet but now it came to the moment, he hated the thought of wrapping his friend as a corpse. He and Jude exchanged wary glances.

'It would be less distressing for all of us, I think, if we simply folded it around him, like a babe in a blanket,' Fisher whispered. 'It will disturb him little in his drugged sleep.'

'You know?'

'We both read your letter, Master Foxley.'

Together, they folded the long length of linen until it was the size of a bed sheet, then Jude and Fisher lifted Gabriel on to it. As they tucked it firmly around the limp body, Seb was still reluctant to cover the face but Fisher did it swiftly, making sure the end was pulled tight. It would not do for the cloth to be seen to move as the incumbent took a shallow breath. Then they lifted the shrouded form gently, out onto the landing and into the waiting coffin. Stephen put the lid in place and affixed it with a nail at the head and foot. Seb winced at every hammer blow.

The burial cart trundled slowly out of Paul's Yard. Seb's shoulders were still afire from the effort of carrying the coffin down so many stairs. Much as he'd expected, a couple of guards, carrying torches, were to accompany them, to see the corpse safely interred, though they did not come too close to the cart and its dangerous load. They wore Bishop Kemp's own livery. He clearly wanted to be sure the heretic was gone into his unhallowed grave.

The cart and its escort went up Ivy Lane, passed the church of the Grey Friars and out through Newgate, turning right, passed St Bartholomew's hospital, to Smithfield.

'There.' One of the guards pointed. 'Beyond the great pile o' faggots we heaped up fer him, that's where we dug the grave.'

Seb was becoming anxious. Where were Emily and Rose? They should be here by now. And where was Jack with the manikin? Sweet heaven, they couldn't let it go so far as to put Gabriel in the ground. He would have to think of some other means of diversion. But what?

'Oh, look, my lady. A pauper's burial. How quaint.' It was Rose who ran forward from the shadows of Bartholomew's wall. 'And see, they wear the bishop's livery.'

'The bishop's? Well, then surely 'tis not a pauper they bury but someone of importance. Say, fellow, you! In his grace's livery. Pray tell us who you bury here in unhallowed earth?'

'Just a...'

'On your knees, oaf. Where are your manners? Do you not know better than that how to greet a lady?' The gold braid edging of Emily's cloak caught the torchlight. 'And you! Bumpkin,' she said, prodding the second guard with a kid-gloved finger. 'Do you think this is how a lady of high birth should be treated? Do you know who I am? Rose. Tell them.'

'You have the honour of being addressed by the Lady Margaret Stanley, wife of Lord Thomas Stanley, Steward of the King's Household. You must make a proper obeisance before her ladyship. Come. We do not have all night.'

As the bewildered guards went on their knees in the dirt with heads bowed, Jack rushed out from behind a clump of gorse with the barrow. Quietly as he could, Stephen prised open the coffin lid.

'So who is it you bury like sneak thieves in the night? I demand to know.' Emily sounded imperious as any queen.

'Just a heretic, my lady.'

'A heretic! In London! How dreadful. Rose. I fear I shall swoon with horror.'

'Help, my lady, you clumsy codpiece,' Rose yelled.

'Now. Hurry,' Seb whispered.

In haste, they lifted the manikin from beneath the straw in the barrow and dropped it, without ceremony, into the empty grave. Then, as gently as they might, Gabriel's limp form, in its shroud, was taken from the coffin to replace the manikin beneath the straw. Tom was about to uncover the face but Seb prevented him.

'Let it lie. We cannot have him breathe in straw and choke upon it.'

They swiftly rearranged the straw, then Jack was gone, returning to the shadows with the barrow and its precious load.

More slowly now and with decorum, Seb, Jude, Tom and Stephen stood around the grave, heads bowed in the fading light. The first drops of icy rain began to fall as Stephen took up a spade and began to refill the grave. Jude and Tom assisted, using their feet to move earth from the mound, into the hole.

'Are you quite recovered, my lady?' Rose was asking.

'A momentary thing was all. I am quite recovered now from my brief indisposition,' Emily assured her.

'We can escort you home, my lady,' one of the guards offered.

'That won't be necessary,' Rose said, thinking quickly. 'Lord Stanley awaits us within the church of St Bartholomew the Great. Come, my lady, you know what your lord husband would say if he knew we had conversation with such people as these. Let us hasten.'

The two women moved to the great Norman portal of the church but, as soon as the guards turned back to see how the makeshift funeral was progressing, they hitched up their skirts and ran towards Newgate where the keeper was preparing to close the gate. They straightened their gowns and walked demurely beneath the archway, neither deigning to acknowledge the keeper's bow as they passed through. Rose was biting her nether lip to keep from giggling aloud. Once beyond Grey Friars, they broke into a run again, back to Paternoster Row, breathless but laughing all the way.

Seb could not be easy in his mind until the last vestige of the white linen doll was hidden from view. With a final Latin prayer from Seb and each making the sign of the Cross, the little cortege formed up around the Stephen's cart.

Back through Newgate, they split up: Stephen with the empty coffin in his cart, returned to his home in Cheapside. The others made their way to Paternoster Row, keeping their heads bowed low in grief until the guards left them at the gate into Paul's Yard, eager to report their duty done.

'God be thanked, that is over,' Seb said as they went into the yard by the side gate.

Emily, Rose, Nessie and Jack were there with the barrow. As the sleety drizzle began to soak them, they discarded the straw and Emily folded back the corner of the shroud.

'Jack, hold the torch closer,' she said. As Gabriel's face was revealed, she gasped and began to sob.

For one horrible moment, Seb feared that all their efforts had been in vain. The face was deathly pale, the lips grey. It seemed not to notice the icy drops falling upon its skin. Seb reached out to touch the pallid cheek. It was cold.

And then Gabriel took a breath.

Relief was a tangible thing, more definite than the sleet.

'Get him within, beside the fire,' Emily said, drying her eyes. 'We must warm the life back into him.'

Hours later, Gabriel was tucked up in his own bed, cosseted by Emily and Nessie. He was groggy and complained of an aching head, but the colour had returned to his face and the warmth to his limbs.

Tom and Jack had finally been encouraged up to their attic, though they could be heard talking still, too excited to sleep.

Seb, Jude and Rose still sat in the kitchen, supping ale and eating oatcakes.

'You think it's safe to have him here, in his old chamber? Will it not be the first place the bloody bishop's men might search?' Jude asked.

'Why would they search for him? He lies dead in his grave, so far as they know. And where else may we hide him? 'Tis only for one night. He will be gone on the morrow. We have to trust in the Lord Christ, Jude; that be all we can do.'

'It was but good fortune that we succeeded, you know that. And we still have to get him to Queenhithe in the morning.'

'Then we may worry about that then. For the present, I be too weary.' Seb yawned. 'I'm for my bed.'

'And I'll take my leave,' Rose said.

Seb rubbed his eyes to banish the sleep that had almost claimed him.

'Forgive me, Rose. I near forgot. I'll fetch my mantle and...'

'It's so late, brother, you'll both attract notice,' Jude said.

'We can play a courting couple,' Rose suggested.

'No. You can sleep in my bed.'

'Rose will do no such thing,' Seb said, indignantly.

'I meant alone. Fear not, I wouldn't turn your house into a brothel. I can have a pillow and blanket in the parlour. God knows, I've slept with less bloody comfort than that before.'

'You are very kind,' Rose said, resting her hand upon Jude's, 'I will be glad of it and leave before first light, so none shall know I stayed.'

'I'll show you the way. The stair may be icy.'

'No, Jude. As master of this house, I shall escort Rose,' Seb said.

'The chamber is untidy.'

'I'll manage,' Rose said, 'And thank you, Master Jude.' She kissed him upon the forehead, a touch so light it might have been brushed by thistledown. Yet Jude could feel the heat from it long after Seb had taken a taper to light her way across the yard and up the outside stairs to the chamber. *His* chamber. And his cold empty bed. What a bloody waste. But he stared at the back of his hand, where she had touched him for the first time, rubbed at the kissed skin upon his brow and smiled as he had not done in a very long time.

Chapter 18

Thursday, the twenty-first day of November
The Foxleys' kitchen

A KIND OF sleety drizzle was falling beyond the shutters, as though daybreak was as yet too early for the weather to have decided betwixt rain and snow. Rose had departed already without breaking her fast, leaving a small wooden box upon the kitchen board, accompanied by a scrap of paper on which she had inscribed in charcoal 'for misstres emerlly', in her best hand.

Gabriel was already up, washed and had found fresh clothes in his coffer by the time Seb went up to the chamber to see how he fared this morn. Youth and strength had aided him in a swift recovery; the slight pallor that remained could have been caused by his imprisonment, as much as by the potions he had swallowed. If he felt any after effects, he hid them well.

'I've made a bundle of a few of my belongings,' he told Seb, 'But there won't be room on shipboard for much. What remains in my coffer is yours, to do with as you will. Sell the stuff, for there is no other way I can repay you all that I owe.'

'It was I that owed you my life for saving me the other day,' Seb said. 'Here are your wages for last week. You will need them.' He gave Gabriel a pouch of coins – more than were his due but no matter. 'As for the rest... you can pray for us all.'

'I do that any way, every day. I pray that you too will become a man known to God.'

Seb gasped.

'Gabriel! Are you telling me y-you be a Known Man? You truly are a...'

Gabriel looked him in the eye. The truth was all.

'A heretic? Aye, if that's what they call one who would study the Word of God in his own tongue. Yes, Seb, you saved the life of a heretic. Do you regret it now?'

Seb felt the need to sit and slumped on the unmade bed.

'No. You are still my dear friend. 'Tis just a shock. I always thought you to be a true son of Holy Church.'

'Even after I destroyed Master Honeywell's relics?'

'Aye. I suppose now that was a strange thing to do. I believed you to be out of sorts with the world and excused your actions. I've been wilfully blind, it seems.'

'Would you have gone to so much trouble for me, if you had realised the truth before?'

There was a lengthy silence.

Seb rubbed at his face.

Gabriel waited.

'In all honesty, I do not know, Gabriel.' Seb stood up. 'There are too many questions to which I do not have answers.'

'I believe I can put your mind at rest with one answer, at least. I have indeed broken the Lord God's Tenth Commandment, in my head and heart, in that I envy you and covet your wife and I admit my fault, to you and to God. But in no way did I break the Seventh. I never committed adultery. I cannot control what my heart desires but I can determine whether I act upon those longings. I never betrayed your trust, my friend.'

Eventually, Seb nodded.

'I suppose I'm partly to blame, for being wedded to a pretty wife. Thank you for telling me. Come, you must be hungry. Nessie has been stirring a pottage for you since the small hours.'

'You've got a bloody good appetite for one so recently coffined and buried, Gabe,' Jude said, grinning as he watched their friend put away a second bowl of pottage and yet another oatcake.

'The bishop had little thought for filling my belly. Food was in short supply and by no means so good as Nessie's cooking.'

'You want more, Master Gabe? There's plenty left.' Nessie bustled over, bearing the pottage pot and ladle. 'I made it special with extra leeks and ginger, the way you said you like it.'

Gabriel smiled and held up his bowl.

'Did I? Just a little, then.'

'Oh, master, you lost your crooked tooth.'

'Aye, Nessie, but I dare say I'll manage without, though it does feel strange.'

Emily came down from her chamber. Lady Josselyn's cloak was folded beneath her arm.

'I must take this to Dame Ellen directly, Seb. She is waiting upon it.'

''Tis like to snow, Em, you may want these.' He gave her the wooden box Rose had left.

'Rose's gloves. She has forgotten them. I cannot return them as yet. I know not where she lives.'

'They are a gift to you.' Seb passed her the note.

'Oh. How generous. I fear I was mistaken in her, Seb. Rose is a good woman. I got to like her last eve.' Emily pulled on the fine gloves and admired them. 'They look very well, do they not? Now, I shall be in haste.' She turned to where the journeyman sat at the board, wiping his bowl clean with a piece of bread. 'You will still be here when I return, won't you, Gabriel?'

Seb and Gabriel exchanged glances.

'No, mistress. 'Tis better that I leave now.'

'Oh, but I cannot...' Tears started in Emily's eyes.

'Nessie,' Seb said, 'Master Jude's bedding in the parlour needs folding and tidying.'

'What? Now?'

'Indeed, now, you impertinent maid, and do it neatly. Jude, I have a matter to discuss with you in the workshop, if you wouldn't mind?'

Alone in the kitchen, Gabriel took Emily's hands in his.

'We mustn't, Gabe, not here.'

'Your husband knows and is kind enough to permit us a moment to say our farewells.'

'He knows?'

'I told him of my feelings for you but that it had gone no further betwixt us.'

'He believes you?'

'Aye, he's a trusting soul. A good friend.'

Gabriel pulled Emily close, enfolding her in a final embrace. Both closed their eyes, breathing in each other's dear scent, a memory to cherish. Their lips met.

'I've tidied the parlour,' Nessie said. 'What shall I do with the bedding, mistress? Shall I put it for washing?'

The couple broke apart.

'I'll never forget you, Gabriel, never.'

'What about the washing?'

'Nor I you, Emily. Pray for me, as I shall for you.'

'Well, I don't know,' Nessie huffed, dumping the sheet, pillow and blanket down on the floor. 'It's not fair. You get to kiss and I don't. And after I cooked all that pottage for you. You're fickle, Master Gabe. Men! You just can't trust 'em.'

Towards Queenhithe

BY THE time they departed Paternoster Row, the sleet had turned to snow, forming slushy puddles to soak unwary feet. Seb feared anything that made his steps less certain, always afraid of falling – a legacy of his past – but the steady descent of white flakes did mean folks kept their heads down and he, Jude and Gabriel had good reason to wear their hoods pulled close. Gabriel had added a length of woollen cloth, wound about to conceal his face. It also gave protection from the cold and would be of great use on shipboard.

The steep slope of Garlickhill was becoming treacherous, so Jude took Seb's arm to aid him while Gabriel went on ahead. All three men were lost in their own thoughts as they passed the Pewter Pot tavern. Jude pictured an enticing wench. Seb yearned for a safe place to set his feet. Gabriel wondered who had betrayed the Known Men and their place of worship and study. He realised he would probably never know.

The *St Christopher* rode at anchor, rising and falling with the swell of the river. Seb eyed the undulating gangplank with misgivings. The crew scurried about the business of preparing to sail but it seemed Raff Scraggs had set a watch for his expected visitors.

'You Foxley?' some fellow called down.

'Aye,' Jude answered.

'Come aboard then. Captain Scraggs is waiting.'

'You go,' Seb said. 'I'll wait here. I can't be doing with a floor that does not stay still – again. I learned my lesson last time.'

'I thought my eyes deceived me,' said a voice, 'But they do not.' Roger Underwood, tavern-keeper and sometime espier in his red cap, sidled over, taking up position betwixt them and the gangplank. 'Gabriel Widowson: risen from the dead. I should have known a case of plague was too convenient by half. The bishop will pay me well for a second chance to see you burn.'

Jude stepped in front of Seb and Gabriel.

'And you fancy your chances? Three against one?'

Underwood laughed nastily.

'Better than that. Here!' he called, beckoning to someone.

Under-sheriff Nox and the two guards from last eve appeared through the veil of snow. 'How fortunate that they were at my tavern, sheltering from such weather with a cup of ale. And then there you are: a ghost, in company with those who aided and abetted you in your escape. Bishop Kemp will be so pleased.'

'You betrayed us, you Judas Iscariot!' Gabriel cried, elbowing Jude aside.

'I admit it but I did a good deal better than a miserly thirty pieces of silver for it, I assure you.'

'I've long since broken the Fifth Commandment to honour my father and, I warn you, as the Lord God stands my witness, I be sorely tempted to break the Sixth and kill you, Underwood.'

'Seize them all! Nox! What are you waiting for?'

Gabriel's fist caught the espier full in the mouth with the force of so much heartache and anger.

Underwood staggered and fell back, into the arms of Raff Scraggs.

'You deceiving, conniving devil. A quick death will be too merciful for you,' the new ship's captain snarled.

Of a sudden, fists and curses flew. Jude leapt upon Nox, giving him a bloody nose for a second time. Gabriel sent Underwood crashing against a mooring post while Scraggs boxed the ears of one guard and Seb managed to grab the other guard's staff and clout him with it, fending him off for long enough that members of the ship's crew – eager for a fight as mariners always be – came in sufficient numbers as to settle the matter.

When Underwood had struggled to his feet and could focus his eyes anew, he saw that Nox and both guards were being manhandled up the gangplank by the crew of the *St Christopher*.

'You didn't suppose I'd let you take my brother a second time, did you? Tie them to the mast,' Scraggs called to his crew, 'And make sure there be room for Judas here, when I've done with him.' With that, Scraggs balled his meaty fist and took pleasure in smashing Underwood's nose. 'I know not which commandment forbids that but it was worth the breaking,' he said, nursing his bruised knuckles. 'Go aboard, Gabe. I'll be there shortly.'

'We are both greatly in your debt, Master Foxley,' Scraggs said, embracing Seb so hard it knocked the wind from his chest. 'You too.' Jude received the same.

'Your captaincy warrant arrived then?' Seb said, not knowing quite what else to say.

'Aye, belatedly. And if I ever get my hands on whoever killed Captain Marchmane... well, no matter. But 'tis late in the season to be making our voyage. This'll be the last of the year, afore the winter storms.' Scraggs squinted up at the falling curtain of snowflakes. 'Snow we can manage. At least I don't sense no gales coming for a week or two. We'll pass the Christmas season in Bruges. Then we'll wait upon the Lord God's intensions for us.'

Scraggs loped away, up the gangplank, sure-footed as a goat, and the crew pulled the plank inboard after him.

'Farewell!' Seb shouted, 'God be with you. Send us word if you ever be in London again.'

Briefly, both Gabriel and Scraggs appeared. Gabriel raised his hand one last time and then was gone.

'Cast off aft; steer a'larboard!' Seb heard Scraggs yell. Whatever that meant. The *St Christopher* was leaving. Gabriel Widowson was gone.

The Panyer Inn

'PHEW. THAT was a near thing, Seb. Bloody hell, we could all have been flung in gaol.' Jude sat toasting his feet by the tavern's bright hearth, a cup of hot spiced ale in his hands.

'We weren't.'

'Your wondrous damned plan was nearly the end of us all.'

'But, mercifully, it was not to be.' Seb rubbed his palms together. His fingertips had yet to regain feeling. 'What do you think will happen to them all?'

'Huh, you know Gabe. He will do well enough; he always does. Flanders women'll be throwing themselves at his feet, as ever. I wish I knew his secret. Not as if he's good looking, is it?' Jude drank his ale, smacked his lips. 'That's better than medicine, that.'

'I mean Nox and Underwood and the guards. What will Scraggs do with them?'

'Toss the buggers overboard, if he's got any sense. That's what I'd do. Who cares? I doubt we'll ever see them again. More ale here, if you will?' Jude called, raising his arm. 'Where's that lazy bloody tap-boy got to? Anyhow, more important: we need a new journeyman. I'm not going to do his work as well as my own.'

'Not sure about a journeyman. Aww...' Seb waggled painful fingers as feeling began to return. 'But I have in mind someone who shows a deal of promise as a scrivener – a more likely apprentice than Jack, at least – one who works hard.'

'Who?'

'A certain tavern wench of our acquaintance whose employer has but lately departed the city, for the foreseeable future. She will need some new respectable means of earning a living.'

'You mean Rose?'

'Why not?'

'That will certainly have my blessing, little brother. What about Jack? Boot him out on his backside would be my advice, the useless worm. And that damned flea-infested dog of his.'

'I cannot be so cruel Jude. It was you who took him in in the first place.'

'A serious misjudgement on my part.'

'Besides, he serves us well in his own way, though a scrivener he will never be. But none other could have climbed that tower to get my letter to Gabriel. We owe him better than to throw him back on the street. Our home is his home.'

'Not for much longer. Ah, here's more ale. A farthing for you.' Jude tossed a coin to the tap-boy who caught it, snapping it from the air whence it disappeared. 'I'm feeling generous, indeed.'

'What do you mean, Jude: not for much longer?'

'I told you. Em's right, the pair of us – me and her – we don't belong under the same roof. I'll be looking to move elsewhere.'

'Oh, no, Jude. I don't want that.'

'Your marriage will work out better without me, cluttering up the place. You know I'm right. Do not fear. I won't go far.'

'Where would you go?'

'A place we both know well enough. I hear Dame Ellen takes in lodgers for a reasonable rent and has a spare room since Nessie returned home.'

Seb sighed with relief and laughed.

'Our old rooms. Oh, Jude, that would be the perfect solution.'

'I'm quite wily in my ways, Seb,' he said, 'I do use my head occasionally, whatever you may think to the bloody contrary. Let's drink to it. Dame Ellen's place!'

'What are you thinking about now?' Jude asked, seeing Seb staring at naught, letting his mulled ale go cold.

'Em and Gabriel. He told me they never committed adultery though he wanted to. I think Em felt the same.'

'You believe him?'

Seb blew out his breath.

'I have to Jude. How else can I go on with Em?'

'He lied to you about being a heretic.'

'No, Jude. He never did. He said naught either way and I never asked. I preferred to believe what I wished to be the truth: that he was a son of the Church, as we are.'

'And it's the same with the question of adultery, isn't it? You'll believe what you want to be the case. Well, I hope matters will prove that way with that wife of yours, little brother. I couldn't bloody trust her, I tell you.'

'With Gabriel gone, I think the situation be resolved now. I pray 'tis so.'

'Masters Foxley, may I join you?' Father Thomas shook snow from his cloak. 'What a time to require my services, in such weather. Plays havoc with my rheumaticks and my chest complains with every breath. Still, none of us may choose the time of our passing, I suppose, and thus the moment when we require the Last Rites. At least this poor soul received them as needed, not like those who be victims of foul murder.'

Seb and Jude crossed themselves and moved their stools to make room for the priest beside the hearth.

'Ale, father?' Seb offered.

'Most welcome; welcome indeed.' The priest eased himself down onto a low stool, wincing and putting his hands to his back. Then he suffered a bout of coughing. 'Cannot shift this chest complaint. A week abed has done naught to aid me. All that has happened of late, I missed it all. And I haven't heard that the authorities have caught anyone for the deaths of those unfortunate women yet, have they? Have either of you heard more than I? Intriguing mystery, is it not?'

'No, father, we haven't,' Jude replied, 'Anyway, the murderer is probably miles away by now.'

'You may be right. I pray God it be so, for the sake of poor harlots in the city. They must be afeared, indeed. I wonder you're not looking into the matter, Master Sebastian, you've had success in solving crimes afore now.'

'We must leave it to the sheriffs,' said Jude, 'When they can be bothered to shift their fat arses. Isn't that so, Seb?'

'Aye. I suppose so.'

'And how is the new psalter progressing? Is it nigh finished yet? It would be pleasant if Father Hugh could have it in time for Advent which is not so far off now.

Seb hid his guilty expression behind his ale cup, taking a long draught.

'I'll have it completed by then,' he said, hoping that would be the case.

'Good. Then I'll thank you for the ale and be upon my way... if you'll be so kind?' The elderly priest held out his arms and Seb and Jude took one elbow each to lift him up. 'They make stools so low these days.'

'That was a rash promise to make,' Jude said, 'Advent is, what, twelve days hence? The book will never be ready on time, will it? How far have you got with it? Last time I looked, you were doing the initial for Psalm Sixty-One. How many more have you done since? Seb! Are you even listening to me?'

'What? Forgive me, my thoughts were elsewhere.'

'Will the psalter be finished on time?'

'If naught else occurs to distract me.'

'Yet something does distract you. I can see that already. What is it now?'

'What Father Thomas said, about solving crimes.'

'It's hardly our place to go hunting for murderers. Best keep out of it, Seb.'

'It was just that something I saw reminded me of... I don't know what. I cannot recall it, but 'tis like a shadow just out of reach in my mind, if only I could grasp it.'

'Well, leave it be then. We've had enough trouble of late without bloody searching it out. Now, you going to finish your ale or not?'

Jude had gone to Dame Ellen's house, to see about returning to his old lodgings. He and Seb had been content enough there in the past. There was room aplenty for two persons and the first inklings of an outrageous idea were sneaking around the dark recesses of his mind. It just might work out upon some far distant day and it certainly raised his spirits to think on it. Yet it would require the shattering of every promise he'd ever made to himself upon the matter: Jude Foxley was not the marrying kind. But promises could be broken.

Seb stopped to speak with Old Symkyn. Though the snow had ceased for the present, the air was bitter with cold and a sky the colour of an unshined pewter trencher foretold more snow to come. The beggar sat hunched on the low wall opposite Seb's house that backed on to St Paul's Yard. His wispy hair was dusted with snow, the heat from his body insufficient to melt it.

'Symkyn, please come dine with us. 'Tis hardly the weather for sitting here.'

'Ah, Master Seb, too kind as ever. I'm an outdoors fellow, you know that. Always was, even afore this.' He held up his mangled arm, earned at Barnet Field six years earlier, that together with an ill-mended knee had ended his craft as a thatcher. 'But I shall accept your invitation, this time. Even my newly won shoes are not enough to keep out the chills this day, but a full belly surely will.'

'Come then. The hour for dinner must be nigh and I smell onions and bacon cooking, or is that my wishful thinking?'

The Foxley kitchen

DINNER WAS indeed a bacon and onion pudding, served with turnips. Though Seb noticed that Em wrinkled her nose behind Symkyn's back as she served him, she had manners enough not to complain about the beggar's ripe odour as his body warmed in the heat of the kitchen. Jack wouldn't notice and Tom was too courteous to say ought but Nessie was another case.

'It stinks in here,' she said, not taking the trouble to lower her voice, 'Like wet sheep and dog shit, it is. If one o' you lads has trod shit on this floor, after I scrubbed it this morn, then I-I'll have something to say about it.'

'Weren't me, wos it?' said Jack, looking to the soles of his shoes.

'My shoes are clean,' Tom said. 'Damp but no muck.'

Everyone inspected their footwear, even Symkyn.

'Naught amiss with my new shoes,' he said, holding out his feet for a second opinion. 'Worn but serviceable... and clean, apart from that stain upon the leather. Pity that, but 'tis probably the reason they was left in the alms box and I have the benefit. Oh, by the by, Master Seb, I believe I owe you this.' Symkyn rummaged within the folds of his ragged clothes and produced a coin: an angel. 'I knew ye never meant to put so much into my bowl. 'Tis far too much for the likes o' me. If only the king was half so generous to those who once fought at his side. So I haven't spent it.'

But Seb ignored the coin upon the table cloth. He was still staring at Symkyn's shoes. That illusive memory had been retrieved.

'Tell me again how you came by these, Symkyn,' Seb said, kneeling at the beggar's feet to look more closely.

'Please get up, master. No one should be grovelling at my feet. I was a humble craftsman and a soldier, not a royal duke.'

'Jack, go fetch my scrip from the workshop. Now, Symkyn, please tell me who gave you these shoes.'

'Father Thomas at St Michael's. Like ye, he's a kindly man and saw my old shoes had no soles left, hardly. He said he thought there was a pair that might fit in the church alms box. And, as ye see, they do me very well indeed. I was in honest need, or I wouldn't have accepted them, in case someone else's need was greater than mine. I didn't steal them, if that's what ye be thinking.'

'No, no. I did not think that for a moment. Jack! Where is my scrip?'

''Ere, Master Seb. Wot you want it for?'

Seb opened the leather bag and sorted through the pile of papers within. Most were drawings and sketches with a few notes. He found the paper he was searching for. Not an exquisite drawing of a bird or a cobweb, nor a sketch of an ecclesiastical arcade or lancet window. It was just a hastily wrought outline of a footprint. One he had found imprinted in the bloody earth beneath a hedge at Smithfield.

And Symkyn's right shoe fitted its likeness exactly. As for the left one, Seb could see that the stain which so spoiled the look of it was precisely the colour of cold blood. To his mind, there could be no doubt but it was a most troubling revelation.

St Michael le Querne church

SEB HESITATED at the church porch. Perhaps it would be wiser to wait for Jude – except that his brother had gone to Dame Ellen's and not come home to dine since. Seb feared that if he delayed any longer, his nerve would fail him, so he pushed open the door and went in. He breathed deeply of the incense-laden air in order to calm himself. St Christopher upon the wall by the door still bore his burden stoically and Seb murmured a short prayer that the saint might keep Gabriel in mind as he sailed the seas. Belatedly, he recalled that the Known Men didn't hold with the intercession of saints. Oh, well, too late; the prayer was said now and would surely do no harm.

He determined to speak with Father Thomas upon the matter of Symkyn's shoes but his misgivings were legion. Jude had previously said he thought the murderer of that poor woman at Bishopsgate – if it was not some drunken imagining – might have been a priest. Seb couldn't think for one heartbeat that dear Father Thomas was capable of killing anyone. But Father Wessell was a man of quite a different humour and hadn't he been wearing new shoes yesterday? Seb had had his mind on the matter of Gabriel's escape but he half recalled someone – Dame Ellen, maybe – remarking upon the Weasel's fine blue footwear.

A door banged, making Seb jump. Father Thomas came from the vestry.

'Ah, Sebastian, my son. Well met for the second time this day. How may I help you?'

'Er, I, er, have some small matter I would discuss with you, father.'

'Not a concern about marriage, is it? Only that truly is not my realm of expertise, although I'll do my best, of course.'

'No. 'Tis about a pair of shoes.' Seb took Symkyn's shoes from his scrip. 'These shoes, to be precise.'

Father Thomas squinted in the gloom to better see the shoes.

'They look in good repair, my son. Did you wish to donate them to the alms box for the poor? I'm sure someone among the needy will make good use of them.'

'I do believe they came from the alms box in the first place. Symkyn the beggar said you gave them to him because his old pair was beyond saving.'

'Did he?' Father Thomas scratched his tonsure. 'Not sure I remember that. Was it recently? I've not given out anything from the alms box for a while, seeing there's little in it but a solitary holed stocking, some swaddling bands for a babe – of which none have been born of late and I think 'tis time that you and your goodwife looked to doing your part to rectify that – oh, and a pair of knitted mitts which be half unravelled.'

'But no shoes such as these?' Seb had been so sure the priest would be able to shed light upon their previous owner.

At first, the priest gave no answer but then he avoided the subject somewhat.

'If Symkyn has no need of them...'

'Indeed he does, father. I left him at my house, warming his feet before my fire, whilst I brought them here. If they were not in the alms box, you do know from whence they came, don't you, father?'

'Aye, I do. I fear that I was in error to give them to Symkyn. You are correct: they were never in the alms box, not really, not until I put them there, at least. But I could not see that their owner had much further use for them. They were just sitting there and when I saw poor Symkyn without soles to his shoes in such freezing weather, I thought the Good Lord must have seen fit to have those shoes abandoned for a better purpose. But I was mistaken.'

'Whose were they?'

'A man who has no heart for charity. He was so angry with me, ranting and raving about the few pence he could have got for them, if he had sold them, instead of which I had given them away. For a few moments, I even feared for my safety, and then for Symkyn's, if he ever learned to whom I had given them. Yet there he stood, as well shod as a king in his fine blue shoes, but newly bought from a cordwainer in Lombard Street. I know not how Father Wessell can afford such luxuries and begrudge a beggar...'

'Where are you going, Sebastian? I was about to offer you ale...'

Chapter 19

Friday, the twenty-second day of November
The Foxleys' kitchen

NOBODY WAS paying heed to breaking their fast, except Jack, for whom food was the most important thing in life.

'Bloody hell, little brother. And you're sure of this?' Jude said, waving his spoonful of pottage with no concern for the consequences.

'As sure as I can be without hearing him confess.'

'So I didn't dream it? I really did see that stinking son of Satan kill the woman I was with and he tried to kill me too.'

'Aye, that's possible, Jude.' Seb put down his oatcake, untasted. 'But the shoe print is only evidence that he murdered Bessie, since it fits exactly the one left in the bloody mud by the hedge at Smithfield. It does not prove he was also at Bishopsgate. On the other hand,' he said, the oatcake almost reaching his mouth, 'I cannot see that there could be two priests committing such similar felonies in the city at one time, can you? Besides, proof that he killed one woman should be enough to...'

'To what? Hang the bugger? He's a priest: he'll get away with a bloody bread-and-water penance and a stern telling off. You know the Church takes care of its own and does so too damn well when justice ought to be done.'

'So what would you have me do? Ignore the fact that I – we – have proof of his guilt? You want me to forget it?'

'Of course I don't. It's just that there must be some other way, Seb, a means of ensuring he gets what he deserves. The city will not be a safer place until he's gone – for good and all.'

'Are you saying we should take this matter into our own hands because I'm not of a mind to do that, if you are? The law is the law to be upheld by the authorities.'

'That may apply to the law of the land but not to the bloody Church, as you well know. They condemn good men like Gabe and let bastard priests go unpunished. Church law isn't good enough, Seb. Can't you see that?' Jude went back to his bowl of pottage. 'And to whom would you report it anyway? Bishop Kemp? Tell him his own nephew is a killer? No, little brother, if we want him to pay for his crimes, we'll have to exact the price ourselves out of his worthless hide.'

'No, Jude. 'Tis not for us to seek retribution.' Seb stood up, abandoning his food.

'Wot's reterbussion mean, then?' Jack asked but no one answered him, if indeed they even heard the question.

'Well and good then. You hide under the bed and I'll go find the devil and make him suffer. He nearly killed me, Seb. It's only right that I see justice done. And not weak-and-watery Church justice, either. I want that bastard to dance the bloody hangman's jig and cheer whilst he does it.'

Seb took down his mantle from the peg on the wall.

'And where are you going without any breakfast?' Emily asked. 'You're wasting good food, here, and it costs coin.'

'To show my evidence to Lord Mayor Josselyn. He'll know what to do for the best.'

'Don't, Seb,' Jude said, grabbing his arm, 'Don't tell anyone of this, not yet.'

'Why not?'

'Isn't it obvious? Three reasons. Firstly: if Wessell gets to hear of it, we could all be in danger. Secondly: he'll run and never be brought to justice. And thirdly...'

'Thirdly?'

'Work it out for yourself.'

'If Wessell is found dead in some dark alley, we will be the first to come under suspicion. Aye, I'd concluded that much already which is precisely why I'm going to the mayor, so that you won't do anything so reckless and foolish as to deal out the sentence of execution in person. We are law-abiding citizens, Jude, or had you forgotten that?'

'Law-abiding? Huh. Those words aren't worth the breath it takes to say them. You've seen enough of the workings of the bloody law, Seb. Can't you see that sometimes it works in the felon's favour? Was I not once accused of a crime I didn't commit and near paid for it on Tyburn Tree? Remember?'

'Of course I haven't. How could I ever forget seeing you with a noose about your neck?'

'Well, then, don't let this matter end likewise, with the true murderer getting away with it.'

'She didn't: we caught her.'

'But it was a close run thing.'

'Aye, I'll grant you. Too close.'

'Can I 'ave yer oatcakes then, master?' Jack piped up.

'Put them down, you greedy rascal,' Emily said, slapping the lad's hands away from Seb's platter. 'Master is going to take off his mantle, sit back down and eat them himself.'

'I am?'

'You are indeed. And you will not be going to the mayor until Monday next at the earliest.'

'I won't? Why not?'

'Because I agree with Jude, just this once. The Weasel needs to be punished for killing Rose's best friend and the other woman at Bishopsgate and to protect all women in the city from a man who obviously thinks we are all of us contemptible because of Eve's sin – a fact I don't much hold with myself. We have a right not to go in fear of the likes of him and it would serve him right.'

TONI MOUNT

'Have you quite finished, Em?' Seb said, removing his mantle, as ordered.

'Aye. I've said my piece. Why? Don't you think I should have an opinion because I am a woman?'

Seb shook his head and pulled a wry mouth.

'Did I ever say that?'

'No. And, if you know what's best for your health and comfort, you never will. Now eat your food.'

Jude smiled hugely as his brother meekly ate his oatcakes.

'Serves *you* right too, for marrying a firebrand. Now eat up, like a good little lad, else mamma will take her broom to your backside.' He burst out laughing when Seb scowled at him.

Later that morn, in the workshop, Seb had a chance, betwixt customers, to speak briefly with Jude out of hearing of the lads.

'Whatever you intend, you must be careful, Jude. I know you might regard it as justice to take a life for a life but, if you do, you'll be no better than he is. I cannot condone it.'

Jack came in from the street with Little Beggar whence they'd been so the dog could do the necessary without getting into trouble with Master Jude for befouling the floor.

'P'raps me an' Beggar can condown it for you, Master Seb, whatever it is?'

'You can stop giving ear to other folks' conversation, for a bloody start,' Jude complained. 'Can't you find something useful to do?'

'I ain't tidyin' the bloody storeroom agen, am I? I already done it, ain't I?'

'Watch your tongue, Jack, and no, the storeroom will do as it is,' Seb said. 'However, you can sweep the slush from the front step to keep our customers safe upon their feet and I would have you run an errand for me in a while. I promised Rose another lesson this afternoon, as usual, but I be so behind in completing Father Thomas's new psalter, I must work on that whilst the light is good enough. Seeing the sullen sky out there, more snow will likely fall sometime soon and the light be hardly adequate to paint by. For now, I must work. After dinner, I would have you go tell her that I shall come when I may, most probably later than I normally do. Can you recall that message?'

'Course I can. I ain't noddle-'eaded, am I?'

Seb settled down to work on the psalter, content to lose himself in the glorious hues of a goldfinch perched upon a bramble bough, within the capital 'O' that commenced Psalm One-hundred-and-eight: 'O God, my heart is fixed...' And, indeed, such employment was the only sure thing upon which Seb's heart could be fixed. There was such an excess of turmoil and worry in life, otherwise.

His brushstrokes were delicate but unerring as he painted the bird's plumage, edging each saffron yellow feather with the gleam of powdered gold. Who would not find delight in attempting to copy the wonders of the Lord God's own creations, though they could never equal them? The tiny creature looked real enough. It could never chirrup, nor sing nor fly but Seb was content to make a fair likeness of it which, he hoped, would be pleasing to both God and man.

After a fish-day dinner, Seb went straight back to his painting, unwilling to waste a moment of fair daylight.

'I'll go t' Rose's place now, shall I? Give 'er your message.' Jack asked.

'Aye, but take care, lad, the ways are bound to be slippery 'neath your feet. I would not have you come to harm.' Seb, busy with his brush, didn't see how Jack rolled his eyes at that. Slippery was fun. He might be able to slide all the way down Garlickhill. 'And come back directly, as soon as you have delivered my message. 'Tis like to snow again.'

Jack knew exactly why master wanted him back soon. It was because master – never so sure-footed – would be needing a steady arm to rely upon when he went down to see Rose. Jack didn't mind. Visiting Rose twice in one day was fine by him.

'It's snowing a bit,' Jude said. 'You want me to put up the shutter? The snow is wetting the counter-board.'

'Aye, may as well. I can hardly see what I'm painting now. Is Jack returned as yet?'

'No. The young bugger never heeds what you say, does he?'

'He ought to be home by now, surely. How long does it take to walk to Garlickhill and back?'

'For you, in this weather? Best part of an hour, I'd say. For him: the time it takes to say a score of Paternosters, maybe less. I shall go myself and find him and woebetide him if I discover him playing in the bloody snow.'

'If you be using Jack's tardiness as an excuse to see Rose,' Seb said, raising his eyebrows and grinning at Jude, 'I'd like to go with you; make use of you as a stout staff, if you do not object?'

'No, I'm used to it,' Jude said with a mock sigh, 'Serving as my little brother's prop and guiding hand. Come on, then, before the snow gets too deep for you.'

Garlickhill

AS HE feared, Seb found the steep way difficult. Cart ruts in the mud had frozen solid and were now disguised by fresh snow – the likelihood of a twisted knee or a turned ankle increased by the moment. Garlickhill was treacherous underfoot and Seb kept his eyes cast down to see where he could best make the next step.

They were close by the church of St James when Seb stopped abruptly.

'Jude,' he said, bending down in the snow, 'Look at this.' He pointed out a footprint in the fresh whiteness and traced the outline with his finger.

'What of it? We're hardly alone in walking this way.'

'I know that but can you see how the weight has been put down all uneven along the toes of the right foot?'

'So? Come along, Seb, I'm freezing my bloody bollocks off out here.'

'Wait.' Seb fished in his scrip and found the now-dog-eared image of the Smithfield footprint as he knelt in the snow. 'See? I know it isn't the same shoe but the pattern of wear is somewhat similar. Wessell has new shoes, we know, but the beginnings of the same uneven tread on the right foot is showing here.'

'So, you're saying that bastard priest has been here?'

'Aye, Jude, and within a few minutes, else the print would not still be so distinct and clear.'

'And why would he be here? To visit a fellow priest at St James, perhaps? Or...'

The scream startled them both.

'Bloody hell! That's Rose.' Jude abandoned Seb, still kneeling, and raced towards the steps that led up to Rose's room.

'Leave us alone, you brute! Get your hands off me.' Jude heard her cry. Then another voice:

'Yer a bloody bastard, ain't yer? I'll set me dog on yer, I will.'

Jude burst into the room. A glance took in the scene of chaos. Rose lay upon the bed. Blood stained her ripped bodice. Jack was trying to pull the priest away from her. The dog barked wildly, running in circles.

'You should have kept silent, you filthy whore. Yet you already yapped to that idiot Nox, didn't you? Told him you saw a priest. Now you'll suffer the consequences, you disgusting, slack-mouthed...' Wessell caught sight of Jude and stepped back from the bed, a bloodied Irish knife in hand, dragging Rose by her hair.

'The harlot must die, seeing the bitch recognised me at Low Mass this morn. Confound Father Thomas and his ailing chest. I told him I never conduct Low Mass for 'tis not worthy of one of my standing but, having done so out of my generosity and consideration for that simpleton Thomas, see what I am now forced to do.'

Jude moved into the room. There was hardly enough space.

Abandoning Rose who had slumped to the floor, limp and helpless, Wessell grabbed Jack instead, holding the blade at the lad's throat.

'One more step, Foxley, and I warn you, I'll slit his skinny neck.'

Jack's eyes were wide, pleading.

'Do as you will,' Jude said with a shrug, 'He's a bloody nuisance anyway. You'll be doing me a favour.' Jude made a move, slow and deliberate, to the bedside. 'Rose?'

She struggled to pull herself up and Jude lifted her back upon the bed, setting a pillow behind her head. He brushed her soft hair from her forehead.

'Rose, you need a surgeon. I'll go straightway to Dagvyle.'

'It's not so bad. Looks worse than it is,' she whispered. 'But Jack...'

Wessell seized the opportunity to slip past the bed to the door, dragging the lad with him.

Jack, too terrified to think, went without a struggle.

'Fear not, lass, Jack will do well enough. Seb's outside and the dog will aid him. Beggar,' Jude said, taking the dog by the scruff, 'Listen you fleabag, go, see the bugger off, you hear.' He set the dog down and it raced out of the door and down the steps.

Wessell had stopped halfway down the stair.

'You make a move and the lad's dead meat,' the priest shouted at Seb who stood at the bottom. 'You let me by and he lives.'

Seb moved back, out of the way.

'Please, don't harm the lad. Just let him go. He has done naught. Please, I beg you. Release him.'

The dog came hurtling down the steps and took a hold on the priest's dark cloak, ripping it with his teeth. Wessell kicked out at it, cursing, and near fell. The dog yelped in pain and Jack, roused from his terror, bit the priest's arm. But the man held on, pulling Jack's head back by his unruly hair, exposing his neck once more to the knife.

Using Jack as a hostage, Wessell dragged him into St James's church.

'Stay back, or he dies,' he snarled.

Seb, now joined by Jude, advanced, matching Wessell's retreat.

'What do you hope to achieve by this?' Jude asked. 'So far as I know, St James does not have a licence to grant sanctuary. You need to go to St Mary le Bow, if that's your plan.'

'I am a priest. I claim benefit of clergy.'

'That's an option, I suppose, but you'll have to go to your uncle for that, won't you? Only the bishop can hear your case and... let me see. Oh, how unfortunate for you, your uncle isn't here. What do you think, Seb, do we let him go to the bishop?' Jude shook his head in answer to his own question. 'Nah, I say not. So where to now?'

Keeping the blade at Jack's throat, Wessell pulled the lad through a doorway from the nave. It led to a stairway up inside the church tower. Jack tried to squirm free but cried out as the steel blade nicked his skin.

'Help me, masters, pleeease,' he wailed.

'Shut up, you, or I'll end it now,' the priest told him.

'What do we do, Jude?' Seb asked as Wessell disappeared up the tower. 'We must save Jack.'

'Follow them?' Jude was doubtful they could do anything.

Seb braced himself for the worst and went up first, with no idea what was to be done. He was no hero and grateful to have Jude with him. The stairs ended at a trapdoor and Wessell was perched there, uncertain.

'Let the lad go,' Seb said, drawing his eating knife from its sheath at his belt. He wasn't sure why but it seemed the thing to do.

Wessell pushed up the trapdoor and an icy blast blew in a flurry of snow. He manhandled Jack out onto the roof and pushed him out across the frozen wooden shingles before clambering out after him.

Seb followed, awkward and uncertain until Jude gave him a shove from behind. The shingles were treacherous but Seb tried not to think about that.

'There's no way out now,' he said as he inched away from the safety of the trapdoor so he and Jude confronted the priest, both now with dinner knives in hand.

Wessell backed away, across the roof, briefly losing his footing as he slipped on the ice, his fashionable new shoes unable to grip.

'I'll throw the lad off, unless you let me go, I warn you.' The priest sounded desperate indeed now. 'I'm warning you. I mean what I say.'

'What in the name of all that be holy is going on?' A young priest came up onto the roof. 'It's too cold for such pranks and japes, you silly lads should...'

'Stay back, all of you, or he dies.' Wessell took another step. And then another.

'Beware the edge!' cried the newcomer.

But Wessell took one more step back, slipped and skidded. He fought to regain his balance. The knife flew from his grasp. With a screech of terror, he tumbled off the church roof, into oblivion.

And Jack fell with him.

Time was turned to stone.

No one moved.

And then the young priest began pattering a hasty Latin litany.

'Lord Jesu have mercy,' Seb cried and, forgetful of danger, he hurried across the shingle roof to peer over. 'Jude! Give a hand here!'

There, just a few feet below the roof, Jack dangled by his fingertips from a gargoyle.

'Elp!' he squeaked, 'I'm slippin'.'

Seb, with Jude clutching his belt, leant out, desperate to reach Jack, stretching as far as he could.

A crowd was gathering in the street below, summoned by Wessell's cry. They were staring up, shielding their eyes from the falling snow.

'I cannot get to him. Lower me further.'

'I can't. Wait. Hey, father, cease your prayers and aid us.'

The young priest, seeing their efforts, took a hold around Jude's waist so he too could lean out.

'I trust your belt is well made,' he said, taking the strain. But Jude's weight had them both slipping, sliding along the roof towards the edge. Jude wedged his boot betwixt two shingles, breaking one with a snap but then his foot took purchase in the hole.

'Can you reach now?' he called to Seb.

'Almost. Another inch or two.'

'Pleease,' came a plaintive wail, 'I can't 'old on any more... I'm gonna fall.'

'No, you are not, Jack Tabor. That is an order.' Seb was gasping with the effort. 'There. I've got your hand. Pull us up, Jude.'

Jude and the young priest were doing their best but cold hands were becoming numb. Then Seb's belt broke.

As his brother slithered over the edge, Jude lunged, grabbing fistfuls of clothing, anything he could lay hold of. Cloth tore. Eventually, all Jude held was Seb's ankle.'

'Christ on the bloody Cross save us!' he swore.

'Amen to that.'

Seb was being pulled, pressed against the gable by his own weight and that of the terrified lad to whom he clung. He felt his ribs give way and such pain shot through his shoulder like an arrow shaft. Yet he held on to Jack by the power of his will alone.

Of a sudden, there were folk hauling them up, back onto the roof.

'Saw you wos in trouble there,' a stout fellow said. 'Quite a show you put on fer the crowd below.'

At last, Seb lifted Jack to safety, holding him close. Both were trembling from shock, cold and exhaustion.

'There, I've got you. You be safe now, lad,' Seb said, wrapping one arm around Jack's narrow shoulders. Someone put a blanket about them both as Seb sank down upon the icy shingles, too weary to move another step. Jack sobbed softly against his chest as he stroked the lad's hair. 'All is well, lad, all is well.'

'Come, Seb. Let's all get out of this weather,' Jude said. 'We need to tend to Rose, too. If that bastard has killed her...'

'You cannot do worse to him, Jude. Did you look down? He won't trouble anyone but Satan now.'

'Aye. Well that's as good as we might have hoped. Now, come...'

'Take the lad.' Seb roused Jack and gently gave him into Jude's care.

'And you.'

'No, Jude. I'm hurt. I cannot climb down.'

'Hurt? How? You can't bloody stay up here. I'll carry you, if I must.'

'The joint in my shoulder be out of place.'

'The surgeon can put that to rights.'

'But I fear I have other hurts less easily mended, inside.'

Jude told Jack to go fetch someone to help with Seb and the lad stumbled towards the trapdoor, still in somewhat of a daze.

'What's amiss, little brother?' Jude said, kneeling beside Seb as the snow settled upon them.

'This.' Seb pulled the torn lacings of his doublet apart and opened his shirt a little with his good hand. Black and purple bruising spread upwards. 'I felt something happen as my belt broke. I know not what but I have no strength left. I just want to lie down, Jude.'

'Aye. But not here on the bloody rooftop.'

Though his own arms already felt nigh wrenched from their sockets, Jude gathered the blanket around Seb and lifted him, carrying him to the trapdoor. There, other willing hands waited to take his burden and get his brother, somehow, down the stairs to the nave below.

Seb knew nothing of it but a brutal crimson storm of pain.

Jude was torn betwixt concern for his brother and anxiety about Rose. But there were now hands aplenty to tend to Seb; a surgeon had been sent for and the injured man lay swaddled like a babe in blankets with a cushion at his head. So Jude made his way to the room above the Pewter Pot.

Rose was also being cared for by an elderly woman, a neighbour.

'Rose. A-are you safe?' Jude asked, sitting on the narrow bed beside her feet.

'And who might you be?' the woman demanded. 'If you be the monster what done this to the poor lass...'

'I'm not, I swear to you. And the monster is no more. My name is Jude Foxley. I'm a f-friend.'

'A friend?' the woman queried, clearly aware of Rose's means of earning her living.

'Not that kind of friend. Rose is very dear to me – to us.'

Rose opened her eyes sleepily.

'Jude,' she murmured, 'Thank you for...' Her voice trailed off.

'I gave her a draught to help her rest. She'll be sore for a few days but the cuts didn't go too deep. She's young; she'll heal well enough, though there will be some scars on her breast for always. Pity. She has such fine skin otherwise. But, no doubt, you know that for yourself.'

'I know no such thing,' Jude protested. 'And damn you for thinking ill of me. I love Rose.'

There. He had spoken the dreaded word and it could not be unsaid.

'I love her,' he repeated, as much in wonder at himself as to assure the old woman.

The attic room in the Foxleys' house

'AN' THEN Master Seb saved me when I were that close t' fallin', Tom. That close t' bein' a dead 'un, I wos,' Jack said, telling his fellow apprentice the tale for the fourth – or was it the fifth? – time, as they lay in their attic bed, staring up into the darkness of the eaves above.

There was little chance of sleep. Jack was still overwrought with the day's events. 'Saved by a bloody gargoyle, wasn't I? Who would've thought it, eh? I never knowed Master Seb were that strong but 'e 'eld me safe fer ages, didn't 'e?'

'So you said before,' Tom muttered, turning on his side and pulling his pillow over his ears.

But the pillow could not mute the sound when a door banged to below. Someone was going into what had been Master Gabe's chamber where Rose now lay sleeping. Probably it was Master Jude who seemed to have a soft spot for her, Tom thought.

The household had been turned upside down since they brought Master Seb home upon a hurdle, pale as death. Tom had remembered master in his heartfelt prayers and mentioned Rose as well. But it was Master Seb whose injuries had caused such distraction.

Surgeon Dagvyle had spoken of 'internal bleeding'. Tom wasn't certain what that meant but everyone was tip-toeing about the house as though a sudden noise might cause master's end.

Except Master Jude, of course. The door into Gabe's old chamber below banged shut again.

Mistress Em was in a state of anguish such as Tom had never seen before, wringing her hands in her apron and hastening from one room to another, upstairs and down, without any purpose or reason, so it seemed.

Then Dame Ellen had arrived, come to see if mistress needed assistance in nursing her husband – or, more likely, to learn of events first hand, in order to set the gossip-mill grinding. At least the old dame had calmed mistress for a while.

And what would you know? In all this chaos and turmoil, Father Weasel was the villain of the peace! A killer! There was news indeed. Little wonder they couldn't sleep.

'Hear that, Tom?' Jack whispered in the dark, clutching at his bed-fellow.

'No. Go to sleep.' Tom didn't want to hear anything.

'That's Mistress Em. I think she's weepin'? Do you s'pose Master Seb might be...'

Author's Notes

The heresy of the Known Men was real and dated to 1476. In that year, Thomas Underwood preached 'All priests since our Saviour were heretics. In Christ's time, there were no priests and many Known Men wish there were still none today...' Bishop Thomas Kemp did attempt to come down hard on the heretics but on a number of occasions had to seek a royal pardon because felons had escaped from his prisons. The Lollards' Tower stood at the south-west corner of Old St Paul's, although there is a later tower, similarly named and still standing, at the Archbishop of Canterbury's Lambeth Palace, south of the Thames. The Known Men were betrayed by one of their own members, Roger Habraham, much as told in the novel.

Perhaps the most exciting and unlikely event in my story also happened – Gabriel's escape from prison as a supposed plague victim in a coffin. In 1681, when cases of plague still occurred and were greatly feared, the highwayman, John 'Swift Nick' Nevison (1639-84) was arrested and incarcerated in Leicester Gaol. Nevison pretended he was ill and a physician friend confirmed this, saying it was most likely the plague and the prisoner should be removed to some solitary place to avoid infecting everyone, inmates and gaolers alike. Then another friend, an artist, daubed Nevison with spots of paint to support the claim that he was dying of the dread disease and no one dared look close enough to dispute it. Finally, the physician administered a potion to feign death for a couple of hours, the coffin was brought and Nevison's 'corpse' removed for burial.

Apparently, Swift Nick then returned to his criminal ways but word of his demise had spread, so he had a hard time convincing his victims they were not being robbed by a ghost and ought to take his threats seriously. Obviously, I couldn't resist using this tale [Paul Buck, *Prison Break*, 2012].

Bishop Thomas Kemp, Lord Mayor Ralph Josselyn and Surgeon John Dagvyle were all real people and I apologise to any of their descendants today for the liberties I have taken with their characters and reputations. As for Father Hugh Wessell and Under-sheriff Valentyne Nox, the villains are wholly fictitious and any similarity of name or occupation with anyone, living or departed, is purely accidental.

I also hope that nothing in this story offends the *real* Sebastian Foxley, whose mother made his existence known to me recently and asked how I came to choose the name for my hero. My inspiration was a fifteenth-century wall painting of St Sebastian. Shot full of arrows, he yet had such a gentle, long-suffering expression, he was perfect for the part. As for the surname Foxley, incomers to London often took their place of origin as their second name and I found a village called Foxley on a map of Wiltshire. However, quite by accident, last summer we discovered Foxley in Norfolk and just had to visit its medieval church of St Thomas. The small congregation was so welcoming and showed us their church's fifteenth-century screen with its portraits of saints – of the right date and just the kind of thing Sebastian might have painted as a gift to his ancestral home, if he went on a visit. So, apologies to Wiltshire; the Foxley brothers now come from Norfolk.

Sebastian is also the saint to ask for protection against plague and, as for Jude, he is the patron saint of lost causes.

I should like to dedicate this story to Glenn without whom my new career would probably have been a lost cause too and never have got off the ground.

Toni Mount
2nd October 2016

Toni Mount

Toni Mount earned her research Masters degree from the University of Kent in 2009 through study of a medieval medical manuscript held at the Wellcome Library in London. Recently she also completed a Diploma in Literature and Creative Writing with the Open University.

Toni has published many non-fiction books, but always wanted to write a medieval thriller, and her novels "*The Colour of Poison*", "*The Colour of Gold*" and now "*The Colour of Cold Blood*" are the result.

Toni regularly speaks at venues throughout the UK and is the author of several online courses available at www.medievalcourses.com.

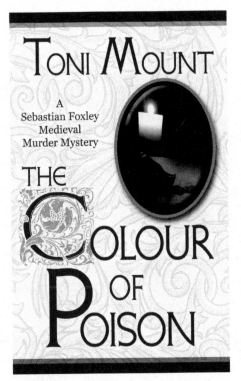

TONI MOUNT

A
Sebastian Foxley
Medieval
Murder Mystery

THE

COLOUR

OF

POISON

978-84-944893-3-4

**The first Sebastian Foxley
Medieval Mystery by Toni Mount.**

The narrow, stinking streets of medieval London can sometimes be a dark place. Burglary, arson, kidnapping and murder are every-day events. The streets even echo with rumours of the mysterious art of alchemy being used to make gold for the King.

Join Seb, a talented but crippled artist, as he is drawn into a web of lies to save his handsome brother from the hangman's rope. Will he find an inner strength in these, the darkest of times, or will events outside his control overwhelm him?

Only one thing is certain - if Seb can't save his brother, nobody can.

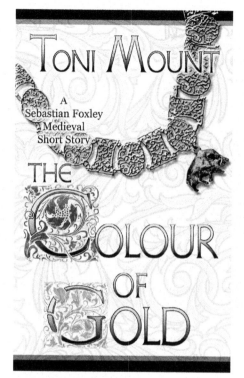

978-84-946498-0-6

**The second Sebastian Foxley
Medieval Mystery by Toni Mount.**

A wedding in medieval London should be a splendid occasion, especially when a royal guest will be attending the nuptial feast. Yet for the bridegroom, the talented young artist, Sebastian Foxley, his marriage day begins with disaster when the valuable gold livery collar he should wear has gone missing. From the lowliest street urchin to the highest nobility, who could be the thief? Can Seb wed his sweetheart, Emily Appleyard, and save the day despite that young rascal, Jack Tabor, and his dog causing chaos?

Join in the fun at a medieval marriage in this short story that links the first two Sebastian Foxley medieval murder mysteries: *The Colour of Poison* and the full-length novel *The Colour of Cold Blood*..

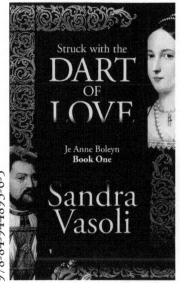
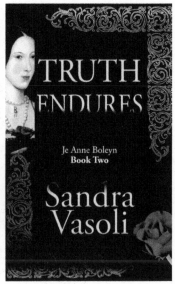

978-84-944893-6-5

978-84-944893-7-2

The *Je Anne Boleyn* series is a gripping account of Anne Boleyn's effort to negotiate her position in the treacherous court of Henry VIII, where every word uttered might pose danger, where absolute loyalty to the King is of critical importance, and in which the sweeping tide of religious reform casts a backdrop of intrigue and peril.

Anne's story begins with *Struck with the Dart of Love*: Tradition tells us that Henry pursued Anne for his mistress and that she resisted, scheming to get the crown and bewitching him with her unattainable allure. Nothing could be further from the truth.

The story continues with *Truth Endures*: Anne is determined to be a loving mother, devoted wife, enlightened spiritual reformer, and a wise, benevolent queen. But others are hoping and praying for her failure. Her status and very life become precarious as people spread downright lies to advance their objectives.

The unforgettable tale of Henry VIII's second wife is recounted in Anne's clear, decisive voice and leads to an unforgettable conclusion...

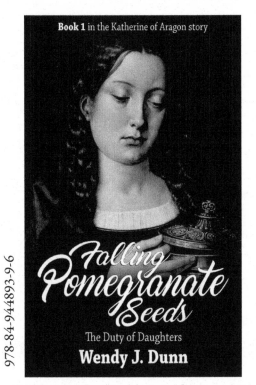

Book 1 in the Katherine of Aragon Story

Doña Beatriz Galindo.
Respected scholar.
Tutor to royalty.
Friend and advisor to Queen Isabel of Castile.

Beatriz is an uneasy witness to the Holy War of Queen Isabel and her husband, Ferdinand, King of Aragon. A Holy War seeing the Moors pushed out of territories ruled by them for centuries.

The road for women is a hard one. Beatriz must tutor the queen's youngest child, Catalina, and equip her for a very different future life. She must teach her how to survive exile, an existence outside the protection of her mother. She must prepare Catalina to be England's queen.

A tale of mothers and daughters, power, intrigue, death, love, and redemption. In the end, Falling Pomegranate Seeds sings a song of friendship and life.

www.SebastianFoxley.com

Why not visit
Sebastian Foxley's web page
to discover more about his
life and times?
www.SebastianFoxley.com

Historical Fiction

Falling Pomegranate Seeds - **Wendy J. Dunn**
Struck With the Dart of Love - **Sandra Vasoli**
Truth Endures - **Sandra Vasoli**
Phoenix Rising - **Hunter S. Jones**
Cor Rotto - **Adrienne Dillard**
The Raven's Widow - **Adrienne Dillard**
The Claimant - **Simon Anderson**
The Truth of the Line - **Melanie V. Taylor**

Non Fiction History

Anne Boleyn's Letter from the Tower - **Sandra Vasoli**
Queenship in England - **Conor Byrne**
Katherine Howard - **Conor Byrne**
The Turbulent Crown - **Roland Hui**
Jasper Tudor - **Debra Bayani**
Tudor Places of Great Britain - **Claire Ridgway**
Illustrated Kings and Queens of England - **Claire Ridgway**
A History of the English Monarchy - **Gareth Russell**
The Fall of Anne Boleyn - **Claire Ridgway**
George Boleyn: Tudor Poet, Courtier & Diplomat - **Ridgway & Cherry**
The Anne Boleyn Collection - **Claire Ridgway**
The Anne Boleyn Collection II - **Claire Ridgway**
Two Gentleman Poets at the Court of Henry VIII - **Edmond Bapst**

Children's Books

All about Richard III - **Amy Licence**
All about Henry VII - **Amy Licence**
All about Henry VIII - **Amy Licence**
Tudor Tales William at Hampton Court - **Alan Wybrow**

PLEASE LEAVE A REVIEW

If you enjoyed this book, *please* leave a review at the book seller
where you purchased it. There is no better way to thank the
author and it really does make a huge difference!
Thank you in advance.

Lightning Source UK Ltd.
Milton Keynes UK
UKOW01f0112100917
308850UK00001B/172/P